THE DUKE IN QUESTION

AMALIE HOWARD

sourcebooks
casablanca

Published by Sourcebooks Casablanca, an imprint of Sourcebooks
P.O. Box 4410, Naperville, Illinois 60567-4410
(630) 961-3900
sourcebooks.com

Printed and bound in the United States of America.
OPM 10 9 8 7 6 5 4 3 2 1

For Ally,
namer of the Willingtons,
and a real-life unicorn.

One

The SS Valor, Atlantic Ocean, 1865

LADY BRONWYN CHASE GASPED FOR BREATH, TUCK-
ing her body into the narrow alcove and not daring to
breathe. *He* was here. On her brother's ship. She had
only met the Duke of Thornbury once, during her step-
brother's wedding ball last season in London, and it had
been enough to make a lasting impression. He'd struck
her as sharp and intelligent, a man whose piercing gaze
missed nothing.

And handsome too, she reminded herself.

Her memory wasn't wrong. In the year since she'd seen
him last, his striking looks hadn't changed. They'd grown
more pronounced. Or maybe that was because she'd idol-
ized him in her dreams…an unreachable fantasy lover
with tawny hair and citrine eyes. Bronwyn let out a silent
breath to calm her racing heart that was pounding for a
variety of reasons—fright, fatigue…and pure womanly
fascination. *He should not be here.*

Why was he here?

Had she made a mistake? Perhaps she'd mistaken him
for someone else. But even as she thought it, she discarded

the notion. It was him, no doubt of that. That thick, sun-gilded, tawny-brown hair still curled around his angular face in unruly locks, a jewel-gold stare and a hawklike nose combining to make most people wary of the hunter prowling in their midst. The duke was attractive in a throat-drying, fierce way; everything about him made her silly heart thrum. Even dressed in formal evening wear, he stood out like a tree in a field of pretty flowers.

Most steered clear of him.

Not her, obviously, because she had rocks in her head. Too bad he was taken, though like everyone else in the *ton*, she'd heard the whispers of estrangement, if they were to be believed. Bronwyn hadn't seen anyone resembling his wife before fleeing the salon earlier, how-ever. Then again, she'd run at the first sight of him. The girlish infatuation she'd quashed a year ago had returned in full force. The urge to throw herself in his path, look up into that sultry stare, and offer herself up like a too-willing Andromeda displayed on a rock for his pleasure had been too compelling.

Good gracious, her thoughts were absurd.

Not that she hadn't dreamed of being swept off her feet and shamelessly seduced by a man who greatly resembled her pursuer. Bronwyn scowled. Now was not the time to be reminiscing about *private* fantasies that had nothing to do with *him* whatsoever. The dratted duke was here to arrest her or worse. What were the odds that he was on *this* ship while she was in possession of documents that could get her thrown into jail?

Or executed for treason.

Perhaps Thornbury had only seen her in the dining room and recognized her as Ashvale's sister. Perhaps he only wanted to say hullo. Then why were her nerves on edge as though she were teetering on the edge of a dangerous precipice? Her instincts were screaming at her to flee. Not that she could jump off the side of a massive ship and swim to safety. She would have to act, pretend to be taking a pleasure cruise or some such. And hiding in an alcove off the main salon only made her look guilty.

Sucking a breath into her tight lungs, Bronwyn eased from the space, peering up and down the corridor. He hadn't followed her, thank God, though she'd felt the visceral tug when he'd set her in his sights in that room, eyes lighting with *something*. Recognition? Suspicion? She was letting fear get the best of her, and that was never good.

With a toss of her head, she smoothed her skirts, lifted her chin, and walked down the hallway. She wanted to run, but she cautioned her trembling legs to take a pace that didn't stamp her as someone suspicious, just in case the duke was watching. The hairs on her nape stood on end at the thought. She walked until she came to a door that led to one of the main decks, her lungs filling with salty chilled ocean air and her gaze greeted by a twilight sky with stars beginning to glimmer in the distance. The endless horizon over the dark, white-crested sea was beautiful in a stunningly vast way, one that made her feel small.

Insignificant.

Bronwyn wanted to make her mark. A mark…*any* mark that would deem her worthy, that would be a reminder that she had been here on earth at this time. It was perhaps what had pushed her to agree to this whole scheme. Using the nom de guerre "the Kestrel," at first she had done small tasks in London. A delivery here, a word there, all with the goal of helping the oppressed to lift the yoke of subjugation. She had started out fighting for women's rights with the suffragettes, but the world was so much bigger and broader than England.

Her brother, Courtland, and his wife lived in Antigua.

His duchess's best friend hailed from India.

There was more she could do…a better way she could make a difference with her time and her efforts. Despite the stringent rules impressed upon her as a woman in England, Bronwyn was acutely aware of her own privilege and the fact that she held power that others might not have. While she could not own property or vote, she still had *some* self-governance. Little actions, no matter how small, could have big ripples. And so, here she was, en route to Philadelphia with sensitive documents.

Bronwyn had known what she was getting into when she had agreed to ferry the packet across the Atlantic. She did not know what was in the letter, only that it would aid in the cause of the Northern states during the American Civil War. Seeing some of the opposition her brother had endured as a man of mixed heritage in England, despite his status as a peer, a fire had been lit beneath her to *do* something.

But unlike her brother who was the Duke of Ashvale, Bronwyn did not have a seat in the Lords. She wasn't a *man*. She might not have the power he had at his fingertips to effect change, but she wasn't incapable, and so she had agreed to hand-deliver the package, despite the personal risk to her person, her reputation, and her family name. Though right now, the thought of being caught and imprisoned by a man rumored to be the greatest spy in London left her cold.

Should her mission be compromised or the documents fall into the wrong hands, lives would be endangered and innumerable losses encountered. The packet was safe in her stateroom, thank God, hidden where no one would find it, but she felt the weight of her choices with every breath. Bronwyn swallowed, resting her fingers on the metal railing.

You're doing the right thing.

She hoped.

"Lady Bronwyn, I thought that was you," a low voice said.

Bronwyn didn't have to turn to know who had found her, even as that lush baritone shivered over her senses like raw silk gliding over bare skin. The greeting wasn't untoward, considering they'd been properly introduced in town, but her heart kicked against her ribs all the same. She'd been wrong to come out here alone. At least in the dining room, there were other people.

Other *barriers*.

Scolding herself silently, Bronwyn lifted her chin. She

could do this. She wasn't some ingenue fresh out of the schoolroom. She was a woman grown and more than capable of handling a simple gentleman. There was only one problem with that logic—the Duke of Thornbury was hardly *simple*. No, he was highly intelligent, distressingly alert, and nobody's fool. Least of all hers.

Act natural, Bee.

Pasting a demure smile on her lips, she turned and took him in up close. Fitted bespoke clothing, tremendous height—he practically towered over her smaller form—those angular cheekbones, hooded golden eyes, and lush mouth all conspired to make her lungs squeeze. His pale skin took on the silvery gleam of the moonlight, making him appear more chimerical than he should be...some fantastical sultry specter from her imagination come to taunt her. She'd take that option if it meant she didn't have to speak to him, but alas, he was indeed real.

"Your Grace, what a surprise."

A thoroughly unwelcome one.

He leaned against the railing and perused her. "It is, isn't it? Fancy seeing you here. I thought I had been mistaken in the dining salon, but here you are...in the flesh. Are you alone?"

"My chaperone retired with a headache," she replied, thinking quickly. Her flighty lady's maid, Cora, who was prone to the vapors and disappearing at the most inconvenient times was hardly a proper chaperone, but beggars could not be choosers. Particularly beggars turned international spies. Though Bronwyn wasn't a spy, per se; she was more of a discreet informant. "Is your wife here as well?"

He cleared his throat. "The lady is, though we are no longer married."

Goodness, her heart shouldn't have raced so violently at that, but Bronwyn could feel it hammering like a bird about to take flight. His marital state had nothing to do with her. He was her brother's friend! And a former British undercover agent. A man who would put her in handcuffs without blinking. A different scenario involving restraints—a much naughtier one with rather less clothing—crept into her mind, and she felt her face flame. *Did* he carry handcuffs?

Stop it, stop it, stop it.

"I'm sorry to hear that," she managed to say.

The duke nodded. "Where are you headed?" he asked. It was a casual inquiry, and yet, Bronwyn recognized that nothing was casual for this man. A seemingly basic question could lure out secrets, ferret out clues. He was a master at interrogation and artifice…while she was a mere novice.

She feigned a coy look and fluttered her eyelashes. "Did the Duke of Ashvale send you to follow me, Your Grace? Very well then, I am visiting an aunt in Philadelphia."

Speculation gleamed in that shadowed gaze. "I didn't realize that you had family in America."

Gracious but he was quick. Bronwyn shook her head, smile pasted on firmly. "On my mother's side, I fear. She is ill, and Mama thought I would be able to offer some comfort."

Now, *that* was a mistake. She almost kicked herself when those heavy-lidded eyes narrowed.

"Lady Borne sent you to play nursemaid to an ailing relative," he murmured slowly. "Unless she has changed in temperament, that is a rather surprising kindness."

Bronwyn stopped herself from gritting her teeth in frustration. A man like Thornbury, an expert in body language and human behavior, would not miss it. Her mother was not known for being the most generous or *kind* of ladies. In fact, she was a terrible person to her core. It still astounded Bronwyn that her mother had attempted to oust Courtland—the legitimate heir to her dead husband's estate—by sending him away from England in hopes of elevating her own son. Perhaps that was another reason why Bronwyn felt so compelled to do what she was doing…to make up for the grievous wrongs within her own family.

"Surprising or not, Your Grace, it is the reason for my journey. Now if you'll excuse me, I must check on Cora." She moved to walk past him, only to be stopped by a firm grip on her elbow. Heat spread across her skin at the contact, even though he wore gloves and she wore long sleeves. Bronwyn couldn't help the gasp that passed her lips, nor the instant tightening of her belly. A wild gasp throttled in her throat, the sensation of his grasp almost too much for her wayward brain to handle. She glanced up, and the moment their eyes collided, something all too visceral shot between them.

"Does Ashvale know you are here?" he asked.

No, because her brother would hardly approve if he knew she'd name-dropped him to commandeer one of the owner's suites onboard. Hiding out in a common stateroom would not have been ideal—what if she'd been recognized?—so she'd elected to travel in plain sight. A loud and obnoxious heiress was dismissible. She had no doubt that Courtland would hear about the incident, but she hoped to have delivered the packet and be on the return voyage by that point. As far as anyone was concerned, Lady Bronwyn Chase was a vapid nuisance, abusing her brother's connections and wealth and visiting an ailing family member.

It was a thin camouflage at best, but the only one she could come up with.

"Ashvale doesn't keep track of my every step, Your Grace," she snipped, her stare dipping pointedly to the long fingers still pressed in the crook of her elbow. He did not take the hint, damn the man, one corner of that indecent bottom lip kicking up in a way that suggested he was well aware of what his touch was doing to her. Bronwyn pushed a haughty smirk to her lips. "And besides, it's not as though everyone onboard doesn't know who I am. My brother owns this vessel, after all."

Distaste flickered across his face, and she winced. Better he think her a shallow, frivolous excuse for a chit who was using her brother's title and property than the reality. Still, something inside of her rebelled. She *wanted* him to keep her in some esteem.

Duty won out over pride, of course, as she widened her coy smile. "Don't tell anyone, but I cannot wait to see Philadelphia. Do you know how much they fawn over aristocrats? As if our blood is so blue, it's gold. Perhaps I shall find myself an obscenely rich husband for my efforts. I suppose that's why Mama agreed to let me go. Fatten the coffers and all that."

"Indeed." The word dripped with derision.

Heavens. She almost loathed herself in that moment, but the unguarded disgust blooming on the duke's countenance was like a blow. She ignored it...his instant and unguarded contempt. Bronwyn felt her cheeks heat, but played into her performance. Her gaze canvassed him in an almost covetous way, lashes dropping bashfully. "I hope you don't think me forward, Your Grace, but perhaps we should have dinner one night. For my brother's sake."

The hefty flirtation worked like a charm.

He released her like a hot coal and bowed, the slightest dip of his head as though he couldn't muster much more than that, his face going studiously blank. Cold. Untouchable.

"Perhaps. Enjoy your trip, my lady."

———

God but she was a spoiled, abominable brat.

Valentine couldn't fathom how the girl who had so courageously helped the Duke of Ashvale and his duchess claim his birthright had turned into this...this avaricious nitwit who'd looked at him like a spider eyeing her next meal. The expression of greed on her face as she'd contemplated her marital prospects in Philadelphia had sickened him. Perhaps he'd become too jaded in life.

He pinched the bridge of his nose between his thumb and forefinger as hard as he could until spots danced in his vision. He had a job to do, and babysitting the younger sister of one of his friends was not in the cards. Valentine hadn't expected her to be on the ship, and he was certain Ashvale would be surprised to learn that she had bandied his name about to secure passage.

He wondered if the ailing relation was real, or whether that was some pretext to leave her mother's clutches. He shook his head—that adder of a woman wouldn't let her spawn go far, not if it endangered her chance to make an exceptional match. Her young, nubile daughter was much too valuable a commodity for that. Then again, money was as attractive a lure as a title these days.

Valentine recognized the initial pulse of interest for what it was. Lady Bronwyn was a comely girl, there was no denying that. Ash-brown hair with hints of rich chestnut was coiled into an artful arrangement that framed her oval-shaped face to perfection. Darkly lashed crystalline blue eyes were the jewels of a creamy porcelain countenance, overshadowing the small bow-shaped mouth that resided below a sloping nose.

She wasn't even his type. He preferred his women bashful, buxom, and brainless.

While she had the last going for her, Valentine couldn't

explain the vexing pulse of attraction. Thankfully, the early spurt of it had evaporated the moment she'd opened her mouth. And he had more important things to do than worry about some silly chit, though he did feel a beat of responsibility to his friend, the duke. Ashvale would pummel him to a pulp if he found out that Valentine had left his friend's younger sister in a compromising situation.

He palmed his face and frowned. So *was* she lying?

No. She had likely used the Ashvale connection to occupy the owner's accommodations onboard. He sighed, rethinking his early thought that she was the shallowest sort of woman. A pity, really. Or perhaps a blessing in disguise. Not that he required any temptation while he was working. He had one job—he needed to find the rogue operative known as the Kestrel.

And his prey was on this ship.

From his years in covert operations, Valentine was well aware that a handle could by definition be anyone. The Kestrel could be a man or a woman, but they had intelligence that it was most likely a man. Though never apprehended, the Kestrel had been seen and described once or twice—a narrow-faced, rangy man of average height with a sparse beard and mustache—and a passable sketch had been rendered.

Halfway into the voyage, however, Valentine had been unable to unearth any more clues as to the man's identity or find anyone matching the likeness. He'd perused the ship's manifesto, but of course no names had jumped out at him. Criminals rarely did.

He blinked. Come to think of it, Lady Bronwyn Chase hadn't been on there either.

The cheeky little liar! Spotting her in the dining room had only been by chance, and though their eyes had met, she hadn't seemed to recognize him at first. And then she'd run off toward the necessary. Valentine went over the names in his memory, stopping at a Miss Bee Chase. It was a common enough last name, but he should have paid it more attention. In truth, he'd been more concerned with the men onboard. A mistake a novice would make. Now, he'd have to go over the list again with a more discerning eye. Still, it had to be a nickname so he couldn't fault her for using it to assume some clandestine deception.

Lady Bronwyn was much too on the nose for that.

Dinner, indeed. He'd stay a far step from the twit if he could help it, or he'd find himself leg-shackled by the end of the journey. Lord knew the grasping Lady Borne wouldn't turn her nose up at the title of duchess for her daughter.

Making his way back inside, he had just entered the vacated salon when footsteps tapped on the polished wooden floors toward him.

"There you are, my darling. Thought I'd lost you."

His fake former countess when he'd been earl and an operative like him fastened herself to his side. While Valentine was officially retired, she was not. In fact, Lisbeth was the one who had asked him to take on the assignment. She was convinced that the Kestrel was a peer, and the only way to uncover a peer was to be part of aristocratic circles.

A year ago, they had started the rumor that they were estranged and a fake divorce to a hitherto fake marriage had been procured and granted by the Home Office, but now she needed him and his connections. It was no hardship. In truth, he'd been bored out of his skull playing duke these past few months, thanks to Uncle Bucky's sudden demise. Valentine had yet to visit the ducal seat in Scotland—a task he hoped to put off for as long as possible.

"Lisbeth, dearest. Weren't you supposed to be playing cards?"

Her lips curled, her eyes flashing with chagrin. "It was a bust."

Damn. He felt his frustration rise. They were both sure that the mysterious Lord Kestrel would show his face after being at sea for three days. Dinner, a dance, or a hand of cards, but no, nothing. Peers, even treasonous ones, enjoyed their entertainments.

"Everyone in the cardroom has been cleared," she said. "Did you find your little diversion? You took off like a bat out of hell when you saw that chit. Who is she?"

"It's Ashvale's sister," he said in a dispassionate tone.

Her brows rose in surprise. "Lady Borne's daughter?"

"One and the same, and suffice it to say that that apple is firmly still part of that beetle-bitten tree."

"Wasn't she the one who helped the duke?" Lisbeth frowned. "She seemed to have a good head on her shoulders despite her sorry parentage."

"A year is a long time to change a person," he said, lip hooking in a repulsed sneer.

"*That* bad?" Lisbeth asked.

"Worse, if you can imagine it."

"I cannot."

Passing another couple and exchanging pleasant nods, Lisbeth hooked her arm in his and peered up at him. It was all a farce, of course, but it was like walking in a worn, comfortable shoe. The pretense came easily to both of them. Though they had been lovers in the past, that had been a long time ago. Valentine kept his liaisons short and detached, while Lisbeth preferred female company these days. Still, they remained close friends, and he suspected that that would never change.

"She wants us to dine together," he said.

Lisbeth grinned as he led her back to their adjoining chambers. "Will you?"

"I'd rather take my chances with the sharks, thank you very much." He shook his head and scowled. "It's only because of Ashvale that I'm even considering it. She claims to have a sick aunt in Philadelphia, but I expect it's more than that. She could be running away the way the Duke of Embry's sister did."

"Do you blame her?" Lisbeth asked when they stopped at her door. "With a mother like that threatening to marry her off to the highest bidder, if I were her, I'd slip away too the first chance I got. Leave her be, Val. You remember what it was like to be young once, don't you?"

"She'll only ruin herself," he said.

His partner patted his shoulder with a laugh. "I think you gentlemen put too little faith in us women. If she's anything like her elder brother, that girl won't allow herself to be ruined. Or perhaps she's the sort who doesn't put much stock in ruination—we're quite a popular set, you know. Keep an eye on her, if you must, but I suspect that Lady Bronwyn might be made of much sterner stuff than we know."

"I won't hold my breath," he said drily. "The chit's head is full of matrimonial ribbons and conceited delusions of grandeur."

Lisbeth laughed at his droll reply. "She sounds delightful! I could do with some entertainment after the last few days. Invite me to your little dinner and I'll be the judge. Twenty guineas says you're overreacting."

He entered his room and nodded just before closing the door. "I'll take that wager. Don't blame me when your ears start to bleed, and remember that you brought this on yourself."

A pair of limpid crystal-blue eyes formed in his head with a face like an angel. She had the body of a siren and the wits of a gnat. Despite the former, Valentine felt a beat of distaste. He'd never been a man ruled by base passions. He wasn't about to start now. Lady Bronwyn might be beautiful, but she was a pest and a grasping sycophant just like her mother.

He scowled with dispassion. He would not allow her to filter into his thoughts...or his dreams. Some strong physical activity was in order so that he could work himself to exhaustion and fall into a dreamless sleep. After putting his body through a grueling bout of exercises that left his muscles weary and shivering, he was finally fatigued enough to crawl into bed.

He needed rest.

Hopefully, one unplagued by blue-eyed angels intent on wedlock.

Two

BRONWYN'S HANDS TREMBLED AS CORA PUT THE FINishing touches on her coiffure. When the maid was done, Bronwyn dismissed her and expelled a labored breath. Why, oh why hadn't she gone incognito? Purchased a ticket for a smaller stateroom. Worn a disguise. Not been so in-his-face bold. Because that was the problem with catching the attention of a man like the Duke of Thornbury. It could not be *uncaught*.

A cold shiver rolled through her. Over the past two days, she had felt his piercing gaze upon her the moment she entered any shared space on the ship. In the cardroom, he'd watched her instead of his cards. In the ballroom, she'd felt his looming presence, even though he'd never approached for a dance.

Bronwyn felt *exposed*.

Worried that she'd make a misstep and give away her true purpose, instead of embracing the role of witless heiress, she'd gone all stiff and jumpy like a nervous ninny. On top of that, she had removed the correspondence from its very clever hiding place—though probably not from an expert spy like the Duke of Thornbury—inside her mattress and had yet to find another spot for it. Nowhere seemed safe.

She glanced at the folded piece of parchment sitting atop a sheet of paper on her dresser. The wax on the seal had nearly come unstuck, likely from the humidity in the salted air of the ocean. Perhaps she could commit the details to memory and then she would not have to worry about someone finding it.

Her pulse raced. *Should* she? It was exceedingly sensitive information, she knew, especially since the page beneath was from a report on Brent Sommers, an American man who had been arrested by Thornbury himself for smuggling, treason, and other crimes.

She'd read *that* with no compunction.

Fascinated by the neat, meticulous handwriting, she'd practically memorized the information that detailed Brent Sommers's extensive network of accomplices on both sides of the Atlantic. Snatching up the sheet, she traced the lettering. How did the duke have such precise, beautiful calligraphy? Strong and controlled. Much like him. Her fingertip brushed over the initials at the bottom. V.A.M.

Valentine Alexander Medford.

Even his name sounded like it had a giant stick lodged up its arse. Bronwyn stifled a snicker. Not that hers was any better. Perhaps their parents had been cut from the same cloth—pretentious and affected. It was why she had preferred the much simpler nickname Bee, given to her by Rawley, Courtland's cousin from Antigua, though her mother detested the shortened sobriquet.

"It's *common*, Bronwyn," the marchioness had sneered with such disdain that Bronwyn had tasted it. "You are a highborn lady and you will conduct yourself as such. No more of this nickname nonsense. And you will stay a far step from Ashvale's contemptuous relations. The nerve of him, sullying your father's good name with the lower classes from the *islands*. The horror."

"What makes them contemptuous to you, Mama?" she had shot back without thinking. "The fact that they might not have money or the fact that they are not white?"

"How dare you speak to me so, you wretched child?"

Bronwyn had dared because her mother was wrong.

She rather liked her brother's family, particularly Rawley, whose easy humor, incisive intelligence, and unswerving loyalty to her brother had won her over. Bronwyn had been so tempted to call herself Bronnie just to aggravate her mother, but the punishments were never worth the overstep. The last time Bronwyn had gone toe-to-toe with the marchioness had been by betraying her, as her mother called it. When Bronwyn provided the documents of birth for her half brother's claim to her grandfather's dukedom, the marchioness had cut the family's season short and taken everyone back to the country in a fit of pique.

Bronwyn and her younger sister, Florence, had been confined in seclusion for weeks. Florence had blamed her, of course, but Bronwyn would not have changed a thing. She'd done what was right. Courtland Chase had been the rightful heir, regardless of her mother's unlawful machinations to make her own son duke. Bronwyn loved Stinson, but her full-blooded brother had always been their mother's puppet. He had a thing or two to learn from their half brother, Courtland, who was a decent and honorable man.

She had a feeling that Courtland would *not* endorse her actions now, however.

Heiress turned international spy was a scandal in itself.

While they had been in Kettering, the marchioness had relented, driven by a desire to see her daughter marvelously wed. They had attended a few country house parties, including a daring masquerade, whereupon Bronwyn had discovered her latest purpose.

Always a magnet for trouble with a curious eye, she'd seen one of her old finishing-school mates, Miss Sesily Pleasant, with her mask askew and arguing with a well-heeled gentleman in an alcove off the retiring room. Sesily was a Black heiress from San Francisco whose business-owning and very wealthy mother had sent her only daughter to England with an immense dowry.

Like most of the American "dollar princesses" who came to England to marry into the nobility, Sesily had been sent for the same reason. However, unlike many of the other young ladies of their acquaintance, she had been kind and sweet, and one of the few girls Bronwyn had counted a friend at school. Sesily's entrepreneur mother had also been an empowering influence on Bronwyn—that a free Black woman could amass such a fortune on her own was a testament to women everywhere.

A bored Bronwyn had shamelessly eavesdropped on the conversation.

"He won't listen to me, Wentworth!"

Bronwyn hadn't recognized the mysterious Wentworth who was masked, but he had been agitated, his palm slamming into the wainscoting. "This is our only window before Ashley leaves for London. Find a way to get the message to him, Sesily. He cannot be on that train." Bronwyn had been thoroughly intrigued by the hushed urgency in the man's tone, but what had interested her even more was the mutinous look on Sesily's face. She was most distraught. "I do not care what you have to do," Wentworth had commanded in a brutal whisper before striding away. "Get it done!"

Bronwyn had approached quietly and handed her friend a handkerchief when she pressed the heels of her palms into her eyes with a groan. "Can I help?"

"Oh," Sesily had said, startled and looking up, tight ebony spirals springing into her brow. "No, you couldn't. It's… Never mind."

"Tell me what to tell him and I will."

"Tell who?"

Bronwyn had canted her head. "Ashley."

Panic had ensued, Sesily's dark-brown eyes going wide, her breathing rapid as though she was going to swoon at any second. "Oh, no. You cannot!"

"Tell me the message and I will take care of it, Sesily," Bronwyn had whispered, determined to help. "I'm masked. No one will recognize me, I promise. Now tell me what to do."

Clearly torn, Sesily had wrung her hands, but then her

spine had straightened and she'd swallowed, her pretty face drawn. "See the man over there in the gray mask? That's him. There's a raid planned to attack his train to London tonight. Tell him not to get on."

"A raid?" Bronwyn had blinked her confusion. Whatever she'd expected, it hadn't been *that*. She'd thought Sesily's distress had had to do with courting or some such. Silly her. "Are you in some kind of trouble, Sesily?"

"No, nothing like that. I help deliver messages from time to time." Her face had gone more pinched if that was possible. "But I made a mistake. I thought Wentworth could get me an introduction to Lord Cupid, er, Pam."

"Pam?" The word had emerged on a gasp. Lord Cupid was a moniker printed by the *Times* about the prime minister, and Pam was yet another of his nicknames. What on earth were Sesily and this mysterious Wentworth into? Surely she did not mean...

"If Ashley gets on that train, he will *die*." A hand had gripped her elbow as her brain whirled to connect the obvious dots. Dear God, Ashley was Palmerston's private secretary. This intrigue was beyond anything Bronwyn had ever imagined. The excitement in her blood had spiked to dangerous levels.

"I'll do it."

And she had, and never looked back.

She'd pretended to approach the Honorable Anthony Evelyn Melbourne Ashley, with her dance card in hand and looking suitably shy.

"I believe we might have this dance, sir," she had murmured. When he'd looked confused, she had pressed a gloved hand to her lips, eyelashes dipping in fabricated mortification. "Oh, I do beg your pardon. I'm mistaken. I must have muddled the masks." Embarrassed laughter had tumbled out of her. "And it appears I have mistaken the dance as well because this is the polka and it's blank. I don't suppose you wish to dance?"

His look of shock had been comical. "This is a bit untoward, Miss...er..."

Rather untoward since they had not been introduced, but it was a country masquerade and rules weren't as stringent as they would have been in London. Her fingers had brushed the edges of the feathers on her mask. "Miss Bee."

"Yes, well, I..." Looking decidedly uncomfortable, he'd tugged on his collar and his voice had trailed off. Clearly, Ashley wasn't nearly the type of womanizer his much older employer was purported to be.

"Never fear, sir, I shall let you off the hook then, but I have a message for you." Voice low, she'd brushed passed him so close that her feathers had skimmed his arm. "Do not get on the train to London tonight. I'm told to advise you that there will be a raid."

She'd left him gaping and melted into the crowd.

The Honorable Anthony Evelyn Melbourne Ashley had not boarded the train that evening and lived to see another day.

For Bronwyn, the rush had been indescribable.

From then on, Wentworth had named her the Kestrel

on account of the spotted-brown-feathered mask she had worn that night. And as the sister to a duke, her connections offered them access in places among the *ton* that they didn't have before. It had started in much the same vein as it had with Sesily...a message here, a coded letter there, and soon, the Kestrel quickly became a notorious informant. Thankfully, it had been Sesily's brilliant idea to leak a male description of the Kestrel to Scotland Yard, which had given Bronwyn some breathing space.

This trip to Philadelphia, however, was the biggest and most nerve-racking assignment she had ever done. Bronwyn fingered the waxed correspondence. The seal was almost lifting off the parchment but remained unbroken. With a little effort, it could detach. She let out a breath. Wouldn't it be better if she knew what was inside? Then at least the information would be protected.

But you *would be at risk, you ninny.*

That was also true. Being able to plead ignorance was always important in her line of work. With a huff, she tucked both sheets into her corset and rose. She'd be late for dinner if she didn't get a move on. It was the farewell celebration before the SS *Valor* docked on the morrow in America. Perhaps the heat from her bosom would make the decision for her and the missive would miraculously open.

Breasts...not just for decoration.

She bit back a laugh. While her mother had made sure she was always dressed in the best of fashions, Bronwyn had never taken much pleasure in it herself. Tonight, however, the Marchioness of Borne would have approved of her garments. The silver-threaded indigo gown was one of her newer ones, the scalloped bodice daring in itself, and one that the scatterbrained Cora had packed even though Bronwyn had specified plain clothing only. Clearly, the maid did not understand what that meant since she had included the extravagant gown. Though Bronwyn was grateful for it now.

Thornbury won't know what hit him.

She blinked at the odd thought. The dress *wasn't* for him. It was the last night on the ship and she had to look her best. The sister of the Duke of Ashvale had to embody the right appearance. As though Courtland cared one whit about appearances. She bit her lip, her excuses so thin even she could see through them, and tossed her head.

It wasn't for Thornbury and that was that.

―――――――

Valentine was irritated.

That was nothing new, of course, but the fact that the blasted Kestrel continued to avoid detection was making him more provoked than usual. The window of opportunity would narrow once they disembarked the next day in Philadelphia and whomever he was would have a greater chance of escape. Valentine had hoped to have the man in custody by now and the missing pages from his report back in hand, but he had nothing to show for his efforts. Even Lisbeth was frustrated, and it took quite a lot to ruffle her equanimity.

On top of that, a certain young lady whose blood had to be a nauseating blend of coyness and coquetry, had burrowed under his skin like a frayed splinter. He'd had to endure watching her flirt and simper with nearly every gentleman onboard, their collective infatuation almost impossible to bear. Yes, she was an heiress. Yes, she was beautiful. But by God, she had nothing but dust motes in her brain. Could they not *see* that?

He was inordinately grateful that she was not in the ship's first-class dining saloon at present. Perhaps she was ill and would bless him while disappointing all her fawning toadies with the lack of her imperiously vapid presence this evening. Oh, to be so fortunate! A whisper of shame swamped him at how uncharitable he was being. It was a good thing his thoughts were private and he was not in the habit of sharing them. In truth, he pitied the poor gentleman who would eventually be caught in the young lady's witless snare.

"Are you well, Val?" Lisbeth asked in a low voice so their other dinner companions would not overhear. There were only two of them, an older couple, with two chairs remaining empty. "Thinking of the Kestrel?"

He set down his spoon from the first course and reached for his whisky that a servant had thankfully refilled. "Yes. The Kestrel."

"Do you think he's here?"

Valentine shook his head, eyes scanning the crowded room. No, he was not keeping an eye out for a shining mop of chestnut and ash-brown curls wondering what

could have befallen his comely nemesis. Irritation returning, he scowled at himself. A flash of a face caught the edge
of his vision and his head whipped back. Tall, thin, black
top hat. He could have sworn he'd seen the man from the
portrait. Bloody hell!

"What is it?" Lisbeth asked.

Valentine hissed through his teeth. "I think he might
be here, but I'm not certain."

"Did you see him?"

"I think so. It was fast." Furious at himself for being distracted, he pointed to the left side of the saloon. "Over
there somewhere."

"Are you sure?" Lisbeth asked.

Valentine's teeth ground together. "No, God damn it."

Eyebrow arched in faint surprise, she stared at him. He
was not a man known for an inability to remember detail or
be uncertain about anything, especially a mark. "Let me take
a stroll to the retiring room and have a look. I'll be right back."

When she rose gracefully and picked her way
through the tables, Valentine released the hold on his
strained jaw. His attention was all over the place. It was
her fault. Ever since he'd run into her a few days ago,
Lady Bronwyn had taken up more space in his head
than she was due. He wasn't a man run by his passions,
but that hadn't stopped him from being fascinated by
whorls of glossy brown hair and rosy, soft skin. His
fantasy version of her and the reality were two different things, however. The reality required cotton to be
stuffed into his ears.

"Here you are, my lady," the footman said, interrupting his thoughts.

"Oh, is this my seat? Thank you, Harry, you are my dashing hero." A breathy voice chuckled, the sound making Valentine's skin tighten. With horror, of course. "Goodness, I do apologize for joining you this late." The footman blushed and Valentine rolled his eyes before standing and settling his stare on their latest arrival. Fate was a cruel, *cruel* mistress as he watched the footman pull out Lady Bronwyn's chair beside a sea of dark-blue skirts. He and the other gentleman at the table resumed their places once she took her place. "Your Grace, what an unexpected pleasure! I was starting to think you were avoiding me."

Like the plague.

Valentine swallowed the curt reply. "Lady Bronwyn, you look..." *Stunning. Elegant. Gorgeous.* He huffed an annoyed breath at how well his brain seemed to categorize details now, despite its lapse earlier with the man who could be the Kestrel. "Well."

"Thank you, kind sir," she replied, dark lashes dipping over clear blue eyes. "You look *well* yourself." She made the word sound lascivious, like a dessert to be relished. With a warm smile to the older couple at the table, she canted her head. "Lord and Lady Willington, how marvelous you both look this evening, and how lucky I am to have been seated with you."

They clucked at her sweetness—which made *him* want to retch in patent disgust—and fawned over her appearance and dress. It was just a gown, one that she wore quite well, admittedly, but so did the countless other ladies having supper here. *They* were all dressed impeccably.

He tore his gaze away, lest she should notice his fatuous perusal, and focused on the second course. Braised beef with morels in béchamel sauce with roasted potatoes, but even the smell of the rich broth could not overpower the cinnamon-and-spiced-apples scent wafting from his right. Why did she smell like pudding? *Who* smelled like bloody pudding?

Where the hell was Lisbeth?

"Something amiss, Your Grace?" Lady Bronwyn asked with a tinkling burst of laughter that set his teeth on edge. "Is your meal not prepared to your liking? You were glowering so fiercely for a moment there, I feared the tablecloth would catch fire."

No, just you.

That was cruel. He didn't actually wish to set the lady on fire, only that she would move elsewhere. Far away. Where he couldn't see, hear, or inhale her maddening scent. Valentine tugged at his collar, sweat beading over his neck. "Of course not, my lady. My meal is fine. How is yours?"

"Lovely! Better now that my sweet Harry is here with wine. Huzzah!" She grinned up as the fawning footman—*how was she so familiar with him as to know his name?*—poured her a full glass of wine. "Thank you, dear one. Aren't you a gem?" She lifted her glass in a toast and the older couple was quick to follow. He lifted his with no small amount of reluctance. "To my lovely companions, and of course, wonderful Harry, who has seen fit to save me more than once."

Valentine had the distinct urge to throw the lovesick, smitten Harry overboard when he went fiery red and stammered his thanks. Valentine's scowl grew teeth. Devil take it, was no man onboard safe from her flirtatious attentions?

"How has he?" he bit out.

Winsome blue eyes met his. "I beg your pardon, Your Grace?"

"How has a footman saved you more than once?" The way he repeated it sounded in no way how she'd said it, given the way Lady Willington's face tightened with displeasure. Lady Bronwyn, however, didn't lose her smile.

"Oh, dearest Harry led me here! I was so late, you see." She took a liberal sip of her wine. "I simply could not decide which gown to wear, and then there was the matter of jewels. Pearl earbobs or diamonds? A necklace or a choker? It's enough to give one a megrim, I swear."

Good God, she was so shallow, she set his teeth on edge.

"Anyway, after much ado about everything, we finally came to an agreement, and here I am at last, thanks to Harry, of course." She lifted her glass again, though the footman had disappeared. "To Harry!"

"To Harry!" the Willingtons chorused with fond smiles.

Valentine did not lift his glass, only stared and cursed

his fate, his life, and his foul luck. He was going to stab himself with his own fork, just to put himself out of his own misery. Hence, it was no surprise that when he saw Lisbeth returning, his skin crawled with relief, despite her expression that told him she hadn't found their target.

"Lady Bronwyn, what an unexpected pleasure," she cooed, retaking her seat.

"My lady," Bronwyn said. "How lovely to see you. It has been an age, hasn't it?"

"Yes, I believe it has been, though I'm sure that Thornbury has told you the news of our separation." She waved a hand. "All amicable, of course. We remain dear friends."

"I was sorry to hear it," Bronwyn replied.

"Thank you and nothing to be sorry about." Lisbeth grinned. "He's an absolute bear most days, which I don't miss. Getting a smile out of him was like working my way past a thorny hedge without getting scratched."

"Ironic, given his name," Bronwyn replied and then frowned as though she hadn't meant to say that. Valentine swallowed a bark of mocking laughter. It was surprisingly clever for her, considering she might not even know what irony was.

"Oh, that's droll," Lisbeth said, while he fought the urge to kick her in the knee. She patted his shoulder. "I don't remember her being so witty, did you, Val?"

He swore that Bronwyn's eyes darkened, flicking to Lisbeth's hand, but in the next blink they were back to their cheery, sunny hues. "No," he bit out. "Not in the least."

"What are you heading to Philadelphia for, my lady?" Lisbeth asked.

"A sick relative," she said without hesitation.

"Oh, I am sorry, is it serious?"

"No, not at all. It's only to be a short trip. I shall return with the *Valor* in a week hence."

Bronwyn shook her head, the rich curls catching the light in a way that Valentine tried not to notice. *Focus on your meal*, he told himself, attempting to block everything about her from his mind. Her pretty face. That provocative, smiling, *vexing* pout. The hint of décolletage that trembled with every breathless laugh. Her irritating scent that should not make his mouth water to have a taste; she was a person, not an autumn suet pudding.

Get a hold of yourself, you fool.

His grip tightened on his fork, but it was no use. His infamous, stony control was nowhere to be found. Rather than rebuke himself for being a surly curmudgeon in the middle of supper, glaring at everyone and answering in unintelligible grunts, Valentine did the only thing he could. He cleared his throat with a mumbled "Excuse me," rose, and nearly bolted for the nearest exit.

Three

Bronwyn drew the first real breath since she'd been shown to the table.

"Was it something I said?" she asked, watching Lisbeth, who barely managed to stifle her snort of amusement at the duke's rapid departure.

"Perhaps it was something he ate," Lord Willington said. "I had an inkling that the sauce tasted a bit bitter. Did you, dear?" he asked his wife.

The lady frowned at her half-eaten plate. "No, it seemed fine to me. A dash more salt, perhaps."

Thornbury's former wife blinked. "I'm sure it's nothing. He hasn't been feeling well the past few days. I expect he's gone to get some air. He'll be back soon."

Or never, Bronwyn hoped.

Being so late after getting lost in her own thoughts had meant that she could not choose her supper partners, and when Harry had led her to one of two open seats left in the crammed dining saloon, she hadn't protested... until she'd viewed her companions. Or rather, *companion*. Luckily, she had met the Willingtons before, who were both adorably pleasant.

But the Duke of Thornbury. Of all the rotten luck. She had hoped to put her performance as the bubbly, brainless Lady Bronwyn to rest for five minutes during dinner before the pretense started back up in the ballroom for the last ball of the trip. In truth, she could have stayed in her stateroom, too.

You wanted to see him. Admit it.

Shut up.

Yes, perhaps in the ballroom from a good measure away, so he could look at her and long for what he couldn't have! *Not* directly across from him, so close that she could lift her slipper and touch his person beneath the table, if she so desired.

Yes! No!

She'd had to keep her traitorous feet glued to the carpet to prevent an international incident. The breathiness of her voice hadn't been a pretext—she could barely form two words together with his unwelcome proximity.

A man so dour shouldn't be so handsome. But even with a scowl on his full lips, Thornbury was unfairly, sickeningly attractive. Curse them all if he had dimples! But if he had any secret indentations in his cheeks, she wouldn't know because the man never smiled. His exwife was right about that. But even his surly demeanor didn't detract from his sinful looks. There was definite padding beneath that finely tailored coat; there had to be. No man was that...perfect.

He's not perfect, she reminded herself. *He's a jackass.*

Yes, the lord of the jackasses.

King of the jackasses, in fact.

"So are you really going to Philadelphia to visit a sick aunt?" A low voice interrupted her internal tirade.

Bronwyn blinked for a beat and then nodded. "Yes."

The lady chewed a mouthful. "You know, I ran from my home once, too. I could not bear the monotony a second more."

"Where did you go, my lady?"

"Please call me Lisbeth." Her smile was warm. "I went south. Stole my father's carriage and took it all the way to Brighton." She shook her head at the memory. "I barely had a farthing to my name when I arrived, but I found work as a governess. I shared a flat with three women of rather questionable morals, though they were kind, and by the time I came back home, I was a different girl. I'd seen the world and I wanted to see more."

Bronwyn longed to give a fervent nod, those words striking a deeply resonant chord inside of her. However, she wasn't stupid. This woman had been married to the Duke of Thornbury for years before he'd inherited his dukedom. She had to know he was a spy for the Crown. Perhaps, she might be one, too. A year ago, if someone had asked her if highborn women worked as surveillance operatives, Bronwyn would have laughed, and yet, here she was…running sensitive documents across the Atlantic while trying to outwit a retired master spy who might ferret her out in an instant.

With a hand to her chest, she feigned a horror-struck look. "That sounds positively dreadful, Lisbeth dear. I couldn't do without my gowns and my necessities for a moment. And share? Goodness, how awful. I can barely tolerate my little sister as it is, and Florence has her own wing." She shook her head and shuddered, rambling on. "No, this trip was only bearable as I had my brother's luxurious rooms to myself. It's been marvelous. I shall visit Aunt Tillie, the poor dear, and then return for a repeat experience. The only part of the world I truly wish to see, my lady, is my future husband's ballroom."

For a moment—Bronwyn could not be sure—there was a shimmer of what looked like admiration in the lady's eyes before it was gone.

"Is that all?" someone drawled.

Bronwyn nearly leaped out of her skin when that mocking voice came from directly behind her chair. She'd been so wrapped up in her tale of vacuous narcissism that she hadn't heard him return. A cringe crept through her, but the pretense was necessary, she reminded herself. She did not *need* to impress him...only impede him.

"Your Grace, you move like a ghost," she teased with a fluttery laugh when he retook his place at the table. "If you were ever to remarry, your wife shall have to put a bell on you. I know I would."

"Oh, my dears, how lovely!" Lady Willington burst out, clapping her hands in delight, obviously catching—and misinterpreting—the last part of the conversation. "Is there to be a marriage announcement between you two? How positively delightful!"

They both froze at that. Lisbeth looked like she was about to split her sides with mirth, while the duke seemed to be caught in Medusa's stare. A look of revulsion crossed his features. Bronwyn's stomach dipped. To her dismay, she wasn't at all relieved that her ploy had worked so well.

Squashing down her confusing feelings—she should be pleased, not dejected—she lifted her chin and giggled again. Did the duke just flinch? In truth, even she was getting sick of the trilling, high-pitched sound she'd perfected over the past year. One of her many suitors onboard had said it sounded like musical wind chimes, but she wasn't so sure, given the duke's constipated expression.

"Not yet, Lady Willington," she replied in a singsong tone. "The poor duke has yet to have the courage to ask me for a dance, much less my hand in marriage. He's rather shy, you see, and probably intimidated by the competition." She leaned forward conspiratorially, her voice a stage whisper. "One of the men who might declare his intentions is connected to a prince!"

Bronwyn didn't have to look…she could *feel* the duke's disdain. She was laying it on rather thick. But the older woman nodded, eyes bright with the idea of being a matchmaker. "Thornbury, you should remedy that forthwith and ask Lady Bronwyn to dance at the ball. The first waltz would be perfect. You simply must ask her right this moment."

"Must I?"

"Yes, I insist," Lady Willington said. "Sometimes the most excellent match needs a little nudge."

Bronwyn couldn't quite hide her glee at the aghast look on Thornbury's face. Would he say no and dash the hopes of a sweet older lady? Of course he would. The man was made of glass splinters and crystal shards.

"I've promised the first waltz to Lady Lisbeth."

To everyone's surprise, his former countess groaned. "Your Grace, I cannot dance because of my recent…toe injury. I stubbed it on the upper deck earlier this morning, do you not recall? It is providential that Lady Bronwyn might take my place."

The deadly look he shot her would have felled her in an instant, Bronwyn was sure, but the woman only grinned wider. She could have sworn that Lisbeth showed no sign of foot injury earlier when she'd sauntered back to the table, her graceful presence making everyone in the dining saloon take notice.

"Very well then, it seems I should thank you, Lady Willington," the duke bit out, his smile mocking. "Lady Bronwyn?"

She licked dry lips, watching those citrine eyes lower and flare before he dragged his gaze away. Bronwyn's breath faltered, her flirty persona failing her for an alarmed heartbeat. Good gracious, did the Duke of Thornbury desire her? He *loathed* her, she could tell. He didn't deign to hide how shallow and insubstantial he thought she was, but that sharp glint had been unmistakable. Her heart gave a silly, girlish squeeze in her chest. Was *that* why he'd left earlier?

Inasmuch as gratification filled her, dread followed.

No, no. She had to dissuade him. She drummed her fingers on the table, a nervous gesture that she instantly quelled.

"Alas, I shall have to check my dance card, Your Grace. The pleasure of my company is rather in demand, you see."

"*Quelle surprise,*" he muttered darkly.

Bronwyn lifted an amused brow. "Why should it be a surprise? I didn't think a fine, upstanding gentleman like you would be so afraid of a little competition, Your Grace."

"I was being sarcastic," he said and took a sip of his whisky. The liquid matched his eyes, she noted, a single drop glistening on the fullness of his bottom lip. Mesmerized, she watched as his tongue flicked out to collect it. What would his lips taste like? Coated in whisky?

Like sin and stupidity.

She needed to stop before she made a fool of herself yearning for a pair of lips she had no business yearning for.

"Truly the lowest form of wit," she tossed back and turned her attention to the last course, smiling up at a still-blushing Harry who had delivered the plate with a poached pear drizzled in chocolate. "Why am I not surprised, Your Grace, that you would be so disagreeable? I'm not surprised that you had to take the air if your disposition is this bad." She tapped her chin. "Have you considered whether it might be gout?"

"I do not have gout," he bit out.

"I say, lad, gout causes constipation," Lord Willington put in. "You have to regulate your bowels before your feet start swelling. Tart cherry juice will do the trick."

Bronwyn's eyes went wide, and she pinned her lips so tightly to keep from bursting into laughter that her teeth ached. Oh God, she was going to die! "Prune juice," she pronounced sagely, despite the laughter bubbling up into her throat. "For the bowels. I understand if you must excuse yourself from our waltz."

His stare should have set her on fire. The smothered guffaw from Lisbeth, who coughed into her napkin, made the duke's scowl deepen, and Bronwyn nearly lost her battle with her composure. Poor Lady Willington looked confused as if she couldn't quite comprehend the undercurrent beneath what seemed on the surface to be easy conversation. Her husband had returned to tucking into his dessert, too busy to notice any metaphorical bloodshed at the table.

"This is easily settled." The growled words were barely audible, but when the duke let out another dark rumble, reached over, and took hold of Bronwyn's wrist, her next breath went captive in her lungs. The heat from his gloved hand seared her as if he'd touched her with bare skin, and the sheer size of those long fingers encircling her wrist was enough to make her pulse kick up a few notches. He took hold of the dance card and its attached pencil that dangled from a silver ribbon.

Bronwyn knew what he would find—the space for the waltz was marked with her own name. It always was. She could flirt and dance ad nauseam, but the thought of being held so closely by any gentleman did not sit well with her. Not that any man would be untoward, but she was guarded with her person for good reason. And besides, except for Cora, she was alone on this ship.

She tried to tug her hand away, but the duke's grip

subtly tightened. Not enough to hurt, but enough for her to know he wouldn't release her so easily, now that the gauntlet had been thrown. One heavy eyebrow rose as he flipped the booklet open to the marked space and wrote his name over Bee in a heavy scrawl. "This Bee person will have to wait his turn. I look forward to it."

———

Valentine was *dreading* it.

Sod his life choices to the pits of purgatory.

Couldn't he have declined like a normal man and not risen to the challenge and the salty bite of that mouth of hers? The lady was toying with his head—one minute the flirtatious, vain, empty-headed miss who made his stomach recoil, and the next, a vicious, sharp-tongued termagant who pushed his normally unflappable buttons. She'd written her own name in the space, and if he hadn't known the moniker from the ship's passenger list, he wouldn't have written over it.

But why had he? The space was already taken.

He could have bowed out with no one the wiser.

Valentine sighed as he and Lisbeth took a turn around the ship's opulent ballroom. One would never know that one was on a ship, with the enormous oak dome rising high toward a spectacular skylight. The starlit sky above was magnificently romantic, if one was given to such tendencies, which he was not. The spectacular decor resembled that of a posh London hotel, the painted murals beneath the skylight depicting frolicking cherubs and dancing nymphs. Valentine had to hand it to his friend—Ashvale's sense of taste was impeccable.

If only Ashvale's sister was cut from the same elegant cloth, but no, the woman had the personality of a burlap sack.

That reminded him. He shot his former countess a circumspect look. "Your toe seems quite fine to me, Lisbeth."

"Oh, it comes and it goes. Toes are capricious things, aren't they?"

"Are they?"

She nodded. "Indeed."

"Why are you doing this?" he asked when their steps led them closer to where Lady Bronwyn stood in delighted conversation with no less than half a dozen of her swains. He had the sudden desire to sweep them all overboard.

"You know why," Lisbeth replied, laughter in her voice. "It's amusing to see her get through that ice shield of yours."

"Ice shield?"

"Nothing and no one ever gets to you, Valentine, not in any of the years I've known you, much less a woman. Even me, you would only let in so far and yet I barely scratched the surface. I have never seen you so...ruffled over a lady."

He scowled. "She's not a lady. She's a bloody nightmare draped in satin and sapphires."

"But you *are* ruffled," Lisbeth said grinning.

"I am aggravated."

One shoulder lifted, eyes drifting to the source of the aggravation in question, as Lisbeth tapped her lips with her fan. Tinkling laughter like the sound of broken glass drifted toward them as one of the bucks dropped dramatically to one knee, a hand pressed to his chest.

"Good God, she's preposterous."

"Why? She's not the one dropping to her knees, is she?" Lisbeth remarked, and that unleashed a different spool of thoughts in his head, ones which he did *not* want to entertain. "How can you fault her for the actions of a few infatuated gentlemen?"

"She is encouraging them!"

"No, she is not." Lisbeth huffed a laugh. "You truly are ruffled. Why *are* you so annoyed by some harmless amusement, Val?"

He tugged on his collar, annoyance spiking as yet another fop fell to the floor in mimicry of the first. Didn't they have any dignity? "Ashvale is my friend. If his fool sister goes and gets herself compromised by the end of this voyage, who do you think he will blame, if he learns I was also on this ship?" Valentine clenched his fingers into fists. "But we should be looking for the Kestrel, not watching a charming chit put on a show for all the witless idiots in this room who only want a rich heiress to fund their diversions."

"So she's charming now?"

He ground his molars. "Charmingly dim."

"I think there's a lot more to Lady Bronwyn than meets the eye, to be honest. All women put on a mask in one way or the other, especially women of the *ton*, but she's different. The mask she's chosen doesn't quite fit."

"How so?"

"I don't think she's as empty-headed as she pretends to be." Her gaze returned to him. "Especially when she's around you. She tries too hard to put you off."

"Not hard enough," he muttered.

The polka on the ballroom floor came to an end and the strains of the waltz began. Valentine's feet were glued to the floor, a feeling of reluctance swelling inside of him. His instincts were screaming and he'd learned to listen to them over the years. They didn't warn of danger, but they warned of *something* all the same. This dance he never should have agreed to would be pivotal.

"Enjoy your waltz," Lisbeth said with no small amount of mirth.

"I'd rather go for swim in the Thames at the height of summer."

She snorted. "It won't be that bad."

"You're right. It will be much worse."

Valentine saw the moment Bronwyn took notice of the change in music as well as the transformation that came over her. The animation melted away. Eyes darting to the orchestra, her spine went ramrod straight, the delight fading from her expression and a studious blankness replacing it. Her throat worked, that full bottom lip disappearing between her teeth. Was she dreading the interlude as much as he was?

Valentine blinked, his brows drawing together as he

watched her make apologetic excuses to the gentlemen around her. Those upturned lips shaped words that were easy to read even from where he stood—*This dance is taken, I'm afraid.* She gave an absent smile to the last of her admirers before he went to find his promised partner and wound her hands in her skirts to lift them slightly. Then she turned as if sensing his focus.

Brilliant blue eyes met his and held.

A handful of emotions bled through her gaze— curiosity, interest, trepidation, panic—before those skirts lifted higher and she whirled on her heel to dash through the doors behind her. The little minx was running!

"Guess she'd rather a swim as well," came Lisbeth's droll assertion.

But he didn't stay to retort; he followed Bronwyn's flight with swift footsteps. She wouldn't escape so easily. A flick of indigo skirts caught his peripheral vision at the end of the corridor leading to the upper deck, the delicious cinnamon-and-apples fragrance teasing at his nostrils. He lengthened his stride, but she must have caught on to his pursuit because when he climbed the staircase to the deck, she wasn't there. On the prior level, there was a library as well as a number of quiet, elegant first-class lounges. She could be in any one of those.

Valentine retraced his steps, peering into each of the dimly lit rooms only to be frustrated time and time again by unfamiliar occupants, when another whisper of her mouthwatering scent wrapped around him, leading him to a narrow staircase that led to the lower levels. Surely she wouldn't go down there unaccompanied? Worry seeped through his veins.

The foolish twit was silly enough to do just that. While Ashvale's staff tending to the ship were well paid and well treated, that didn't mean she would be safe there. It would be like a lady venturing into a tavern in Whitechapel in the dead of night.

Bloody hell. Disquiet turned to something else in his churning gut.

Valentine ran.

Four

OH DRAT IT, SHE WAS LOST!

Bronwyn had known that someone was on her heels. She'd felt the pursuit in the hairs rising on her nape when the steady echo of a long stride reached her ears. Those frenetic nerves of hers had fired again, an anxious, unsteady version of herself storming to the fore, instead of practical, capable Bronwyn.

Heart pounding, she changed her mind about taking some air outside at the last minute. It might have been Thornbury, or it could have been any of the other persistent gentlemen from the ballroom. Once she realized that some-one was trailing her, instead of turning and confronting her pursuer in a public space as she should have done, she had panicked and taken the next staircase she'd seen.

It had led her to the servants' quarters. The space was tighter on the lower levels of the ship...the hallways nar-rower, the chambers smaller, and the sturdy furniture chosen for practicality rather than elegance. It was much warmer, too. Bronwyn could feel the beads of perspiration making her underclothes cling to her skin. She did not want to end up in the boiler room by accident!

Another set of stairs beckoned at the end of one hall-way, and she gratefully climbed it. To her surprise, it led to yet another staircase. Curiosity overtook her fears. She'd seen the upper decks while strolling on the main sundeck of the ship and had always wondered what was up there.

As she grew closer to the door at the end, the boisterous sounds of a fiddle filtered down from the upper level, the sounds of laughter and stomping feet growing louder as she approached. Where on earth was she going?

Taking that chance was a much better option than wandering back down through a maze of corridors and inviting trouble. Too much drink could turn the sweetest man into a cheeky scoundrel, and a public space was always safer than being trapped in a private one. She had been told too many stories by her mother of young ladies being compromised by unscrupulous gentlemen to ignore those warnings.

Bronwyn pushed open the heavy door, the delicious smell of salt and ocean blowing into her overheated face. Oh, that was lovely! Her trek upward had led to a private deck, she surmised, and a crowded one from the looks of it. She blinked, taking in the sounds as well as the sights. Her mouth gaped. Dear Lord, was that Lady Finley dancing near the railing? She was a widowed marchioness and looked to be having the time of her life.

The more Bronwyn parsed the crowd, the more familiar faces she caught sight of—lords and ladies whose normally stiff-upper-lipped mien seemed to be much more relaxed up here out in the open air. How had she not known *this* revelry was here? This was where the real party was, not in the staid ballroom downstairs.

"My lady!" a frantic voice hissed. "What are you doing?"

Bronwyn whirled to find her aghast lady's maid, whom she had dismissed for the evening, standing just inside the corridor. Given her intention to go to supper and then only the ball for a short while, she hadn't needed Cora, and since the girl had been somewhat seasick, Bronwyn had left her to rest. "I got lost. Why aren't you abed?"

The maid blushed. "I felt better, and Rawley thought I might enjoy a diversion."

"Rawley?" Bronwyn croaked in slow-dawning horror. Her brother's man of affairs was here?

No, no. It couldn't be him. But what were the odds that someone onboard would have the same name? Bronwyn's heart quailed but her brain rallied. It was a common name in the islands, wasn't it? This had to be a fluke because if it was the same man, there wasn't one chance in hell that he wouldn't know exactly who she was, which meant that Courtland himself would be well aware of her impulsive transatlantic journey.

Not what her purpose was, of course. She'd been much too careful in covering her steps, but she hadn't exactly hidden *who* she was. Once more, Bronwyn cursed herself for choosing the hide-in-plain-sight route. She should have worn a disguise. Too late now, however, when she'd thrown the name Lady Bronwyn Chase around like gold coin in a gambler's den.

There's no reason for him to be here.

It's a coincidence, that's all.

"Hullo, Little Bee."

Oh, hell in a dratted handbasket. Her luck was absolute shit. Bronwyn's heart dropped to her feet. Biting her lip, she turned to see the huge, handsome man leaning propped against the wall with his arms folded against his chest. Rawley resembled her brother with his close-cropped dark curls and midnight eyes, though his burnished skin was several shades darker than Courtland's. Rawley favored Courtland's mother's family—the first Marchioness of Borne had been a mix of Indian and African descent—and he, too, was a striking blend of the two.

Normally, her beloved half cousin was pleased to see her. However, the easy smile that he usually had for her was conspicuously absent.

"Does Courtland know?" she blurted out.

Black brows rose. "That you're on his ship right at this moment? Of course he does. You're his sister. He knows where you are at all times."

Damnation. Did that mean Courtland also knew what she was up to? Despite her instant dread at the thought of her mission becoming compromised because of her overprotective brother *and* his cousin, she hoisted her chin. "Why did you not make yourself known to me?" she demanded imperiously.

Those thick brows nearly shot into his hairline. "Don't take that hoity-toity tone with me, Little Bee. It might work to cow everyone else onboard, but not me. I did not tell you I was here because Ashvale did not want me to."

She squashed down the burst of shame at her

pretentious behavior and being called out for it so baldly. "Do you do everything my brother tells you?"

He smirked. "Perhaps as much as you do."

Bronwyn had the decency to blush. Clearly not, then. So that meant Rawley *was* spying on her, watching to see what she was up to. Thankfully, she'd hidden the sensitive correspondence from everyone, including her lady's maid, while in the privacy of her stateroom. Bronwyn bit her lip, attention flicking back to Cora who had moved to stand close to Rawley and stood wringing her hands and blushing. It was obvious there was something between them, especially from the soft looks her maid was sending Courtland's cousin.

Bronwyn narrowed her eyes. "How long has *this* been going on?"

Rawley relaxed. "For some time."

The expression of tenderness that crossed the big man's face was impossible to ignore. A *long* time, if Bronwyn had to guess. Something like envy curled through her. She was happy for them, just as she was happy that Courtland had found Ravenna. Love was a rare gift, not that she would ever be given the opportunity to receive it. Her mother intended to marry her off to the richest, most well-titled peer in London, and the chance of a love match for her would be like wishing for rain in purgatory.

It wouldn't matter if her future husband was old or ugly or cruel, or gained his wealth in an untoward manner. As long as he was part of the peerage, he would do. Bronwyn didn't have any illusions about that. And while Courtland was her guardian, her mother was devious in ways that could not be fathomed. No doubt upon her return, Bronwyn would be locked away in Kettering at the country seat until she could be safely married off to a man of her mother's choosing, right underneath her brother's nose.

In truth, that had been one of the reasons she'd agreed to the assignment in the first place.

Bronwyn wanted to make a real difference, yes. But she also knew her wings would be clipped soon enough, and she would be trapped in a fate she would not easily escape. Born and raised to be a peer's broodmare, her future was sealed. And if the Marchioness of Borne had her way, that would be sooner rather than later.

No thank you.

Suddenly, Bronwyn wanted nothing more than to stay with Cora and Rawley. She did not want to return to a ballroom and a world that promised only superficiality, superiority, and eventual suffocation—a mirror of the life waiting for her upon her return to England.

"Might I join you both up here for a little while?" she asked in a small voice.

There was that smile of his, finally. Rawley nodded, one large arm drawing Cora closer to him. "Of course you can." He grinned. "If you can keep up."

A weight lifted from her shoulders. "I might not be from the islands like you, but I assure you, Big Man, I can dance circles around you."

Nobody looked askance when she exited onto the

upper deck with Rawley and Cora, not even Lady Finley, who was being swung around in a rousing Scotch reel, or some of the other aristocrats Bronwyn recognized. As with most of the people in Courtland's circle, a wide mix of ethnicities greeted her. Men and women with skin varying in tone from as milky as hers to rich hues darker than Rawley's. The scene was a far cry from the ballroom below, but the sight of it made something inside of her come alive.

She might not be of mixed blood as Courtland was, but she felt a camaraderie lift her spirit all the same. Bronwyn knew that her brother hired anyone with the necessary skills for open positions on his ships and his estate, especially people from his mother's homeland. It was one of the things she most respected about Courtland. He judged people by the strength of their character, not their appearance or lineage.

Bronwyn didn't hesitate before jumping into the joyous fray, her smile wide as she paired up for a rousing polka with a sweaty young man with reddish-brown skin, long dark hair, and an open smile. "My lady," he said with a smart bow.

"It's just Bee," she said.

"And I'm Rishi."

She grinned. "Where are you from?"

"Trinidad."

She'd heard about the island in the southernmost West Indies. "I'm from London."

He pulled her into the first skipping turn, drawing a

breathless laugh from her as they hopped and then took three swift steps before another spin. "I know who you are."

Bronwyn frowned a little at that. "Truly?"

"I do some business with your brother, and he speaks quite fondly of you. He showed me a portrait of you once." Rishi winked. "I have to say, it hardly does you justice, Miss Bee."

She flushed at the compliment and gave herself over to the wild rush of the polka. The music was different, she noticed. Still at double time, but with the hollow, rhythmic sounds of the guiro, the bongo drums, and the maracas complementing the fiddlers.

After the first rousing round, she thanked Rishi for the dance and guzzled a tumbler full of something fizzy and sweet. Sweat poured off her body, but she'd never felt more energized in her life. Breathing great lungfuls of briny ocean air, she dragged Cora to the side and pulled her into an alcove. "Help me get these off," she said, reaching underneath for the tapes on her petticoats.

Cora's eyes rounded. "My lady!"

"It's much too hot and no one here will care."

"What if one of the guests notices, like the lady over there?" she asked.

"Then she does. Besides, Lady Finley has her hands full at the moment and doesn't seem to give a whit about propriety. Neither do the others for that matter. Quickly, Cora, I want to dance without sweating to death." Her maid grinned and released the ties. As Bronwyn shimmied out of the constricting layers, she whipped off her stockings and air kissed her bare calves. Heaven. She could have done with removing the tight corset as well, but no need to tempt fate. "Loosen the laces if you can."

Lastly, she pulled the butterfly-and-lily-tipped hairpins from her hair. Laughing with relief, she rejoined the line of dancers, mimicking Rawley's quick footwork in the country dance and letting the joyous music flow through her body. There were no rules, no expectations, no marriage noose hanging over her neck.

She let that bliss take her far away from reality.

———

Lady Bronwyn Chase was the most glorious thing he had ever seen.

Though she hardly resembled the lady from the ballroom downstairs at the moment. Hair brazenly down, the glossy brown waves skimming rosy shoulders and her flushed bosom with each jubilant bounce, hips swaying like a seasoned dancer, and her face—God, her *face*—wore an expression of such pleasure and delight it was breathtaking. *This* wasn't anything like the silly chit from before who simpered and preened. This was a mythical creature in her domain.

Valentine had never seen anything like it.

Like *her*.

Mesmerized, he barely took notice of the others on the crowded deck, though he had marked most of the people,

THE DUKE IN QUESTION 57

both passengers and crew, in his memory over the past days. Upon boarding, he had toured the entire ship, cataloging the faces. It was part of his process—always good to know who was in his space at all times. Finally, he tore his gaze away from the dancing goddess in a blue dress to the man who whirled her in a giddy circle and blinked in utter disbelief.

What the *hell*?

He was a hardened spy, and Rawley, Ashvale's man of business and cousin, had eluded his notice all along? What the devil was *he* doing here? And why was he dancing with Bronwyn? Ignoring the blast of possessiveness that heated his blood, Valentine narrowed his eyes. Ashvale trusted his cousin implicitly, which meant he had to know his marauding sister was onboard this ship. Why Rawley wouldn't have made his presence known nagged at him, however.

His eyes met Rawley's and the man showed no surprise to see him there. So *he* had also known that Thornbury was onboard. That realization bothered him even more, but as much as Rawley stood out because of his size, he could be undetectable when he chose to be. Valentine had his suspicions that the man was a covert operative himself, working for the Antiguan government as well as the Americans in the North fighting to abolish slavery.

Noel Rawley's name had come up in the British War Office with ties to Alexander Augusta, a field surgeon and one of Lincoln's highest-ranking Black Union officers in the Civil War, as well as Frederick Douglass, a fiercely outspoken activist in the abolitionist cause. The sudden thought of whether Rawley could be the Kestrel hit Valentine, but he dismissed it just as quickly. Rawley didn't fit the description. The Kestrel was a white English peer.

When the grinning man picked Bronwyn up by her waist and spun her, making her howl with laughter—not the nauseating tinkling sound from earlier but a full, throaty belly-laugh that had Valentine's jaw gaping loose—he almost started forward, but stuttered to a stop. What was he doing? Why was he reacting like a territorial creature? He had no claim on her, and Rawley cherished her like a sister.

It's your duty.

His duty to what? Protect her? Rawley was closer to her by a blood connection through the Duke of Ashvale than he was. The man was honorable and trusted by the duke. Rawley was family. It was *his* duty to look after the chit, not Valentine's. He should leave. Go back to the ballroom downstairs. Return to his job of finding the Kestrel.

Bronwyn was safe. Rawley would take care of her.

She was in good hands.

But the longer he stood there, the more he was inured to reason or logic; a man never ruled by passions of the flesh was fast becoming an alacritous disciple. Valentine was transfixed. She moved like blue flame, the dance so joyous that she gleamed. There were no masks, no pretense.

Just *her*.

And he wanted nothing more than to stay right where he was.

Valentine swallowed, muscles clenching and unclench-
ing with indecision as he watched her dance. Watched her
body undulate in ways that made his abdomen constrict
and did away with the fact that she was his best friend's
sister. She was a woman. A beautifully dangerous one
whom he was beginning to crave with a visceral, endless,
avid need.

When the music shifted to something different—
resembling a slower Viennese waltz that had couples
moving scandalously close, including Rawley and
Bronwyn's slip of a maid—Valentine found himself
pushing through the crowd. He stared down anyone
who dared to get near to Bronwyn, baring his teeth. Men
retreated, understanding that there was a much larger
presence in the room. She, however, was oblivious, eyelids hooded, gilt-tipped lashes leaving shadows over
flushed cheekbones as she swayed with a radiant smile
on her face.

When he slid a palm over the warm, damp fabric covering her torso and drew her back to him, she didn't shove
him away, only continued to sway gently to the three-
count measure. It took his stupid brain a second to see
that her slender body was unencumbered by its usual ring
of petticoats. His other hand went to her hip and the confirmation of what he suspected nearly unmanned him. No
other layer rested between the satin and her hot, bare skin.

The sweaty heat of her sweet-apple fragrance seduced
him as much as the shape of her did, but then Valentine
blinked when she remained silent. Did she know who he

was? Her lashes were still downcast. Would she be this familiar with anyone? With Rawley?

A husky voice pierced his thoughts. "Did you enjoy the show, Your Grace?"

His breath rushed out on a tide of relief. "Valentine."

"I beg your pardon?"

"My name is Valentine," he rasped. "And yes. Was that for me?"

Valentine had been all over the world on his travels in service to the Crown, and while he'd encountered many different cultures and their styles of dance, the sight of Bronwyn—the demure, sheltered, haughty English daughter of a marquess and sister to a duke—dancing with such unbridled enthusiasm had been a shock to his senses.

"It was for *me*, sir." She turned in his arms to face him, one palm going to his shoulder in the standard waltz position. "Did you know that the locals in the West Indies, in countries like Antigua and Trinidad, took English country dances, quadrilles, and reels, and turned them into their own according to their cultural traditions?" That low, rich laughter so unlike the tones from upstairs reached him again. "My sister-in-law said that she loves to dance in bare feet." Without warning, she kicked off her own slippers.

He frowned. "Don't. You could cut your soles."

"Yes, I could, and this ship could get caught in a freakish storm and sink. Sometimes, Valentine, you must seize the moment."

His fingers flexed on her hip. "Who are you?"

"Out here, I'm…Bee."

"You're nothing like you were during the past week," he rumbled, unable to reconcile the two very different versions of her.

Her shoulders shook and the curve of one cheek rose as she turned in his arms to face him. Blue eyes glittered like aquamarines, a sheen of sweat coating her rosy, over-warm skin. Moonlight wound through her hair and shone off the glistening apples of her cheeks while damp tendrils clung to her brow, her temples, and her neck. He didn't dare look lower, though her bodice gaped perilously, a glistening ribbon of sweat catching his eye.

"Women have many layers, Your Grace. We don't give up all our secrets for just anyone. Otherwise, they are not worth the discovery. Surely a man of your persuasion would know such a thing."

"A man of my persuasion?"

"Are we still playing games, Your Grace?" The taunting words drizzled through him and he frowned at the question. Was Lisbeth right? That she was sharper than she seemed? He fell back to his usual dismissal.

"I am a duke, Lady Bronwyn," he tossed back, distracted by the renewed motion of her body that followed the slightly quicker tempo than a usual waltz and the purposeful gleam in her gaze. "That is all."

"Then you're on your way to Philadelphia for a pleasure trip?"

Valentine studiously ignored the unguarded reaction that word claimed from his already too-interested lower half. "No, I am looking for someone actually," he said and then frowned, wondering why he'd volunteered that information. Her body seemed to tense, but then she relaxed on the next beat of music and quarter turn.

"So the huntsman *is* on the hunt, even if he's been put out to pasture."

His eyes caught hers, amusement winking in their azure depths. The little minx was teasing him. "I'm not on my last legs yet, my lady."

"Clearly."

When the music came to a lilting crescendo and couples separated with enthusiastic clapping as a heart-thumping reel began, she rose to her tiptoes and pressed a kiss to his cheek, so close to the corner of his mouth that the heat of her breath mingled with his. A miniscule shift and his lips would be on hers. Valentine froze, the brand of her mouth imprinting on his skin like a trail of fire before she broke the connection.

"Why did you do that?"

"Why not? I wanted to."

The husky reply had him looking at her mouth and then dipping to the pulse that fluttered at the base of her throat. He wanted to taste it beneath his tongue, suck on the cinnamon-apple salt of her skin, follow that tempting, glistening trace that led to the deep valley between her breasts. Valentine's eyes snagged on the edge of what looked like a piece of parchment tucked into the corner of her bodice, the hint of a waxed seal almost visible, and he frowned.

"What's that?"

Her eyes followed his, and she let out a laugh—not the kind from just before—but that tinkling sound he'd heard so many times over the past week. *Odd.* The shift from the full, gut-clenching laughter from earlier made him frown. "Your Grace! That is a lady's private treasure." Something about the sudden coyness in her voice gave him pause and set off a few alarm bells. "But if you must know, it's a love letter. To you, actually. I meant to find the courage to give it to you in the dining room, but then I could not."

He stepped back, cool sea air rushing between them, cooling both his ardor and his fogged brain. "A love letter?" he repeated carefully.

"Surely you must know of my feelings, my dear sweet duke." Her sigh of longing seemed forced, at odds with the sudden stiffness of her carriage. A mask had crept back into place, though he did not know what had caused it or what its purpose was, only that it unsettled him. "Valentine, wherefore art thou, sweet Valentine. You have given me leave to address you thusly, haven't you?"

His skin itched. Something definitely wasn't right.

But then she'd ducked under his arm and was gone before he could collect himself, slipping past him in a blur of filmy satin skirts toward the staircase that had brought him here. He turned to follow, but was blocked by none other than Rawley.

"Thornbury."

His jaw clenched. "Get out of my way."

"No." Rawley had the audacity to smile.

"You know who I am, don't you?"

"I also know who *she* is."

Valentine fought the urge to put the bigger man on his arse. It would be hard, but he could do it. His muscles rolled beneath his skin in readiness, driven by a wild impulse he didn't care to investigate too deeply. He was *this* close to breaking his own hard and fast rule of never making a scene in public when Rawley's eyebrows rose as he crossed his arms across his massive chest and laughed at him. Valentine blinked.

"Where has this infamous control of yours gone, Thornbury? One dance and you'll let your cock make your choices for you?"

"Like you weren't doing anything different a minute ago," he replied in a testy tone, though reason—along with a healthy amount of embarrassment—was starting to seep in through the red smog of lust that blanketed his brain.

"I love Cora and plan to marry her," Rawley said mildly. "Do you love Lady Bronwyn and plan to do the same?"

Valentine opened his mouth. "I..."

Want to debauch every part of her. Lift those damp skirts, discover those long, silken legs, and lay waste to the treasure between her thighs.

He closed his mouth, the hunger dissipating from his veins like ice melting on a summer day. Ashvale would kill him if he debauched his younger sister. And Rawley wouldn't hesitate to put Valentine's head through a wall if he suspected an inkling of his corrupted private thoughts. His temper ebbed as quickly as it had risen.

Clearly, his intentions weren't in the least bit

honorable. A lady like Bronwyn deserved to be wooed and wedded, and the truth was that marriage—outside of the contrived kind for clandestine Home Office purposes—wasn't for him. At least until he was forced to find a duchess for the sake of the dukedom…which would be in the very distant future.

Hell, he'd been besotted by a brilliant smile and nearly fallen into a snare as old as time because, in the heat of the moment, he'd forgotten who she was and what she represented.

A lady of the *ton*…and a surefire marriage trap.

It wasn't her fault. She'd been clear about what she wanted all along. Thank God he hadn't read that love letter, though perhaps that would have been the precise incentive he needed to stay far away.

Five

Twenty-four hours later, Bronwyn's heart was still racing. She couldn't believe that the Duke of Thornbury had nearly discovered the letter that she'd tucked into her corset and completely forgotten was there. She had been lost to the music, lost to the dance, and when he had taken her in his arms, she'd been lost to a delicious desire that had nearly derailed her.

Nearly derailed her *mission*.

Because God forbid that he discover what she was hiding.

And not just the arousal under her skirts. In truth, she hadn't been above dragging the man to the nearest alcove and demanding that he ruin her properly. The only thing that had stopped her—that had kept her from carrying on like a seasoned courtesan—was the watchful eye of Rawley, even though he'd had his hands full with Cora.

Like *that* wasn't a surprise in itself. The normally talkative maid was tight-lipped about her torrid affair with Ashvale's cousin, though she did admit that she was deeply in love with him. Love was a far step from the emotion Bronwyn felt with Thornbury.

More like carnal dementia, thanks to all the blood from her brain that had descended to intimate regions in tune to the throbbing beat of the drums. She'd felt that thundering pulse everywhere...behind her breastbone, at the points of her nipples, between her drenched thighs.

She *had* been wet for him, there was no denying that fascinating force of nature or the fact that he made her body thaw to liquid with just a word, much less than his touch. The moment she had sensed him enter the room, every hair on her nape had risen. The awareness had been instant and visceral, like a shock of lightning to her nerves.

No doubt Rawley would be reporting back to her brother about her scandalous behavior and the fact that she had been practically writhing on his longtime acquaintance in a public space. Anyone could have seen them, including the handful of aristocrats and gentry who'd been on the upper deck, and the fact that everyone had been of a similar mind to dance beneath the stars would not stop juicy gossip.

Then again, it wasn't like the other passengers and off-duty crew weren't wrapped up in their own little worlds. Perhaps no one had taken notice of the two of them. Heat rushed through her at the memory. She hadn't been able to curb herself, not when she'd felt that strong palm sliding over her trembling belly and then her waist, the tip of his thumb so very near to her needy, aching breasts.

She'd wanted that thumb to go higher. To squeeze. To pinch and roll.

You were lucky it didn't before he discovered what was really inside your bodice.

The solemn voice was a reminder of how close she'd

come to being found out. The lie about the letter had been easy enough. If she had said it was nothing, his curiosity would have been piqued. A love letter had been nothing short of a stroke of genius because now he was back to thinking she was a witless, smitten idiot with a misplaced infatuation who was intent on declaring her heart.

She let out a low laugh.

Nothing like the threat of undying devotion to send a man scurrying for the hills.

Regret sluiced through her. For once, she had wanted him to *see* her as she was, and he had. Gods, that moment of being stripped to her elemental core had nearly cost her everything, but in hindsight, she did not regret the choice to dance, knowing part of her performance *had* been for him, despite her protest to the contrary. The duke had desired her.

She'd seen the glint of hunger brightening those golden eyes, felt the possession in those large hands.

All for her.

What would it be like to couple with a man capable of such passion?

"My lady?" There was an edge of impatience to Cora's voice as though she'd tried to get through to her several times. Blushing at the indecent swerve of her thoughts, Bronwyn blinked and gestured for her to continue. "Shall I ask the footmen to come for the luggage?"

"Oh, yes. Please do."

They would be disembarking in short order, and with some luck, she would not cross paths with the disturbing

Duke of Thornbury. Something occurred to her as she watched the maid flit around like a distracted bird.

"Cora? Did you tell Rawley that I would be on this ship?"

Wide eyes met hers. "No, my lady." Bronwyn relaxed, seeing only earnestness in the girl's stare, but then her stomach sank at her next words. "He already knew."

Shit.

What else did he know? And if by default her brother also knew, which was obvious, then why did he not put a stop to it? Courtland might be coiled around the finger of his very daunting duchess, but he was exceedingly protective about family, which included Bronwyn.

Heavens, what if he told Rawley to forbid her from leaving the ship? He wouldn't, would he? The answer was there on the heels of the denial. Courtland would, and could, given he was a duke and accustomed to being obeyed. And it wasn't as though she could fight Rawley. The man was the size of a mountain, and in truth, he was just as protective and probably even more so than her elder brother.

She would have to tread carefully and quickly. As much as pushing the limits thrilled her in addition to doing what she could to make the difference in the world she so wanted, she did not want to lose the esteem of the brother she'd only just found.

How important could this message be?

Perhaps she should just tear it to pieces and dispose of it in the ocean.

The thought didn't sit well with her. She'd come this far. She had to complete what she'd committed to for Wentworth's sake. He believed in their cause of righting the wrongs that the British Empire had wrought through colonization. What they were doing would help those who remained oppressed and enslaved in the American states. Who knew what rested upon the delivery of this letter that she had been tasked with?

Wentworth hadn't been sure to trust her, but her brother's passenger liner had been the fastest way to get to Philadelphia, and he'd been trapped between the devil and a hard place. Bronwyn had sensed her handler's indecision.

"Perhaps, I should go," he'd said.

"No, you're too well known," Bronwyn had insisted. "I'll do it. I'm Ashvale's sister. No one will suspect me."

"This is important."

"I know, Wentworth."

He'd scowled. "Sesily might be a better option. She's American. This is America's war, isn't it?"

Bronwyn had blinked, frowning at the blunt, harsh reply. "It's *everyone's* war, Wentworth. We all have to live in this world. I want to go."

He had scrubbed at his face. "I don't need to explain to you what will happen if you're caught with this."

"I *know.*"

A shiver rumbled through her. She could be arrested. Detained. Thrown into prison. Worse. It would be a public scandal that no one, least of all her or her family, would recover from. She might be protected by a powerful name, but that would not stop her from being ousted from British society. None of her friends would be allowed to be seen with her for fear of damaging their own reputations by association. She would be completely and utterly shunned.

But some risks were worth it. Sometimes, putting oneself on the line for the sake of others who needed one's help was worth it. That was the definition of a true ally. She could take the easy way out and walk away— she would not be harmed regardless and that choice was hers to make—but what would that make her? Complicit. Weak.

A coward.

You asked for this. People are depending on you.

Once the porters had cleared the stateroom on the heels of her lady's maid, Bronwyn was alone. She retrieved the folded parchment, which had come open thanks to the heat of her own body the night before. She could read it, reseal it, and no one would be the wiser.

Sod it. Better to know what she was getting into than not.

Bronwyn opened the correspondence and sagged against the paneling as she read. Oh, dear God above. It wasn't *nothing*. It was everything. Damn, damn, *damn*! She couldn't walk away from this. Rereading the missive, she committed the details to memory. A man named John Wilkes Booth, an acquaintance of the deported Brent Sommers who had been arrested by the Duke of Thornbury, was planning to abduct President Abraham

Lincoln on March 17 from a place called Campbell General Hospital in Washington, DC.

Bronwyn's stomach curled in upon itself. It was already the tenth of March.

She couldn't fail.

Good gracious, what if she *did* fail?

Courage, Bronwyn!

Her contact in Philadelphia was Mary Richards, a free Black woman who worked with the notorious Elizabeth Van Lew, an abolitionist and head of the espionage network out of Richmond, Virginia. Mary had been north several times at the behest of her employer. Wentworth had told her that both Mary and Elizabeth were indispensable to the Union cause, sending coded invisible correspondence north that could only be seen when milk was applied. Unfortunately, that was not the case with Bronwyn's message, which was written in clear, black ink and visible to all. Should it be discovered in her possession by the wrong forces, the repercussions would be horrific.

Taking in a calming breath, Bronwyn smoothed her skirts and made sure her bonnet was properly affixed. Moving to the small grate, she struck the flint to the tinder and held one end of the parchment to the fire until it burned away to nothing. The date, name, and place were in her head. *She* would be the message. She tucked the remaining sheet from Thornbury's report into her corset—she couldn't memorize all the names and that would be safe enough there for the moment—and left the room.

The wharves lining the Delaware riverfront, which was thankfully not frozen, were crowded. Philadelphia was a less popular port than Boston or New York, given the river that tended to freeze often so it took much longer to navigate around Cape May, but luckily the SS *Valor* was a private ship and did not depend on set timetables or routes. There was no sign of Rawley or Thornbury, but that didn't mean that they weren't both lurking somewhere. At the end of the ramp, Cora was waiting near a carriage, and Bronwyn pulled her cloak around her to ward off the chill in the air.

"Where's your paramour?" she asked the maid.

Cora's cheeks brightened. "He has some business to attend to."

"Does he know where we are going?"

"Yes, my lady."

The news didn't bother her. In fact, she was glad that Rawley knew. Despite her desire to do her job and finish the mission, Bronwyn had no intention of courting danger and putting herself *or* Cora in harm's way. A little extra brawn never hurt. The rooms Wentworth had secured on her behalf were at a nondescript but clean hotel, near her ailing "Aunt Tillie's" house just north of South Street. As she checked in, the clerk handed her a folded message that only listed an address of a tavern. The Bell in Hand Ale House.

She would have to find a way to get there unseen by Rawley.

Or a certain meddlesome duke…

Valentine's posterior was sore from sitting in a carriage outside Lady Bronwyn's hotel for the better part of six hours. His stomach let out an obnoxious growl as well, but he couldn't risk letting her slip through his fingers. He *knew* she was up to something. Lisbeth had remained onboard, visually checking each of the hundred and three passengers leaving the ship against the portrait they had of the Kestrel, while he was here in a cramped carriage snooping on a woman.

Valentine was 90 percent sure there was no sick relative, but what was she up to? Philadelphia wasn't exactly a popular hub, and America was embroiled in the middle of a civil war. Was she meeting a gentleman? A lover? A future husband? The thought irritated him more than it should. Why should he care if she wanted to tie herself to a wealthy American? Perhaps she hoped it would get her away from the unpleasant Marchioness of Borne.

Rawley had gone missing the moment the ship docked. Given Valentine's knowledge of Rawley's close ties to men like Augusta and Douglass, he wasn't surprised in the least. Valentine had hoped to pawn off the responsibility of keeping an eye on the chit to the Duke of Ashvale's cousin, but when he'd seen Bronwyn getting into a carriage with her maid, he'd had no choice but to follow or lose track of her. Lisbeth had rolled her eyes, but told him to go. And so, here he was.

Stuck in a carriage.

Spying on a woman who was most likely having a rendezvous with a libertine.

Was she? Valentine blinked, pondering the question. It wasn't any of his business, but he was curious. After working with a firecracker like Lisbeth who flaunted her lovers across three continents, he was the last person who would tell a woman what to do with her body. The world of the *ton*, however, was a different story. If a lady, especially an unmarried one, dared to break the rules, she was excoriated faster than one could say *scandal*.

What if she was already betrothed to someone here?

He hadn't even thought to ask if she was. *That* notion didn't sit well either.

Clearly, his hunger was making him irrational. It was *good* if she was engaged. Best for everyone. The sight of a tall, lithe figure in a bulky, dark coat coming out of the dark alley adjacent to the hotel had him sitting up, but it wasn't her. The brim of a top hat obscured the person's face, but from his vantage point, the figure was most definitely a man. Valentine blinked, peering at the disappearing shape of the person and a sensual gait that seemed all too familiar. Unless that wasn't a man…

Bloody hell, it was her!

Swearing aloud, he descended from the coach and kept to the shadows until she got into a hackney a few streets away. He waved down another hansom with curt instructions to the coachman to follow her conveyance. His clever quarry didn't go far, only a few streets north to what looked like a tavern. The wooden placket on the wall read BELL IN HAND.

"Here we are, sir," the driver said. "McGillin's, best place for an ale and a cottage pie. Ask for Ma or Pa and tell 'em Beckett sent ya."

Valentine nodded and paid the man. He had no interest in food. His stomach gave a loud growl as if in defiance of that last thought, but he ignored it. First, he had to make sure that the daft chit didn't compromise herself by meeting with a strange man alone. This wasn't the place for aristocratic young ladies. Though maybe he was mistaken about Ashvale's little sister. It wouldn't be the only time he'd ever been wrong about a woman.

She's not Lisbeth.

No, Lisbeth had been raised by strict, pious, wealthy parents, but her father had often done business in seedier parts of London. She'd given her virginity to a flashman when she was fifteen and then robbed him blind. To her, sex and seduction were tools to be used, and use them well she did. It was Lisbeth who had told him that sheltered girls were usually the most repressed, and they tended to act out when offered a modicum of independence.

Was that what Bronwyn was doing? Acting out?

Fulfilling her fantasies?

Keeping the collar of his own coat high, Valentine waited a few minutes near the entrance before shifting to an empty table with a view of the room. It was crowded and dim, but he spotted her quickly. Now that he was on to her disguise, his attention was instantly drawn to where she sat in a shadowed corner of the ale house. Facing the door, he sipped on a mug of ale, one gloved hand clasped around the tankard.

Her face still remained partially obscured by the hat brim, but he had no doubt it was her. That imperious jut of her chin and the impatient flutter of her fingers were dead giveaways. She did the latter when she was nervous. He frowned. Sitting hunched as she was and in profile, she reminded him of someone else, too, but for the life of him he couldn't put his finger on it.

"What'll you have, boss?" a buxom girl asked, the look in her eye stating that she'd offer a lot more than tavern fare if he was interested.

"Ale." His stomach rumbled as he threw a few coppers onto the table. "And a sausage pie."

"Comin' right up. Ya let ol' Dolly know if ya need anythin' else."

He nodded, never taking his eye off Bronwyn. How long did she intend to wait, and who was she meeting? The minutes turned into a quarter of an hour, and when his drink and food were delivered, he devoured them. She didn't do anything but nurse that mug of hers, eyes trained intently on the doorway.

When nearly an hour had passed, cold air whisked past him as a strapping man stalked from the entrance straight to where she sat. Her fingers instantly stopped moving when he took the chair opposite. Valentine was sitting too far away to hear their conversation, but he could see the strain around Bronwyn's mouth as her lips grew translucent.

"Where's…Richard?" He couldn't quite make out her words, but it seemed like this wasn't the person she was supposed to meet. The man shook his head and answered something that made her hands go to her lap, her entire body much too still. Her shoulders went up into a slow shrug, that vapid look that he was much too used to coming over her face. The man's hand slamming on the tabletop quickly put an end to whatever game she was playing.

What the hell was going on?

Valentine stood and quietly slipped around the periphery of the room to where he could better hear the conversation. It was a risky move. If Lady Bronwyn glanced up in his direction, she would see him, but she was much too focused on the man at her front.

"You're not who I expected," she was saying.

The man, an ugly-looking brute with pockmarked, pale skin, scowled. "Change of plans. Hand over the list." From the sound of his accent, Valentine deduced he was American.

"I don't know what you're talking about. I'm here to meet a friend."

"Stop playing games, lovey. We know you have it."

We? At that, Valentine's eyes darted around the tavern. Other than the man, no one else had entered, but that didn't mean that others weren't lying in wait. It could be anyone in there, including the barman or any of the patrons. Bronwyn's stare narrowed, too, and then hardened as though some deeper, survival instinct was kicking in.

Every sense in his own body grew heightened,

alerting him to the threat. After so many years, he'd honed his nature to recognize trouble, and it was there in the form of this hulking man who was growing more agitated by the second. However, Valentine couldn't tell if he was more agitated because *she* had noticed the signs of danger and was about to act or whether the instincts were his own. Both, probably.

"I believe, sir, you have me confused with someone else. I am not in possession of any list." She paused, a thoughtful, calm stare returning to the man. Her posture had changed again. Instead of being rounded with submission, it had become straight and keen like a knife edge, as though crossing her would get a man slashed to ribbons. Who was this girl? "However, if you have a message for the Kestrel, please let me know."

"The fuckin' what?"

The man took the words right out of Valentine's mouth. Surely he didn't hear that right? Brain whirling, his mouth fell open. Lady Bronwyn was in league with the Kestrel? Had she met with him on the ship? The questions raced through his head like wildfire. Had the Kestrel been one of the young bucks she'd been flirting with, and he'd somehow not noticed because he'd been insensibly distracted by *her*?

"Never mind," she said coolly and placed both hands on the table to show she wasn't a threat, but the man's aggressive mien didn't change.

This was going to go sour very quickly.

Just as Valentine made the decision to intervene—he'd

come up with some plausible story as to why he was there—the table between them went flying as the lady flipped it, clipping her companion in the face and dousing him in a tankard three-quarters-full of ale. The man shoved upward with a roar, crashing into the man behind him in the process, and within seconds, pandemonium erupted into a bar brawl. Fists and curses flew in tandem.

In the commotion, Valentine saw Bronwyn duck under a meaty arm that reached for her, nearly catching on the back of her coat, as she slid into a narrow servants' hallway that led to the back of the establishment.

Punching out blindly at the two drunks who tried to block his way, he shoved past the throng of surging, flailing bodies and followed where she'd disappeared into the narrow hallway that lead out to a filthy alley. But she was gone, nothing but a hint of cinnamon and apples left on the wind. Curse his luck that he hadn't been closer.

Reaching for the pistols clipped into the holsters at his hips, Valentine took off.

She couldn't have gotten too far.

Six

"Oy, LITTLE BUNNY RABBIT," A VOICE CALLED FROM behind Bronwyn. "Where're you runnin' to?"

Damn and blast! Of course there would have been others waiting. He'd said as much: *We know you have it.* Bronwyn lengthened her stride, her lungs screaming in her chest. She'd been smart to put on the gentlemen's clothing beneath the heavy coat that she had discarded as soon as she'd begun running. She had learned the hard way that a lady's gown led to much less economy of movement, especially when fleeing for one's life. And she definitely was doing just that at the moment.

That man from the tavern was most certainly not Miss Mary Richards.

And even if Mary had sent him in her stead, he had not known Wentworth's secret code they had agreed upon to confirm each other's identity. It was a rather simple question about the quality of the hops in the ale, and he had looked at her as if she were daft. That had been the first clue. His appearance had unnerved her, not to mention the way he'd scrutinized her like an insect he wanted to squash under his boot. Every warning bell in her body had rung from the moment he'd sat down, but she hadn't wanted to misjudge someone on account of their appearance.

War made strangers and monsters of everyone.

As the minutes had crawled by, however, she'd realized that somehow she'd been found out. How, she did not know. She hoped that poor Miss Richards was not in harm's way or hadn't been hurt and forced to give up any information that might hurt her. That man didn't look like he had a kind bone in his body, and Bronwyn had no doubt he would have done dreadful things had he gotten his hands on either of them. Had he come to *kill* her? Her blood ran cold.

Clenching her teeth, she willed her legs to pump faster, the soles of her shoes snapping against the gravel of the road. She had no idea where she was going, tearing down darkened street after darkened street. Unlike London, this wasn't familiar territory, after all, but if she could find a safe place to hide, then she could figure out her next steps. For now, she had to avoid her pursuers. If they caught her, she was dead. Or worse. She didn't want to become a sorry casualty in a hole somewhere.

She cursed again.

Why hadn't she left a note for Cora, letting her know where she was going?

It wasn't that she didn't usually do that, but tonight she had been preoccupied, her nerves nearly shot to death. Her confidence that Rawley might be present and watching her every move hadn't helped either. It was almost as if a part of her had expected the adept islander to follow her. She had foolishly hoped he would.

A stupid, *stupid* assumption on her part while she was

in a foreign country meeting with unfamiliar people…and now she was going to pay a horrific price for the mistake. Her lungs were going to collapse in her chest, her breath streaming white fog from the deepening chill in the crisp air. Every muscle in her body burned from exertion.

There!

A slab of wood lay open on one hinge, leading to an underground space. From what she could tell, it looked like a root cellar—the kind that merchants or farmers stored food and produce in to keep them cool. She could hide in there. The streets were deserted and quiet, but beyond this residential-looking square, the area opened up into the docks and that would be much too exposed for her liking.

No, she had to hide here and pray for some luck. Running toward the opening that some good soul had forgotten to close, she climbed down the crude, uneven steps and pulled the door shut, enclosing herself in darkness but for a meager sliver of light through the crack. Bronwyn tried to ease her breaths as best as she could, the panting sounds sawing through her throat loud and harsh in the quiet. She dug in her pockets for the pistol she carried, feeling its comforting weight in her palm. At least, she was armed. The small weapon was only good for one shot, but she'd make it count if she had to.

It would have been so easy to shoot the man in the tavern, and she had almost done so, but getting arrested and detained was not part of the plan. Not while she didn't know who she could trust. The sound of clopping footsteps echoed beyond the doors, and Bronwyn held her breath. There had to be at least two men from the number of footfalls. Maybe more. They went past as she had hoped they would, but she didn't move. Not yet. It was a good thing she waited, too, because those same treads returned, only slower. Bronwyn strained her ears, wishing she could see, but she didn't dare move.

"Come out, li'l darlin'," a gravelly voice called out much too close to her hiding spot. "We won't hurt you."

"She's gone, Carl."

"Little bunny was fast."

Raucous laughter rung out. "You're just too fecking slow."

The second voice sounded garbled. There were a few scuffling sounds and then the scent of cigarette smoke wafted inside. They had to be close if she could smell it through the doors. Goodness, her legs were beginning to cramp. Bronwyn inched forward slightly, shifting the pressure off her thighs, but it sent a small scatter of gravel down the stairs that sounded like gunshots to her ears. She held her breath.

"Did you hear that, Ralphie?"

"Fecking rats."

"Let's head back. Larry and Frank went the other way."

God, Bronwyn hoped there weren't any rats in the cellar she was hiding in. She could think of nothing more horrible than one of them crawling up her leg. She blinked, remembering what had brought her here in the first place. Never mind, capture by Carl and Ralphie would be *much* worse. After a few minutes, their voices got fainter, and with no small amount of relief, Bronwyn realized they were walking away. And then a shout made her freeze.

"Oy, he was in the tavern!"

"A rich toff by the looks of him. At least we won't go home empty-handed."

The sounds of a scuffle reached her ears, punctuated by dull thwacks and grunts. What sounded like a moan pierced the air. She couldn't tell if it had come from her two pursuers or whatever poor sod had happened upon them by accident.

It's none of your business, Bronwyn. Stay hidden.

There were more out there, including the brutish lout from the tavern, who she knew would want a personal reckoning after she'd upended a table at him. But she couldn't stay hidden, not when some innocent soul was getting mugged by those two unpleasant criminals. Carefully, she eased upward, cringing when more gravel skittered beneath her feet. She pushed the door upward, hoping that the hinges would not be old and rusty and loud. Thankfully, they weren't. Her eyes adjusted to the gloom, she saw three shadowy, grappling figures taking center stage.

One bearded redhead lay groaning on the ground, while a man—a tall, well-dressed, hatless man with a cap of light-brown curls—kicked a knife out of his hands that went skating halfway across the courtyard. The other man ran at him from behind, and she couldn't help it, she shouted out a warning. But it was too late. The man looked directly at her and Bronwyn shuddered with the wallop of recognition just as the knife in the second man's hand came down.

The Duke of Thornbury was here.

With unearthly, catlike speed for a man of his size, he dodged the brunt of the strike and slammed upward with his own fist right into the man's throat. Crimson welled over his neckline, spotting his white cravat with red, and Bronwyn realized with a cry that the assailant's knife had found his skin after all. He'd avoided a killing blow, but gotten carved from chin to collarbone in the process. The sight of that blood did something to her.

"Valentine!"

"Stay there," he growled. "Don't move."

It was in slow motion that she saw the fallen man pulling a gun from his boot. Bronwyn didn't think; she pulled the pistol from her pocket, aimed, and pulled the trigger. The bullet caught the man right in the thigh, but it was enough for him to drop the weapon and collapse.

———

Valentine stared at her in mute shock before rushing over to where she stood like a deer frozen in the shine of a lantern, frowning ferociously at the man she'd shot as if daring him to rise. "Run!" he rasped, taking hold of her arm in an unyielding grip and ushering her from the open square. "There are more of them, including that big beast from the tavern."

"What are you doing here?" she bit out over her shoulder as she hurried to keep up with him.

He glared down at her. "Looking out for your fool self."

"Last I checked, I didn't need much looking after, Your Grace," she shot back, even though he'd seen the gratitude and the fear in her expression. "I'm not the one bleeding like a stuck pig or who would have been shot through the gut. I was quite fine in my quiet little hiding place."

"These men are not playing parlor games."

She let out a gasping snort. "Is that so? Because I could have sworn he invited me to play whist right after a game of blindman's bluff."

"Put that vigor toward running instead of nattering, and we just might make it out of here."

"You're bleeding," she panted, eyes slicking over him again.

His neck stung, but he could pay it no mind. It was in one of those places that bled profusely because of the thinness of the skin, but he hoped the injury wasn't anything more than a scratch. He suffered worse and lived.

And besides, they were moving much too slowly. While the lady was commendably fast on her feet, he could hear the indistinct shouts of their followers, which meant they weren't far behind. Thankfully, he knew Philadelphia well enough to figure out which routes to take, but they wouldn't have a hope in hell if they didn't pick up the pace.

The big man from the tavern hadn't been that far from Valentine's heels, but he'd managed to throw him off near Market Street. In the process, he'd lost Bronwyn, and it was only by sheer luck that he'd come upon the two bully ruffians who'd stopped for a cigarette in that square. Was it also by luck that *she* had saved his life twice now? The first time with the shout and the second with that rather excellent shot. Had she meant to shoot the man in a place he might survive?

Valentine shook his head. She was a witless chit with nary a skill beyond chattering the ear off the nearest gentleman. She'd probably pointed and shot, and hoped for the best. He revised the opinion as soon as he made it. No, her hold on that weapon had been one of confident skill, not the grip of a novice. He attempted to reconcile the versions of her he'd seen—the flighty coquette, the carefree dancer, and most of all, the marksman in disguise who met strange men in taverns and referenced a notorious person of interest. Valentine intended to get to the truth of the matter sooner or later.

If they made it through this alive, that was.

A sharp cry tore through the air just as Bronwyn stumbled on a crooked section of cobblestone. "My ankle," she gasped with a pained hop. "I think I've twisted it."

"Shit!" he swore, glancing around. They were nearing the Schuylkill River, heading west. "We need to cross, if we can. There's cover of parkland there toward the Fairmount Water Works from the old riverfront grounds."

"You lead. I'll follow. I won't slow us down."

Bronwyn's face was contorted by a grimace, but she hobbled along, wincing each time she put pressure on her injured ankle. Valentine had to admire her sheer mettle. He added this side of her to the list he was compiling in his head. The Bronwyn he had expected based on the version of her from the ship would have swooned, wept, and demanded he carry her. This woman gave no quarter to what had to be sizable pain.

"Here, let me," he said, swooping her up in his arms, bridal style.

"Thornbury, what are you doing?"

He grinned down at her and increased his pace. "I liked it more when you called me Valentine."

"And I like it more when I'm not treated like a sack of potatoes," she panted, pushing a hand into his chest. "Put me down this instant. I can see to myself."

He narrowed his gaze on her, taking in the red cheeks and mussed hair as well as the stubborn line of those plush lips. "Sack of potatoes? You're right, that would be much better."

Without losing a step, he swung her up in his arms so that her belly was resting up over his shoulder and bracketed by his arm behind her thighs, ignoring her rumble of outrage. Given her choice of clothing, there were no ridiculously wide underlayers to navigate, nor was he blinded by copious numbers of ruffles.

"Put me down, you insufferable oaf," she wheezed, head hanging down while she kicked her legs.

"This insufferable oaf is about to save your hide." He slapped her on the rump, some lusty and deranged part of his brain taking in the fact that it was round and pert beneath the snug twill of the trousers she wore. "So quiet and stop wriggling."

"Did you just spank me?" Her voice was ripe with indignation.

"I will again if you keep making that racket." Valentine grinned, driven by a new burst of energy, brought on by the spitfire he held over his shoulder. "And that wasn't a spank, it was a tap. Trust me, you'll know the feel of my hand over this luscious, bared arse of yours."

She went quiet suddenly, and his grin widened when a sound like barely shuttered rage tore past her lips. "You are vile. How dare you? Put me down this instant."

"Stop bloody squirming." He punctuated his words with pats of his palm. "Or I'll drop you and leave you behind for those men to find. With your injury, how long do you think it will take them to catch up?"

"I'll hide again," she said in defiance.

Not wanting to squabble with her or deal with her struggles, he stopped, nearly losing his hold over her thighs in the process. "If that's what you truly want, Lady Bronwyn, I will do it. Tell me, but we don't have much time."

She didn't have much of a choice, and as stubborn as she seemed to be, Valentine was hoping that she would not substitute common sense for pride. "Run, damn you, Thornbury!" she spat.

It was just as well because more shouts reached them, but before he'd taken more than a dozen steps, more shouts reached him from the other end of the street. He sat Bronwyn on a crate that was half-hidden by a short wall. "Stay here."

"Where are you going?"

She pulled on his sleeve, halting him. "Valentine." He turned, one brow lifting at the troubled expression on her face that was quickly hidden. "Don't die."

"Worried about me, imp?"

"Just worried about losing my very capable beast of burden."

His grin was wicked when he grasped her chin in his hand and crashed his lips to hers. "You can ride me anyway you want, my lady."

Bemused and thoroughly scandalized, Bronwyn touched a finger to her tingling lips.

It'd barely been a kiss, more of a violent meeting of open mouths with a single wicked swipe of a sleek, hot tongue over her lower lip, but it had rocked her to her toes. One because it was *Thornbury*, the man whose two favorite emotions were grim and grimmer.

And two because now she wanted much more than that small taste.

It didn't matter that they were in a race for their lives or what was at stake. All she could think of was the firm press of his lips, the delicious scrape of his stubble on her chin, and that dark, sinful flavor that was all his. And his parting remark…what did *that* mean? It was some sexual innuendo, it had to be. Cheeks going hot, her core fluttered at the lewd images that flooded her brain.

Stop thinking about straddling him, half-wit, and focus!

Gingerly, she rolled her foot and winced. Curse her sodding ankle! They might have been in a much better position if she hadn't gotten hurt and slowed them down. And now, they were trapped, and she wasn't much help, not with a spent pistol and injured body.

Gritting her teeth, Bronwyn scowled. She wasn't completely helpless! She still had a knife tucked into her boot, if worse came to worst. Looking around, she reached for a piece of wood that had broken off one of the nearby crates and shifted to crouch behind the wall.

She peered over. Thornbury was nowhere to be seen. But she did recognize the man keeping to the shadows with a gun in one hand—the ugly knave from the tavern. A shiver ran through her. He looked mean, and that pistol was cocked and loaded, ready to be used. He wasn't a hired rogue like the other two men who had chased her. Despite his pugilist face, his eyes had been sharp. Intelligent. He'd known what she'd been there for.

She slid a finger over the folded page in her pocket wondering if one of the names from Thornbury's report on Sommers's accomplices included him. Once more the thought shot through her brain. Who had been the leak? Besides her and Wentworth, who else would have known the nature of what she carried?

Or that *she* was the informant.

That man had come straight toward her. He had known exactly who she was, even with her gentleman's disguise and the fact that he hadn't seen her leave the carriage house. Someone had described her to him. Someone on the *inside*.

Suddenly, in a blur of movement that made her gasp, the Duke of Thornbury flew from his hiding place and swept the man's legs from under him. The gun in his hand skidded across the cobblestones. It wasn't that far from her. It was a miracle it hadn't gone off, but perhaps she could even the odds and get hold of it somehow. Thornbury was out of his league with that enormous brute. The two of them rolled in a flurry of fists and grunts. The man had a few stone over the duke and he knew how to fight. He used those ham-sized fists like a prizefighter.

She had to get that gun!

Bronwyn rolled her ankle, which didn't ache as much though it was still tender, and sucked in a bracing breath. She crept out from behind the wall, only to be yanked back by her hair. Her eyes burned from the sting.

"Where do ya think yer goin'?"

The smell of tooth rot filled her nostrils as an unwashed man restrained her, and she fought not to retch when he pulled her against him. From her angle, she couldn't reach the knife in her boot, but the piece of wood was right there. Without any hesitation, she inhaled, stood on her injured foot with a shudder, and stomped down on his instep with all the strength she had in her good leg. When his hold loosened, she shoved her elbow back, connecting with his stomach. Bronwyn didn't waste time in grabbing the wood and swinging it like a cricket bat going for the boundaries. It cracked into the man's ribs, and he crumpled with a grunt to the cobblestones of the square.

She turned, distracted by a pained shout from where

Thornbury and his opponent were wrestling. The duke looked a little the worse for wear, his elbows up trying to protect himself from the relentless assault to his head. If one of those punches landed just right, he would be dead. She had to help him! Where was that gun? Bronwyn peered down at the stones where it'd been last and frowned when she couldn't see it.

"Looking for this?"

Bronwyn whirled. It wasn't the man she'd brought down who still lay in the fetal position, groaning and clutching his middle. It was another of the unwashed cretins, and he was pointing the discarded pistol right at her. Heavens, how many of the little bastards were there? She bared her teeth but moved her hands out to the side in reluctant surrender.

"Slow," he warned her.

The sharp sound of cracking bone filled the air, and her stomach dropped in horror.

Please don't be Thornbury.

Unable to help herself, she glanced over her shoulder. The duke was standing over the body of the man who was lying insensible on the ground, clutching a wrist that was bent at an unnatural angle. He was alive! Her relief was quick but eclipsed by a gurgle of fear when the man with the gun wrapped his arm around her neck and pressed the cold muzzle into her temple. Her blood turned to pure ice in her veins.

"Bronwyn, eyes on me," the duke said.

The command was soft but she obeyed. Thornbury

held his own gun pointed toward them, but there was no chance of her surviving a shot to the brain at such close range. She couldn't take the chance to fight her way out of her attacker's hold, knowing his finger was already on the trigger. One wrong move and he would fire.

Her breath hissed out in shallow pants as terror took hold in the pit of her stomach.

She was going to die.

"Drop it," the person behind her snarled, using her body as a shield. "Or she's got a head full of fuckin' lead."

That rhymed. The inane thought made a hysterical half-giggle, half-sob rise to her throat. She was about to meet her maker and she was *rhyming*. Lord, the idiocy!

"Who sent you?" Thornbury asked in a soft, deadly voice.

"Your mother. Drop the gun or yer ladybird dies right now! Or maybe I'll kill you and keep her for fun." His left hand dropped from around her neck to fondle her midriff. She stiffened, revulsion filling her, but didn't dare move with the gun still in place.

The duke's eyes narrowed, his face grimmer than she'd ever seen it. Bronwyn had never beheld a look like that come over a man, like Death himself had slid into his soul. A shiver of pure fear coasted through her. Thornbury didn't look afraid or worried. His flesh could have been made of the ice she'd always accused him of being, but those nearly feral, golden eyes of his burned with lethal promise.

"You shoot her and you die," the duke said.

The man huffed. "I wouldn't be makin' threats if I was

you." The muzzle of the gun tapped against her skull, making her flinch.

"Valentine." No sound came from her lips as she breathed his name. It felt like goodbye, like this was the end.

"Do you trust me?" he asked.

Those eyes pierced her, saw through her, held her. Bronwyn wanted to laugh. It wasn't as though she had much of a choice. "I—"

The discharge of the gun was deafening, cracking through the air just as the body holding hers was yanked backward by the force, nearly taking her with him. Delayed heat seared the crown of her head and her cheekbone, something warm splattering her skin before Bronwyn could gather her wits and register that she wasn't, in fact, dead.

Or that Thornbury was gathering her shuddering, boneless body into his arms, scooping her up, and running once more for their lives. Or that he hadn't just shot a man dead center in the middle of his forehead with cool, unerring precision.

On silent, fast feet, he left the streets for the cover of the woods near the riverbank. Her thoughts and faculties came back to her in sluggish spurts as the duke ran, her eyes taking in the thick cover of trees and her dulled ears registering the lack of any pursuit. The sound of the gunshot would have drawn other unsavory types as well as the local police.

When the skies opened up and a deluge poured down, Thornbury didn't reduce his pace. A little rainstorm wouldn't stop people who wanted to kill them, but it was a bit of a silver lining in itself. Rain covered tracks, deadened sound, and washed away scents. Most of all, it would wash away the blood she knew was on her face. Her assailant's blood.

Bronwyn didn't know how long they ran, only that the duke's shoulder felt safe and warm, and despite the rain, the jostling of his pounding strides, or the metallic scent of blood from his cravat, she rested her head against him, face to the sky, and closed her eyes. When they finally slowed and stopped, he slid her to her feet.

"Bronwyn, look at me. Are you well?" His words came through her in a low, dim echo, her ears still ringing from the blast and her brain still fogged with shock. The patter of raindrops hit the pine tree cover above them.

With one masterful, controlled shot, he had saved her bloody life.

"Don't think we're even now," she whispered. "I saved you twice."

His chuckle warmed her. Heart pounding and blood rushing in her veins like a storm tide, Bronwyn felt her body sway. Oh, dear Lord, she would *not* swoon. She wasn't a swooner. She never swooned. To counter the ignominy, Bronwyn did the only thing she could as blood rushed like a river through her veins. She launched herself forward, grabbed his lapels, and yanked his head down to hers.

Seven

WHAT COULD HE DO BUT SUCCUMB?

They weren't out of danger, but no one would find them for the moment, shrouded under the cover of evergreens and darkness as they were. His sodden arms wrapped around her—this brave, wicked hellion who had turned his life upside down in a matter of days—and he pulled her close as her sweet mouth sought his. It slanted open, a brazen tongue courting his, licking inside his own mouth with frantic surges, her teeth almost grinding into his.

God, the taste of her was sublime.

The kiss itself was destructive. Chaotic. A gnashing of lips, teeth, and tongues as if they were desperate to climb inside each other. To celebrate the fact that they were alive! His hands roamed her back as hers wound and wrenched on his damp hair. Water dripped down his cheeks and warmed from the heat of his skin as passion flared, burning away any cold.

Blood, excitement, and primal desire tore through his veins on the heels of the fight, his cock surging painfully in his trousers. Valentine knew what she was feeling. After any kind of life-and-death situation, particularly in his line of work, he always felt the need to release. To *fuck*. It was a post-survival emotional trigger, rising from perilous conditions leading to a frenetic kind of lust. Sex was a natural outlet, and years ago, Lisbeth had been a willing enthusiastic partner. But this was *Bronwyn*.

"Wait," he said.

She nipped at his lip, her teeth dragging along his sensitive skin, hard enough to sting. Walking them backward until his back was pressed against the bark of a tree, she ground her pelvis into his body, making him groan. "No, Thornbury, you don't get to tell me what to do. I need to erase his touch from me. I need *this*."

He understood that, too.

Fear and anxiety deepened physical attraction, and God knew, after the interlude in the bowels of the ship that the two of them had that in spades. The flames between them could set the entire copse on fire. But he had to be better. He had to think for both of them when the haze of lust was blanketing her brain. He was the trained operative in this situation and she was not.

"Don't," she warned. A glimmering dark gaze speared him.

He let out a breath when she went still, her body still glued along his front. "Don't what?"

"Think for me. I've had enough of people who try to do that. I'm capable of making my own decisions, no matter what's running through that deeply logical head of yours."

"Not logic, I assure you."

Moments—an eternity—passed between them. Her pulse hummed wildly at her nape, her heartbeat drumming at a pace as chaotic as his. Her hand slid from its hold around his neck, sliding ever so slowly down his chest. She leaned back slightly to allow it room to move, and Valentine caught his breath when she reached his waistband. Eyes holding his with complete clarity, though dilated with the same lust likely consuming his, she dropped her hand and gripped his rigid length in her palm. They both inhaled.

"Do you want me, Valentine?" she asked, her thumb stroking over the tip of his achingly sensitive crown.

"It's obvious, no?" he hissed. "This erection isn't for the man I left in the alley."

Her lips curved at his caustic tone. "I want you, too."

"Bronwyn."

She squeezed, making him gasp, and then stroked down. "Will you deny me?"

"You're a—"

"I would caution against saying 'lady' with my hand where it is." She dragged her nails upward along his rigid length, earning a growl from the depths of his chest. "I am a woman, and I know what I want."

Without warning, she dropped to her knees, and before he could stop what she was doing, she had the placket of his trousers opened, the fabric yanked down, and the full head of him engulfed in her warm mouth. Valentine's eyes rolled back in his skull when she lapped at him, a needy moan rumbling from her. No, she wasn't a lady…she was a temptress sent to lure him to purgatory with that sweet, sinful tongue.

"Bronwyn, you can't."

In response, she sucked. Hard. And he nearly spent right there.

Unwilling to spend and very near the verge of doing just that, Valentine reached down to drag her up, his mouth sealing over hers, and his hands wrapping around that round arse. She fumbled at the buttons of her own fly before he took over, unfastening the wet fabric and peeling it over her hips. Skirts would have been preferable in this situation, but he wasn't about to complain, not when he slid his palm inside against the heart of her and was rewarded with copious amounts of wet, delicious heat.

She was drenched, and not from the rain.

"Bloody hell," he muttered. "You're..."

"Wet," she supplied on a moan when he slid his fingers through the silky dampness of her arousal. "Don't be so shocked, Your Grace. It's a natural reaction to desire."

"Not shocked. Delighted."

"I never realized how much of a chatterbox you are," she said. "One would think you intended to talk me to death instead of fucking me to death."

Her vulgar words shocked him. Thrilled him. *Inflamed* him.

"I didn't know you had such a filthy vocabulary."

She rolled her pelvis into his. "There are a lot of things you don't know about me, Your Grace."

"I won't be gentle," he said on a ragged kiss that toyed with the edge of violence, his tongue desecrating her mouth with carnal plunges that left her in little doubt of what he wanted to do.

The saucy little minx raked her nails over his bared buttocks and hauled him closer. "I don't want you to be."

Growling, he dragged his mouth down the column of her neck, sucking on that tantalizing little pulse that teased and tormented, before lifting her shirt to knead a handful of a luscious breast. He bit at the rigid nipple through the layers of fabric. Blast, he wanted her fully bared to his view. *Later.* This would have to do.

"Turn," he ordered in a voice made of gravel. "Hold the tree."

His hand traced the length of her spine, depressing right before the swell of her buttocks, making her arch. He couldn't see her bared bottom in the gloom, the curves gilded in shadows making his mouth water, but his hands more than made up for his lack of sight. He filled them with the fleshy globes before freeing himself from the confines of his own trousers.

"Valentine?" There was a breathy question in her voice, and he stilled for a moment, reason intervening in his lust-addled mind. She must never have done it this way.

"Trust me," he said and reached around to where she was wet and wanting. A few circles of his fingertips on that needy little bud and she was writhing back against him, seeking the completion that only he could give her in this moment.

Valentine did. He notched himself to her entrance and pushed inside. They both groaned at the intensely snug fit. She was tighter than he expected, but in this position, she would be. He wasn't going to last as it was, the heat of her body making his wits scramble, but he was determined to make it good for her. He wasn't selfish when it came to pleasure.

Gritting his jaw, he inched back and thrust forward while simultaneously pulling back on her hip bone with his palm. Her body gave way beautifully, enclosing more of him in a pulsing sheath that had him gasping, but he still wasn't fully seated. Sweet damnation, she was tight. *Too* tight. A soft whimper was broken by a sharp inhale. Of pleasure? Of pain?

He wished he could see her face to know.

"Bronwyn," he rasped. "Are you well?"

She shuddered, her passage fluttering around his cock, her voice breathy. "Don't you dare stop now, Thornbury." He quickened his circles with his fingers at the apex of her sex and withdrew his cock, only to slide back in on a long stroke that had them both groaning in tandem. "Like that, yes," she whispered. "More. Harder next time."

He gave her what she wanted, impaling her slim body with a powerful thrust, and it only took a few more strokes for her to go hurtling over the edge with a ragged sob, her walls convulsing around him in a way that had his own vision going white. With a shout, he withdrew and clasped himself in his fist to spend in the earth beneath them. Valentine pulled her back against him and braced his arm on the tree, feeling his heart beat pumping a mile a minute as beatific lassitude replaced the embers of his release.

After a beat, Bronwyn caught her breath and

straightened. She stepped out of his loose embrace to put herself to rights and yank up her trousers. Before she could fasten them, Valentine removed his handkerchief from his pocket and handed it to her. She stared at it with a quizzical look before realizing what it was for.

"Oh, right." He was certain she was blushing, though he couldn't tell in the darkness. "Thank you," she said, the rustle of clothing the only sound before she handed the neatly folded square back to him. "Do you need it as well?"

"Yes, thank you."

It was all very polite as if they hadn't fucked each other to the edge of oblivion moments before. But that was the thing with this kind of sex. It was raw, quick, and a hundred percent about physical release. In the past with sex like this, things had always gone back to business as usual, but now Valentine felt painfully hesitant about how to respond. Nor did he want to acknowledge that he hadn't come so hard in…ever.

In silence, he cleaned himself and pocketed the soiled handkerchief.

When they were both calm and reassembled, she peered around, squinting in the darkness. "What now?"

"We won't get far in the dark. We should try to get some rest and wake up in a few hours when it's light."

"Out here in the open?"

He shook his head. "I saw the top of a folly or a rotunda to the north, I think. It must have been part of the old Lemon Hill estate. At least, that will give us some shelter if it rains again." Valentine glanced at her. "How's your ankle? Still sore?"

"I can manage."

―――――――――

They picked their way through the trees by the meager light of the moon whenever the clouds parted. It was slow and tedious, but Bronwyn was too tired and too cold to complain. Her ankle ached, but there was no way in hell she was going to whine about it, only to end up in the duke's arms...not after what they'd just done. She might not be able to control herself if he touched her again.

Good gracious, she'd made a hash of things.

She'd bloody lain with him! Though technically, they had been vertical.

Heat filled her cheeks, and once more, Bronwyn was glad for the cover of night. This brazen, demanding version of herself had shocked her to the core. She had practically ordered him to do the deed. *Palmed* his hard male organ and then dropped to her knees like a seasoned doxy. Her cheeks scorched at the memory. And then, he had taken her like a wanton up against a tree, and she had liked it!

Loved the raw, explosive nature of the release he'd given her...the release she had *begged* for like her body needed food to function or air to breathe. She'd felt his need in the uncontrolled movements of his hips that had sent her onto her tiptoes with every decadent, forceful plunge.

That had to be a novel position for deflowering. Most of the books she'd read had virgins being introduced to the marital act in the customary man-on-top-of-the-woman position. She hadn't even thought such an act could be possible or even pleasurable.

But it *had* been.

The orgasm had felt nothing like the furtive ones she'd given herself, all quiet and civilized and unseen beneath the bedclothes. This release had been almost primal in nature, climbing from the most primitive depths of her like a beast in heat being unleashed. She bit back a giggle. And *in* actual nature, too. Oh, the audacity of it.

Sex in a public park in the middle of the night after nearly being murdered.

There was an explanation for it, she knew. Something to do with heightened emotion, terror, and physical relief. It was the reason that every time she did a job in London for Wentworth, she had to do something to get the coiled energy out of her body. A ride on her horse, if it wasn't too late, or a very long, hot bath, followed by a personal release in the privacy of her bedchamber. There was never any shame in it.

There was no shame in this now. They were two consenting parties.

Bronwyn squeezed her thighs together, clenching on emptiness. Nothing would ever compare now. Not to the substantial length and girth of him or the expertise with which he'd worked her inexperienced body. She hadn't seen him, but she had certainly felt him inside her in multiple places. Her sex. Her *mouth*.

Cringing in mortification, Bronwyn nearly tripped over her own feet. She'd done the *thing*. The brazen, fascinating thing she'd once read about in a gothic novel and wondered what could ever drive a woman to taste a man *there*.

Well, now she knew.

Lust derangement. It had to be a medical condition. Because *why* on earth was her pulse galloping anew and her stupid mouth salivating at the mere thought of the act? The salty-sweet taste of the bead of liquid she'd found had made her nipples tighten to taut, painful points. If he hadn't yanked her up, she would have quite happily stayed on her knees.

"Cat got your tongue?" the duke asked, making her jump.

"A girl isn't allowed to think?" she shot back, horrified that she'd been in the middle of reminiscing about the feel of his male organ in her mouth. Silky *and* hard. And utterly delicious.

Oh, shut up.

"There she is. The imp we all know and love."

"Oh, you poor thing. One game of pully-hawly, and you've gone and tumbled head over heels in love. I thought you were more worldly than that, Your Grace."

Her companion laughed, the sound humorless. "I would never be caught in such a noose."

The reply left her oddly bereft, not that she was looking for love either. Maybe one day, and most definitely not with a man like the Duke of Thornbury, who would probably welcome a wife with the same frigid disdain he had for everything else.

He wasn't frigid half an hour ago.

No, he'd been hotter than a brush fire. Her cheeks heated anew and Bronwyn pressed her chilled fingers to them. A bone-deep shiver ran through her, and she was hard pressed to say whether it was due to the memory of what they'd done or the fact that her body felt numb from the night air. She wished she hadn't discarded her topmost layer in her haste to escape.

Suddenly, a warmth engulfed her. Thornbury's coat, she realized, cozy from the heat of his body, though the outside was still damp. She pulled the lapels closed, her frozen skin soaking up the warmth. Had he been watching her and seen her shiver from the cold?

"Won't you freeze?" she said with a slight chatter to her teeth.

"I should have offered it to you earlier," he replied gruffly, his arm moving over her shoulders and drawing her against him. "I have endured much worse with much less."

It made her think of what he'd done for the sake of his job. She knew his travels had taken him all over the world in service to the British Crown. Had he been in situations like this before? Running for his life? Escaping death? Seeking a passionate outlet? Her thoughts flicked to the gorgeous woman who'd been married to him, and Bronwyn's stomach soured. Had the two of them ever shared that kind of near-violent, frantic intimacy? Had the former countess known the lithe thrust of those strong hips, the feel of those hands, the wicked, erotic taste of him?

Bronwyn's stomach wound into ugly jealous knots.

Of course she had. She'd been his *wife*.

A vision of them coiled naked together in the throes of sexual congress assaulted her. Bronwyn pinned her lips, bitterness surging into her throat, its fingers clawing upward and making it hard to breathe. She had zero claim on him. What they had shared had been sex, nothing more. She needed to get her head out of her arse, especially where this man was concerned.

"What is wrong?" Thornbury asked.

"Nothing. Why?"

"You made a strange, angry sort of noise," he said.

She bit down on her lip. "My ankle hurts."

"It's not far, I don't think," he said and tugged her closer. "Here, if you won't let me carry you, lean on me a bit more."

He was right. It wasn't much further until a dark structure came into view. It did resemble a pile of old, gothic ruins, with what looked to be a square base with a cylindrical tower looming above them. Follies on estates in England were built to be admired, depending on the tastes of the gentlemen who owned them. Gentlemen who had returned from travel abroad took creative liberty on their estates. There was a folly at her family's country seat in Kettering that resembled an ancient temple and another that was a dovecote.

This one, however, looked like it was in danger of crumbling apart, as if it had been forgotten and left to its own devices. Bronwyn wrinkled her nose, though the promise of shelter made her giddy.

"Stay here for a moment," Thornbury said. "Let me check that it's safe and empty of vermin."

The duke might be hard and unfeeling most of the time, but he was a born-and-bred gentleman. If he wasn't such a horse's arse, he might have made a good husband. Bronwyn frowned, remembering the lady's comments at dinner. Why had he and the former countess petitioned Parliament for a divorce and been granted one? It wasn't any of her business, but suddenly, she wanted to know.

"Why did you and Lisbeth get a divorce?" she blurted out, softly, but she knew he had heard because the rustling a few feet away had stopped. When the silence stretched out, she thought he wasn't going to answer and wanted to kick herself for prying or making it seem like she cared to know.

"We wanted different things," he replied after a while. "I suppose that everything eventually runs its course and our marriage did."

"That's cold even for you."

A bark of laughter flew on the air. "What offends you more, my lady? That we didn't stick it out and take other lovers like everyone else in the aristocracy, exchanging one or two words over dinner and sleeping in different rooms once we produced an heir and a spare? Or that we decided to go separate ways because our paths diverged and it was the most sensible option?"

He had a point. Most marriages in their circles were arranged in the interests of fortune and power. It was rare that couples got along. Her own father had preferred captaining his fleet of ships to his marchioness's bed, though he had doted on his children until his death. Her brother and Ravenna had been lucky. They were a love match. Envy bled through her and she banished it in the same breath. Yearning for something well out of her reach was not only impractical, but also useless.

"Was your former wife like you?"

The silence grew until it felt heavy and sticky. Bronwyn couldn't see his face from where he stood near the entrance to the folly, but suddenly she had the feeling that he was watching her from wherever he stood in the shadows. "Like me?"

She swallowed. "A spy."

Eight

"You truly do have a fertile mind, Lady Bronwyn Chase."

She ambled toward the entrance of the building where she could detect the long shape of him propped against one side. "You know, my mother always called me by my full name whenever she was prevaricating."

"I am a duke, *Bronwyn Madeline Charlotte Chase.*"

The mockery was subtle despite the knowledge of her name that made her heart kick against her ribs; the fib, however, was not. "What are you doing with your former spouse in Philadelphia then? Don't tell me, you're on a pleasure trip. An attempt at reconciliation? Wait, wait, I've got it. Shopping!"

"Business."

It irked her that he was so smoothly evasive and so blasé about the fact that he was clearly here on some clandestine mission. Then again, what did she expect? That they would trust each other because they had been joined in the biblical sense? That they would sit over a fire and trade secrets, hold hands, and stroke each other's hair?

Lord Iceberg was back and in fine form...or perhaps he'd never left. He had kissed her and taken her as though she'd been the air he needed to live, but she had rocks in her brain if she thought he'd ever go soft. The man was frost through and through.

And a gifted deceiver.

She didn't need to see him to know that his impenetrable face would give away nothing, with falsehoods falling so naturally from his lips. He lied as easily as he breathed. It was by default of his occupation, of course, no matter his calm, mocking denials. Bronwyn swallowed a puff of laughter. It wasn't as if he would have readily admitted such a thing. *She* wouldn't. If he guessed who she was—if *anyone* guessed—life as she knew it would be over.

So what was she so peeved about? Trust went both ways.

As a covert operative, one had to be ready to hide the truth and cover one's tracks at every turn. Even from curious friends or nosy sisters-in-law. Bronwyn had become quite adept at deceit herself. She had lied about this trip, about a nonexistent sick aunt, about where she was going and who she was. About everything. Discomfort filled her. Her grandfather, the late Duke of Ashvale had always told her that once a person told a lie, all their truths became suspect.

Even the poet Lord Byron had called a lie the truth in a masquerade.

Bronwyn suddenly wanted to take the folded report with his initials from her pocket and wave it in the duke's face as indisputable proof of his profession. But then *she* would have to explain how she came to have a confidential piece of correspondence on her person in the first place, and wouldn't that be a pickle? *Hullo, guess what, sir? I'm a spy, too. Let's do the secret handshake and swap stories!*

"Why were you in that tavern?" she asked instead. "Were you following me?"

"McGillin's," he replied. "Best cottage pie this side of the Atlantic, apparently. Can't beat a good pie, my Uncle Bucky always said. Kidney pie, apple pie, fruit pie, mince pie. Pie is the true key to a blissful existence."

"Stop saying 'pie,'" she snapped.

"You don't enjoy pie?"

"I hate it," she said, blood boiling. "Answer the question. Why were you on that ship? You didn't come to America for the pie."

"Maybe I did *come*...for the *pie*."

She faltered when the cadence in his deep voice shifted to something low and much too sultry on two particular words in that sentence. Did...the Duke of Thornbury just make a filthy, bawdy joke at her expense? Her mouth opened and closed, ears going hot. Surely he wasn't referring to *her* as the pie. Heat drizzled through her like thickened honey. "If you're using sexual congress as a decidedly unclever metaphor, I assure you that my pie is burned and completely inedible."

"I'll withhold judgment until I can savor at my leisure."

Oh dear heavens.

If she wasn't already half-frozen, she would melt, starting from the place between her thighs that felt like it was currently incarnating a waterfall. "Shall we go in?" she asked, changing the subject before she did something stupid like drag him to the floor, mount his face like the lusty heathen she was, and demand to be eaten.

"It's safe."

Entering through a low archway that was just a darker shadow, her fingertips drifting over the old stone, Bronwyn found herself inside a roomy ground floor that was miraculously dry, despite the dilapidated appearance of the structure. And not freezing! Vermin or not, this was much better than being cold and clammy.

"I think this might once have been a water tower," Thornbury said from her right, making her jump. She hadn't heard him move and she could barely see now that he'd closed the heavy, half-rotted door, shielding them from the bitter bite of the outside air. "But it's not connected to the old waterworks down the way. It's clean and should do for the night."

"Do you think those men are still after us?" she asked softly, rubbing her hands over her stiff arms that felt like two columns of ice. Now that she wasn't arguing with him, or being stupidly seduced by him, she felt every painful tremor of her tired, cold muscles. Beneath Thornbury's coat that had lost every ounce of its warmth, her shirt and trousers felt as though they had been frozen directly to her skin.

"Not tonight and not with their injuries."

Relieved, Bronwyn nodded. "Would a small fire draw notice?"

"No, and there are some pieces of wood over here that should do. Some woodsman or worker must have been in here before us. Either that, or the beams above are old. There's a pile in the corner."

Within minutes, Bronwyn busied herself gathering some of the chunks of wood that might have been left behind or fallen off the half-rotted beams in the ceiling—she fervently hoped no more would come tumbling down upon their heads—and stacking them into a small pile, along with dry leaves and small twigs. Moving mostly by touch and the faint moonlight from the narrow cutouts above, it was slow going, though her eyes were growing used to the darkness.

She stumbled upon a few pine cones strewn near the entrance of the folly and nearly whooped with joy. They were the best kind of kindling. Lastly, she removed the knife from her boot and found a flat stone that she struck the knife down. Her hands were trembling so badly, however, that she could barely manage a spark after a few tries.

"Let me," Thornbury said, taking both from her. He replaced the stone and her knife with a box from his pocket that contained safety matches, and it wasn't long before the small pile caught fire.

She shot him a baleful glare. "You had those in your pockets all along?"

"I wasn't sure they were dry." He grinned, his teeth shining in the firelight. "And I wanted to see what you could do. Quite intrepid of you, I must say."

"Wonderful," she replied drily at his tone. "I have earned the everlasting admiration of the great Duke of Thornbury. However shall I cope with the weight of all that shining esteem?"

"What did you say about sarcasm again? That it was the lowest form of wit?"

"Touché, sir." She sat cross-legged in front of the small blaze, as close as she dared, and reveled in the delightful, if scant, heat. "How cunning of you to use my own words against me. I didn't think you were paying that much attention."

"I always pay attention."

The way he said it made her pause, but then he started to remove his waistcoat and then untucked his shirt, making her frown.

"What are you doing?"

"Trust me, you should do the same. I know the heat feels good, but your clothes will dry much more quickly off your body, and you won't catch a rotten, dangerous chill in the meantime."

"Surely you don't expect me to undress in front of you?" she asked, her cheeks flaming. Bronwyn had no reason to be mortified, especially when the dratted man had been *inside* her, but for some reason the idea of undressing seemed much more intimate than their impassioned interlude in the wood had been. Then, they had mostly been dressed, with the exception of one or two key areas. He opened his mouth and she lifted a hand. "Don't say whatever it is you're thinking."

"How do you know what I was about to say?"

She huffed. "You have that look on your face, and your lip is curling in the corner the way it does when you find something amusing and no one else does."

That blasted lip curled even more into something that almost resembled a smirk. Good Lord, was that a *dimple*? The shallow never-used indent in his cheek vanished almost as quickly as it had appeared, making her question whether it had been the flickering flames and not her besotted mind trying to trick her into thinking that he might be, indeed, human. And besides, he did not need any more armor against failing female wits.

A dimple on such an undeserving man would be the last sodding straw!

"That tiny fire is not enough to get you dry whilst covered in layers of wet clothing. You'll catch your death," he explained as he kicked off his shoes and unrolled his stockings before shucking off his shirt.

Bronwyn's breath snagged in her throat as a brain-melting expanse of firelit muscled skin was unveiled. She'd known he wasn't a man of excess, apart from the occasional glass of whisky, and she'd seen that lithe, powerful body in action against those men in the square, but nothing…*nothing* had prepared her for the sight of him without a shirt.

He wasn't perfect, that sinewy body marred by faded scars that traversed his skin like a pattern of ragged lace. Old wounds and newer ones, some deep, and some like the scratch on his neck that was now only a dark line of dried blood, painted his body. But scars were the marks of a warrior, and Thornbury wore his without shame. With pride.

Her eyes devoured the ridges upon ridges of lean

muscle stacking from his wide shoulders to a corrugated abdomen and narrow hips. A spattering of bronze hair dusted those sculpted pectorals, a thicker line trailing from his navel to his waistband. Traitorously, her eyes dipped to the bulge at his crotch, widened, and darted away. Dear Lord, he wasn't even erect and it was heart-palpitatingly prominent.

Of course, it's big, you twit, he nearly split you in two.

Her thighs quivered at the memory, and she bit her lip as her core went molten. Thankfully, the duke hadn't noticed her drooling over his person when he turned to drape the articles of clothing over the half-crumbled wall behind him. Her mouth practically fell open as he kicked off his trousers, leaving him standing in transparent knee-length linen smallclothes that left little to the imagination.

Of course his back had to be as powerfully built as the front, the flex of muscles bracketing the deep channel of his spine catching her attention anew. And those buttocks... She'd dug her fingers into those hard globes, but her hands hadn't done the reality a lick of justice. Were all men hiding such lush posteriors beneath their tailcoats? She looked away as he turned, but now she couldn't unsee the damn, entirely too luscious thing.

Forcing her eyes anywhere but on him, Bronwyn belatedly glanced over the inside of the folly, which had probably been divided into four or five rooms at one point, not to mention the upper levels that led to the tower. "What do you think is up there?"

"Not sure. The stairs have fallen in. Probably just a bird

or two, I imagine." One brow raised, he stared pointedly at her. "Don't dawdle. Your turn."

"Fine." She breathed out. "Face the other way."

———

Valentine thought she would put up more of a fight. What they were doing was truly scandalous in the eyes of British society…especially for an unmarried couple. But they weren't in England and this was a matter of actual survival. If the chill took root in her lungs, she could become quite ill, and they had already avoided being grabbed and gutted. It made no sense to give in to something completely within their control for the sake of propriety. Not on his watch.

The rustle of clothing reached his ears.

"I'm finished."

"Give me those—" Without thinking, he turned and promptly lost the power of speech. She looked like a Titian painting, all dewy, creamy skin and long, sinuous limbs. Thick, loosened brown hair tumbled over her shoulders in a riot of waves and curls nearly to her waist. Her bare knees were curled to her chest, arms wrapped around them. A sheer shift hid all of the delicate, feminine parts from his view, but the hollows and lines of her body left him breathless. He cleared his throat and finished what he'd been about to say. "Clothes, please."

With a blush on her cheeks, she pointed to the bundle beside her. Silently, he took the discarded apparel, including his coat, and hung them over the wall next to his. The faint scent of cinnamon and baked apples wafted from the clothes, and he fought the instant urge to lift them to his nose and breathe them in. That would not do.

He scowled. "Why do your things smell like a harvest festival?"

"I visited an apothecary once that made perfumes and soaps. I chose a scent I liked and a special soap was prepared for me. It's a bit too sweet, I think, and everyone seems to think I'm hiding a Marlborough pie in the pockets of my skirts."

With a huff, Valentine didn't answer. It wasn't too sweet at all, and he didn't want to dwell on the slew of lascivious images that rushed into his brain at the thought of what truly lay beneath those skirts and had nothing to do with apple and custard whatsoever.

"This is not so bad, is it?" he said, settling himself a good distance away from any tantalizing scents on the other side of the fire.

She chuckled, that rich real sound that he preferred over the false one she put on for her admirers. "Better than being dead, I suppose. How's your wound?"

Valentine reached up to the dried line of blood and winced. It wasn't deep, but it stung. He didn't want to touch it, but it probably needed a good cleaning, just in case, once they got back to civilization. He'd seen sepsis set in from an insect bite that had gotten infected. "It's fine for now."

"You were lucky it wasn't worse," she said.

"Thanks to your shout of warning."

Valentine blew out a breath, all of his questions rising to the surface again. They had skirted long enough around the issue of how they were in this predicament in the first place, and now it was time for some answers. It was clear that she knew what he was, even though he had avoided admitting anything with his usual, automatic deflection. Technically, *he* wasn't a spy any longer. It was Lisbeth's mission, though that was splitting hairs at best.

"Exactly what kind of trouble are you into?" he asked bluntly.

She exhaled. "I'm not in trouble. Well, not technically."

Valentine fought the bubble of frustration at her stubbornness. He couldn't help her if he didn't know the scope of the mess she'd found herself in. He'd long revised his earlier speculation that she was meeting a lover, unless it was a tryst gone wrong. A disagreement on terms or jealousy or some such. He had seen it a thousand times in the rookeries. But this wasn't that. Back at the tavern, there'd been no desire on her face at all.

"Bronwyn, you nearly got killed by a group of hoodlums. You're dressed in clothes that no lady of your station should be caught wearing, and you're sneaking off to meet with strangers in seedy taverns three thousand miles away from where you should be."

"Snug in my bed like a good little girl?"

Hell if her words didn't make his traitorous blood simmer. She was a paradox, this woman. Sweet, and cloyingly innocent one moment and then a saucy hellion with a sword for a tongue the next. Who was Lady Bronwyn

Chase? Had he been wrong about her all along? Lisbeth had sensed there was more to her, but he'd been so blinded by antipathy that he'd missed all the signs. Blinded by obvious misdirection. Devil take it, the little minx had pulled one over on *him*.

"Was it an act?" he asked with a narrowed glare.

She eyed him back, her shadowed blue gaze glimmering with yellow and red tones from the flames. "What?"

"The flirtations. The intrigues. The love letter."

Valentine didn't miss the way her eyes widened and flicked toward where her trousers were drying over the wall. Was the letter in there now? He shook his head. Whether it was or not was her business. For all he knew, that had also been part of the performance and nothing but a blank sheet of paper she had planted to support the illusion.

"Why were you at McGillin's?"

Her face tightened, though she gave nothing away. "Same reason as you. For the pie."

Valentine admired her pluck, but he'd worn down men more hard-bitten than her. He could wait her out or catch her in a trap of her own making. She would tell him, if he had to pry it out of her truth by truth, and he wasn't above intimidation to get his way. "Does Ashvale know of your secret obsession for pie or assignations in seedy taverns?"

Her nostrils flared, the threat obvious. "No, and I'd like to keep it that way."

"You have to give me something more here, Bronwyn."

She glowered at him, head cocking slightly, and he

could see the wheels turning in her head. How had he ever thought of her as vapid or unintelligent? She was as sharp as a tack and as inflexible as one, too. Normally, he was an excellent judge of character, a skill honed over countless years in service and surveillance, but she had fooled him so completely that his own dependable instincts had faltered. Dark lashes hooded over her eyes, hiding them from view.

"A trade then," she said eventually. "A secret for a secret."

He frowned. "You seem to forget that I'm holding all the cards."

"Are you?"

She adjusted herself, her arms falling from around her knees as she tucked them beneath her in a cross-legged position. The soft lawn of her shift gathered in her lap, the lace edges tracing along the enticing curves of her thighs. Her hair, lit gold in the firelight, thankfully hid most of her upper body from view. Valentine sucked in a breath as a clear gaze met his, not an ounce of guile or guilt in it, only an astute fortitude that made him take notice. In truth, that sharp stare was more of an aphrodisiac than her state of undress, but what came next was a blast of cold water to the face.

"I doubt my brother would look any more favorably on *your* current flavor of pie, Your Grace." Her eyes glittered like shards of ice. "In fact, one single bite just might lead you down a rather disagreeable path that you seemed so eager to escape the first time."

Valentine almost laughed aloud at her sheer cheek. The ballocks on her! A slip of a girl was going toe-to-toe with him, throwing the fact that they had coupled back in his face along with the threat of wedlock. He had no illusions that she would divulge all to her brother, if push came to shove and that was really her game, and then he would be forced to do right by her. "Which path is that?"

"I think you already know, one heralded by wedding bells."

"If I recall, my lady, you consented quite enthusiastically to the act."

A dark flush crested her cheekbones but she nodded. "I did. That doesn't change the fact that should the Duke of Ashvale learn that you joined giblets with his younger, unmarried sister, even with her consent in a public wood, we would both be expected to do what society demands of us."

Valentine drew in a clipped breath at the unrefined slang falling from such aristocratic lips.

"Which neither of us wants," she added.

"That mouth of yours," he murmured.

That puckish pout quirked upward. "I rather thought you enjoyed this mouth of mine, Your Grace. At least, it *felt* like it."

Goddamn his fool self, now *he* was blushing like a schoolgirl, if the heat filling his face was any signal. Heat was tormenting other parts of him as well. Thank God his propped knee blocked most of his distended crotch from her view. The thin underclothes would hide nothing, and the last thing he wanted was to upend a necessary conversation with more lust. He was already in enough of a bind as it was, especially if she decided to make good on her threat. Sealing his fate with another round of mind-numbing, gratifying sex was certain stupidity. His gaze flicked to her lips, the barest flick of her glistening tongue making a low growl climb up his chest at the memory of her soft, wet mouth on him.

"Where did you learn to do such a thing?" he rasped out and nearly kicked himself. Some focus.

"A library."

"Does dear Lady Borne know of your wicked preference of reading material?"

Her brows lifted. "There are many things my mother does not know about me, Your Grace. I gather she would be shocked, if she suspected." Face unreadable, she peered at him. "So are we in agreement? A trade for a trade?"

"Very well," he agreed. "Why have you come here? Are you really visiting a sick relative?"

"No, but I am here to help a friend who might be in trouble."

"That's vague and tells me nothing," he said.

The imp grinned. "Ask better questions next time. You know for a supposedly unrivaled big, bad secret operative, you're rather easy to sidestep. Were you any good at your job at all?"

"I am not a spy." Valentine set his jaw. "And I'm very good at my job."

Two could play at this game. Her blush heightened

when his stare canvassed her body in a leisurely, heated sweep. The pulse at the base of her throat visible through the parted curtain of hair fluttered to life, though to her credit, she didn't drop her stare.

"My turn. Were you following me?" she asked.

"I've already answered your allotted question, imp."

"I didn't ask you a…" She pressed her lips together, recalling her mistake about asking whether he was good at his job. Something like vexation flickered in her eyes. If he had to hazard a guess, she was worried about the slip. "That was devious."

"How do you know the Kestrel?"

She thought on that for a moment and then shook her head. "I don't. I'm tired and we should probably get some rest, if we can."

Valentine had an inkling she could be a vise when she wanted. Instead of pressing the matter, he nodded and rose. His coat was already dry enough. He spread it out and placed it on the ground near the fire that was already burning down faster than he'd hoped. "Lie on this."

She stood up in a graceful movement, the shifting of her silky hair affording him a tempting glimpse of the curve of one breast. Hell, she was lovely. Situating herself on his coat, she propped herself up to her side on one elbow and gazed up at him. "Where will you sleep?"

In reply, he sat down next to her, his back to hers. "Right here. We need to keep warm when the fire goes out. I'll keep it going for as long as I can, but body heat is better than no heat."

Bronwyn stiffened but didn't move. She might refuse to tell him her secrets, but she wouldn't argue the logic of staying alive. For long moments, he pondered the puzzle that was his beautiful, mysterious companion until her even breaths of sleep finally filled the air. He drew his dried shirt from the wall and placed it over her.

Whatever trouble she was in—and he didn't doubt for one second that she was in way over her head—he would get to the bottom of it.

Whatever it took.

Nine

"WHAT THE INFERNAL *FUCK*, BRONWYN!"

The bellow was enough to wake the dead. Bronwyn's eyes flew open and she sat straight up in complete confusion, eyes squinting in the stark light of day. Every muscle in her back and posterior hurt from the hours spent asleep on the unforgiving ground. Blinking, she focused her blurry vision on the fully dressed man standing in front of her holding up a square of linen, one she sluggishly recognized as his handkerchief.

"What's the matter?"

"You were a virgin?"

Bronwyn narrowed her gaze on the unfolded swatch of fabric, reality chasing the fog of sleep from her brain when the pink stain on its snowy-white surface came into focus. She wrinkled her nose as understanding hit. A blush filled her cheeks. Oh, the cloth must have been what he'd used to clean them both up after their frenzied interlude the evening before.

"Nothing gets past you, does it," she muttered and when he kept glaring, she shrugged. "Clearly, the evidence suggests that a minuscule amount of blood was involved during the, er…deflowering process."

"*Deflowering?*" A muscle throbbed in his cheek as she

took in the fact that he was already dressed. "Then it's true. What have you done, Bronwyn?"

She lifted a brow. "Are you going to go all histrionic on me?"

"I am *not* histrionic."

Her brows went higher. "You sound histrionic to me."

"You have been compromised and we shall have to marry. There's no other course of action." He scrubbed a hand through his hair and then over his face, which was covered in a delicious layer of bronze scruff. Then again, he wasn't so delicious when he was behaving like an over-bearing jackanapes who thought he had the right to tell her what to do.

Bronwyn frowned. She had a foul taste in her mouth, she felt dirty from the smoke and ash of the fire, and she was exhausted. But not too exhausted to take offense. "No one is marrying anyone, Thornbury."

"We are."

She glared and rose, fists at her side. "No, we are not. *I* will not. I fail to see how it was well and good for us to do what we did when you thought I had done the act before. What is the difference?"

"You were untried. And I took you like a beast up against a tree—" He broke off in horror, the normally implacable duke clearly worked up into a lather. "Like an animal."

"And I liked it. We both needed that."

"Bronwyn," he began. "I took advantage of you."

Before he could continue, she raised a hand and

stalked toward him. "Enough. You give me little credit, Your Grace, to think that I don't have my own willpower or control over my thoughts and my person. I wanted the outlet as much as you did. I took as much advantage of you as you did of me. We are equally responsible. Stop trying to assume blame for *my* actions."

The muscle in his cheek flexed. "Then we must take responsibility and do the right thing here."

"The right thing by whom?"

A scowl split his face. "By *you.*"

"For the love of God, no." She scowled fiercely back at him. "I will marry someday, and it will be with a man I choose and can grow old with. As much as I desire love and a true courtship by a man who might esteem me someday, I am also a realist. What happened between us was sex, Your Grace, and that is *all* it was. Please do not make it into this grand catastrophe with an ending that will ruin two lives. We were two people seeking comfort in the moment, that's all." She exhaled, watching him fight with his own sense of honor even as his pride felt the sting of her rejection. "Don't escalate this into more than it is."

Chest heaving, he raked a hand through his hair and exhaled on an irritated sigh. "This isn't right. I should have known better. I *do* know better."

"Perhaps, but a convenient marriage to placate denizens of society who are not here isn't your decision to make. I offered, you accepted. Regardless of my state of chastity, the desire was mutual. Leave it be."

Well awake now, Bronwyn attempted to make some

sense of the tangle of her hair. The pins were somewhere about. There! She cringed at the dirty condition of her favorite hairpins with the jeweled lilies and butterflies but had little choice. When they got back to the hotel or the ship, she intended to take the longest, hottest, soapiest bath known to man. She reached for the pins, cleaned them on her shift as best she could, and twisted her locks up into a bun that she secured in place.

"Will you hand me my shirt and trousers?" she asked a still frowning Thornbury.

He nodded and retrieved them both, giving the shirt a good shake before holding it out to her. His eyes fell to her front and something dilated in his gaze before he flushed and averted his head. Following his gaze, Bronwyn looked down and squawked in dismay. Now that her hair was up, her nipples were at proud attention in the cool morning air, the darker areolas of her breasts visible against the transparent fabric. She grabbed the shirt and wrenched it over her head.

The duke shook out her trousers next, and something tumbled from the pocket. What it was didn't quite register until much too late when she was poking her head through the neckline of her shirt. "No, wait," she blurted out as he bent to retrieve the item. "That's private."

A slow, aggravating smile that made her panic curved one side of his mouth. "I believe you said this love letter was to me. Doesn't that make it mine?"

"That's something else!"

He unfolded the paper before she could protest or

snatch it away, and she could only watch in abject horror as the smile faded, to be replaced by confusion and then anger. His brows snapped tight, face going hard. Bronwyn knew what he was seeing—the typeface of the British Home Office and his own handwriting.

"What is this? How do you have this?"

Deuce it, why hadn't she burned that, too? It was just her luck that *he*, the owner of the document, would be the one to discover it. "I can explain," she said.

Waving the parchment, he closed the distance between them. "Yes, explain to me why you have a confidential report from the Home Office in your possession, part of a report that I compiled. Did you steal this? Who are you? Where did you get it?"

She bit her lip and took a step back. "Are we still doing a question for a question?"

"I'm not playing games, Bronwyn. Answer me."

Too soon to joke, clearly, from the furious pull of his mouth, the clipped rage in those last two words, and the fire turning those amber eyes a dark gold. Her stare dipped to the trousers he still held in his other hand and narrowed as if they were at fault. They were! Why couldn't the dratted things have kept her secret? Snatching the pants from him, Bronwyn yanked them up her legs. If he was going to interrogate her, she wasn't going to do it half-naked. When she was covered, she met his livid stare.

"You will talk right now, Bronwyn, or so help me."

The threat hung in the air, and she bristled at his high-handedness, ready to retort that she didn't have to tell him a damned thing, when a faint shout resonated from outside the folly. It came from some distance away, but much too close for comfort.

"Shit," he bit out, a muscle flexing in his jaw. "We need to go."

Panic overtook her irritation. "Is it them? The men from last night."

"Probably. We shouldn't stay here to find out."

As much as she was grateful for the reprieve, he wouldn't forget. Bronwyn exhaled and reached for her waistcoat and stockings, putting them on as quickly as she could. They were cold to the touch but had thankfully dried overnight. She bit her lip. Despite the discomfort of the ground, she had slept soundly enough, and the duke's body heat had been enough to keep her from shivering. She was certain that she'd either cuddled him or he'd cuddled her. Their legs had been intertwined at some point, too. It was a small mercy she hadn't woken up to *that*.

The duke grasped her arm at the door, his eyes promising the retribution that was still forthcoming. "This isn't over."

Her jaw clenched. "Let me go."

He did so, and then set about kicking the cold ash of the dead fire into a dark corner. The char on the ground could not be hidden, but it was only visible if someone looked closely. The duke picked up the coat that they had slept on and shook it out as well, beating the dirt off with one hand. With a grim scowl, he put it over her shoulders and she frowned at the unexpected caring gesture. "It's still cold."

The small act of compassion, despite his ire, warmed her. "Thank you."

As if he could read her thoughts, his mouth flattened. "Don't read anything into it, my dear, or mistake my kindness for weakness. Treason is treason, even in the form of beautiful young ladies."

Treason? Bronwyn blinked and then felt a boulder of pure ice form in the pit of her stomach. She was in possession of a document from a confidential government report. How had Wentworth gotten his hands on it? Had he stolen it? "It's not what you think, I swear."

"Save it," he growled. "You can tell it to the Metropolitan Police when we get back to England."

She let out a hollow laugh, despite her dread. "How quickly we have gone from marriage to prison! I suppose they equate to the same kind of cage for a man like you."

"What the hell is that supposed to mean?" he growled, seething. "You have confidential Crown documents in your possession. One of *my* private reports. Are you working with the Kestrel? Who is he? Did you get this from him onboard your brother's ship?"

Bronwyn blinked, her mind whirling. She almost laughed in his face but didn't want to push her luck. The man looked like he was on the verge of coming apart at the seams, and she needed his help and knowledge of the city to get back to the *Valor*. She would figure out a means of escape once she was safely on her way back to England.

"I have no idea what you're talking about."

The look he gave her was fulminating. If she were a

man, Bronwyn had no doubt she would not be standing right then. "You'll give up all those pretty secrets soon, love. I swear it."

The endearment was spat with such loathing that she almost shuddered but lifted her chin. "You can try."

———

Fearing that the shout had been from one of their attackers, Valentine moved them quickly. It would be impossible to retrace their steps from the night before, considering they were deep in the woodland of Fairmount Park and had floundered around in the dark before finding the folly that had sheltered them overnight. However, from the position of the sun in the sky, he could at least determine which way was east as well as the direction of the docks.

The page from *his* report was burning a hole in his pocket.

Who the hell was she? And how had she become embroiled in this mess? What was she doing in Philadelphia, and most of all, could she identify the slippery Kestrel?

Valentine kept a close eye on her as she trudged along beside him. She knew better than to try to escape, especially in an unfamiliar place and with men at their heels. The maze of streets started to become wider as they walked into the city. No one was following them for the moment, but there were eyes everywhere, and Valentine didn't want to take any chances that someone would be alerted to their presence.

He glanced down at Bronwyn, whose head was low-ered, but he sensed she wasn't missing a thing. Bitterness sluiced through him. How much of what had happened between them had been a lie…a sodding deception? If he hadn't seen the blood on his handkerchief himself, he would never have known. She had played him like a god-damned fiddle and he had been completely oblivious. Thank God he'd found evidence of her treachery and she had not accepted the protection of his name.

Or then he would be branded a traitor, too!

Bloody hell, what was Ashvale going to do? The scandal would be interminable, unless there was a way he could con-tain the mess with the Home Office. If Bronwyn was will-ing to cooperate and give up the names of her cohorts—*the identity of the Kestrel*—maybe he could help keep it quiet for his friend's sake and obtain some leniency.

But first…they had to get back to England.

He shook his head to clear it, recognizing the street of the Bell in Hand Ale House, the start of this foul adventure. The sound of a cocking gun made him shove Bronwyn to the ground, and he dodged the cracking shot right at the last moment. She scrambled to the other side of the street, watching him with frightened but clear eyes as he loaded his own pistol and took aim.

"Stay down," he told her. "I don't know how many there are."

These men were relentless. What kind of information did Bronwyn have, and why did they want her so badly? Before he could think more about it, he was attacked on both sides by three men. None of the three were ones he fought before, but they were clothed in rags and dirty. Hired ruffians. But hired by whom?

He shot one in the leg and kicked out at another who tried to get an arm around his neck. With intense focus born of years of training, he dispatched the second man and then the third. It was daylight and someone would have reported the gunshots to the police. Considering he wasn't officially employed by the Home Office, he didn't have much leverage, and this wasn't England. They could both be tossed into the stocks.

Valentine turned and ran back to where he'd left Bronwyn, but the bloody chit wasn't there. Had she been attacked? Taken? A quick glance over the space showed that there was no sign of a scuffle, and rage spun through him. She'd run! Where would she go? She'd either get a hansom back to where she was staying or head for the ship.

Or… He glanced down the street to the tavern.

No, she wouldn't do something so unreasonably reckless, would she? He exhaled. Of course she would. Valentine sprinted as fast as he could, stopping just before he barged in with the force of a bull in a shop full of china. If she was meeting the Kestrel, he had to know, and that required stealth not a commotion. He slipped in the side entryway that he'd exited the day before—which seemed like a lifetime ago—and crept along the quiet corridor. It was early yet, but the tavern was already open for business, given the low murmur of voices.

He spotted the slight figure still wrapped in his cloak,

but he tamped down the urge to rush over and demand answers. That wouldn't help anyone, and if her companion wasn't the Kestrel, there would be no point. She was speaking with someone he couldn't see from the back, though they appeared to be small in stature. Curious. He couldn't get any closer without attracting attention so Valentine crept back down the corridor and put his ear to the thin wooden wall on the other side of where they sat until he could hear hushed snatches of the conversation.

"Thank you, sorry...yesterday," the other voice was saying. "Couldn't come."

"Was an attack. A man tried to take...message by force." That voice was Bronwyn's, and it was trembling. Was it because of fear or worry that he'd catch her? Or that someone else would? "Glad...you were here. Lucky."

"Waited for you," the other voice said. "This information...is paramount."

Valentine frowned, straining to hear more. What information? He wished he had gotten there sooner to learn whatever secret it was Bronwyn had shared. And paramount to what? Shit, this went much deeper than a stolen page from his report after Brent Sommers's arrest.

"Paper with names was...lost. They...John Surratt... also Powell. They...league."

Valentine blinked and reached for the page from his pocket. At the very bottom, it detailed names of Brent Sommers's network, all men who were known spies and criminals. Both those names were on it. What the devil was Bronwyn up to? There was no way he was going to be able to help her, or her family, if she didn't tell him the truth. And that had to start right now.

"That is helpful. Be safe…Kestrel…thank…."

Satisfaction gusted through him. Valentine knew it! He knew that blasted man was involved somehow. There was the scrape of two chairs along the floor, which meant that they were leaving. Hurrying from the corridor, he rounded the room and nearly crashed into his quarry, her beautiful and treacherous blue eyes widening in recognition. The person she'd been whispering with had already gone.

"Thornbury."

"Who was that?" he growled.

"My acquaintance," she said softly. "The one who I needed to meet with. I was coming back to you, I swear. I took a chance that my contact might be here and I was lucky. I wasn't running away, I promise you."

"I don't care about your promises." His jaw clenched. "What was his fucking name?"

"*Her* name," she whispered. "Mary Richards."

Valentine frowned, the name not ringing any immediate bells, but that didn't mean anything. He'd been out of the game for some time, and Sommers's case had been handed off to another operative. "Who is she?"

Bronwyn shook her head. "Not here."

If he clenched his jaw any harder, his teeth were going to shatter, but she was right. This was an open public space and anyone could be listening. He'd just done it himself. "Fine. We are going back to the ship, and you are going to tell me everything from start to finish, do you understand me? No more lies, no more detours, no more games."

"My things are at the hotel."

"I'll send Lisbeth for them."

The sound of the woman's name—and what she clearly represented—made Bronwyn flinch as if she had an inkling of what was coming her way. She gave him a weak nod, though resentment glinted in her eyes before her lashes dipped to hide her expression. The Bronwyn he had come to know in less than a day would have something up her sleeve. She was not the sort to capitulate so quickly and so easily. In another life, he might have admired what the Americans called gumption. She had it in spades, but she was on the wrong side of things. The wrong side of *him*.

Why did that grate more than it should? He barely knew her.

You know her well enough to have been inside her.

That had nothing to do with anything, but the reminder didn't help. He'd coupled with a thief, a turncoat, a liar, and God knew what else. Inexplicably enraged at his own stupidity in falling for a master thespian, Valentine took her by the elbow and she didn't protest his unyielding grip as he led her to a hansom.

"The docks," he ordered the coachman.

In the carriage, he stared at her. His jaw ached from holding it so tightly, but if he didn't keep himself under rigid control, who knew what might happen. Even covered in streaks of ashy grime, brown hair falling loose from her bun, and wearing filthy men's clothing, she was stunning. The combination of wide-eyed innocence and innate sultriness had been his downfall.

She's not innocent.

No, she had played him like a child's top. Spun him around until he'd been dizzy, addled with lust and desire. Valentine could not recall the last time he'd been so bamboozled by anyone, much less a slip of a girl. It itched under his skin like a festering pustule.

"How did you get my report?" he asked in a curt tone.

She licked her lips and he fought not to respond. "Someone in London."

"The Kestrel?"

She turned her head toward the window, her throat working. Her chin jutted in mutinous silence. In that moment, he saw it. The sight of that profile and the reason he'd had such an odd feeling that he'd seen her somewhere before when she'd first left the hotel dressed like a thin, young buck and sitting at the tavern. It was the profile of the portrait that had been drawn…because the damned Kestrel wasn't a man at all.

Now that it was clear, everything seemed to fall into place all at once. The mysterious peer who had access to all of the exclusive events and parties in London, the fact that he could elude authorities so easily, and all of the many faces worn for the sake of the assignment.

This beautiful young charlatan had fooled them all.

Valentine went cold. "You're the Kestrel."

Ten

BRONWYN WAS DONE FOR.

She'd had that same thought many a time before, of course. One did not tangle with dangerous people and do dangerous things without feeling backed into a corner with no way of escape once or twice. But this was *Thornbury*. His reputation of being a ruthless bloodhound was something she hadn't seen in person until now. Sure, he'd been stony and sour, but that had been his general disposition. He wasn't a man given to warmth or docility.

But *this* man, this hard, hatchet-faced statue who had locked her in her cabin the minute they'd set foot on the *Valor*, was. But he had gone unnaturally still, his face so hard that the only thing moving had been the occasional flicker in his stubbled cheek. It hadn't even looked like he was breathing. Not one more word had come out of him after his pronouncement.

Not a sound. Not a single expression.

Nothing.

And oddly, that had chafed more than anything else. Those piercing eyes had communicated it all—frustration, resentment, betrayal, aversion, disappointment. The silence had been unendurable, and she would have given anything to know what was going on in that head of his.

Admittedly, the stolen page of his report looked bad. It put her in the wrong, and she couldn't defend it because she had no idea how Wentworth had come into possession of it. And the message she delivered… How could she explain her actions about thwarting a possible abduction of the American president without clearing it with her own people first? Thornbury wasn't going to harm her if she didn't talk. At least she hoped so.

She was trapped between a rock and a hard place. Wedged between Thornbury's judgment of her conduct and her duty to her chain of command. One would break…she just wasn't sure which.

"My lady," Cora said, opening the stateroom door and startling her. "Do you wish for some hot tea?"

"Yes, please," she said. "And a bath."

Bronwyn's body itched beneath the unwashed, filthy clothes. It had only been a day and a night, but so much had happened. A blush warmed her face as she recalled using Thornbury's handkerchief and the anger over the loss of her virginity that had been eclipsed by her supposed treachery. Was being in possession of confidential—possibly filched—reports worse than safeguarding one's chastity?

If a tree fell in the forest and no one was there to hear it, did it make a sound? From her own reading, the philosopher George Berkeley seemed to think there wouldn't be if there were no means for listening. So by default, wouldn't virginity be the same?

Then again, hers hadn't gone quietly. It had left

in a carnal symphony of indelicate moans. Bronwyn burst into soft laughter, earning herself an odd look from Cora who was busy getting the bath prepared in the adjacent chamber. Dear God, she was losing her mind. No one knew besides her and the duke, and he wouldn't be going around proclaiming that anytime soon. He probably couldn't wait to wash his hands of her and move on.

"Did Rawley say anything, Cora?" she asked.

"I haven't seen him, my lady."

Bronwyn blinked. Where was he? Though that was a small mercy, at least. She didn't know if she could take Rawley's disappointment as well. She let out an aggravated huff. What did Thornbury have to be so disappointed about anyhow?

If he had been in her position with a way to stop an important man from being assassinated, he would have done the same thing. She'd bet if Lady Lisbeth were the operative, he would not have had a single issue with that. He'd probably praise her…and then reward her with his masterful prowess in bed. Jealousy warmed up in Bronwyn's belly like a horde of angry bees.

Oh, stop. The duke doesn't matter. Nothing matters but the pickle you're in and how to get out of it.

A silent housemaid brought in a tea cart, poured the steaming tea, and left as quietly as she'd come in, a red tinge on her cheeks as though she was uncomfortable or frightened…or given strict orders not to make eye contact or say a word. That was outside of enough. She was a lady! Bronwyn stiffened. Obviously, the maid was under instructions not to talk to the prisoner.

In fact, her nemesis was probably standing guard outside her stateroom door and glaring at anyone who came too close. Her stomach growled at the delicious scent. Mutinously, she sipped the tea and munched on the delicate sandwiches beside the teapot. At least he wasn't trying to punish her with starvation. She would need her strength. For what, she didn't know.

Cora gave an approving nod at the empty tray. "The bath is ready, my lady."

Bronwyn stood and nearly ran into the antechamber. Stripping out of the grimy clothes, she almost wanted to instruct Cora to get rid of them, but they were the only suit of men's clothing she'd packed. "Will you see that these are laundered, please, Cora? Without that meddlesome duke knowing, if possible?"

"Yes, my lady. I'll go now while he's with Lady Lisbeth."

Bronwyn bit her lip hard, unwelcome images arising of the two of them lying in flagrante delicto in his former countess's room, his beautiful lean body, laced with its network of scars and sinewy muscles, intertwined with hers.

Stop thinking about him. He's not thinking about you.

Scowling, Bronwyn stepped into the steaming bath and winced at the ache in her muscles as she slipped under the cinnamon-and-apple-scented water. The singular scent of her soap brought a comfort she hadn't realized she'd needed. Sighing with relief, she washed and rinsed her hair, and then leaned back for a moment. Heavens, she was sore. Sore in her back, her neck, her legs... She froze. Between them as well. Bronwyn flushed, a hand wandering down to cup her mound.

It had been less than a day and perhaps such soreness was to be expected. She was untried and her lover hadn't been under-endowed. Nor had he been docile. No, his strokes had been hard and demanding, working her body to an explosive release. Bronwyn could feel the memory of his palm against her spine, forcing her lower half to arch toward him more fully and then moving to draw her hip to him. Beneath her hands, the aching flesh tingled.

Goodness, *why* was she obsessing about the man or the act? It was to be expected, she supposed. He'd been her first. She was bound to associate some deep-seated, useless feelings with him. Those would fade in time, and once she found another lover to replace him, none of it would matter.

You don't want any other.

The duke had been her fantasy lover for so long that imagining someone else in his place was impossible. And now he wanted to arrest her. She was lucky he hadn't thrown her in the brig. Bronwyn let out a hard sigh. Did her brother's fancy liner even *have* a brig? Given the caliber of its few passengers, no one would ever dare put a toe out of line. Though most ships had a place where misbehaving crew or travelers could be kept. She was certain of that. If Thornbury had put her in such a place, she would have demanded that he lock himself in there with her like the gothic heroines did in her racy novels. *Naked.*

Sighing at her foolishness, Bronwyn smiled. A man like Thornbury would likely be immune to female seduction, though he hadn't resisted when she'd dropped to her knees like a practiced lover. *That* thought filled her with gratification. His desire hadn't been fake in the least. Nor had hers. She skipped her fingers up her ribs on each side, leaving goose bumps. Her breasts begged for stimulation. *Should* she touch them? No one was here.

Her body prickled from the coarse direction of her thoughts, her nipples still obscenely tight. Bronwyn's eyes fluttered closed. The pads of her fingertips brushed over the taut peaks, and a ragged pant hissed out of her. Gracious, she had never been so sensitive. Her thumbs and forefingers pinched in tandem, the sound of the water sloshing against the sides explicit when she arched upward, a needy sigh bursting past her lips.

"Want me to come back?" a low voice growled.

Bronwyn nearly jackknifed out of the tub, her hands falling guiltily to her sides as she sank back into the water, though it hid nothing. "You need a bloody bell."

"I knocked. Twice." Leaning against the doorjamb, his hands in his pockets, Thornbury looked clean and put together in a fresh suit of clothes. He'd bathed and shaved as well, the angular planes of his face no longer softened by bronze stubble.

Apart from the faintest of flushes against those high cheekbones, he didn't look in the least bit affected by her impromptu performance. It irked. Here she was fantasizing about him, and he had probably put her from his mind like yesterday's leftovers. She wanted to cover herself and scream at him to leave. This was her *private* bath! But a more perverse part of her wanted to make him react. Wanted to deconstruct that careful expression of cool boredom.

"What do you want?" she asked, meeting his unreadable eyes as she reached for the washcloth on the side of the tub and began to wash her already clean body in leisurely circles.

Those hawklike eyes flared, but he didn't move, ever in complete control. "We need to talk."

"And that couldn't wait?"

He glared. "I couldn't take the chance that you would coerce a servant to assist with your cause."

"To do what?" she asked, moving the cloth to her neck and her collarbones before trailing it down her torso. "Push me through a porthole?"

"I wouldn't put that past you."

"I might be imprudent, Your Grace, but I am not stupid. Where would I go? I have no good soul in Philadelphia to help me."

"No aunt?" he shot back.

"You know there's no aunt," she said mildly and drew the rag over her breasts. The moan that crept past her lips was inaudible, but she sensed rather than saw him tense.

Bronwyn had half expected him to avert his gaze, but the competitive creature in him wouldn't, recognizing her ploy for the game of seduction it was. His eyes were riveted as the cloth dipped through the valley between her breasts and lower down the expanse of her belly, still moving in small, maddening circles. When that muscle slowly flexed to life in his cheek, she hid her glee.

He glared. "Who was your contact? Richards?"

"She's a free Black woman with her own troubles. She's gone."

"Where?" he demanded.

"Back to Richmond, I expect. To the home of Elizabeth Van Lew."

Bronwyn saw the moment recognition glittered in that saturnine gaze. Thornbury might not have heard of Richards, but anyone worth his salt as a British operative would have known the name of the abolitionist who had freed her father's slaves after his death over twenty years ago, brought food and medicine to Northern soldiers incarcerated at Libby Prison, helped them escape, and ferried secret messages to Union leaders.

"Do you mean Mary *Bowser*?" he asked softly, eyes piercing.

"I suppose that is one of her names, yes."

"The spy?" Thornbury pressed.

"As much as I am, I suppose."

Recruited as part of an enormous espionage network, Van Lew was the one with ties to Wentworth, but it was Mary whose bravery had stuck with Bronwyn. Risking discovery and her own neck, the courageous Black woman had posed as a domestic servant behind enemy lines and passed on critical information to Van Lew. A huge part of how she avoided exposure was by pretending to be insensible and witless, fooling dozens around her, when the fascinating truth was she possessed a photographic memory. The information she gleaned was vital to the cause. Mary was one of the true unsung heroes of the war.

In truth, Richards's efforts were the reason Bronwyn had agreed to do this in the first place. She had seen the opportunity as a chance to do *something*. To be part of a changing tide and the revolution that women like Richards so bravely led.

The duke frowned, his brows dipping so harshly that she swore she heard a crash of thunder. "You are not a spy, Bronwyn. You are a girl playing at grown-up reconnaissance games."

His words stung, but Bronwyn hardened herself against them. It wasn't the first time she'd faced the disdain of men in her chosen line of work. Some of the long-time operatives who worked for Wentworth had been openly contemptuous of her ability—as a decorous lady of quality—to do anything worthwhile. But she had! She'd risked life and limb to get that message to Richards.

"Think what you will, Your Grace. You have already formed your opinion of me."

"What did you talk about?" he ground out. "What was the missive?"

Bronwyn ran a hand down the edge of the tub. "There was chatter about an attempt to abduct the president on a certain date at a certain location."

The duke's eyes narrowed, likely in disbelief or anger at her prevarication, but she didn't care what he thought.

She'd done what she had to do. The message had been delivered.

"Who do you work for?"

She smiled. "Now that will have to wait until we are back in London."

"I can get it out of you."

"What are you doing to do, Your Grace? Starve me? Torture me? Punish me?"

His eyes widened at the lowered inflection on that last word, but nothing else moved, not even the muscle in his cheek. He could be a statue for how rigidly he held himself, but Bronwyn knew better. He was fuming underneath that frigid facade.

"I might be a silly girl in your eyes, but underestimate me at your own peril." She slid the cloth between her legs and arched lewdly, giving voice to the erotic moan crawling up her throat. "Do. Your. Worst."

"You're playing with fire." His reply was barely a rasp, eyes fixed on the swirling cloth. He couldn't hide the raw quiver of need in his words, and Bronwyn dropped a bold gaze to the crotch of his trousers that was already crudely jutted. He might be made of ice and able to put on an impassive mien, but he wasn't immune to her down there.

"But I do so love a good game. Don't you, *sir*?"

Eyelashes flickering down, she abandoned the cloth, her hands reaching indelicately between her thighs. Gracious, she was so aroused, her body started to shudder at the faintest brush of contact. The primal growl that rumbled out of the duke's chest made the paroxysm hovering just below the surface break free. Bronwyn gave into it like the wanton she was, soaking up every undulation of pleasure that came forth.

The slam of the door was the only sign that he had gone.

That round of battle went squarely to her.

Was that *disappointment* she felt? Bronwyn threw an arm over her face and sank below the water. She hadn't meant to do what she'd done. She had only hoped to rattle him a bit, but then she'd lost control of the very game she had been playing. She might have won the battle, but him leaving hadn't meant he'd flown a white flag of surrender.

No, this conflict was just beginning...and all she had succeeded in doing was to provoke her opponent. Bronwyn had no intention of giving in without a fight. She was clever and she was persistent. There had to be a way off this ship once they got closer to London.

She would find it, if it was the last thing she did.

Eleven

VALENTINE FELT NO GUILT AT STROKING HIMSELF TO vicious completion, bathing for the second time today, now that his spend was coated all over him. He'd barely been able to get his excruciatingly hard cock from his trousers. After watching her in that bath, two delirious pumps were all it had taken to feel like his entire insides had shaken loose from their mortal trappings.

Panting, he leaned his head on the porcelain side of the tub, images flowing through his mind of her sprawled in decadent display, breasts bobbing above the water and begging for his mouth. Valentine had no idea how he had remained upright at the door and not crouched at the side pleading for favors. Imploring for a taste…wanting his tongue to be pressed where her fingers were.

Hell! He was growing hard again.

How had he been brought so low as to this base version of himself, driven by carnal need? This uncontrolled, wild creature that he loathed. *This* was why he kept his emotions firmly buried beneath layers and layers of pure frozen will. A man should not be ruled by his passions, especially not a man in the bloody business of espionage.

A chit who fancied herself a spy.

Valentine's laugh was guttural. Did she have an ounce

of sense in that fool head of hers? Gallivanting off with stolen reports and secret messages to America where she could have gotten herself killed or incarcerated, which would have had her wishing for death! He knew of the ills that went on in those places for prisoners of war. It didn't matter if one was female. In fact, the cruelties of war were much worse.

God damn it! She made him see red. *Burn* red. He found her infuriating and intriguing in equal measure, but it was evident that she was in over her head, and whatever she was doing had to stop before she got hurt.

What on earth was she thinking by colluding with Van Lew? Who had put her in touch with the woman in the first place? He'd heard whispers of the infamous spy known as Crazy Bet in the last two years since she'd been recruited by Union General Benjamin Butler, thanks to some of his former associates in the know. Bronwyn was nothing like her. She was young, inexperienced, and untrained. A sheltered, delicate, highborn aristocrat.

She's not so delicate.

Valentine recalled her grim determination and shot to the man's thigh in the square, and he scowled. That could have been by pure accident, and if it wasn't, so what if she could shoot a gun? Being a good marksman didn't make her an expert in deadly situations. Now, she had a target on her back.

His anger returned full force. It wouldn't compare to that of her brother's however. Valentine didn't want to have to be the one to tell the duke what his younger, *unwed* sister had been up to across the Atlantic with no chaperones or protection. Ashvale would have her hide the moment they docked and lock her away in a remote convent somewhere.

If she was lucky...

She was so maddeningly immovable, refusing to confess who her contact in London was. There was either a traitor in the Home Office or someone was running a clandestine operation under the authority of the one person who could approve something like this...the queen herself. Then again, nothing went without Palmerston's sanction, so who the bloody hell was it? Who would endanger a duke's sister?

She knowingly endangers herself.

Good God, his thoughts were all over the place. Valentine was all for any woman following her dreams and doing whatever she wanted, but he was thinking like a caveman when it came to Bronwyn Chase for some reason. He wanted to protect her...by keeping her under lock and key. Would he have done the same with Lisbeth? He knew the answer before he even finished the question. Of course not. Lisbeth was a seasoned, trained assassin, if she had to be. She could speak half a dozen languages, blend into any situation, and seduce the hell out of anyone.

Bronwyn is capable all those things.

Of course she was.

She was the fucking *Kestrel*.

Valentine scrubbed a palm over his face. That thread of guilt beneath all the self-recrimination pulled taut. The tangled web seemed to constrict with him squarely at the center. His unruly emotions veered from being furious that he hadn't recognized her for what she was more quickly... that he had been so blinded by his lust for his *best mate's sister* that he hadn't been aware of what was right in front of him all along. She dulled his very reliable senses, and perhaps that was the most frustrating part of it, because she also made him feel the most alive than he had in months. Years, even.

Good Lord, the *audacity* of her in that bath.

He'd wanted to pluck her from the water like a rosy, freshly washed fruit and devour her. Show her how to make that luscious body writhe and squirm. But the lady was squarely off-limits. At least until he decided what to do with her. The ship had already left port, so unless she jumped over the side into frozen water, she wasn't going anywhere.

Damn and blast. He raked a hand through his hair and palmed his nape.

Valentine had to figure out how much to say and who to confide in because if the gossip got out, the scandal of an unmarried, unchaperoned lady being on her own in America would be insurmountable. Loose lips would sink more than ships. They'd sink whole futures. And while Bronwyn had deceived him and led him on a merry chase, he was loath to bring more ruin down upon her head. He really was going soft.

After finishing up in the bath and dressing in a new set of clothing, he made his way toward one of the lounges where he'd arranged to meet Lisbeth. She would have to know the truth in order to keep an eye on his clever little captive. Lisbeth sat at the pianoforte, fingers drifting over the keys in a lively melody. As usual, she was surrounded by a throng of admirers, male and female. She wouldn't have lacked for company even though he was unforgivably tardy.

"I was beginning to think you had forgotten our rendezvous, Thornbury," she drawled when his dank expression scared off most of her hangers-on, who retreated a safe distance away. "I almost had to stop a duel from happening over who would be my new escort in to dinner."

"Sorry I'm late. Something came up."

An amused brow lifted, a smirk drifting over her mouth. "Does that something have brown hair, bright blue eyes, and a body made for an artist's canvas?"

Positively. Valentine ignored the rush in his blood and schooled his features to remain blank. He couldn't, however, keep the flush from heating the tips of his ears. Predictably, Lisbeth's smile widened, but she kept those opinions to herself.

"Yes and no," he replied. "She's a nuisance who's only going to get herself killed."

Lisbeth ran her fingers over a scale and then turned to face him. "You have blinders on where the lady is concerned, Val. She's more accomplished than you think."

Didn't he know it now. Valentine loosed a breath and resisted the urge to tug on his cravat. He leaned in, voice low. "We need to talk."

Lisbeth rose, much to the disappointment of her audience who had retreated to a safe distance but were still present. She had a way with people. They fell to her charms like blocks of dominoes. *Like Bronwyn.* Valentine's scowl deepened. The two women were nothing alike.

When he led Lisbeth to a quiet set of armchairs in an alcove that wasn't in the middle of the room, she frowned at his expression as she took the seat opposite him. "Do I even want to know what this is about?"

Best to just get it out. "She's the Kestrel."

Whatever she'd been expecting him to say, he knew it wasn't that. Her mouth went slack, her eyes glittering with shock bleeding into mirth, and then she started to laugh. Those light, airy chuckles drew attention, but Valentine couldn't bring himself to care. He'd laugh too, if the whole situation didn't paint *him* in the worst possible light.

He'd missed all the signs.

He'd been led like a dog following a meaty bone.

He'd taken dreadful advantage and deflowered a lady.

"It's not that funny," he growled.

Lisbeth wiped her eyes and shook her head. "Of course the Kestrel is a woman," she said. "I had my suspicions, but the Home Office was so adamant it was a man. And of course they were. No man could be so elusively brilliant. My hat is off to her. Honestly, I think I'm half in love with her already."

"The Home Office might have done that on purpose," Valentine said, ignoring the dreadful fact that a part of him—a very small, very insignificant part—admired

Bronwyn's ingenuity as well. She was smart, persistent, dangerously clever, and as stubborn as a mule. Even his threats to make her confess had been futile. Those traits were to be admired. He scowled. In any other woman *but* her.

Lisbeth frowned. "How so?"

"I believe that the Kestrel may be a double operative, or at least someone working for the British Crown in some other capacity." He went on to briefly explain what had transpired, leaving out the frantic half an hour in the woods, but by the time he was done, her eyebrows had climbed to her hairline.

"Val, you slept in the same building alone," she said softly. "She's the sister of a bloody duke. What were you thinking?"

The guilt was instantaneous, considering they'd done much more than sleep. While it'd been by mutual consent, the fact that they had passed an entire night together unchaperoned meant that British society would hold them both in contempt. They might as well have been copulating all night long for what it would look like to the denizens of the *ton*.

Valentine raked a hand through his hair for the tenth time. "I *know*. I couldn't very well find a chaperone in the middle of nowhere while we were running for our lives, could I?"

"What will you do?"

"Take her back to London and hand her over as quietly as possible. Ashvale will have to deal with any fallout at that point."

An odd look crossed Lisbeth's face. "You'd just abandon her?"

"Did you not hear a word that I said?" he whispered furiously. "She's the bloody Kestrel! A spy you have been searching for and dragged me in to help you find. If it were any other person, trust me, neither of us would be this... concerned. I've done my part and it's finished."

"Just like that."

"What are you getting at, Lisbeth?" he muttered, the decision not sitting well with him at all but his hands were tied. "It's always been just like that. We apprehend the bad people and turn them in to our superiors to face sentencing. She's not any different."

"And you're fine with her being treated like a criminal?"

"She *is* a criminal."

Confusion crossed her face. "You just said that she could be a double operative working under a different set of orders for England. Which is it?"

"Damn your eyes, I don't know."

"Good God, Val, you *want* her to be guilty," Lisbeth deduced, leaning closer and watching his face with an intensity he was used to seeing when she was interrogating others. It had never before been directed at him, and Valentine fought not to move from the uncomfortable force of it. "What happened out there? What was the message?"

"She claimed it was to foil an abduction attempt of Lincoln. I doubt it was real, though she met with Mary Bowser, part of Crazy Bet's intelligence ring." He glowered harder, banishing his misgivings. "And don't ignore the fact that she stole *my* report."

"Or someone gave it to her," Lisbeth mused. "You said it was the page that had the names of Sommers's contacts? What if it was a credible threat?"

"There's no way for us to know until we get back." He exhaled. "She won't say who her contact is."

"I wouldn't either, until I was certain of immunity." A small smile curled her lips as she sat back in her chair. "Told you she was smarter than you gave her credit for."

"I never said she wasn't smart."

"Oh, please," she scoffed. "You should have seen yourself whenever the girl came anywhere near your sphere. The infallible Duke of Thornbury scurrying for cover, in case her perceived witlessness was an infectious disease. I believe the words you used to describe her were 'charmingly dim.' She sure had you fooled."

He pressed his lips together. "I never scurry."

But she'd had him fooled. And that rankled.

Something like a whisper skated across his nape, and Valentine looked up just as the object of his unfortunate obsession entered the lounge. He hadn't expressly told her that she wasn't on ship's arrest, but her maid hadn't been given orders to keep her to her stateroom. Besides, locking the sister of the owner away would draw too much attention. They might not be in London, but most of the passengers were English and tasty gossip was still a meal course.

A pair of brilliant blue eyes met his and held. Every

nerve in his body leaped to attention at the challenge in that stare.

"Feel like scurrying now?" Lisbeth teased wickedly.

With a glare, Valentine signaled a hovering footman and ordered a whisky, hoping it would take the edge of whatever *this* new feeling was. When had the sight of her become as important as breathing?

The moment he was sure that Lisbeth's attention was elsewhere, he stole another glance. Bronwyn looked nothing like the urchin of the past few days, dressed in a sumptuous lavender gown trimmed in delicate embroidery. Her curls were draped in an elegant updo, amethysts winking in and out of the glossy strands. Lady Bronwyn Chase was every inch the lady.

Every inch the consummate actress.

That tinkling laughter he so loathed broke out across the room as she found herself surrounded by fawning admirers. He kept his feet firmly planted so that he didn't go over there and make an ass of himself. Though he might have been her first lover, she wasn't his to keep. He held no claim over her.

When he tore his hungry gaze away, Lisbeth's attention was on him. "You know, you retired honorably from service for a reason, Val."

"What's your point?"

"The Kestrel isn't your responsibility," she said.

He shot her a sidelong glance. "Are you saying I should pretend she isn't an international damsel-turned-spy who stole *my* confidential Home Office documents?"

Valentine felt his blood boil, as if Bronwyn had committed the offense directly against him.

"We don't know how she came into possession of them." Lisbeth tapped her fingers against her chin. "What we need to do is find out who the real instigator is. It's not her, clearly. She's not an official British operative. When we get back to London, I say we let her go and see what she does."

It was a sound plan. An excellent plan. But once more, the idea of letting Bronwyn out of his sight made his skin prickle and itch. Lisbeth was right—this had become more than personal. More of those bell-like sounds reached his ears, and he fought not to ground his teeth together when two of the men mimed having a duel in front of her. The so-called winner dropped to his knee before the lady and begged loudly for a favor.

Valentine was halfway across the room and on the edge of her space before he stopped himself from hauling the idiotic young buck to his feet. A pair of startlingly blue eyes met his and his breath constricted in his lungs. "Your Grace," she said with a dip of her head, lashes falling demurely to her cheeks. "To what do we owe the pleasure?"

He fought not to groan as the inflection on that last word arrowed straight to his groin, reminding him of the provocative scene in her bath chamber he'd escaped by the skin of his teeth. The young gentleman genuflecting in front of her skirts shot him a fulminating glare, which Valentine ignored. "A word, Lady Bronwyn," he said, and then choked out the last word. "Please."

A slim brow rose, amusement trembling over those lush lips that he had kissed many a time. "Will you excuse us, kind gents," she said to her avid entourage, who erupted in sighs and protests. "His Grace is a dear friend of my brother's, you see, and I'm certain that if I'm not exceedingly polite, word will get back. Ashvale will be very cross with me indeed if he hears I shunned the man." She gave an audacious wink when the most ardent of the toadies shot him a look of mistrust. "Don't worry, he's no danger to me. He's more of a fond nuisance."

Valentine blinked. A fond nuisance.

They groaned and complained, all the while shooting daggers at him for spoiling their fun, but she smiled charmingly and offered a gloved palm to the sullen, kneeling buck who was the most vocal. He stood and pressed his lips to her knuckles, which set Valentine's teeth firmly on edge. He clasped his hands behind his back and reminded himself that he had no claim on her, despite his body's propensity to think otherwise.

She's not yours.

Well, she was his prisoner. *That* thought let to an unholy swarm of lewd thoughts– including the lady being deliciously restrained—that had no business seeing the light of day. He blinked and gave his head a rough shake.

When those thoughts dispersed, he glowered at her. "Is that all I am to you? Your brother's friend?"

"Do you wish to have a deeper designation, Your Grace?" she asked and signaled for a glass of champagne from a waiting footman. Her voice lowered. "Would you rather I introduced you as my lover? As the gentleman who was buried so deeply inside me, I couldn't form a coherent thought? That would have done wonders for my reputation."

His cock twitched. It wanted to be buried in her right now. Nape heating, Valentine's eyes shot to hers, noting the mischievous glint as she sipped, regarding him over the crystal rim. Hell, why had he marched over here in the first place as though she needed rescue from a bunch of overeager young rogues?

"Walk with me," he said, desperate to escape the many eyes watching them, including Lisbeth's. When she nodded, he led her out of the room to the cool air of the main decks.

"Oh, how beautiful," she murmured.

He glanced up, following her wide-eyed stare. Bright stars twinkled against the immense backdrop of a twilight sky, glittering over the slumbering stillness of the Atlantic Ocean. The moon was large and full, casting a silvery sheen over the polished floorboards. It was, indeed, lovely, but Valentine had other things on his mind. There were a few couples with the same idea strolling near the bow, so he led her toward the more deserted stern.

"Your Grace, are you trying to get me in trouble?" she teased. "I promised my gentlemen friends that you would not lead me astray, and here you are, guiding me to a very solitary part of the ship with no care for my poor reputation."

"Your reputation will survive."

"Will it?" she asked, voice low and husky in indecent invitation. Hell, he should have stayed in the lounge where he would be in control by default of everyone else's observation. He huffed a breath. He'd say what he meant to say and escort her back inside.

Valentine throttled his spiking desire. "Is this some kind of game to you?"

"All life's a game, Your Grace. If one doesn't play, it passes you by in a blink."

"You think what you're doing is some amusing diversion?" he asked, furious, though a part of him sensed that she was baiting him. "People can get hurt. You can get hurt."

"I'm well aware of my limitations, Your Grace," she replied coolly. "I'm also aware of my merits. I'm sorry that with your blinkers on where I'm concerned, you cannot possibly see past the satin skirts and the proper manners to realize that I am perfectly capable of not being foolish." A hint of red touched the tops of her cheekbones, indicating she wasn't as cool as she pretended to be, but he was too busy being insulted to care. "Give me some small credit, sir."

"Blinkers," he echoed softly.

"A horse wears them to focus for a race, blocking out all other distraction."

"I know what they are."

She smiled. "Then you take my meaning."

The breath left her in a gasp when he took her by the

arms and ushered them both around the sternpost and then into some kind of crew alcove where a ladder led down to the engines. His much bigger frame crowded hers in the narrow space, but she did not cower or back away. No, the little minx reached for his lapels and erased any space between them. Her face tilted upward. "Are you going to kiss me, Your Grace?"

No. He had absolutely no intention of doing so.

His hands trembled on her elbows and slid over her arms to her shoulders and up in a slow, measured glide until he cupped her slender nape. His thumbs grazed over the sides of her delicate jaw. Her lips parted in invitation, and he had to force himself not to sample them for the sake of it. No, he wasn't interested in those lips.

"Lift your skirts, Bronwyn."

Twelve

BRONWYN'S THROAT DRIED AT THE EXPLICIT COMMAND.
Every time she thought she held the reins and was in control of the seduction, he demonstrated so easily that she wasn't. Because, dear heavens, he was going to debauch her out here in public view where anyone could come upon them, and she couldn't stop from shivering with equal parts of excitement and alarm. This wasn't like their coupling in an abandoned shelter in the woods, even though this part of the ship seemed to be mostly abandoned. Any and all crew would be readying for the dinner service. At least, she hoped.

The duke stared at her with hooded, expectant eyes and removed his gloves. The sight of those long bare fingers did something to her... Would he use them on her? Graze their calloused edges over her goose-pimpled skin? Touch her beneath the skirts he'd commanded her to lift? Her breath hitched with desire. With tentative hands, she tugged at the satin of her gown, grabbing handfuls of the thicker petticoats beneath until her stockings came into view, then her garters, and the embroidered edges of her drawers.

"All the way up," he said and she complied. "Loosen the tapes of your drawers," he said, voice so guttural her own core clenched with need.

In silence, she did as bid, feeling the material sag from her waist to her knees, cool ocean air kissing her heated skin beneath her thin chemise. He knelt and dragged her drawers down further, lifting each leg out of them. Watching her, he held the fine-spun silk undergarments up, fingers easing over the slit in the middle. Bronwyn shuddered in mortification when his eyes dilated. "So damp already."

It was a fact—she could feel the slickness between her thighs.

Her mortification grew when he lifted them to his nose and inhaled deeply before folding the voluminous silk and tucking it into his coat pocket. Hissing a raw sound of arousal, the duke placed his hands at her waist and lifted her to the low metal ledge that snaked the circumference of the space, before dropping to his knees.

"I *am* going to kiss you." Warm bare palms skated up her thighs just as she'd hoped. She trembled when he widened her knees and caressed her dewy skin with the backs of his knuckles. "Here."

Oh God.

She rolled her bottom lip between her teeth and bit down hard when he settled those broad shoulders between her splayed legs, baring her to him. Bronwyn wasn't a prude, but she didn't dare watch, the feeling of him staring at her too much to handle. Her eyes fluttered shut when she felt his breath on her. He was having none of it though. "Look at me."

The sight of him perched in front of her was decadent,

but the hungry expression on his face even more so. Fabric pooled over her hips, her thighs spread indecently wide, his face so close to her most intimate parts that she quivered.

"You're so pretty and glistening," he whispered, and she didn't even have the wherewithal to be embarrassed at that. Golden eyes burned into hers, his nostrils flaring with lust as he breathed her in and licked his lips in anticipation. She'd never seen a man look so...ravenous. So full of desire and wicked intent.

Keeping his eyes locked on hers, he leaned in for a long, slow lick with the flat of his tongue. Bronwyn couldn't help it; her eyes rolled back in her head, her hips nearly coming off the ledge at that first scintillating touch. Gracious, it was filthy and incredible what he was doing to her. He licked her again, swirling at the top of her sex in a move that had her whimpering.

"Perfection," he pronounced. The growl of approval that burst from his chest was primal when he set himself to her, as if that first taste had been his utter ruin. His tongue licked and laved, swirled and sucked while pleasure built along her nerve endings. It was near intolerable, the feelings surging inside of her, her veins going molten as he stoked the fires of her arousal with every flick of his tongue and scrape of his teeth on her wet, throbbing flesh.

"Valentine," she begged.

"Yes?" he said, a deeply feral gaze catching hers, though he did not stop in his ministrations.

"I need..." Her voice trailed off when his lips closed

around the peak of her sex, the soft suction making her writhe. She couldn't form a single articulate thought.

"I know what you need," he promised.

She almost toppled off the ledge when his finger probed her entrance while his tongue continued its sensual assault on her body. He slid inside, thrusting once and then twice, and suddenly, the combined sensations were too much. With a gasping moan, Bronwyn felt her entire body seize, her core clenching around him as pleasure crested in waves upon crashing waves. Her head slumped back onto the porthole, stars in the sky merging with the stars going white in her vision as she rode out the storm he'd ruthlessly wrought upon her.

Damnation, the taste of her was to die for—all silken, tart sweetness, much like the apples she smelled like. Their coupling in the woods had been fierce and frantic, and there'd barely been any time to appreciate her form. But now, he reveled in the beauty of her feminine shape, the fragrant scent that lit his body on fire, and the sublime banquet that would send him quite happily to his maker with that as his last meal on his tongue. He'd seen her beneath the water in her bath, but those glimpses had only hinted at the perfection of her.

Valentine's cock was so distended, it hurt to move, but he stood anyway, wincing as his sensitive shaft grazed against the constraining fabric. He was certain he'd soiled the crotch of his trousers with the amount of fluid he'd leaked while gorging himself on her.

Languid, passion-drenched dark-blue eyes met his, even as reality intruded between them, the haze of lust clearing somewhat. It didn't diminish his arousal, but his ardor retreated. Valentine had no reasoning or excuses for what he'd just done—the untenable position he'd placed them both in, and this time, with no acceptable justification. They had both known exactly what they were doing.

He exhaled. He'd come out here to clear the air, to remove her from her vexing sycophants, and instead he'd made yet another unspeakable mistake. Ever his fate, it seemed, whenever he was around her. He opened his mouth at the same time she spoke, probably to make the same apologies he was about to.

"I need you inside me."

Valentine blinked. Had he heard that right? "I beg your pardon?"

"You gave the orders before," she said huskily. She lifted one heel and swung it around his legs. The other wrapped around the back of his thigh, propelling him forward so that his swollen groin pressed right up against her center. When she hooked her calves over his hips, they both groaned. "And I obeyed you without question. Now it's your turn. Unfasten your trousers and fill me."

Heaven help him, her *words.*

"Bronwyn, we—"

"Damn it, Thornbury, if you're about to tell me that we

can't do this, so help me, I will pitch you over the side of this ship and let the sharks have their way with you." She tightened her muscles, dragging her core over him again. "And I guarantee you that it won't be as pleasurable as if you let me have my way."

Nimble fingers reached for the fastenings, and with a few quick snaps, he sprang free. Blue eyes widened at the sight of him, lips parting on a gasp of air. It would be her first look at him as well. Glancing down, he winced at the sight of his engorged cock, fluid glistening over the crown, veins lining a shaft that was angry and pulsing and excruciatingly hard.

He let out a grunt when her palm slid over him, thumb spreading the moisture over his skin. "Sorry, I've changed my mind. The sharks can't have this. It's mine."

"Is that so?"

"It is."

A dark laugh left him, one that was quickly throttled to a groan as she pumped her hand down and then back up. At this rate, he wasn't going to last. She drew him back to her, lining the tip of him up with her body, and when her calves pulled tight against his buttocks, he had no choice but to slide into her warm, willing heat.

"Oh, fuck me," he groaned as the exquisite pressure enveloped him.

She felt like goddamned paradise.

"Are you well," he whispered when he was fully seated, her walls clenching around him in erotic, needy pulses. He definitely wasn't going to last.

"Harder," she said. "Like in the woods, but keep your eyes on me. I want you to do this as if it isn't a mistake. Like you know exactly who I am and whose body is bringing you to pleasure."

He froze, his confused gaze meeting hers, trying to read her expression and failing. His cock didn't soften, but cold logic was present in his mind, ever lurking. She was right. This was different. *This* would change everything, and yet, he couldn't stop. He didn't want to leave the haven of her body, logic and sensibleness be damned.

"Who am I, Valentine?" she asked softly, rocking her hips up and making him lodge deeper into her.

She was a liar. A spy. A cheat. The bloody Kestrel.

She was a woman. A siren. A warrior.

His lover.

"Bronwyn." Valentine pulled back from the clench of her body and thrust back in, the slick glide making them both gasp. "Bronwyn," he said again before his mouth took hers in a drugging kiss, their bodies grappling below in a race to completion. One hand wound into her hair, cupping the back of her head and tugging just enough for her to gasp into his mouth at his handhold. His other hand went to her hip, securing her to him down there.

He felt as though he could never let her go.

Would never let her go.

Her pelvis ground up against him as if she couldn't control herself, whimpers leaving her each time he stroked deep. Hell if it didn't feel as though she were made for him. They both froze as faint voices filtered toward them, but not close enough to convince either of them to stop. They were out of the way as it was, and the risk of being seen in this little nook was low.

"Kiss my breasts," she panted.

He lifted them from the confines of her bodice, his mouth closing over one of her dusky, taut nipples as a fresh surge of lust poured through him. She whimpered, arching toward his mouth and crying out when he bit down gently. He soothed the abused flesh with his tongue, and then turned his attention to its twin until she was writhing in his arms.

"I'm close."

So was he.

Valentine slid his hand down between their straining bodies to where they were joined and angled his thumb to circle her firm peak. His hips pistoned faster, the sound of their frantic coupling loud in the narrow space as she cried out and dug her heels in harder. "Yes, *yes!*"

Heat lit the base of his spine while she convulsed around him, her mouth parting on a soundless scream as she shattered. It didn't take long for him to follow into bliss, her release spurring his into completion. With a labored groan, he pulled from her body and yanked her drawers from his pocket before spending into the soft fabric.

Panting, she stared at him, laughter in those sated blue eyes. "Did you just soil my drawers?"

"They were already soiled," he said with such a prurient look that she blushed.

"I cannot go back to the dining room without undergarments, Your Grace," Bronwyn said primly, when he helped her off the ledge and tucked himself away. She smoothed her skirts and tried not to look. It was odd to see his cock in such a flaccid state, when he'd been so huge and hard and intimidating only moments before. Then again, her own body seemed to bloom and contract from pleasure in a matter of minutes as well.

She wasn't going to lie. The sight of his male organ had snatched the breath clean out of her lungs. She'd taken him without any issue, obviously, but seeing his over-engorged length had sent her body into a mild state of panic. Thank God she hadn't seen his size their first time. She might have had second thoughts about offering up her virginity.

But the *feel* of him when he was inside her had been sublime. So thick and long that the fullness of him had penetrated everywhere. A twinge throbbed from her well-pleasured center and a blush heated her cheeks at how wanton she'd been, propped up on the ledge like a doxy on the docks while a gentleman had had his carnal way with her.

Not that she was complaining. She'd wanted him, too, with a hunger that had shocked her. The salacious images in her head during their walk had been summarily banished for her own sanity, but they'd seen her bent over the ship's railing with him plowing her from behind. This way had been infinitely better.

Bronwyn secured the pins in her hair that had come loose when his fingers had been buried in the strands. Heavens, had a little hair-pulling ever felt so wickedly divine? She sniffed and smoothed the tendrils away from her flushed cheeks.

Desperate for space and clarity, she cleared her throat and exited the alcove, walking to the rails at the rear of the ship to enjoy the cool sea air coasting over her hot, damp skin. "That was an interesting way of marking your territory."

"I beg your pardon?" She felt him join her and she glanced up at him, a shuttered stare meeting hers.

"Your jealousy could not have been any more obvious, Your Grace."

Those eyes narrowed. "I was not jealous. I simply did not think that a woman who is a prisoner and a traitor to the Crown should be surrounding herself with fawning admirers who have no idea of her true identity."

"Oh, so you were concerned for *their* well-being? How generous of you. What was this, then?" She hooked a thumb over her shoulder to the nook they'd just commandeered, brows rising as anger tore through her. "Punishment? Your way of putting the prisoner in her place as judge and executioner? Seems rather self-serving to me, Your Grace, considering the gratification you gained from your methods."

That muscle ticked to life in his cheek, a hint of his own ire flashing over his features at the awful accusation. "You know damn well that was not what this was."

"Then what was it?" Bronwyn swallowed, her eyes falling to the glassy ocean and the white swaths left in the wake of the ship. Moonlight sparkled over the surf, the beauty of it distracting from the certain deadly hazards that lay beneath. That was what Thornbury was to her—attractive on the surface, mortal danger underneath. Like a deadly iceberg. She'd always known that, and yet, she'd been drawn to it...drawn to him.

"I can't control myself around you," he muttered and raked a hand through his already mussed hair. "I don't know why."

Neither did she, for that matter. It was raw and consuming, whatever this connection was between them, but Bronwyn had no earthly definition for it. Lust at its most base? Primal attraction? Whatever it was, it was powerful enough to not stop him from condemning her and craving her at the same time. Or vice versa, considering how he'd brought her back on the ship like a lowly criminal. She *should* hate him.

"Well, at least you are honest about that."

"When have I not been truthful with you, Bronwyn?" But even as he replied, shadows descended over his face. His whole life had been a lie, just as hers had become. There was no room for truth, not when one's existence depended on the fabrication of false identities.

"Who is your contact in the Home Office?" he asked. "If you even have one."

Her gloved fingers clenched around the metal of the railing. "I cannot tell you."

"Cannot or will not?" he asked.

"Whichever suits your narrative, Your Grace," she replied. "You've pegged me as a traitor who is deserving of your contempt in your less-than-humble estimation."

"The Kestrel is a rogue operative, Bronwyn, acting beyond any official capacity that I am aware of, and that person, astonishingly, is *you*. The sheltered, highborn sister of my friend. How else would you have me respond? If you were any other, I would have you locked in the brig. Contempt is not even close to what I feel. I am furious you've put yourself in this position!"

"And again, that is my decision," she said quietly.

"Yes, you've said. It doesn't stop me from worrying about your safety, and it won't stop Ashvale from fretting about it either. You do understand what's going to happen when we get to London?" He exhaled. "Your brother will be the worst of it, and with his new position in the Lords, the repercussions upon him will be challenging."

"Repercussions?" Bronwyn asked with a frown.

"Come now, my lady. Clearly, you have a very intelligent brain in that head of yours. What do you think will happen when the sister of a mixed-race duke is accused of treason? How do you think that will reflect upon him?"

"This has nothing to do with Courtland!" she retorted.

"Doesn't it?" he asked softly. "He's your brother. A duke many still don't recognize as the rightful Duke of Ashvale because of his heritage. They will say your actions are obviously reflective of *his* character and *his* influence, and all the work he has put in to change ignorance and biases will be lost."

Those quiet words lodged like blades between her ribs as Bronwyn sucked in a horrified breath. Of course she'd considered what would happen if word got out about her activities—protecting her sister, Florence, and her family was paramount—but she'd never thought about how her reputation as a female spy would reflect upon her brother's work in Parliament, should her identity come to light. And besides, she'd been guaranteed protection by Wentworth. He could make this go away. "That's preposterous. You're being unfair. They won't use me to unseat him."

"You think *I'm* being unfair? They will vilify you—and by association, him—in every way possible to support their own dogmatic views. Surely I don't have to remind you of what some of the peers in the *ton* are capable of, especially in the protection of their own very selfish financial interests? They will not hesitate to tear him down by reference to what you've done. A lady of your stature gallivanting all over England and across the Atlantic?" The duke cursed under his breath. "Ashvale has been very vocal about the practices in the Southern states, but he does not have the support of everyone in the Lords."

Her eyes widened. God, he was good. Now Bronwyn understood why the Duke of Thornbury was such an excellent operative. His quiet intensity and impassioned list of her purported transgressions made her feel as if he were on her side, made her want to confide in him...to beg for *his* help. To trust him.

Was he on her side though? Or was he simply rooting for information?

Her mind whirled with possibilities. She didn't want to hurt Courtland, but she could control only her own actions, not anyone else's. Right now, only Thornbury and Lady Lisbeth knew of her identity. They were not yet on English shores, and once they arrived, things would change. She might be arrested, her brother would be informed, and Wentworth would have to bail her out. Bronwyn blinked, considering that last point. What if Wentworth wasn't the man she thought he was either? What if he left her swaying in the wind to protect his own identity? She'd always trusted him, but she'd never been in this much trouble.

Was saving his own skin more important than hers?

He was a man. Of course it would be.

Letting out an aggravated sigh, Thornbury scrubbed his hand over his face and stared out into the moonlit night. "How did you even come to do something like this? It's not normal fare for a lady of quality."

Bronwyn bit her lip, recognizing the ploy for what it was and admiring how casually it was asked in the same breath. "Why? Because I'm too 'sheltered?' I won't drop a name by accident if that is your hope, Your Grace, but I asked to be involved at a country party in Kettering some while ago."

"Care to share more?"

She blew out a breath. It wouldn't hurt; it was already done, and perhaps it might go a little way to dispel the thinking that she was a vile criminal. "I helped foil a plot to blow up a train that Palmerston's private secretary was supposed to be on."

His head whipped to hers. "Ashley?"

"One and the same." Her shoulder lifted in a shrug. "That was the first time, and it was addictive."

"I remember hearing about the report on that incident. It was the Fenians, they said," he murmured. "There was no mention of you, however."

"Why would there be? I did it as a favor to a friend."

"A friend."

She huffed a laugh, though she could sense his brain mulling over all the details, trying to narrow down the event and the timing. Perhaps she'd erred in confessing anything at all, but a part of her didn't want him to equate her with some treasonous creature. What she was doing was for Crown and country. Her efforts had not been for naught. "I think we've shared quite enough for the evening, Your Grace. I wouldn't want you to be late for dinner."

Thirteen

DEUCE IT! SHE WAS GOING TO CLIMB THE BLOODY walls of her stateroom!

It was her own fault. After the incident on the stern, Bronwyn had been dead set on avoiding her warden at all costs. Not for any other reason than she was tangibly weak for him. Her body was already at his mercy and she feared that her brain would follow. She would not betray Wentworth, or believe the worst of him just yet, but the Duke of Thornbury was too clever by half.

Bronwyn flopped back onto her bed and stared at the painted mural on the ceiling that she'd long since memorized: one of a woman on a swing surrounded by peacocks. The symbolism was not lost to her. In the *ton*, husbands and fathers controlled every aspect of a woman's life—when she was to smile, to speak, to act. Her purpose was to look pretty and fetching. The joy of the swing was a trap because once one was on, one could never escape. The peacocks with their beautiful tail feathers and sharp beaks kept her in place.

Or perhaps she was over-reading into it. Perhaps it was just a lady on a swing.

She'd taken her meals in her room, and only went out for brief walks to stretch her legs when Thornbury was at dinner or Cora was sure of his whereabouts. Bronwyn had managed to avoid Lady Lisbeth as well, but she knew the other woman was watching for her. The former countess and the duke used to be a team; they would be in cahoots naturally, burning both ends of the candle. Bronwyn had to be vigilant…and come up with a plan.

A knock on the door made her fly up.

"Cora, where have you been? I've… *Oh.*"

Because the person at the door wasn't Cora. It was the man she wanted to see least in the world, even less than the duke, in fact. Rawley. Bronwyn gulped as he entered with her maid on his heels and closed the door behind the two of them. She stiffened, expecting a beratement of some sort, and opened her mouth, but before she could speak, he held a hand up. "We need to get you off this ship."

Her jaw gaped and shut. "What?"

"Preferably without Thornbury knowing before you can get to safety."

Eyes rounding in shock, she blinked like an owl. "I beg your pardon?"

"The minute we get to England, you will most likely be arrested by British operatives or snatched by very bad people, likely on our heels in another ship as we speak."

Bronwyn frowned. Someone was following them? "What do you mean? No one beyond Thornbury and Lady Lisbeth know anything."

"That's where you're wrong, Little Bee. I sent a telegram to your brother before we left. When the duke brought you back on the ship, there were eyes and ears on you. You've put yourself in an inordinate amount of danger by running off as you did. Meeting with Richards was a risk."

"You followed me?" she demanded.

He scowled. "And lost you for an entire night until you returned. I tracked you until the river and then lost the trail. When you turned up at the tavern, I was just about to involve the local police and cable your brother that you were missing."

Bronwyn gulped. "I wasn't in danger."

"Weren't you?" Thick black brows drew together into a thoughtful frown. "You know who Richards is, don't you?" When she stayed quiet, he went on. "Mary Bowser—also known by many other names…Henley and Jones, to name two—is a wanted woman."

"Yes, I know. She's also a hero and only wanted because she's fighting for basic human rights."

Face unreadable, Rawley eyed her. "Is that what you think you are as well? A hero swooping in to save the day?"

"No," Bronwyn replied aghast. "I'm not. I'm only trying to do my part to right the wrongs of the past. Is it wrong to want the world to be better? I might be limited in my own power, but I still have a voice and the agency to act. The value of being an ally is ceding the space to the oppressed. You taught me that." She sucked in a breath. "Isn't that what you're doing, too? Providing funds and information to the Union cause?"

His nod was short and he regarded her seriously.

"This is dangerous, Bee."

"No more dangerous than Mary Richards surviving in an unsafe space," she shot back and then bit her lip hard. "My life shouldn't carry more weight than hers. I had to do this, Rawley. People were at risk." One important person in particular, not that she could admit that to him. *Oh, Rawley, putting myself in danger might have saved the life of the American president.*

He didn't speak for a few moments. "In a perfect world, the value of human life would be the same, but we're not in a perfect world, are we? We're in one that makes race a reductive device, used on the oppressed by oppressors, for profit."

"That's why I want to help," she said fiercely. "That kind of thinking has to end."

"It does, but power is never given," he murmured. "It's always taken, by strife and by blood." When she didn't speak, he exhaled and ran his palm over his short hair. "Your decisions are your own and I respect that. However, your brother wants you safe, and while I understand your motivations, those men at the tavern are out for blood. Your blood. Last I heard, there was a bounty on your head for your capture along with a list of names you carry."

She flinched. "On my head? I assure you, Rawley, I am not carrying—" She broke off at the vexed look on his face and swallowed the rest of her protest. She'd had the damn thing in her bosom the night of the dancing in the lower decks. Thornbury wasn't the only smart man with a pair of eyes.

"Keep your secrets, if you must," he said. "I wanted to

take you home to Antigua, but it was impossible to get you away from Thornbury without drawing suspicion to us both before the ship left port. And he knows I am from there, which meant it would have been the first place he looked." His face tightened with frustration. "And so now we have to divert the ship for an alternate plan."

"Divert the ship?" she asked, matching his frown. "We're a day to England, if that."

He nodded. "Hours. The captain has directions to stop at Brest in France, citing emergency engine repairs."

"Thornbury will know something's amiss."

Rawley shook his head. "He won't. I've been filling his ear with crew complaints with the boilers for the past few days. It will not come as a surprise." He grinned, a lopsided quirk that she knew foretold mischief. "And besides, I have a fun little explosion planned."

"An explosion!"

"Contained, Little Bee. Don't you worry. Just enough of one to be convincing. Your duke has an uncanny attention to detail."

"He's not my duke," she said without much heat.

Rawley only lifted a skeptical brow at that and then glanced over to Cora who was busy packing her things into a small portmanteau. "Whatever is going on with you and Thornbury is another problem for another day. In the meantime, Cora will be with you. She has all the information about where I will meet you in Paris. From there, we'll await your brother's instructions."

Bronwyn bit her lip. "Is Courtland very angry?"

"He's not happy, I'll say that." Rawley shrugged. "It's more for your safety than anything else. That and the fact that your mother has been hounding him with fear of your absence. You know how he feels about the Marchioness of Borne."

Bitterness flooded her. "She's only worried about how she will look to her friends if I've gone and ruined myself. Trust me, it's not out of any actual concern for my welfare."

"Regardless, Ashvale wants you safe."

She let out a breath. This was a good plan, and it would do until she could figure something out for herself and possibly get in contact with Wentworth. However, contradictory emotions were at odds in her body when it came to the duke—the thought of deceiving him felt wrong. "Rawley, do you think I can trust Thornbury?"

He didn't answer for a bit, but then he shook his head. "I'm not entirely sure. The duke is a good man, but he's England's man first. His duty will be to the Crown and the Home Office. Your brother trusts him but says he will follow the law to the letter, and that will be his downfall."

"How so?" she whispered, heart sinking. In other words, he would turn her over, no matter his own true feelings on the matter.

"Just because he's a man of integrity doesn't mean everyone else is." Rawley sent her a compassionate look as though he could guess what his blunt words were doing to her. "And he's no longer active. He will not be able to help you from within. Thornbury might want to do the right thing, but his faith in that office is misplaced considering the corruption running through its ranks." He lowered his voice. "There are those, like Palmerston, who secretly support the American war for trade reasons, and others in the Home Office who disagreed with Thornbury's arrest of Sommers."

Her eyes rounded in shock. "Sommers was a bastard, involved in stolen goods and in the shipping of enslaved human beings!"

Rawley nodded. "You don't have to tell me. The man was scum and deserved what he got, but he'd lined the pockets of many powerful men in England whose wealth was built off the back of such bondage." His voice shook with a hint of its earlier intensity. "But money is king, even if it comes from the blood of innocent men."

"It's despicable," she whispered.

He let out a breath. "Yes, it is, and I don't intend to give up."

"I wish I could do more."

He sent her a soft, fond smile. Then he turned solemn. "Unfortunately, you have drawn the wrong kind of notice this time."

A knot swelled in her throat, both from his words and the obvious warning. "So you're telling me I have to run?"

"Yes. For now."

Bronwyn sighed. Not only was she already a criminal in the duke's eyes, but now she'd be a fugitive as well. And nothing looked as guilty as someone who ran, even if they had legitimate reasons for doing so. "Very well. Tell me what to do."

Gaze narrowed, Valentine stared at the captain, watching a trickle of perspiration meander down the man's temple. His worry was also apparent in the lines of strain around his mouth and eyes that seemed to be in a constant flurry of movement over the dials and gauges of the engine order telegraph. "You mean to tell me we've been slowing for hours because of engine troubles? Will we be able to reach our destination?"

"We should, Your Grace," the captain replied. "We'll just pull in to port a bit later than expected. I've given the crew a bell to slow to half speed and sent men to check on one of the boilers. It's been giving trouble since we left Philadelphia."

Valentine glanced at Lisbeth and Rawley, who stood near the door listening to the update with matching frowns. "So I've heard. Very well. Keep me abreast of the situation, our position, and time of arrival."

"Yes, Your Grace."

Rolling his neck to ease the tension gathering there, Valentine moved past Lisbeth who followed him onto the open deck. Rawley strolled behind them but moved to another part of the deck to speak with one of the crew. "Do you suspect something, Val?" Lisbeth asked.

He shook his head. "We're too close to England, and Rawley mentioned issues earlier. Likely just coincidence. Still, keep an eye on our bird."

The ship troubles didn't bother him. If anything, the

delay gave him time to think about what he was going to do with Bronwyn. Valentine wasn't stupid. He knew the moment they hit English soil, she would be seized and detained by someone who *wasn't* him. The thought rankled.

Lisbeth had said she would do her best to ensure Bronwyn's safety, but even he knew it was a man's world in that office. The capture of the Kestrel would be a coup, propelling whoever took over to instant notoriety, and the newssheets would be in raptures. They already salivated at the thought of the man. The fact that *he* was a *woman* would rock London. It would be the scandal to top all scandals— DUKE'S SISTER EXPOSED AS INTERNATIONAL SPY.

Valentine rubbed at his chest, soothing the queer, piercing ache. Even if he believed her and somehow managed to help her to clear her name by proving she was a secret operative serving her country as she claimed, her reputation would take a thrashing. The newspapers would not be kind. They never were. And no doubt, some of his peers in the Lords would have a field day using the scandal to bring Ashvale low.

You could let her go.

He balked, blinking. Letting her go meant going against everything he'd been taught. Everything he'd ever fought for. But if he did, he could figure out her claims on his own, find out who her contact was, and *then* take her into the Home Office when he had solid evidence. He knew Lisbeth would back him up, whatever he decided, but that meant putting her in an ugly position with her supervisors. She would have to lie to cover his tracks, and that did not sit well with him.

Walking over to the railing where Rawley was smoking a cheroot, Valentine studied the churning ocean. A storm was coming in, darkening the morning sky to an overcast, ominous gray. He was glad they'd escaped bad weather while in the middle of the Atlantic. Even on a ship of this size, those storms could be deadly.

"Did you find out who those men were from the tavern?" Valentine asked the silent man. "The ones after her, who hired them?"

Rawley nodded, flicking the burning end of his cheroot into the waves. "Some chatter, not much. They were local men, but the ones I questioned didn't know anything. Low-end bully ruffians, if that. The big brute mentioned the name Lewis Payne."

Lisbeth let out a sharp exhale and they exchanged a look. That was one of Lewis Powell's many aliases. He was a dangerous man as well as a known entity from Sommers's list of acquaintances. The plot was sprawling wider and wider, giving some veracity to the idea that Bronwyn might have been involved in something much bigger. He slid the page she'd had on her person from his pocket and studied the names. Brent Sommers. Lewis Payne. John Surratt. John Wilkes Booth.

A low sound emerged from Lisbeth's throat. "If Payne is involved, this is beyond us, Val. I would need to get our superiors involved. He's a piece of shit. While we were in Philadelphia, I found out that Lewis Payne was arrested for beating a maid who ousted him as a spy." She frowned. "Coincidence? I think not. It has to be him."

"We have no proof," he said. "Beyond a cad's word."

"What do you mean to do?" The question came from Rawley, whose face showed concern, obviously for his cousin's sister.

"If these men are after her, then we have to take her in for her own safety," Valentine said, the pain at the base of his skull expanding to a deep throb. "It's the only way."

Lisbeth's face pulled tight. "What if we don't?" When he gaped at her, she lifted a palm and dragged him a few feet away, presumably out of Rawley's hearing. "Hear me out. What if we let her go home, post a man on her heels at all times, and find out who her contact is. *Whoever* that is has to be the real ringleader, if there is one. She's just a means to an end to someone. A homing pigeon."

Valentine glared at his former partner, even though he'd had a similar thought just before. *She's the Kestrel*, he wanted to shout. Bronwyn wasn't a simple pigeon that someone had used to send a message. She was a bird of prey! The Kestrel had been setting the Home Office on its collective ear for months.

Lisbeth's idea had merit—he didn't want to expose Bronwyn to his peers or the presses—but Valentine couldn't protect her without more resources. He glanced at Rawley, wondering if the man suspected his plan wasn't to safeguard his cousin's sister once they got to England, but to turn her in. However, the man's face was unreadable. Valentine guessed he would not like it. Nor would

Ashvale, for that matter. His best friend would be livid at such a betrayal.

Then again, neither of them knew of the Kestrel's true identity.

Letting Bronwyn go, as slippery as she had been to track or catch in the first place, would be a mistake. He'd gotten lucky. He hadn't caught her out of his own skill; it had been pure luck that events had unfolded the way they had. In his gut, Valentine knew that she would not let herself be entrapped a second time. She was much too clever for that, which meant that the minute he let her out of his sight, she was as good as gone. He had to do the right thing, and the right thing was trusting in the justice system. And protecting her as well, while he was at it. A tremor slid through the pit of his stomach.

"No," he said. "It's for her own sake."

"Val," Lisbeth said in a low, urgent voice. "Think about what you're saying. She's Ashvale's sister. We can't keep this quiet, even if we tried. There are too many eyes and ears, and someone will want to make a name for themselves over this. I know it. *You* know this. Would you put her through that?"

"I'll reinstate my position," he said, then he peered at her. "Would you really consider keeping this a secret? If it got out, you would be finished."

Her pretty face went ashen, but she nodded. "My gut is saying keep this to ourselves for now. She's a lady, Val... and a friend."

Valentine opened his mouth to reply when something

like a firing cannon blasted through the air and the entire ship rocked, a thick black plume of smoke rising from one of the funnels in the middle of the ship. Lisbeth let out a scream and grabbed hold of the railing, staring up at the mushroom-shaped cloud.

"What the fuck was that?" Valentine roared, eyes roaming the horizon for a ship that might have fired on them, but the seas were clear. "Were we hit?"

"Boiler explosion," Rawley shouted as he ran past.

Hell, the captain hadn't been minimizing the problems. Thank goodness they were near the French coast. Boiler explosions caused by pressure failure due to faulty valves or corrosion were common on steamships, though he knew for a fact that Ashvale took meticulous care to maintain his vessels. Or it could have been a firebox explosion in the furnace caused by vapor accumulation. Either were a possibility and both were dangerous.

Lisbeth composed herself. "I'll go check on the passengers."

While she took off toward the main lounges, Valentine headed back up to the captain's deck where the man was furiously ringing the bell for the engine order telegraph and calling for dead slow. "We'll have to reroute to Brest. It's closer. I won't take the chance that the metal will crack. If the cold seawater touches the hot metal…"

The captain's voice trailed off, his face going pale. Valentine knew what would happen. Ships had sunk easily because of that. England's coast wasn't that far from France, but even a few kilometers could mean the difference between life and death. "Very well," he said. "Do you know what kind of explosion it was?"

The captain huffed. "Hopefully not the sink-to-the-bottom-of-the-ocean kind, but we need to take every precaution."

Rawley burst through the door, face purple and panting from the effort of having run back from the engine room of the big ship. "Furnace fire. Contained. For now." He blew out a breath. "No injured."

The relief on the captain's face was clear. "Thank God."

Valentine pressed his lips together. "We're going to Brest," he told Rawley. "Just to be safe. I agree with that. Once the ship has been checked, we can leave for England. If it's not safe, we will make alternate arrangements for travel."

"A sound plan," Rawley said.

"Everyone should stay onboard," the captain said. "I'll make an announcement to the passengers and let them know it was nothing to be frightened over. These things happen. We have enough provisions on the ship for a week or more, and we can get more supplies if needed in France."

"Very good." Valentine nodded.

There was still the matter of Lady Bronwyn, but the small fire had bought them a few days. He would think upon Lisbeth's advice. There was no point in making a rash decision without considering all the angles. Meanwhile, the Kestrel was going nowhere.

Fourteen

BRONWYN FELT THE THREADS OF PANIC CATCHING IN her throat, making it hard to breathe. She kept expecting to see the Duke of Thornbury around every corner. She was convinced they were going to get caught because the man was *always* watching. Even when she hid in her rooms, she could sense his attention on her. It was infuriating!

"This way, my lady," Cora whispered as they snuck down the gangplank during dinner, while Rawley's men kept a close eye on the duke and his companion, Lady Lisbeth. It was dark, but the ship was well lit enough to see…and to be seen.

The ship had docked in Brest as Rawley had said they would. As promised, the explosion necessitating the change in course had been small, but had still made a screech of fright tear from her chest when she'd felt the walls of her stateroom rumble. Most of the passengers had been assured they weren't in any danger and the stop in France was simply a precaution. The captain promised that they would be en route to England within the matter of a day or two…which meant the window of escape was narrow.

At first the plan had been to sneak off the ship during the first night, but Thornbury had not slept, keeping a keen eye on the decks as though he was expecting trouble.

His vigilance had frustrated Rawley, but he had adjusted the plan without losing a beat. The duke might not sleep, but he did have to eat. Bronwyn had made an appearance at dinner the next evening, flirting with her usual entourage though it had taken enormous concentration to play the part of the coquette, and then on to the gala. During the ball, she'd had to time it exactly when both Thornbury and Lady Lisbeth were dancing, and *not* with each other.

She'd met Rawley's gaze when he'd asked Lisbeth to dance, and made eyes at the silliest of her admirers, Lord Daley. The earnest buck was quick to take the bait and usher her onto the ballroom floor. Bronwyn had made sure to be seen, if not heard, with her habitual tinkling laughter, before she'd excused herself mid-dance to the retiring room.

From there, it'd been a matter of changing her bold, daffodil-yellow gown with the help of a quiet maid—one of Rawley's trusted few onboard, no doubt—and donning a dark cloak over her garments before slipping outside to meet Cora. Precious, hurried minutes later, they were in a coach on the wharf and heading toward the train station in Brest where a private rail car would be waiting. They'd toyed with the idea of traveling in disguise in public, but it was too dangerous. Luckily, Rawley seemed to be quite industrious at making arrangements.

"How did he do all this so quickly?" Bronwyn asked Cora, whispering though she didn't have to, now that they were alone in the carriage.

Cora smiled. "Noel is smart, personable, and has

friends in many places, high and low. There's a reason your brother trusts him with his life and yours. Rawley is almost synonymous with the name Ashvale in England, across the Atlantic, and even here in France."

"Noel?"

Her cheeks flushed. "His given name."

"So it's that serious between you?"

"He has asked me to marry him," she confessed softly. "And I have accepted."

Bronwyn's heart twanged with an odd combination of joy and envy. She'd never been envious of any of her set who announced marriages, likely because her own mother was plotting her nuptials at every turn. Though now, something squeezed in her chest. Perhaps it was because Cora and Rawley's connection was real and the union was not *arranged*. "Oh, how wonderful, Cora! I am happy for you both. Only I hate to be bringing you into this mess. You should be with him."

"Your safety is the important thing at the moment, my lady. I do not presume to know the whys of your decisions, but I do know that you don't do anything without cause. If you are in trouble, then I suppose there's a good reason for it." Cora folded her hands in her lap and shrugged. "You will always have me."

Bronwyn glanced back at the retreating docks through the carriage window, seeing the bright outline of the ship and almost expecting to see a towering form appearing on deck in the wake of her departure. Her heart was still pounding a harsh tempo against her ribs.

It wouldn't be long before her disappearance from the ballroom would be noticed, but another maid had been instructed to inform Lord Daley had she had retired with a megrim. The young man could be counted upon to spread the news faster than a fishwife in the local market. With luck, the hard-to-fool duke would assume that she'd gone to bed, and Rawley would confirm her malady, if necessary.

"So the Duke of Thornbury?" Cora asked.

Bronwyn jumped as if the utterance of his name could summon him like the unholy wraith he was and met her maid's eyes. "What about him?" she mumbled.

"You like him," the maid said pointedly. "You've always held a tendre for him since last season and this is the most time you've spent in his presence, and he's no longer married."

Bronwyn opened her mouth and shut it. It was imprac-tical to argue. Cora had been with her so long that, of course, she would know of her adolescent infatuation. Bronwyn had doodled the man's name many a time in her private journal. It was beyond infatuation now, how-ever. She had *coupled* with the man. Her feelings were complicated.

"He has…other interests," she said.

Like his duty and locking up the Kestrel.

"What happened between the two of you?" Cora asked. "Noel seemed to think there might be an announcement at first, when we left England, and then in the last few days on the return, it was the opposite."

The breath left her in a whoosh. "An announcement?"

Cora rolled her eyes, a smirk overtaking her lips. "That man devours you with his eyes when he thinks no one is looking. I've watched the two of you dance around each other for days. There's something between you. Even the hardiest cynic could see it."

The feeling squeezing her heart spread to the rest of her body. Bronwyn felt guilty for running, but it was clear that the man was married to his duty, even though he was supposed to be retired from his position. His desire for her was caught up on his desire to apprehend his target. "It's too hard to explain or to make sense of," she whispered. "A convoluted mess."

The coach rolled to a hard stop, making them both gasp, and the door was opened by the coachman. "Come now, my lady," he said, putting out the stool.

Cora reached forward and made sure the hood of Bronwyn's cloak was over her head and the buttons were tightly fastened before they descended into the station. It was newly constructed by the looks of it. The hour was late, though the platform still bustled with activity. No one paid them any attention as another man approached, said something to Cora to which she nodded, and handed her a pouch. The coachman took his leave, and the maid gestured for them to follow the second man who carried their bags with him.

"This way," Cora said in a low voice.

A knot in her throat, Bronwyn nodded. Her skin itched. She didn't like not being in control. Normally, when she was doing any of her message deliveries, she knew exactly what had to happen, who the players were, how to extract herself from possible danger. She'd trusted Thornbury in Philadelphia, but that had been instinctive. Now, she had to trust that Rawley had her best interests at heart.

Head down, they weaved between people and walked past the cars until they came to one that was lit by a single gas lamp. Cora thanked the man when he deposited their belongings inside and vanished into the darkness with a bob of his head. They entered the empty railcar, and Bronwyn let out a sigh of relief that they were alone. She didn't know if she could handle being with others, as on edge as she was.

"A private car?" she guessed.

Cora gave a nod. "The Duke of Ashvale cabled a friend to arrange it."

Bronwyn was grateful for her brother's help, but she knew it would not come without a price. She could appeal to her sister-in-law, Ravenna, for support and leniency, but Courtland took his family, which included both his half sisters, very seriously. She'd worry about him being overprotective later.

Right now, she was intent on escaping the man who would soon be on her heels. Thornbury would not let her go so easily; she felt it in her gut.

Paris was a big city, and she had friends there. Family too.

"What's in the packet?" she asked Cora, letting out a breath and attempting to gather her scattered wits. Taking control and regaining her sense of power was the first step in not feeling so untethered.

"Money and an address."

The maid handed her the pouch, and Bronwyn's eyes widened at the blue-printed French banknotes and francs inside. "We should go to my aunt. She lives near the Bois de Boulogne and will naturally be in town for the Parisian season."

Cora frowned. "Noel said to go to this specific place."

Every instinct inside of her, born of reading outcomes and considering scenarios over the past year, told her *not* to go to the address. Not that she didn't trust Rawley. It was *Thornbury* she was worried about. Going into hiding meant she was guilty, and Bronwyn would not back herself into a corner like a mouse for a cat to find. She would not cower. She was the blasted Kestrel.

"We will go to my aunt Esther. We'll hide in plain sight."

The maid blinked. "Do you think that is wise, my lady?"

"I do," she said, feeling less panicky already as her nerves started to settle with the resolution of a plan that worked for her.

"There's food here," Cora said. "You should eat, use the water closet once the train starts moving, and get some rest. It won't be long before we arrive in Paris, about six hours with stops."

"Good." She glanced at her loyal maid, who was preparing her a small plate of food from the basket on the table. "Thank you for doing this, Cora."

She shook her head. "I'll say one thing for you, my lady. You do keep life interesting."

————

"What do you mean, she's not here?"

Attempting unsuccessfully to curb his mounting temper, Valentine scowled at the hapless servant hovering in the doorway.

He'd spent a restless night, tossing and turning and unable to sleep, a deeply unsettling sensation crawling under his skin that something wasn't quite right. Lord Daley had brayed all evening about the love of his life's being so dreadfully ill, and when Valentine had gone to check, unlocking the door to the darkened room with a special set of instruments that opened any lock, he'd been satisfied.

Yes, he knew it was untoward to let himself into a lady's room without her permission, but it'd been for his own peace of mind. Besides, she was his prisoner. He'd caught a whiff of her sweet, distinctive scent, seen the provocative bright yellow dress she'd worn draped untidily over the edge of the chair as if she'd undressed in a hurry.

He had frowned, wondering why her lady's maid hadn't done her job and put away the obviously expensive gown, but maybe she'd been more concerned with her sick mistress. To that end, the Bronwyn-shaped lump in the middle of the mattress had satisfied him enough to creep back outside and take himself off to his own quarters.

Now, however, he frowned, rubbing his gritty, sleep-deprived eyes.

"Begging your pardon, milord. I came to clean this morning as I always do, and no one was here. I thought milady was still asleep, but there were only pillows beneath the sheets." She shook her head with rounded eyes. "Very strange."

Valentine went preternaturally still at her pronouncement before nearly shoving past the maid and letting out a roar of fury when he yanked the counterpane all the way off. She wasn't there because she was never in bed at all. *Damn it!* He wanted to tear into the pillows that he had foolishly assumed had been *her*. He'd fallen for an old childhood trick foisted upon unsuspecting parents. It was already hours later. She could be anywhere. He knew for a fact she wasn't hiding on the ship—why would she be? No, she was gone.

Still, he had to be sure.

He ran out of the room and down the corridor. His first stop was the captain's quarters. Attempting to draw his rage under control, he breathed in through his nose, striving for calm when the man's eyes rounded with surprise and fear. "I need all of the crew supervisors on duty immediately."

Seeing his expression, the captain made no bones about giving the directive to a nearby crewman, and within short order, a small crowd had gathered, including Lisbeth and Rawley. He met the man's concerned stare.

"What's the matter?" Rawley asked, drawing him aside.

"She's bloody gone," Valentine bit out, searching the

other man's eyes for any possible sign that he'd known about the bird's overnight flight. "Lady Bronwyn."

Lisbeth let out a small gasp from where she stood. Rawley's gaze narrowed when he shook his head. "No, she was ill and in bed. I checked last night and again earlier this morning when I brought her a tincture for her headache. She was still asleep."

Valentine exhaled. "It's not her. Pillows, not a body. She's gone. Fooled us all." God, he could barely form the words through his clenched jaw, but at least, he knew that Rawley looked as surprised as he'd been by the news.

"Where would she go?" Rawley muttered. "Why would she leave in the first place?"

Because she's under arrest, Valentine nearly shouted. *And she's the Kestrel, a notorious operative I've been tracking for weeks.* Not that Rawley, or anyone beyond Lisbeth, would know that. He was likely sent here by Ashvale to keep an eye on his sister, without having any clue of her secret, illicit identity.

Valentine stared at the gathered men. "Did anyone leave the ship last night?"

"The footbridge was up, Your Grace," one of the men said. "Captain's orders. No one but workers checking on the boiler can leave. The checks were completed and we were due to leave port this morning."

"I need every room on this ship searched," he commanded.

"Your Grace!" the captain spluttered, but Valentine's glare shushed him.

"I am the highest-ranking peer on this ship, and a lady is missing. If you don't intend to have her disappearance on your conscience, you will do as I say. Every nook and cranny must be searched. Get your men on it, now."

"Yes, Your Grace."

Rawley cleared his throat. "Where do you want me?"

"Was her maid with you?" Valentine asked. "The small blond-haired chit. I did not see her in the room this morning. You two are courting, are you not?"

"Cora wasn't with me as her mistress was ill." He frowned. "You don't think…"

Valentine searched his face for signs of deceit, but the man's dark eyes were heavy with worry. "I wouldn't put anything past Lady Bronwyn. If I had to guess, I would say the maid went with her. They had to have had help. There's no way they could have vanished on their own."

But even as he said the words, Valentine knew that Bronwyn was more than capable of being resourceful. For all his protestations to the contrary, she was a spy. A smart, practical, devious spy. Any of the sailors onboard could have deployed the footbridge and let her off the ship with enough coin or a piece of jewelry. She wasn't poor, and he hadn't thought to confiscate her possessions. Finding who had helped her would be like locating a needle in a haystack. *Impossible.* He ground his jaw and cursed under his breath.

He'd underestimated her…again.

"You go back to London with the ship," he said eventually. "I'll stay in Brest, see what I can find out. She couldn't have gotten far. Someone had to have seen her leaving the docks."

Rawley frowned. "Two heads will make quicker work together."

"He should go with you," Lisbeth said with a nod. "I can stay with the ship."

Valentine wanted to object, but it made sense for him to have help. A part of him wanted to be alone so when he did eventually get his hands on his little fugitive, he could punish her in private for daring to run from him. But two people meant more avenues could be covered. Brest wasn't a huge city but it was a port, and there were other ships. She could have gone on to England on another vessel, or even gone toward to Paris. The train station had been recently built, the leg between Guingamp and Brest finished in the last year.

"Very well," he said. He didn't want to lose any more time. The longer they waited, the less chance he had of catching up or finding her, wherever she'd vanished. It would take at least a good few hours for the ship to be thoroughly searched, but he knew that Lisbeth would have it in hand. This was her operation, after all. "If you find anything, send a cable when you dock in England. I'll do the same."

She tugged on his sleeve, her voice going low. "Val, don't do anything rash."

"What do you mean?"

"Your feelings are tangled up in this woman," she said. He opened his mouth to deny it, but the hard look on her face stopped him. "If I were in her shoes, I would have left, too. It's not personal, but you need to exercise wisdom when you do find her. There are too many open-ended questions. I've thought about it more, and we need her help."

"Do you know who she is," he whispered furiously. "Or have you bloody forgotten?"

"An operative who has foiled nefarious plots against our leaders."

He scowled. "And stolen confidential documents."

"You don't know that," she returned. "They could have been given to her by someone in the Home Office, and that person could be working for the queen herself. You of all people understand how it works—we don't always know who is part of the network at any given time. We need more information to be sure before we expose her to the wolves."

His mouth pulled tight, but she had a point. "Fine. I won't throw her to the ground and restrain her in my handcuffs the minute I find her." Valentine felt the flush flood his cheekbones as his helpful brain supplied a very lewd image to accompany his words.

The small laugh at his expense and the knowing look in Lisbeth's eyes made him blink. "Well, I'll never advise you not to do that in the right circumstance, Your Grace. A little consensual bed sport between friends can be quite diverting."

He ignored that, along with the visions supplied by his vexing imagination. His ears burned at the provocative idea of using the cuffs in a more carnal way. He wondered whether Bronwyn would consent to such a thing and then cursed himself in the same breath. This wasn't the time to be daydreaming!

Valentine shook his head. "Where would you go?" he asked his former partner, who was still watching him with a too-intense expression as if trying to confirm that he could be trusted to do right thing. He *would*! Maybe. Women's intuition was a valuable thing and he respected Lisbeth's opinion. Perhaps she could shed some light on a dismal situation. "If you were her?"

Lisbeth's grin widened. "You mean if I were an intrepid, daring, clever international agent who had thwarted my pursuers by feigning illness and pretending to be asleep in bed by means of a very devious trick, all the while planning my escape off a passenger liner in the middle of the evening when my enemies were distracted?"

"Yes." His humor soured further. "Thank you for the succinct summary."

She lifted her brows. "Of course, I have an idea of where."

"Are you going to make me beg, Lisbeth?"

She laughed and cocked her head. "Do allow me my fun, Val. It's rather entertaining watching a jejune chit wind her frustratingly wily webs around you. If I didn't know you better, I'd say deep down, you were pretending to hate it. Secretly, you admire that she outmaneuvered you, the spymaster prince himself."

His jaw ached from grinding his teeth. "I do not."

She let out a scoffing noise. "Answer me this. Tell me you haven't felt more alive in the past weeks than you have in a long time?"

Valentine had, but that was no one's business but his. He didn't admire the girl; he wanted to lock her in a room and throw away the key. Preferably with him in there.

With a pair of handcuffs.

Growling at his own absurdity, he pinched the bridge of his nose and banished his salacious and categorically unwelcome fantasies. "If you're not going to be helpful, I am leaving."

"Don't be cross, Val," she said, laughing at him and tugging on his arm. "If I were her, I'd go to Paris."

He frowned. "Not board a packet to England?"

Lisbeth shook her head. "My guess is that she would anticipate that you'd expect her to do that. Run back to her brother or whoever her contact is. But you asked me what a woman might do, and it's what I would do. My money is on the City of Light."

Fifteen

THERE WAS SOMETHING ABOUT PARIS THAT FIRED UP the senses. Perhaps it was the way the French lived, or the feeling of flamboyance and élan in the air. It didn't feel as stoic or as measured as England. The French did everything with such flair. Even this ball that her aunt Esther had insisted she attend so she could show off her beautiful, accomplished niece.

As expected, the Comtesse de Valois had welcomed her with open and very enthusiastic arms when she and Cora had shown up on her doorstep.

"You're just in time! My spring ball is this week. You'll be its star!"

The last thing Bronwyn wanted to do was attend a ball or be its crowning jewel, but she'd come to her aunt's against Rawley's instructions and the whole entire point of being in plain sight was not to blend and to be seen as Lady Bronwyn Chase enjoying the season. She didn't plan to stay long in Paris. Just long enough for Rawley to catch up with them as he'd intended and for her presence to be noted by enough people in case he did not. If the Duke of Thornbury did follow on her heels, he would be hard pressed to accuse her of anything in front of the entire French aristocracy.

She hoped.

As such, her take-no-prisoners aunt had commissioned the most sought-after modiste in Paris to fit Bronwyn in a dress in the two short days since she'd arrived, and here she was. Dressed in the most sumptuous confection of a gown she'd ever beheld and being paraded and courted and charmed by everyone with a title, and even a few without, at her aunt's very well-attended party.

"This is my dear friend, the Marquis de Tremblay," her aunt Esther was saying. "He's quite a lovely gentleman when he's not flirting with anything in skirt." She frowned. "Or trousers. Or any clothing, actually."

Bronwyn bit back her horrified giggle. Her aunt was the opposite of her dour sister, Bronwyn's mother, in every way. It was a wonder the two had shared the same womb.

"I do not flirt unless it is invited," the marquis said in charmingly accented English.

Bronwyn's eyes lifted to meet the smiling face of a very handsome man she was certain she might have met before, but all the faces were beginning to merge. Goodness, did her aunt intend to introduce her to all of Paris in one evening? Perhaps she and the Marchioness of Borne weren't so different if she also secretly intended to marry her off at the best opportunity that presented itself.

"Lovely to meet you, Monsieur," Bronwyn replied in fluent French.

His eyes brightened with delight. "Your accent is perfection, my lady."

"Thank you," she replied.

"Will you dance the next set?" he asked.

"I would love to." At least it would get her away from more unwelcome introductions. Aunt Esther seemed ready to embark with a new group of eligible gentlemen she'd summoned. Bronwyn was never going to remember all those names! She supposed her aunt meant well, intending for her to have fun, unlike Bronwyn's mother, whose marital leanings hinged on the match that would serve *her* best.

But Bronwyn wasn't interested in any gentlemen, save for the one she emphatically could not have.

A hard face with amber eyes and sculpted lips filled her vision, and she blinked, feeling a wash of gooseflesh rise on her arms.

He wants you in jail, you nitwit. That's why you ran.

Monsieur de Tremblay offered her his arm with a bow. She and the handsome marquis—though in truth his attractive looks did nothing for her beyond superficial appreciation—strolled to the ballroom floor, where the orchestra was in the midst of the opening chords. Bronwyn gritted her teeth, her feet slowing. The waltz was not her favorite. Too many gentlemen in England saw it as an opportunity to get handsy. Would it be the same in France?

"Do not be nervous," the marquis told her. "I am an excellent dancer."

The flirtatious glint in his eye told Bronwyn everything she needed to know. The hand on her waist would slip down to the curve at the top of her buttocks; he might hold her closer than was appropriate and then brush himself indecently against her at every turn. Cringing, she braced for the inevitable, and then the hairs on her nape rose for no reason at all.

"I believe this dance is mine," a deep voice said over her shoulder, making every nerve in her body come startlingly, shockingly alive.

He was here.

Bronwyn suppressed the shiver winding up her spine. Of course he was here. Deep down, she'd known the duke would come. That he would find her. A hunter like him would never abandon his prey, not when it had so tauntingly escaped his clutches under his very nose.

Bronwyn's mouth dried as she turned, her blue eyes meeting burning gold. It had only been a handful of days since she'd seen him last, and yet she drank him in as though it'd been years. Square jaw, tightened lips, tousled tawny hair tumbling over his collar, and dressed to kill in raven-black superfine. Likely dressed to kill *her*. A hysterical giggle climbed into her throat, the urge to flee making her legs tremble beneath her skirts. At least that was what she thought it was. A desire to run, *not* to tumble headfirst into his arms.

"Your Grace," she said in a delighted voice that hid her fraying composure. "What a surprise."

"I beg your pardon, sir," Tremblay said, a scowl darkening his pretty face. "I am dancing with the lady."

"This dance is spoken for, I'm afraid," Thornbury said without taking his eyes from hers. The possession in them spoke volumes, and she felt the sensitive bundle of nerves at the top of her thighs pulse wickedly in response. "Lady Bronwyn, looks like I've found you just in time to claim what's mine."

Dear God, how could a man's voice wreak such havoc? He meant the dance, of course, acting as though he'd written his name in the space next to it on her dance card. Every word of that last sentence bled with a sultry possessiveness that made her blood heat to sinful levels. She wanted to scream, *Yes, you found me, now take me*. Wanton fool that she was. Bronwyn lifted her chin, resentment at her own weakness for him filling her.

The blatantly ignored marquis glared and spluttered his outrage when Thornbury bowed and lifted a brow in expectation. The music was starting and the other couples were already in position. Heavens, the arrogance of him.

"I'm sorry, Your Grace," she said firmly to the duke. "I've promised this dance to Monsieur de Tremblay. You'll simply have to find me later." She would take a handsy marquis over a man whom her body recognized as its erotic downfall. A waltz would be utterly detrimental.

Those eyes of his glowered…promising *something*. "As you say, my lady. Don't worry, I am not going anywhere."

She couldn't help it; she shivered. The corner of his lip kicked the tiniest bit and she jutted her jaw with a dismissive sniff. As she and the marquis took their positions, she could feel Thornbury's stare on her though she could not see him. She wasn't surprised that he had come. Her intention hadn't been to hide, after all, but still the visceral reality of him had rattled her to her core. Her very warm, very needy core that was begging to be ruined.

Oh, enough!

"Who was that?" the curious marquis asked when they glided into the first turn. "I am not acquainted with him."

Bronwyn looked up to see a pair of sharp green eyes on her. "No one of import. A gentleman from England who fancies himself a suitor, I suppose. He followed me here, hoping to declare his intentions."

The marquis's brows rose. "And you do not welcome those intentions?"

"Why would you say that?"

A grin displayed two dimples on either side of his cheeks. "I am French. I recognize desire when I see it, mademoiselle. It does not only go one way, *non*? He wants you. You want him. But he also frightens you, which was why you did not dance with him."

"You are very perceptive, Monsieur de Tremblay," she murmured. "Though 'frighten' isn't the right word. He is…intimidating."

Fingers flexed at her waist, but not enough to cause alarm, and to her surprise, they did not wander. "I could make you forget him, if you like."

For a heartbeat, Bronwyn wondered whether the touch of a man could erase the one who had imprinted on her soul, but everything in her recoiled at the thought. She exhaled. With time, the attraction would lessen. It had to. Then if a man like Tremblay made her such an offer, she would not be so repelled.

She smiled coquettishly, knowing Thornbury was watching, wherever he was. "What makes you think I cannot forget him myself?"

Delight danced in that green stare. "That's a rather intriguing stance. Tell me more."

"A woman doesn't need a man. They are simply implements to be used when the opportunity presents itself. Most women are capable of rescuing themselves, given the chance."

The marquis laughed, low and deep, a sound that had attention flocking to them, including her aunt's. Bronwyn thought she heard a low growl somewhere in the vicinity of her left shoulder. "I think I might have misjudged you, Lady Bronwyn."

"Let me guess. You thought me demure and proper, the perfect English rose."

"Quite so," he said with a snort. "Though I do know your aunt quite well, so I should have guessed her niece would be as extraordinary."

"How *do* you know my aunt?" she asked, curious.

He waggled his eyebrows suggestively, and Bronwyn nearly stumbled over her own feet. *No*, he could not mean what she thought he meant. But when he grinned and winked at her, she could help a horrified bark of laughter. The marquis was half her aunt's age! Then again, who was *she* to judge? She'd been taken up against a tree and then again in a ship's aft hold by a powerful lover.

"I have a proposal for you," the marquis said, dipping

his mouth close to her ear. "Shall we fan the proverbial fires a bit?"

"What do you mean?"

But instead of replying, the marquis gave a wicked laugh, held her hand tight, and pulled her out the nearest balcony door onto the terrace.

Well, *shit*.

Valentine watched her like the hawk he was. Watched her in that maddening silver gown that left one creamy shoulder bare and clung to every luscious feminine curve. Watched her dance and flirt with that smarmy worm of a Frenchman whose hands were all over her. Heard her simper and laugh. Not the fake laughter she'd given the dandies aboard the *Valor*. No, it was the one he relished, those deep, throaty, decadent sounds that made his skin tighten with lust.

He hadn't known what to expect when he'd come to Paris, whether she would even be here. Part of him had thought she would have found some nook on the ship until they got to England. It was what he would have done in her shoes. Half hoping that Lisbeth was wrong, he'd quickly learned that Lady Bronwyn coincidentally had a very real aunt in Paris, the sister to the Marchioness of Borne, unlike the fabricated one in Philadelphia.

His eyes darted to the woman in question. Unlike her fastidious and unlikable sister, Comtesse Esther de Valois, an enormously wealthy widow, was the undisputed queen of the ball, surrounded by gentlemen and ladies of all ages.

Perhaps that was where Bronwyn had inherited that easy, irritating charm.

Even now, she had that sly marquis curled around her fingers.

Displeasure was quick to follow.

He glanced back to the ballroom floor and froze. Where the hell were they? His eyes combed the dancers, some leaving and others being replaced by new ones as the waltz ended. Perhaps she'd gone to the refreshments room. He quickly made his way over there, perusing the guests near the tables, but the gleam of silver skirts did not catch his eye.

Where could she have gone? The retiring room? His gaze focused on the women crowding that area. She could be inside, meaning to thwart him yet again. Annoyance pulsed through him. She wasn't getting away so easily this time.

But before he could march off in that direction, he was blocked by a very ample figure with blue eyes so familiar that he nearly staggered when they speared him in place. He almost thought it was the Marchioness of Borne, though her face wasn't quite as pinched or looking as if she were perpetually ingesting a lemon. He hadn't realized they were twins.

The resemblance was extraordinary, both to the marchioness as well as her niece, but the Comtesse de Valois had laugh lines around her eyes and bracketing her lips while her sister did not. Bronwyn had inherited the same eyes, stubborn chin, and pale coloring, though she had her late father's brow and cheekbones.

"Who are you?" she demanded.

He bowed. "The Duke of Thornbury, at your service, Madame la Comtesse."

A sniff left her red lips as she regarded him from head to toe in frank perusal. "I do not recall sending you an invitation, Thornbury."

"I am a guest of Lady Bronwyn."

Instead of softening, those cornflower-blue eyes hardened. "My niece whom you've been staring at like a dog waiting at the scullery stairs for scraps?"

God but she was direct. Bronwyn got that from her, too. His brain whirled with an acceptable story that would appease the shrewd old woman who he sensed wouldn't let him off the hook that easily. "Not scraps, Madame. I intend to offer for her."

The lie rolled so easily off his tongue, it could be truth for how natural it felt. Ashvale would refuse his offer, but she wouldn't know that.

To his surprise, the comtesse cackled. "Along with half of the gents in this room by the end of the evening."

"I am aware," he said.

"Walk with me," she said, as she extended an arm that he had to take to avoid causing offense to the lady in her own home.

While his skin needled and burned to find Bronwyn, he might need to be in the Comtesse de Valois's good graces, if he could not get his target alone. She was clever, he'd give her that. Out of respect for his friendship to the Duke of Ashvale, he'd never cause a scene in public. Now that he knew where Bronwyn was, it was simply a matter of getting her alone in his custody and taking her back to England.

They strolled around the ballroom, and irritation streaked through his veins when after nearly a full promenade around the perimeter, the lady did not speak. Valentine cleared his throat, but that did not make one whit of difference. Bronwyn's aunt remained utterly oblivious. He was just about to make up some excuse when she came to an abrupt stop. "Were you not married?"

He blinked. "Yes, but no longer. Parliament granted a divorce."

"Why?"

Valentine debated not answering, but then went with the truth. "The lady wanted other things and our paths diverged. It was amicable."

Bright blue eyes glittered at him, a cunning intelligence shining in their depths, and Valentine had the feeling that she knew more than she was letting on. Then again, maybe he was just on edge and wanted to know where the hell his little bird had gone. And what she was *doing* and with *whom*. Heat crawled through his veins and he resisted the urge to tug at his collar.

"And now you've set your sights on my niece."

"Yes," he said.

She gave a sniff. "I suppose my sister will find you acceptable, considering you're a duke since your uncle died." A grin graced her lips. "I'm sorry for your loss. Bucky and I were friends, you know. Good friends. In my youth, I had hoped he would approach my father before Monsieur de Valois did, but no, it was not meant to be. I was rather saddened to hear of his death."

Valentine's eyes widened. The thought of his old, sedate Uncle Bucky—the previous Duke of Thornbury— with this spitfire of a woman nearly made him chuckle. "He lived out his last years in peace and quiet, doing what he loved. He enjoyed fishing on his country seat in the Highlands, mostly."

The Comtesse de Valois wrinkled her nose. "He spoke of his castle and his loch with such fondness. I always told myself I would visit him there." She waved an arm. "Then again, I could not see myself leaving all this."

Following her movement, Valentine shifted, eyes perusing the crowd again, always on the hunt for that flash of silver. Had enough time passed for him to take his leave? He still couldn't see any sign of Bronwyn, and the dancing had started up again. A quadrille this time with every color in the rainbow *except* silver.

"Have you seen your niece?" he asked.

Her head cocked to the side as she tapped her lips with her fan. "Oh yes, but not for some time. Monsieur de Tremblay, that naughty opportunist, escorted her out on the terrace after the waltz for some air, or whatever it is these young devils do to court a lady." She patted his arm, even as an unholy force nearly drove his body to the doors in question, and laughed at him. "Best not wait too long,

Your Grace, or your prize will be snatched out from under you by a much wilier competitor."

Frowning, he opened his mouth and shut it. Blast it, she'd distracted him on purpose, hadn't she? Had Bronwyn said something to her aunt? Confided that she was running from a feared pursuer? Or was the Comtesse de Valois simply making mischief because she was bored and peeved that he'd come to her ball without an invitation?

"Excuse me, please," he bit out.

Fisting his hands, he marched through the throng, nearly pushing people over in his haste. Cool air filled his lungs, but brought no reprieve as there was no sign of them on the terrace either!

And then he saw her.

Sitting on one of the marble benches with Lord Tremblay, much too close for comfort. Another young lady sat on her left, which gave him the barest modicum of relief, although not enough to deflate the instant surge of possessiveness. A pair of crystal-sharp eyes lifted to meet his as if she'd sensed his presence.

"Your Grace, is something amiss?" her soft voice called out, tinged with amusement. "You look rather tense. Surely you're not still vexed about the mix-up with Monsieur de Tremblay. There'll be other waltzes this evening."

Tremblay—that lily-pated maggot—leaned in to whisper something in her ear that made her blush and smile, and then lifted her knuckles to his lips for a leisurely kiss. Valentine's spine locked, a growl catching in his throat.

With a sweet grin to the marquis, Bronwyn rose and

strolled over to him where he leaned against the stone balustrade leading down into the gardens. Her familiar perfume wafted upward as she stopped within arm's reach and peered up at him, blue eyes gleaming silver with reflected moonlight. "What's the matter, Your Grace?"

"You ran," he demanded in a low voice. "Why?"

"You would have done the same." That jewel-bright stare dropped to the gardens. "We both know what you think of me and what you intended. I will go back to London on my terms."

"I can arrest you right now."

She had the audacity to laugh. "Restrain me and put me in handcuffs? In front of all these good people? You and I both know that you respect my brother too much for that. No, Your Grace. You can hover as much as you like, but if you think you will catch me unaware and alone, then think again."

Deuce it, he wanted to devour the bravado from her lips. Ferry her down into the shadows of the garden and repeat their encounter in the woods until the only sounds coming from her mouth were whimpers and moans for more.

"And what if you're in danger?"

That bare shoulder lifted, drawing his eyes to the tantalizing slope of creamy skin as she scoffed. "You can't have it both ways, Your Grace. Either I'm a terrible danger to all and sundry, and must be taken into custody, or I'm a damsel in need of your strength and manly protection."

Valentine stared at her, so close and yet infinitely beyond his reach at the moment for precisely the reason she'd stated. Arresting her in public would cause no end of scandal. For the moment, his hands were tied. "You can't hide forever, my lady Kestrel. At the end of all of this, you will be in handcuffs, I promise you."

Husky laughter that shot straight to his groin drifted from her as she returned to her friends. "So you say, Your Grace, so you say."

Sixteen

THE DRATTED MAN WAS *EVERYWHERE*.

And Bronwyn meant every single place she went in Paris, she was acutely aware of his presence, as if he were waiting for her to slip up so he could arrest her like a thief in the night. Of course, she could be imagining things, but Thornbury wasn't a man who would leave anything to chance. Which was why Bronwyn was never alone. Poor Monsieur de Tremblay was becoming a crutch as her preferred escort, but the friendly marquis didn't seem to mind the designation.

"I shall have to be extra careful," he'd told her once during an afternoon stroll through the Tuileries. "Or I will lose this rather dissolute heart to you."

Bronwyn had patted his arm. "One cannot fall in love in less than a week, Monsieur le Marquis."

"I assure you, *I* can," he'd replied with a feigned swoon. "You should marry me and put me out of my misery."

The question, jokingly plied as it had been, had jarred her. Why shouldn't she marry someone like the marquis? He was diverting and charming, quite intelligent when he chose to be, and underneath the layers of fashionable dandy, he hid quite a sensitive soul.

Because he's in love with someone else.

Because he's not a sultry-as-sin duke who wants to put you in restraints...as you desperately want him to.

Her knees had gone weak, causing her to stumble.

"Ah," Tremblay had said, watching her like a hawk. "You're waiting for a certain English peer to make his move, is that it? *Mon Dieu*, but that man is a bastion of ice. Your dour duke wouldn't know passion if it hit him with the stick lodged up his arse."

Bronwyn had giggled and then blushed, the reply on the tip of her tongue that beneath his impassive exterior, the frosty duke ran unspeakably hot. His passion would put this Frenchman to shame in a heartbeat. "No, it's not what you think." She had blushed, irritated that she was so transparent when it came to the vexing man. "It's not like that."

"You don't want him?" Tremblay had asked.

Now, that had been a loaded question in itself. Did Bronwyn want him? Yes, it was indecent how much she craved him at any given hour of the day or night. At night, in dreams, her body was his in every carnal way. But beyond her very visceral fantasies, Thornbury was a hardened ex-spy whose progressive views about women would never extend to her, by virtue of who she was. A peer who would never allow her to be who she needed to be.

Not a duke's daughter.

Not a duke's sister.

But a woman operating under her own willpower and her own governance. A kestrel—a bird of prey—was meant to fly, and Thornbury wanted to clip its wings and put it in a cage. Bronwyn wasn't stupid. She'd always known that her identity as the Kestrel could not exist forever, but she wanted to end it as she'd begun…on her own terms.

What if she truly was in danger as Thornbury claimed?

The memory of those men chasing her through Philadelphia made her grow cold, but she was over three thousand miles away now. That threat was now behind her, and until she heard back from Wentworth, she had to stay one step ahead of the duke.

She had sent a carefully worded message to Wentworth via her old friend Sesily in London, letting her know that she had completed the mission and was staying with her aunt in Paris. The message was scrambled and could only be decoded with a special cipher. Bronwyn hadn't dared to expand on the fact that her identity had been compromised by the infamous team from the Home Office, but she hoped that Sesily would reply soon.

In the meantime, she was taking Paris by storm, thanks to Aunt Esther. Her whereabouts might have already gotten back to her mother, whose loathing for her irreverent twin sister wasn't a secret. In fact, it might be just her luck that the Marchioness of Borne would show up in Paris to drag her back to London before Bronwyn ruined herself.

Little did her mama know that that ship had already sailed…

Speaking of the coldhearted ruiner, where was he? The duke had to be here somewhere. Bronwyn couldn't step outside without sensing him on her heels. She peered over her shoulder as she and Aunt Esther walked past the fancy department store, Les Grands Magasins du Louvre, on the Place du Palais-Royal.

These well-lit, spacious *grands magasins* were an immense draw. The shop windows were beautiful with fabrics, novelties, and fashion, and Bronwyn had welcomed the chance to explore and get away for a bit. Thank goodness Aunt Esther wasn't averse to some shopping, as was evidenced by the footmen trailing behind them carrying hatboxes and piles of wrapped parcels. Even Cora had her hands full, though she too was gazing rapt at the lovely displays.

The maid had heard from Rawley, who had sent a messenger to say that he was in Paris. He hadn't been pleased at Bronwyn's blatant disregard of his orders, especially when he'd arrived at the secure residence to find them missing. Bronwyn was certain that he, too, had to be somewhere about, along with Lord Happy Handcuffs himself. Cheeks heating, she snorted at the irreverent nickname.

"Good heavens, I'm quite famished," Aunt Esther announced.

Bronwyn was as well, her stomach giving a little gurgle in agreement, but before she could nod that she was ready to head back to the residence or perhaps visit the nearby tea room, her aunt gave a gleeful little squeal and disappeared into a shop with yet another display of feathered hats. Bronwyn bit back a giggle. Aunt Esther simply could not help herself. Enjoying the warmth of the weather, Bronwyn stayed where she was, in close view of the waiting footmen and the carriage that followed.

She glanced at the closest bay window with its brightly colored cupola. Silk scarves hung down from a line in a jewel-toned waterfall with hues from emerald greens to crystal blue to violet and crimson. The display itself was eye-catchingly stylish and elegant.

"That color is the exact shade of your eyes," a low voice said. "Like the bluest, hottest part of a flame."

Her entire body came alive. Bronwyn stifled the instant shiver as that rich baritone coasted over her like a physical touch.

"Your Grace, I was wondering when you would appear like the scourge you are."

"Scourge?" he said with a low chuckle, and her stupid core fluttered. "You wound me."

She sighed. "If only you took that message to heart."

The heat of him was tangible, pushing into her, warming her skin with fiery need.

"Don't you have anything better to do than follow me around? Surely the feared and respected Duke of Thornbury has more important matters to attend to."

"Alas, I cannot take the chance that you will hop on an omnibus and sneak away as you did off the *Valor*."

She glanced up at the horse-drawn wagons with seats painted orange, yellow, and brown that ferried people to different parts of the city. The liveried driver and conductor were very efficient. A ticket only cost thirty centimes, and the omnibus was indeed an easy form of public transport within Paris, if one did not have one's own coach.

Bronwyn wouldn't admit that it had crossed her mind. It always paid to be informed about exit strategies in a foreign city. She wasn't above crowding in with other passengers if she had to, but if push came to shove, she would hire a fiacre, which was more expensive at two francs but private. She kept her thoughts to herself, however.

"I'm with my aunt, Your Grace. I'm not sneaking off anywhere."

"Where's Monsieur de Tremblay?" he asked with a sidelong glance at her. "I'm surprised not to see that self-involved fop glued to your side. It's obvious what he wants."

"I've told you that jealousy is not a good look on you, Your Grace," she said and then frowned. "Why do you even care what the gentleman wants with me? I do not care what you do with your time and whom you spend it with. We're both free to do as we like. Neither of us has any claim on the other."

Except the rather obvious one that made her body so stupidly, acutely aware of him. It obviously hadn't gotten the message that the duke was off-limits because her nipples were beaded in her bodice, her throat was inexplicably dry, and her lower half felt as though it was immersed in deliciously warm bathwater. It was a wonder she could string any words together that weren't *I'm yours forever, sir*.

The duke's mouth went flat. "By all accounts, the marquis is a rogue who can barely keep his trousers fastened from bed to bed."

Bronwyn laughed. He wasn't wrong about that. Tremblay was an unapologetic libertine. "He very well might be, but his company pleases me and that's all that matters. Why don't you scamper along and find someone to entertain you as well?"

He was deeply annoyed, as evidenced by the muscle only she could seem to get to beat in that stubble-covered cheek. It never seemed to appear for anyone else. Scrutinizing it, she blinked. Normally he was clean-shaven, but she quite liked this scruffy, unkempt side of him as well. Looking like a racy pirate only increased his allure.

How would that stubble feel on her skin? Over her cheeks? Between the much softer skin of her thighs? Suddenly burning hot, she shifted to put some space between them.

"Lady Bronwyn, you are—"

But whatever the duke was about to say was cut short by a boom and the smashing of panes in the bay window near her head where she'd been standing a second before. She barely had time to let out a yelp as a huge body barreled hers out of the way and shielded her from the shattered glass that crunched beneath his booted feet. He dragged them into a side alley, keeping her wildly trembling form behind him. People were screaming and running in every direction. Had that been a gunshot? Where was Aunt Esther? Cora? Panic flew through her.

"Your Grace." She attempted to push past him, but one immovable arm kept her in place. "My aunt. Valentine, I must see if she's well. And Cora!"

"They're safe. Rawley has them," he said. "You, however, are not, so stop fighting me. I'm not letting you out there, not until I know you're not in danger."

She stopped grappling. "What do you mean?"

"That bullet was meant for you, Bronwyn."

━━━━━━━━━

Every inch of him felt numb. *Hell,* she'd almost gotten shot right in front of him.

Thanks to Lisbeth, a team of operatives working with the French government and the national police forces had been following up on his hunch that someone had been on their tail since their journey back from Philadelphia. And the attempt on her life had just proven it. Either some kind of bounty had been placed on Bronwyn's back or someone had a personal vendetta. It didn't matter that she was a highborn lady or the sister of a duke, someone wanted her dead and had come all this way to finish the job.

And they'd very nearly succeeded. If she hadn't moved a fraction away from him, there would be a sea of red mixed in with that shattered glass littering the white-washed cobblestones. His chest squeezed at that terrifying image. Valentine didn't want to begin to dissect what that meant. Of course he cared what happened to her— she was his best mate's sister.

She's more than that.

Scowling, he shrugged off that voice, peeking around

the corner to see if the French police had arrived or if the assailant would show his face and make another attempt. Not wanting to take any chances, he drew his pistol from the holster beneath his coat and cocked it. He reached down for the second smaller gun tucked into his boot and handed it to her. "Take this, just in case."

She stared at it. "I'm not familiar with that kind of gun, only Ravenna's."

He narrowed his gaze. "You shot that man in Philadelphia. A brilliant shot."

"I was trying to save your life, and I was familiar with that weapon."

"I'm very grateful for it. This is a bigger gun so the recoil will be harder. Hold with both hands and brace. Finger over the trigger when you're ready to use it. If anyone you don't recognize comes at you, fire first and ask questions later."

"Where are you going?" she asked.

"To find your shooter."

He hated to leave her, but she would be hidden enough in the alleyway. Valentine had to make sure she'd be in no more danger. He eased from their cramped hiding spot, peeking past the wall to see that the streets were clear, though people were crouched behind walls and stalled omnibuses. When Valentine caught Rawley's eye from where he stood on the other side of the storefront, the large man pointed to his eyes and then to a building a few yards down the boulevard.

It wasn't coincidence that Rawley was there. He

had been scouting ahead when the shot had been fired. Though his vigilance hadn't stopped some cleverly hidden renegade from planning an attack. With some relief, Valentine noticed that both the Comtesse de Valois and the maid were safe. There had only been the one shot, but that didn't meant the shooter wasn't armed with more guns or didn't have accomplices.

Pistol in hand, Valentine eased from his position and rose gingerly. The cream-colored limestone exploded to the right of his head when another shot ricocheted as he ducked for cover, body sprawling flat on the sharp rocks. The answering roar of Rawley's gun discharged from across the boulevard, and then Valentine was on his feet and running toward where Rawley had indicated. On the roofline of the newly built apartments, five stories up, movement caught his eye, reflecting from a pane of glass that had been smashed on the steeply angled mansard roofline, presumably where the person had been firing from.

Valentine took off in pursuit, running along the front of the building and knowing the man might still be inside. He would try to escape from the back. Older Paris was a warren of side streets, but Valentine was not as familiar with these new arrondissements that had been annexed a handful of years earlier. Once the man was out, however, he could vanish quite easily. The rapid sounds of snapping shoes on cobblestones behind him made him slow and look over his shoulder. He expected to see Rawley, whom he could direct to cut the man off, and frowned when striped skirts filled his vision.

"What are you doing?" he demanded, panting and slowing. "Go back!"

"No." Bronwyn's eyes shone with fury as she kept up with him. "I'm not very well going to cower in a corner while you chase a man who was shooting at me!"

"You daft girl, it's you he wants."

"Good, then let's catch him before he does it again."

Torn between hauling her back to Rawley and getting eyes on the criminal, Valentine gritted his teeth and growled his anger. She was going to get herself killed! Or shoot him in the back by accident. Squashing down his protective instincts, he nodded and lengthened his pace. If it had been Lisbeth, he would have been grateful for the help.

Think of her as another operative.

Every nerve in him bristled at that, but he couldn't afford to call her the Kestrel only when he wanted her to be guilty. Reputations weren't built on sand. The Home Office had been tracking her for months with nothing to show for it. That had to be based on some experience.

"Fine," he gritted out. "Stay close and keep your eyes open. Shout if you see anything."

"Is he still inside?"

Valentine nodded. "Yes."

In any other situation, he would direct her to go around the other side of the building so they could cut the man off, but he was hindered by his own panic where she was concerned. He turned to tell her to stay put—extra eyes were always good—but the minx wasn't there. All he saw were striped skirts disappearing through the front entrance.

Bloody hell, she was stubborn at the worst times! Dread pulsing through his veins, he raced down the side street to cut around to the back. There were people here, but not like those on the wide boulevard. A wide-eyed groom stood near a carriage.

"Anyone come out from here in the last five minutes?" the duke demanded.

"*Non, monsieur*," the boy replied. "I heard two shots."

Valentine nodded. "Yes, go hide somewhere safe."

Inside the grand foyer with its enormous ceilings and thick walls for the business, people were murmuring, but smart enough to stay hidden from view. Valentine caught sight of Bronwyn heading up the staircase to the mezzanine above, which was mostly storage for the shop owners.

"Out of the bloody way!" A high-pitched male voice let out a stream of violent clipped English from somewhere overhead, and then came the sound of boxes toppling over and a crashing noise. That had to be him.

"Stop this instant, or I will shoot you!" Bronwyn's clear voice called out, though she sounded uncertain. Nervous.

Valentine didn't think. He leaped over the first few steps and sped upstairs, his legs burning from the effort and his heartbeat making an ungodly racket in his ears. Bronwyn stood at the top of the stairs to the second floor, her gun pointing at a clean-faced, smartly dressed young man of no more than seventeen or eighteen who stood near a window. He carried a rifle case, which made his innocent appearance all the more gut-wrenching. He'd shot at Bronwyn!

"Don't move," Valentine shouted. The boy's gaze darted to him and narrowed. In recognition? In surprise? It was definitely with something, though he'd never seen the young man in his life. "Who are you? Who sent you?"

The assailant's face went slack, right before he kicked open the large pair of ornate windows. "He's coming for her and there's nothing you can do to stop it."

And then he jumped.

Seventeen

"BRONWYN, LET THE DOCTOR LOOK AT YOU, FOR THE love of God," her aunt screeched. "You have blood on your dress."

"I'm fine, Aunt. It's a scratch."

A scratch from a window that had shattered from a bullet meant for her. In fact, she was lucky that she'd escaped with just the thin nick on the underside of her jaw. By all accounts, she should be dead, bleeding out on the boulevard. Instead she was at home, safe for the moment, and being bombarded by a doctor who wouldn't stop pestering her. She wanted to hear what the police were saying to the duke in the foyer.

From what she could overhear, the French Sûreté had confirmed that the shooter was unconscious and had been taken to the local hospital. Despite the fact that he'd tried to kill her, Bronwyn was glad the boy had survived the fall. He was so young. Less than a few years younger than her, true, but still. From the look of him, he wasn't poor, and his crisp English had carried a distinct upper-class accent. Was he gentry? The son of an English peer? Why would *he* shoot at her? Then again, indoctrination began at early ages…and she was the daughter of an English peer.

The tumble from three stories had not killed him, but

for the moment, he could not provide any answers as to who had employed him or why he was after her. And his last words before leaping had been ominous, suggesting that someone else would come. Bronwyn rubbed her arms and suppressed a shiver.

"See! You're catching a chill." Her aunt's voice had risen an entire octave. "It could be the fever setting in, you wretched child."

"I am fine, Aunt Esther, I promise you."

For now, the Duke of Thornbury had taken up uninvited residence at her aunt's domicile and seemed to think that he was in charge of everything, as indicated by his heavy frown in her direction as he strode toward the library. Bronwyn took a few hurried steps back as if that could prove she hadn't been shamelessly listening to every word.

"I heard shrieking. What is the problem?"

Bronwyn clenched her jaw at his tone. "This does not concern you, Your Grace."

"She refuses to be treated," Aunt Esther said with an enormous sniff. Bronwyn felt a stroke of guilt as she met her aunt's red-rimmed eyes. No doubt she'd been traumatized by the incident, and here Bronwyn was, more intent on eavesdropping than reassuring her aunt that all was well.

Thornbury closed the distance just as Bronwyn had resigned herself to the examination, his windblown hatless form making her breath hitch for an instant. "May I?" he inquired in a deep voice.

She blinked at him. "May you what?"

"Check your injury."

It was on the tip of her tongue to retort that he wasn't a physician, but the steely look in his eye stopped her short. Her tongue slipped out to wet her lips and she nodded, tilting her head to the side. "Very well, see for yourself."

Gentle fingers grazed her neck, pushing her hair out of the way, and she winced as the ends caught in some of the sticky, congealed blood. With a soft murmur, Thornbury blew on it, and she swore the entire area caught on fire. Bronwyn froze, her feet glued to the pile of the carpet as his fingers stroked the three-inch length of the laceration from her earlobe to her chin. She felt that touch in between her breasts and all the way down to her abdomen to her tightening core.

"It's not too deep," he said in a low rasp. "But we should clean it to prevent infection. Now we have matching scars."

Bronwyn was too busy keeping her body from combusting into a heap of ash at his feet to do anything but give a weak nod. She didn't miss the look her aunt sent her way either and focused on keeping herself together while the doctor exchanged places with the duke to dab the cut with a damp cloth and apply a thin salve. "Keep it clean," the grump of a doctor told her, likely because she'd quite rudely refused him earlier. "It will likely scar."

"Better than a bullet hole," she replied, and the man's eyes went wide.

Thornbury sent her a wry look as her aunt burst into tears. Bronwyn hurried over to her side and gathered her into her arms. She really had to watch her words. In a man's world, no one would ever worry about a scar or being shot at, and yet have it happen in a woman's world, and everyone went a bit mad. Her life was worth the same as the duke's. If that man had been a worse shot, Thornbury could have been a casualty as well. Amber eyes pierced hers from where he still stood, his face hard and unreadable. Bronwyn was sure he wanted to encase her in wool and ensure her safety at all costs.

"You c-could have been k-killed," her aunt blubbered.

"But I wasn't," Bronwyn said gently. "The police are saying it was an altercation gone askew. It was an accident. We're all safe."

Bronwyn didn't see any need to worry her aunt with the truth, considering her current state, and thank God Thornbury had agreed. Her aunt had been much too terrified to notice that both shots had been in their direction and didn't need confirmation that her niece had been the actual target. When the second shot had gone off, Aunt Esther had already been pulled to safety behind closed doors by Rawley.

After a while, Cora escorted her aunt upstairs for some rest, and Bronwyn poured herself a whisky from the nearby decanter and downed it, feeling the burn of the spirits tear a path to her stomach. She wasn't much of a drinker, beyond the occasional glass of champagne, but it helped to calm her nerves.

"We should marry."

The pronouncement echoed off the paneled bookcases of the library. Bronwyn set down her glass, resisting the immediate urge to tip back the whole bottle, and turned. Thornbury stood near the fireplace, watching her. Her gaze flicked to Rawley on the opposite side of the room. His face remained impassive, though he hadn't disagreed. "You have nothing to say about this?" she demanded.

"He's right," Rawley said. "As the Duchess of Thornbury, whoever is behind this might think twice about their actions, given who *he* is."

Bronwyn bit out a bitter laugh and ignored the small thrill that the title *Duchess of Thornbury* incited in the pit of her stomach. "Why is it that every Englishman feels that the power of his name will magically prevent all manner of terrible things from happening? I assure you, Your Grace, my enemies will still be there, even without binding myself to you in wedlock."

"With my name, you will be under my protection," he said.

Her brows rose. "Am I not under your protection now?"

"Bronwyn, don't be stubborn."

Laughter burst from her again. "You think I'm refusing your suit because I'm stubborn? Good Lord, Your Grace, you have a ridiculously high opinion of yourself."

Rawley let out a noise that sounded suspiciously like a snort and took that as his cue to leave. *Good.* Bronwyn didn't want to make a production of the matter. She walked toward Thornbury and stopped, not trusting herself to be too close. Heaven knew what happened anytime she ventured into that man's orbit.

"It is impractical, doesn't make any logical sense, and I do not wish to wed any man, not even for the sake of protection or convenience."

Those full lips pressed thin. "You're not merely a convenience, my lady."

"Oh, Your Grace, you *do* care," she said with a hand to her breast.

He strode toward her until they were nearly nose to nose. "This is not a joke, Bronwyn. That man was serious. Whatever you did in Philadelphia had repercussions." She did not utter a word when he marched to the door, closed it, and returned a moment later, though she braced at the rather serious expression on his face. "I received a cable from Lisbeth that a plot to abduct President Lincoln from Ford's Theatre in Washington nearly four weeks ago had been foiled. Coded messages urged him to be deliberately misleading about his movements, which might have saved his life."

Bronwyn blinked, relief rushing through her. She *hadn't* failed. At least that was good news. Wentworth would be pleased, if he ever got back to her. She frowned. Was that why these men were after her? They were angry and wanted someone to blame. She was as good a scapegoat as any, and that big brute from the tavern had seen her face. Men of his ilk took things personally, especially if they were bested by a woman. Political tensions and loyalties also turned the most rational of men into monsters.

Hell, she needed to get to Wentworth.

Or marry Thornbury.

Bronwyn swallowed. No, she couldn't. Marrying the duke—the leading man of every dream she'd ever had—would be too easy and would cost her her freedom. She could do this…survive off the merit of her own two feet, her wits, and a bucket of courage. Her spirit had never failed her before. She lifted her chin. "I don't know what that has to do with my current circumstance."

"The Union also sacked Richmond, and the Rebels surrendered on the ninth," Thornbury went on in a low voice, and she frowned. That was only four days ago, but she hadn't seen the latest newssheets in France, which no doubt might have covered the international news. "Those names you passed on from my report were shared with General Ulysses Grant. They're looking for the men. Surratt and Powell might be headed for Canada. They think Booth is in Boston, and they're still searching for the others."

Bronwyn shivered. Booth was the main perpetrator as far as she had discerned. She hoped they would all be caught. The end of the American Civil War was encouraging news as well. War took a toll that could never be forgotten. For now, she avoided Thornbury's astute glare. "I hope they catch them."

"You're still in danger, Bronwyn."

She sniffed. "Marrying you would not be a deterrent to any man with a vendetta. My answer is no, Your Grace, so unless you intend to compel me to the altar somehow, might I propose an alternate suggestion?"

"Which is?" he bit out with a scowl.

"Teach me your methods to defend myself."

The Bois de Boulogne was enormous. The park itself was several times larger than Hyde Park in London, and it used to be a royal hunting preserve, though much of the area had been neatly transformed into acres of walking paths and grassy areas for Parisians to enjoy when it had been acquired by the City of Paris nearly a decade and half ago. Other parts were still thickly wooded and less traveled. Which would suit Valentine's purposes.

"Where are we going?" Bronwyn asked as she cantered beside him.

He glanced at her. "You wanted to learn to defend yourself so here we are."

It chafed that she had disregarded his offer of marriage so cavalierly, though deep down, he had guessed that she would not accept, just for the sake of it. Taking a man's name for *protection* would be the last thing she'd do. Not her. Not the *Kestrel*. While he admired that rebellious streak of independence, he cursed it, too, because even retired, his former name of Waterstone was known across continents and could deter the most hardened of criminals. He'd always been a fair arbiter, but the rumors about him being ruthless weren't unfounded.

While she had admitted to nothing, he knew the foiled abduction in the United States was thanks to her. The only question was…who was she working for? It had to be someone at a high level, considering no one had openly sanctioned her role. Lisbeth had written that she was at a loss. The Kestrel was a ghost. So who had conscripted her?

The prime minister? Ashley? The queen herself?

Valentine didn't know when he'd stopped thinking of Bronwyn as a criminal. Or whether he ever had. Her identity as a disreputable spy had confounded him, but they had to be on the same side. Her moral compass seemed to be in excellent order…and she hadn't tried to stab him yet, though he was certain she wanted to. The funny thing was that he was not thinking of her as his enemy any more, considering what she'd accomplished, and he admired the fact that she hadn't given in to his pressure tactics. Not once.

She was right that she needed to know how to protect herself, however.

In a more secluded part of the woods, he dismounted and secured their horses, before emptying his saddlebags. He brought out a case that contained two pistols and gestured for her to come closer.

"This is a Colt Army revolver, a single-action sidearm, capable of firing six shots, mostly used during the civil war that just ended," he said, pointing to the first which he had given her on the Boulevard Haussmann. He pointed to the second. "That's a Whitney revolver. It's a solid frame with a similar percussion lock. For both, the hammer has to be cocked for each firing. But once each bullet and the paper cylinder with the black powder charge is loaded in the chamber, seated with the lever and the percussion cap set, it's ready to go. These are likely the weapons Powell and his men will have."

Blue eyes widened as she lifted the first gun. "It's heavy."

Valentine nodded. Bronwyn ran a thumb over the walnut grip before carefully placing it back down. Valentine didn't want to think about what it would mean if any of the men on their heels were armed, but Bronwyn was right. Knowing what to do in a situation with an armed enemy was half the battle. When she was finished examining both, he placed the pistols back in the case and into his saddlebags. She frowned at him with a raised brow.

"I wanted you to be familiar with them," he explained and bent to retrieve a broken stick from the ground. "We'll use this piece of wood instead. What's the first thing you do with an assailant who is armed?" he asked.

"Run away."

"If you can safely, yes," he said. "Run, hide, fight is a good rule of thumb. Always stay calm and control your emotions. If you can give them what they want, then do so. Under no circumstances go anywhere with them because the opportunity for escape will lessen."

"Run, hide, fight," she repeated softly.

"This is only a worst-case scenario, if they catch you unaware. Chances are Powell and his men won't want to shoot you because they want something from you and they want to scare you. That's an advantage, a slim one, but one you can use. The first goal is to get out of the line of fire and the second is to disarm them if you can." He lifted the stick and handed it to her. "Here, take this."

"Why?" she asked. "Shouldn't I be disarming you?"

"It's better if I show you first," he said and took a step toward her. "May I touch you to demonstrate?" He glanced down at her. Was she holding her breath? Faint spots of red bloomed over her cheekbones when he settled his palms over her shoulders and maneuvered her body into the position he wanted. The touch was innocent, but his own body acted like it wasn't.

Striving for control, Valentine shifted her stance so that her weight was centered and gently rotated her free arm at the elbow to point the stick at him. "If you're dealing with a knife instead of a gun, it's the same concept. You want to try to get out of the line of attack and aim to disarm by going for your foe's arm. Even if they manage to cut you in the process, it will likely heal."

"Is that what you did in Philadelphia?" she asked, glancing at the reddened scar visible over his collar.

"Exactly so."

She nodded and gave her shoulders a slow roll, settling into the new position. Valentine turned so that the stick was pointing to his back. Before she could blink, he waved his hands slightly in the air as if surrendering, then he stepped in, rotated, and snatched her wrist before breaking her hold on the makeshift weapon in a hard downward motion. "You're smaller than I am, so put all your weight forward and slam downward as hard as you can. If his finger is in the trigger, you can break it by twisting the gun. Now you try."

Watching her repeat the simple moves shouldn't have made him aroused, but it did. Her slim fingers closed over his wrist with enough force to make his breath hiss through his teeth. She did everything with precision and she took his direction exceptionally well. Would she be as compliant and biddable in an actual bed? He snorted. She'd be a tigress in bed as she was with everything else, and he wouldn't change a thing. Not that there was any intimate future for them in beds or otherwise. She'd turned his proposal down.

Why had she? The solution was both logical and pragmatic.

Matters of the heart are never pragmatic.

Was that it? Did she expect sonnets and odes of undying devotion? She didn't seem like the type, but she'd spoken of a dream of a husband once. Then again, he didn't really know Lady Bronwyn Chase. Had he truly ever known the real her?

"What if one of them shoots if I choose to run?" she asked.

"Chances are they will miss a moving target," he said with a serious expression. "Another technique is to try to distract them before running. That was the reason I wiggled my hands before in a show of surrender. That second of distraction was critical. Throw anything you have at them. A reticule, a bonnet, anything, and then run."

Though the image of her in mortal danger made him feel sick to his stomach, Valentine sucked in a breath. He wanted to treat her as though she were made of crystal, like every other lady in the *ton*, but at every turn, Bronwyn showed that she was not breakable. That underneath all that softness, all that upper-crust decorum, she was made of forged steel.

"I won't let you out of my sight, Bronwyn, or let it get to that point," he vowed. "I'll do everything in my power to keep you safe."

Her lips quirked. "No person can be everywhere at all times, but I am grateful that you're here, Lord Spy." She stared down at the ground and twirled the stick between her fingers.

"Why don't you want to marry me?" he asked softly.

She glanced at him. "This again?"

"Answer," he said. "Please."

He saw her shoulders lift, the curve of her cheek as she took her lips between her teeth in aggravation. "Because it's not for the right reasons."

"You don't care for your safety?"

A pair of luminous blue eyes met his when she turned to face him. "Now that you've not deemed me your foe for the moment, I know you will protect me, no matter what, Your Grace, whether I have the protection of your name or not. You just promised you would. For the sake of your friendship with my brother or perhaps the little that you care for me as a friend."

"We are more than friends."

"Are we?" she whispered, standing so close he could reach out and touch the silky brown curl that had slipped from her bun.

If you get arrested, as your husband, I cannot be used against you.

The words were on the tip of his tongue, but he did not say them. When the truth came out, once they were back in London, it could go any which way. If the handler in the British service was a turncoat, she would be guilty by association. If they weren't and he had apprehended her, he would look the fool. He'd take the latter any day.

"I only want to protect you, Bronwyn," he said in a low rasp when she closed the distance between them, the scent of her—cinnamon, apples, and forest air—crowding his nostrils and making his chest constrict. Then again, everything about her enticed him. The way she moved. The way she smiled. The way her sharp eyes stared him down as if they knew every one of his secrets.

So much so that he wanted to take her in his arms and show her without words how he felt. That his true reasons for marriage were the most selfish ones of all. He wanted her for himself, not in the arms of that ingratiating, knuckle-kissing marquis. Besides, as her husband, she would be bound to listen to him. The thought filled him with dry amusement. Who was he fooling? Bronwyn would do whatever Bronwyn wanted to do.

Her irises flared as her lips grazed his in the smallest, meanest of kisses.

God, he wanted to slip that kiss into her mouth. Take it deeper. Lose himself in the tart bite of her. But she pulled away, and he let her go.

"I can protect myself, Your Grace, and now you've made certain I'm as prepared as I can be." She said it as if she had more to say, but then her lips firmed and her lashes dropped to hide her expression from him.

"Bronwyn."

"Valentine," she shot back mockingly and stared at him.

He stared into the blue fire of her gaze and let out an aggravated breath. God save him from headstrong women. This wasn't a battle he would win right then, but he would do whatever was necessary to protect her from herself.

Eighteen

THE MAN WAS A DOLT. A CATEGORICAL TYRANNICAL beast. The worst creature ever to be put on this earth. A veritable duke-shaped plague upon her house!

"Who does he think he is?" she seethed at Cora. "How dare he lock me in here?"

"For your safety, my lady," the maid said softly.

Bronwyn ground her molars together and prowled back to the window. "This is *my* family's residence. Not his! The only reason he's here is at my invitation. God, he's so overbearing, I could kick him right in the teeth. No, the ballocks!"

"The duke cares about you, my lady," Cora said, unperturbed by her mistress's unladylike threats.

"No, that jackanapes only cares about himself!"

The key in the lock turned right at that moment and she whirled on her heel, ready to give her nemesis a piece of her mind. She opened her mouth, tirade ready to explode, and snapped it shut when the person on the other side came into view. Anger ebbed and dismay took its place as the Duke of Ashvale loomed in the doorway.

Oh, hell.

"Brother." She exhaled and folded her arms across her middle. "What brings you to France?"

"You know very well what summons me here, Bronwyn," he said, that familiar voice making her want to burst into tears as though she were a child and fling herself into his arms. But she wasn't a child. She was a grown woman who had made her own decisions. She wanted to stand on her own two feet and she'd face her fate with her head held high.

Courtland glanced at the maid. "Please excuse us, Cora."

She bobbed. "Your Grace."

Bronwyn felt her heart sink as Cora left, suddenly feeling quite vulnerable. But then her fury returned as the Duke of Thornbury followed on her brother's heels. Those amber eyes were as hard as quartz and just as unreadable. Her fingers dug into her palms in aggravation. Why did men always assume they knew what was best? He had to go and involve her brother. This was truly the last straw!

"Did Thornbury summon you?" she bit out. "That cretin thinks he knows what's best for everyone, but I assure you—"

"Rawley," the duke said, interrupting her rant, "informed me about the attack on your life and the dire state of the situation. I suppose I am grateful that the Duke of Thornbury was here to protect you, though I have heard enough about his version of defense to have my own reservations. But that is something I will address at a later date. You can both count on it."

Bronwyn gulped at the intonation, heart slamming

against her ribs. What did he *know*? She didn't dare look over at the duke, though she could feel his unswerving attention on her. She still wanted to kick him in both places. The expression in her brother's eyes as they shifted to the duke was one of deadly intent. Thornbury, for his part, did not bat an eyelash at the obvious menace from his friend.

"What have you gotten yourself into, Bronwyn?"

She licked her lips, not wanting to lie and also wanting to uphold the oath she'd taken. "I cannot tell you."

"Lives are in peril," he said.

"Only mine, and I knew what I was getting into when I agreed to do what I am doing."

"And what exactly is that?" Onyx eyes drilled into hers, her brother's handsome face pulling tight. "I'm not playing any games, Bronwyn."

Well, neither was she. She firmed her lips and stared back, their sheer obstinacy common ground between them. They might not have grown up together, but their similarities in personality were more than evident in that moment.

At her mulish expression, he sighed and threaded a hand through his dark curls. "A letter came for you."

She frowned. "A letter?"

"To my house in London. Addressed to you, which I opened. The sender claimed that they knew your secret identity as the spy called the Kestrel and would go to the presses if you did not pay them the sum demanded."

The sharp exhalation from Thornbury made her

flinch. Clearly, the cat—no, the *bird*—was certainly out of the bag now.

Bronwyn bristled with anger. "You opened my correspondence?"

The look Courtland gave her was so full of veiled fury that she quailed in her slippers. "Contrary to what you might think, dear sister, I have always known of your little escapades. My wife convinced me that with Rawley on your heels, I should let you fly as you wanted, as long as you weren't in any danger." Emotion bled over his face for in instant, letting her see exactly what she had put him through. "But then you decided to go to America and nearly got killed. Twice." His voice shook with strain.

"I had to, Courtland," she whispered. "A man's life was hanging in the balance."

"Yes, I understand, but *your* life matters to me, and you nearly died *twice* at gunpoint."

Bronwyn flinched at the consternation, and felt Thornbury's gaze flutter to her from where he stood leaning against the doorjamb. "No need to make her feel worse, Ashvale. She was doing what she thought was right," he said.

"Don't get me started on *you*," Courtland growled. "When this is over and done with, you and I will have words, I assure you."

"Thornbury didn't do anything, Courtland." Heavens, why was she defending him? The rotter had locked her in her chambers for two days! She could feel his quiet surprise, but ignored it. "In fact you should thank him that I am here in one piece."

That was entirely the wrong thing to say, considering her brother's thunderous expression.

"This has to end, Bronwyn," Courtland said through clenched teeth. She rolled her palms into fists at the curt order, ready to rail at him, ready to scream that she was in control of her own life, until his next softly spoken words. "You have no idea how terrified I was when Rawley's cable came through. I cannot lose you, not when I've only just found you."

Not even attempting to hold back the burst of her tears, she crumpled straight into her brother's arms. "I didn't mean to scare you, Courtland. I just wanted to *do* something. Make a difference. I don't have a seat in the Lords, I can't enact change like you and Thornbury can, but I can help in my own way."

He wrapped her up in a warm embrace. "Not like this."

She sniffed. "You expect me to sit at home? Do needlepoint, play the pianoforte, and twiddle my thumbs? Let the dogmatists win because they're used to it?"

"No," he said. "Your voice is power, Bronwyn, and the fact that you are willing to use it for the sake of those who need it says a lot about your character. But if you die, that proud, strong, compelling voice dies with you."

Bronwyn exhaled, shoulders dipping with dejection. "So how do I help?"

"Small efforts make big ripples. You don't have to be an infamous international spy, though it appears your methods are rather effective. I heard what you did for Lincoln."

"Hardly infamous," she muttered, dismay deepening that he obviously knew who she was and also what she'd done. Some spy she was turning out to be if her brother knew her every move. No surprise now considering the big, silent shadow she'd never noticed on her heels. She narrowed her gaze, thinking about Rawley who was arguably the cleverest spymaster of them all.

Courtland glanced over his shoulder. "Besides, ask Thornbury about his past. Always running for his life. So wrapped up in deception, he doesn't even know the truth of who he is, or what he wants." A dark gaze filled with fondness peered down at her. "I want to hear what you have to say, Bronwyn, and I need you alive to help me amplify as many voices as we can in Parliament."

Of course he did. Because that was who he was—a brother, a husband, a fair and just man who wouldn't placate her with empty words.

Bronwyn choked up. "I love you, Courtland."

"Love you too, Sister."

———————

Valentine fought the envy rising inside him as he watched the siblings. He didn't begrudge his friend for hearing those words from his sister, but deep down, he coveted them for himself. Valentine wanted her affection...and the fervent avowals of love. Two things he would never have. Things he didn't deserve. And clearly she thought so as well because the idea of being married to him was a fate worse than death.

Bloody hell! He needed to do something to rid himself of these sodding useless feelings that had no business being inside his mind. They were digging under his skin, burrowing into the marrow of his bones, and messing with his head in a way that was not healthy. That was the thing with emotions…once a person let them in, they spawned and swarmed until they took over. He needed to take back his shaky control.

You don't want control. You want her.

Valentine firmed his lips. Want was a useless thing that set terrible expectations. Sure, he *wanted* a dozen Arabian thoroughbreds, but that didn't mean such a thing was good for him. He scowled at himself. Bronwyn wasn't a mare in his stable. Admittedly, the analogy was poor. He cleared his throat, watching with forced dispassion as Ashvale and Bronwyn broke apart.

"This letter you received," Valentine said. "Any clues as to who sent it? Where it was postmarked from?"

"No idea to the first, and it was sent from England, not here," Ashvale said, taking the correspondence out of his pocket and handing it to Bronwyn. Valentine suppressed a burst of irritation. It was *her* mail, after all. "Do you recognize the handwriting?" the duke asked.

"No," she said, brows furrowing over the folded parchment. A shocked gust of breath whistled through her lips. "They want one thousand pounds or I will be exposed."

"Extortion," Thornbury said with a frown. "Who else knows about you?"

"Besides you two? And Rawley? No one beyond the man I work with, and I've been extremely careful, considering how long I went undiscovered."

Thornbury prowled forward. "And who would that be?"

"You know I cannot tell you until I've verified that it is well and good to do so," she replied quickly, still studying the parchment as if looking for more clues.

"What if it's that very man?"

A low laugh left her. "It's not him. He has too much to lose."

Valentine's mind ticked over. That ruled out the queen. Bronwyn had said *he*. Though Her Majesty wasn't known for involving herself in clandestine surveillance affairs, the queen had used the War Office for her own ends in the past, especially when she wanted eyes on her own people. He should know—she'd once used him to spy on Palmerston, early in the prime minister's career. It was in the interest of protecting England, she'd claimed, but he guessed that the queen had wanted to make sure she could keep the charismatic, shrewd politician on her own leash.

"We should pay them," he said.

Flashing blue eyes met his as Bronwyn whirled, outrage written all over her. "No! I won't give one cent to someone who hopes to use my situation for financial gain. Extortion is the most cowardly of acts."

"Or a desperate one," Valentine countered.

"Thornbury has a point," her brother said. "We could leave the money as indicated. It is the least problematic route."

Valentine walked over to where Bronwyn stood and reached for the correspondence. When she handed it over, he scrutinized it. There was nothing remarkable about the paper or the hand. The sender's penmanship was neat and precise, so it could be a man or a woman, and the word choice suggested a person of skill and education. Definitely not a servant, if he had to guess, even if they'd paid someone to write it.

Dear Lady B, I know who you are.

If you would like to see your identity as the Kestrel remain a secret and not shared with the gossip rags, jeopardizing both the future prospects of your younger sister and your brother's reputation as duke, you will comply forthwith.

Leave the sum of one thousand pounds in the decorative urn beside the jasmine trellis a fortnight hence.

Yours, a most avid friend.

"Hardly a friend," he muttered. "This is someone who knows your residence. Are you familiar with the urn in question?" When they both nodded, Valentine pursed his lips. "If I had to hazard a guess, I would also say that this person knows your family. He or she knows you have a younger sister and that you recently came into the fold as the Duke of Ashvale."

Ashvale nodded. "They could be using her to discredit

me. The extortion must be the start of it. There's no guarantee that they won't ask for more, or go to someone with deep pockets who wishes to see me deposed."

"Exactly!" Bronwyn exclaimed. "So why pay them?"

"To ferret them out," Valentine said.

"All this person has is conjecture. There's no actual proof that I am anything other than a lady of the *ton*. Slander is also a crime, is it not?"

Valentine lifted a shoulder. "Trust me, the gossips won't care if it's the truth or not. They want to sell their news rags, and this story will be hot for the presses. Anything touching a duke, particularly the already questionable Duke of Ashvale, will be bound to sell newssheets. In our incestuously petty circles, scandal is currency."

Bronwyn's face paled as she shot a horrified glance to her brother. "I am sorry. I didn't mean for any of this to touch you."

Valentine let out a scoffing noise. "What exactly did you expect, Lady Bronwyn? Duty isn't limited to the men of the *ton*. Women are just as constrained by the rules of society and decorum. The barest hint of impropriety can ruin the finest of families. Did you think your little adventures would go unnoticed?" Her face went mutinous, and a muscle had started to tick in Ashvale's jaw at his hard, vicious words, but Valentine didn't stop. "I've said all along you were a little girl playing at adult games."

"I'm not a girl, Your Grace," she snapped. "And no one asked you to be here."

"I asked him," Ashvale said, scrubbing a palm over

his face. "We will contain this situation by whatever means necessary," her brother added before leveling a quelling glare at the two of them, his dark eyes particularly flinty toward Valentine. "And you two will wed to contain any further scandal as to your whereabouts over the past few weeks."

They both turned to stare at him.

"I'm not marrying him!" Bronwyn screeched.

Ashvale's mouth went flat with anger. "Why not?"

"He's an arrogant, self-serving, cold, fractious-to-a-fault, bothersome, controlling, and muttonheaded, taciturn, unfeeling cad. Need I go on?"

God, she was stunning when she was angry, like an avenging angel sent to earth to smite the unworthy. And he was very, *very* unworthy. Valentine lifted an amused brow. "Your command of the language is masterful. I applaud you."

"You can take your sodding applause right to hell." She ground her jaw and approached her brother, whose eyes had narrowed at his sister's vocabulary, which was saying something considering his own duchess was fluent in the vulgar tongue. "I cannot marry him, Courtland. Please do not do this."

Ashvale sighed. "I'm afraid there's little choice left in the matter, my dear. You were seen together without a chaperone."

"By whom?" she demanded. "There were dozens of people on that ship."

"Precisely, and likely more than a few accounts of Lady

Bronwyn Chase leaving an alcove on the stern of my ship with her clothing mussed and looking thoroughly ruined."

Bronwyn's jaw fell open and snapped shut as a bright blush seeped over her cheekbones. "That could have been the hearty sea air."

"I sincerely doubt the sea air has teeth, Bronwyn," her brother remarked drily.

Valentine didn't remember anyone being about, but that didn't mean someone might not have seen her returning to her stateroom with her hair tousled and marks of passion on her creamy skin. Deep masculine satisfaction rode him until he locked eyes with an incensed Ashvale, who looked like he wanted to pummel him into the wall.

The man fairly seethed with rage. "You and I will settle this properly when we get back to London. For now, I need you in good form, without any broken bones, because I have a plan to break quite a few in your body, starting with your legs."

Valentine wanted to point out that it wasn't his legs that had seduced the duke's sister, but very wisely kept his mouth shut. Bronwyn, however, wasn't of the same mind.

"No. I refuse."

Ashvale's icy countenance when he took in his aggravated sister was resigned. "I know this isn't want you want, Bronwyn." He sighed and walked to the door. "Do you think I wish to see my younger sister forced into a union? Don't you think I want you to wed a man who will make you happy?"

Valentine ignored the taste of bitterness in his mouth

and didn't point out the irony that Ashvale had been wed to his duchess in much the same way—through a forced trip to the altar—though their...scandal had been viewed by actual witnesses and not based on assumptions and hearsay.

Though, *he* knew what he'd taken.

She'd been a virgin when they'd coupled. Guilt boiled through his veins like acid. The right thing to do was to marry her, but if Bronwyn was truly opposed to wedding him, he would never force her. Gossip would eventually peter out for something juicier. They would both survive that, at least.

Assassins and bullets were a different story.

But she was right that he didn't have to marry her to protect her. He'd do it anyway.

"Bronwyn, you claim to want to help, to make a difference, and yet, how do you intend to do that as a disgraced woman?" Ashvale went on in a gentler tone. "You will be shunned from ballrooms and ousted from polite society, not because there is any truth in the scandal, but because there will be those who will delight in your misfortune. Think about it and let me know your answer. For now, I am tired, in need of a bath, and we need to get you back home."

"What about the boy who shot at me?" she ground out. "We can't just leave him here alone in Paris. What if he wakes and knows something?"

"Rawley has agreed to stay behind. Right now, we have the pressing matter of your identity to resolve, and you will be much safer in England, clearly."

Ashvale left, but not before sending another seething

look in Valentine's direction that promised nothing but violence. When he eventually demanded his pound of flesh, that was going to be a spectacle of pugilism for the record books. Valentine didn't blame him—if he had a sister, he'd have done the same. He cleared his throat and glanced over to where Bronwyn was wringing her hands with a distraught look on her face.

"What's wrong?" he asked.

"Get out. This is all your fault."

He lifted a brow. "My fault?"

"Why couldn't you have just gone back to England?" she said.

Valentine exhaled. "Because I can't seem to let you go."

The words dropped like lead ballast between them, and her eyes shone with the gleam of tears before she turned her face away. "God, is that all I am to you? A target? A stupid bird to be caught? The fantastic prize of the Kestrel to be caged and lauded as the greatest arrest in the history of time? You probably led those men here when you decided to pursue me, and then you locked me away in here like some damsel in a tower!"

Valentine deserved her wrath, but he'd been out of options and terrified half to death at how close he'd come to losing her. The gendarmes in Paris were looking for signs of the man or any accomplices, though without the shooter's testimony, they didn't have much to go on. The rifle in the young man's possession had been of American issue, but he'd carried no identifying papers. Until he woke up, they had nothing.

Following her brother's footsteps to the door, Valentine paused in the corridor and looked over his shoulder. "If you want me to apologize for keeping you safe, I won't. Get some rest. We'll talk in the morning."

Face unreadable, she closed the distance between them, her throat working as though she had something to say. Her eyelashes fell, hand shaking as she gripped the edge of the door. With her crimson cheeks and trembling lips, she was so beautiful and fragile, he wanted to take her into his arms and comfort her. "Valentine?"

The whispered cadence of his name gripped his heart in a fist. "Yes?"

"You can go fuck yourself right into next week, the week after, and all the other weeks to come," she said sweetly and then slammed the door in his face.

A half-amused, half-aroused Valentine revised his statement. She was certainly beautiful…but she was far from fragile. The sooner he reconciled that in his head, the better off he would be.

Nineteen

VALENTINE PALMED HIS NAPE AND SIGHED. THE JOURney back to England via Calais had been uneventful, thank God. A rather quiet and docile Bronwyn had stewed in her quarters for the entire trip, which had surprised everyone, especially him. The clever little harpy was only biddable when she had some other maggot of an idea in her brain, and he wouldn't put it past her to try something. He'd watched her like a hawk, but she had done nothing to warrant suspicion.

The presence of her aunt seemed to mollify her as well. It had been a surprise when the older lady had insisted on accompanying them, saying it was about time she made peace with her birth country...and her sister, she supposed.

As the boatswains secured the lines, Valentine checked the London Docks while the swift clipper was tethered to the wharf and directed some of the crew to do the same before lowering the gangplank. Though the risk was low, anyone could be an enemy, and the docks were crowded with workers, sailors, fishermen, and people spilling out of the main taverns lining the edges. Thankfully, Ashvale had arranged for transportation, and several unmarked coaches were waiting for them to disembark.

"Scotland Yard has been apprised," the duke said. "We'll have an armed escort."

Valentine raised his brows at the overabundance of caution but said nothing. He would have done the same. *Should* have done the same. Then again, he didn't know who he could trust. Best to just focus on keeping Bronwyn safe and out of trouble. Because he could sense it was brewing. She was too quiet. Too submissive.

She was a gale. A cyclone. Hurricane Bronwyn.

His instincts prickled with heat. He knew more than anyone that she didn't have a submissive bone in her body.

Unless they were alone and tearing each other's clothes off.

He squelched that thought with ruthless force.

Another smart-looking ship had docked to the left of them, also from France, if memory served. He remembered the flashy sails of the clipper and had kept an eye on it. He frowned as a gentleman dressed in a peacock-blue frock coat and fawn trousers strolled off the footbridge and spoke to the coachman of an equally gaudy coach drawn by four snow-white horses.

Beggars and children crowded up to the conveyance, while the tigers in fancy livery fought to keep them at bay. Valentine shook his head. Some people had too much money to spend and not enough sense to go with it. What idiot flaunted his wealth in one of the busiest and seediest parts of London? The fop was begging to be fleeced.

"Oh, we're here," a soft voice said as the lady of the hour joined them.

Valentine turned and gaped. From the top of her

gleaming brown hair to the tips of her dainty polished boots, Bronwyn shone like the lady she was. The periwinkle-blue dress hugged every sinful curve, clinging to her bosom and that tiny waist before flaring in satin folds to the deck. Her eyes sparkled and he'd never seen anything lovelier in his life. "Lady Bronwyn."

"Your Grace." She wrinkled her nose at the pungent scent of the Thames. "Smells like home."

"You should wait belowdecks," he said, the words emerging much harsher than he'd intended. Had she dressed like that to tease him with what he could not have? Heat burst under his collar when those clear blue eyes met his. Not for the first time, he wished he could read what he saw swimming in them, but Bronwyn was fast becoming a master of artifice, or maybe she'd been one all along. A thick fringe of lashes fluttered down as if, she could only hold his gaze for so long.

The Duke of Ashvale made a sound of approval. "Here's the Metropolitan Police now. Give them a few minutes and we shall be on our way."

"Thank you, Brother," Bronwyn said. "But I've made other arrangements."

Valentine's stare narrowed.

"Bronwyn," Ashvale began. "You know what's at stake."

She reached up and pressed a kiss to her brother's cheek. "Relax, Courtland, you will be happy to know that I intend to surround myself with so many admirers and potential suitors that no one will even have the space to get a shot off at me." She grinned at both of them, and that smile had teeth that Valentine recognized. He could feel the prick of them against his jugular, even as he turned in slow motion to follow her gaze, to where the colorful fop from the neighboring ship ambled along the docks.

Recognition dawned like the taste of ashes.

Devil take it.

"I've invited Monsieur de Tremblay to join us in London for the rest of the season," she said airily as they walked down the walkway. "Isn't that lovely? I wasn't sure he would be able to come on such short notice, but well, here he is. My French knight in shining armor."

Valentine gritted his jaw and curled his palms into fists. He had many other descriptors in mind, the least of which stemmed from a sudden surge of misplaced jealousy. Said knight was in armor so bright, it was a wonder everyone wasn't blinded.

"Your Grace," Tremblay said with a smart bow to Ashvale. "How good of you to offer to host me. That is so very kind of you."

Valentine blinked. He watched as Ashvale directed an inscrutable look to his sister who didn't bat an eyelash. "Well, he can't very well stay with me and Mama, and you live right across the street. Besides, you're not even in residence. Ravenna told me at the start of the season that with her confinement, you're spending more time in Kettering than in London."

"Monsieur de Tremblay," Ashvale said with a gracious nod. "Of course, whatever pleases my darling sister. I believe you know the Duke of Thornbury."

The man grinned. "We are acquainted, Your Grace, considering the duke and I are both mutual admirers of your charming sister. If I were a less confident man, I might even be worried about the competition, but the lady has assured me that she thinks of the duke as a dear brother. What a relief!"

Bronwyn put a hasty hand on Tremblay's arm and ushered him back the way he'd come.

Ashvale's brows rose, a hint of amusement glittering in his black eyes when he turned to Valentine. "A brother? How droll."

"You know very well that's not the case," he muttered. "The man is an imbecile. Surely you don't trust her safety in his coach?"

The duke peered at the mounted policemen. "We are all headed to the same place, though I assume you will go to your residence. She will be safe enough."

Valentine stared at him in astonishment. "Do you *know* the marquis? The man is a ferret with hands like tentacles." He scowled at Ashvale's amused expression. "And yes, I know those two things have nothing to do with each other, but trust me that you do not want him near your sister. You worry about her reputation being compromised with me, and yet you send her off to certain debauchery with a libertine for a companion." He bit off the end of his outburst, knowing he was being unreasonable but unable to help himself all the same.

"Tremblay and I have known each other for years," Ashvale said. "He knows what will happen if he thinks of putting one tentacle out of line. And besides, the Comtesse de Valois is with them."

Somewhat pacified, Valentine watched Bronwyn's aunt enter the carriage.

"She invited him on purpose," he muttered.

"Who?"

"Your sister did to aggravate me."

Ashvale grinned and patted him on the back. "I'm beginning to think that I might have to take pity on you and not flog you to within an inch of your life after all. It seems you're being punished quite enough. Who knew my sweet, gentle, harmless sister had it in her?"

Valentine scowled. Given any choice in the matter, he'd take the beating. "If you think she's harmless, you're a bigger fool than I am."

———

The look on the duke's face had been worth coming back to London without any solid answers as to who wanted her dead. Bronwyn trusted Rawley, but she had wanted to be there when the assailant awoke. Things were missed in translation.

You have worse things to worry about.

That was true. Someone in England wanted to expose her. On top of that, she had yet to hear from Wentworth since Sesily had not written, which could mean one of two things—either her letter had not in fact reached London, or Sesily had been compromised in some fashion. Either way, Bronwyn had things to do, but she wasn't above acting like a petty brat when it came to Thornbury.

She didn't even know what she was irritated about.

He'd offered her the protection of his name, but she didn't want it. Bronwyn didn't want to be married to him. Not like that anyway. God, she was a fool a hundred times over. The duke might be an excellent lover and a brilliant strategist, and a man whose mind fascinated her as much as his body did, but he did not have a working heart.

At least one that was capable of love.

Was outstanding sex worth the cost of a loveless marriage? She swallowed around the knot in her throat. She'd watched her mother pine away for a man whose heart had been buried with his long-dead previous wife—Courtland's beautiful West Indian mother—and Bronwyn had sworn from a young age that she would never fall in love with a man who could not love her back. Her breath fizzled in her lungs.

Dear God, was it possible that she was *in love* with Thornbury?

No, this wasn't love. It wasn't sweet and gentle and lovely, and all the things love should be. It was raw and wild and unprincipled. All teeth, nails, and gasping breaths. Naked bodies and fervent demands. Deliciously filthy promises delivered in the heat of the moment. No, this was lust bordering on pure, impassioned attraction.

That was why she had barricaded herself in her room on the clipper. Being in any close proximity to him resulted in a complete lack of willpower where he was concerned, and Bronwyn wasn't sure that she wouldn't yank him into the closest alcove and demand he repeat the carnal acts that had gotten them in trouble in the first place.

The Duke of Thornbury was best put out of her head.

Inviting the Marquis de Tremblay had been Aunt Esther's brilliant idea, and of course, the gentleman had agreed, delighted to charm his way through greener pastures after declaring boredom with Paris. Bronwyn had seen it as the perfect wedge to drive some space between her and Thornbury, and it had clearly worked, considering his thunderous expression on deck. Strangely, it did not feel as gratifying as she'd thought it would, leaving only a strange hollowness in the pit of her stomach.

That was likely nerves. She hadn't seen her mother in a few weeks, and no doubt, she would be in a tizzy. She wondered if Lady Borne would approve of the marquis. Tremblay was handsome and wealthy and ticked all her boxes, with the sole exception that he was French. And of course, the dear friend and possible former lover of the marchioness's estranged sister. Bronwyn glanced at her aunt, whose head rested on Tremblay's shoulder. It was curious that those two had an on-again, off-again relationship, considering she was twice his age, but they got along marvelously well.

Bronwyn lifted a brow at them. "Are you two going to behave?"

The marquis let out a chuckle as her aunt grinned, making her look much younger than her forty-odd years. "We are going to destroy this rigid *ton* with every weapon in our arsenal, never fear."

"Mama is going to have conniptions," Bronwyn groaned.

Tremblay waggled his brows. "And the tight-arsed Duke of Thornbury."

The sound of his name made her core clench, not to mention causing an instant and unwelcome vision of that very tight, very firm pair of male buttocks that she had yet to see unclothed, and she almost cursed aloud when the marquis's soft laughter filled the coach. "Don't worry, dearest. I will make your arctic snow-beast positively melt with jealousy."

"Leave her alone, Jacques dear," Esther scolded. "If there's any melting to be done, I'm sure my niece can handle it."

Bronwyn glanced at her aunt whose own mischievous smile rivaled the marquis's. It was incongruous to think that she and the rather expressionless and haughty Marchioness of Borne were twin sisters. They had the same features, but they could not be more different. Both brown-haired and blue-eyed, Aunt Esther embodied warmth and charm, while her mother had the personality of a weed and the friendliness of a jagged blade. Bronwyn knew she favored both her aunt and her mother in looks. Aunt Esther's arrival was going to be a shock, considering the two women hadn't seen each other in years.

"When was the last time you saw Mama?" Bronwyn asked.

Sadness shadowed her aunt's face. "When your papa died." Bronwyn blinked. That had been over a decade ago. "She made it very clear that I wasn't the right kind of influence to have around you and Florence, and that I wasn't welcome. I don't enjoy going where I'm not wanted so I found myself an agreeable husband in the Comte de Valois and left for Paris."

In truth, Bronwyn wouldn't have known her mother had had a twin sister if she hadn't discovered the portraits tucked away in a drawer of them when they'd been children, whereupon she had nagged her mother to death until she'd confessed the truth of her sister. She had forbidden her sister's name from being mentioned, however, stating that Esther had run off with a scandalous French comte with no morals whatsoever and lived an undisciplined, vulgar life somewhere in Paris.

Of course, a much younger and much-too-sheltered Bronwyn had been fascinated. Thanks to Wentworth, whose network of informants ran all over Europe, she'd found her aunt's address in her first stint as the Kestrel and corresponded in secret for the better part of the past year. They had met during a shopping trip to Paris as well as a delivery for Wentworth and discovered an instant camaraderie between them.

Her mother, however, would not be pleased.

Then again, the marchioness would not be happy about a lot of things.

When the coach arrived in Mayfair, along with their largest entourage known to man, Bronwyn was a froth of nerves. Between dealing with her unresolved feelings where Thornbury was concerned and now handling the certain consequences of her mother and aunt's reunion, she would have preferred being chased by faceless enemies.

The Marquis de Tremblay was ushered into her brother's residence, where she and Aunt Esther made sure he was settled and then walked to the house on the other side of the street. For reasons known only to him, Courtland had purchased the home opposite years ago and had kept it, despite being the true Duke of Ashvale and owning both properties.

"Are you certain I cannot stay with Jacques?" Aunt Esther asked, wrinkling her nose. "I am a widow, and it's not as though we haven't shared a bed before."

Bronwyn bit back a giggle. "Hush, Aunt. No, you cannot stay with an unmarried gentleman, no matter how intimately you know each other." She peered over at her, curiosity riding her. "Are you two courting?"

"Neither of us wants to be mired in wedlock at the moment," her aunt replied and then waved a dismissive arm. "Men are too much maintenance. We have an... indelicate understanding. Call it that."

Bronwyn laughed. Good gracious, she loved the lady. "One day, Aunt Esther, I wish to be just like you."

Her aunt's eyes twinkled. "Marry an old French peer, murder him with arsenic, and become a gloriously unrepentant widow with a score of younger lovers."

"Aunt Esther!" She lowered her voice. "Did you truly do away with Monsieur le Comte?"

Her cackles were infectious, making Bronwyn's lips

twitch. "No, darling. I loved the old codger. His poor heart could not handle me, however. We had ten wonderful years together, and I am grateful for every single one of them."

"Will you marry again?"

Aunt Esther sniffed. "Not if I can help it."

"Not even if Monsieur de Tremblay gets down on his knees and begs?"

Her aunt winked. "If he's down on his knees, it's not to speak, trust me."

Bronwyn's entire face went hot before she dissolved into laughter. The woman was truly irreverent. No wonder her mother abhorred her sister. She embodied everything fun about life, while her mother was the opposite. Bronwyn grabbed hold of her aunt's hand and squeezed, wondering if she was nervous about seeing her sister. The lady didn't show it, but she had to be feeling something to see a sibling she hadn't seen in a decade.

That was how Bronwyn had felt when she'd come face-to-face with her half brother, Courtland, for the first time. Her late grandfather had adored his prodigal stepgrandson and that love had turned into a strange fondness by association for Bronwyn, who grew to know her brother through the copious updates and portraits commanded by their grandfather. She doubted it would be the same between the marchioness and her sister, however. There was too much distance and history between them.

"Mama?" she called out as she walked into the familiar foyer. Servants rushed forward to take her cloak and bonnet. "I've returned."

Her younger sister, Florence, walked down the stairs, her pretty face twisted into a sneer. "You are in so much trouble! Mama is in a lather."

"I told her I was with Ravenna in Kettering." Yet another white lie to placate her mother and to cover up her travels.

Florence bared her teeth in a fake grin. "Stinson went to Kettering, only to return and report that you were not there. So where have you been all this time, sister dear?"

Drat and botheration! She'd hoped to be back in London much sooner, and also before her very controlling mother sent her brother after her.

"I—" Her brain went blank.

"She's been with me in Paris," Aunt Esther supplied from behind her.

Florence's eyes rounded as they fell on their aunt for the first time. She wouldn't have known about their mother's sister or the fact that they were twins. Their mother had sworn Bronwyn to secrecy. "Who are you?" she whispered.

"I'm your aunt Esther. You've grown into such a beautiful girl."

"We don't have any aunts," Florence said, face tight with suspicion, though her voice wavered with confusion. The resemblance was too obvious to think otherwise.

"She is our aunt, Florence. Mama's twin." Bronwyn let out a breath. "I've been visiting her in France for a spell."

Her sister's eyes narrowed, but before she could speak, the marchioness herself appeared at the top of the stairs.

Bronwyn braced herself for the outburst of wrath, but it didn't come. Her mother was much too poised and put together for that, at least in front of the servants. However, the look she speared Bronwyn with, once she reached the bottom of the staircase, ran her straight through like a cold shaft of iron. Disappointment and betrayal were the least of it.

"You lied to me," the marchioness said.

"I didn't lie. I did go to Kettering at first." *Then I went to the United States and then on to France, but that's neither here nor there.* Thankfully, the last half of that stayed in her head.

"You expect me to believe you?" Her mother's thin nostrils flared. "It's that boy and his wanton wife. I've told you I don't want you associating with them."

"Courtland isn't a boy, Mama. He's duke. And he's our family."

"Not my family."

Bronwyn's mouth went tight. "Mine, then. His blood—Papa's blood—runs in my veins and in the veins of all three of your children. And Courtland did not make my decisions for me. I'm perfectly capable of earning your everlasting disapproval on my own."

"You are turning out to be a blight on the family name, just as he is."

"Then I'm in excellent company, Mama. I'd prefer be like him than someone so small-minded they refused to grow or change. I would much rather stand for something, than sit on my hindquarters for nothing at all."

Breathing hard, she attempted to control her temper, but her mother always had a way of pushing her to extremes with the slightest look or smallest word. Bronwyn had run correspondence for Wentworth, carried coded messages, charmed gentlemen for the sake of duty, and never had she felt as skewered by her mother's judgment as she did right then. She bristled, though her eyes stung. She would not cry.

Her aunt cleared her throat. "Come now, Evelyn, don't you think you're being a little harsh on the girl? Surely a little trip to Paris isn't cause for hysterics?"

"Esther," her mother said in a frosty voice. "You look—"

"Happy?" her sister interrupted before some other offense was uttered. "Yes, I am. Much to your alarm, I know."

The marchioness's lip curled. "I was going to say 'old.'"

Everyone froze, but her aunt burst into raucous laughter. "One of these days, sister dear, you will learn to insult me without insulting yourself at the same time. I'd rather be old and happy, than old and full of salt and vinegar."

"Why are you here?" Bronwyn's mother demanded.

Esther sniffed. "My darling niece invited me for a visit. Surely you won't turn away your own blood." Her mouth lifted into a smile. "Then again, the master of the house did offer his hospitality, so I suppose I don't require your approval after all. You're as much a guest here as I am, aren't you, Sister?"

Bronwyn had to work to keep quiet at the astonishment on her mother's face. A completely unperturbed Aunt Esther was deploying the big guns without fear of reprisal. The marchioness sputtered, but then clamped her lips together and turned on her heel, walking back the way she'd come with a rigid spine.

Esther smirked. "That went well! Florence, my dear, how about a tour and you can tell me if you have any handsome beaux."

Twenty

CURSE HER LUCK!

And her overbearing, managing mother!

And sumptuous ball gowns that barely covered any skin at all!

Bronwyn would much rather be chased and shot at than ogled by men twice her age who saw her only as a dowry with lace-covered breasts. She hadn't come back to England to be forced onto the marriage mart like some precious society darling as if she'd never left, but that was exactly what was happening.

Mere days after their arrival, her mother had announced that they were to attend a midseason ball at the residence of some peer Bronwyn barely knew. A bloody masquerade, no less! Apparently, the suitor in question—in line for a solvent marquessate—had expressed interest in Bronwyn's hand, which was why her mother had gone into a frantic state and sent Stinson to Kettering to fetch her forthwith. Needless to say, a wrench had been thrown into the marchioness's marital hopes and dreams for her daughter when said daughter was nowhere to be found. And now Lady Borne was making up for lost time.

"Mama, I don't wish to go," Bronwyn had protested

to no effect. "I don't even know Lord Whatever-His-Name-Is. And I loathe masquerades."

She actually loved them, along with the diverting anonymity they provided, but when there was someone trying to kill her, a party with guests in disguise could include a death sentence with her name on it.

"Lord Herbert," her mother had replied crossly. "I won't hear any excuses."

The only marginally good thing was that Sesily would be at the ball and had sent word that Wentworth wanted to meet. It was the one place where Bronwyn could facilitate a meeting without being followed by half a dozen people, and the disguises would offer another layer of secrecy. She was sure that between Ashvale and Thornbury, a number of the guests in attendance would be there for her protection…at least ones in possession of an invitation.

Not that any part of her scandalous dress allowed her to blend in.

She might as well be a red flag in the middle of a bullpen.

To Bronwyn's shock, the ball gown her dour, unimaginative mother had chosen was practically indecent. Red, lacy, and much too provocative. She had to be truly desperate to barter her daughter off as quickly as possible to the peer of her choosing. And a boring one at that. The masquerade theme was unoriginal in the extreme— Roman gods and goddesses. No surprise there from an aristocrat named Herbert. Bronwyn could point out a dozen Venuses and Apollos.

Thought it was more than likely that Lady Borne had commissioned the bold red gown, long before Bronwyn's disappearing act, with one thing in mind: A splendid— and altogether swift—engagement.

Bronwyn sighed with a discreet tug to her bodice while smoothing the voluminous skirts, and sipped on warm rata- fia. Under other circumstances, such a luxurious gown would make her feel beautiful—the black Venetian lace over the red was truly a work of art—but while she was trying to avoid the attention of one persistent lord in particular, the dratted color was worse than a beacon! Luckily, a large column at the side of the ballroom served as a wonderful hiding spot.

It offered a lovely nook resting adjacent to an enor- mous statue of Jupiter, one of the many sculptures placed all around the massive room. Guests whirled and danced, most wearing masks, and all in grand costumes, but no one took notice of her. Thank *God*.

"The roses in my garden are inundated by weeds."

She jumped at the low male voice, but excitement pooled in her chest. "Perhaps you should invest in a sharp pair of shears."

"When the weather is good, I shall."

With gladness, Bronwyn moved to turn toward Wentworth, but was stopped by a low hiss. "Don't turn too quickly. I'm on the other side of this column. There are too many eyes and ears about."

She lifted her glass and pretended to take another sip, hiding her lips. "Where have you been? I was nearly arrested and shot."

"I heard. I am sorry I could not offer assistance. I was also in hiding, after an assignment gone wrong in Washington."

Washington? He'd been in America as well? Bronwyn blinked. Then why had he sent her to Philadelphia? "Listen carefully. There's a traitor in the War Office. I received word of an urgent cable. The American president was shot an hour ago at Ford's Theatre."

Horror filled her. "Is he dead?"

"We don't know yet. He was taken somewhere for treatment."

Bronwyn's heart went cold. Her actions weeks ago had thwarted a kidnapping but the attackers had persevered. Sadness flooded her at the loss of a man who had been working toward equality for all, something the world desperately needed. "Will he survive?"

"I hope so." Wentworth went quiet as a couple walked past them around the perimeter of the room. "I need the list of names from that report."

"I don't have it with me," she whispered, her stomach clenching at the sound of the duke's name and the report that belonged to him. "Wentworth, what is going on? Is this related to the man after me?"

He made an angry sound. "I'll send word via Sesily for the list."

"Wait," she whispered, but he was gone. Damn it! Things had to be awful if he couldn't help her and was worried about his own neck. Thornbury's list included many names she hadn't recognized. Was one of them English? And possibly the traitor?

The hairs on her nape rose as a new presence drifted over. "Who were you talking to?"

Valentine.

She glanced up at him, her gaze colliding with a burning amber stare and making a river of heat travel to every pulse point in her body. God, what he could do with those eyes alone was indecent! She cleared her suddenly dry throat. "No one."

"There was a man dressed as Neptune in a fish mask on the other side of this pillar."

She feigned confusion. "I did not see anyone."

His lip curled, though anger flashed in his eyes. "But you did *hear* him, did you not? That seemed to be quite an intense, cozy conversation. Was he your contact?"

"If you're so interested in him, whoever he was, why don't you go harass him?" She glared at the duke, even as his full mouth flattened. "Why aren't you in costume? Too uninventive and dreary to come up with an idea?"

"I'm not here for entertainment, Lady Bronwyn."

"Mars, perhaps? With that scowl, you could be the Roman god of war. Ah, I've got it! Pluto, god of the underworld, but that would be too much on the nose, don't you think? I do credit you with a little more imagination than that." Her gaze traced him from the tip of his crown to his raven-black evening clothes and polished boots, ignoring how well the tailored jacket fit his broad shoulders and the snug lines of his trousers over strong legs. "Never mind. I know who you are. You're Janus, the two-faced god of duality, one face to the past and the other to the future."

A grim laugh broke from him. "Clever. And who are you supposed to be?"

When he returned the favor, that hot golden stare swept down the shimmering swaths of fabric that wound over her body, and Bronwyn felt it everywhere. Visions exploded in her head from that one heated look, of bodies tangled together on satin sheets, sweaty, slippery, and hot, coming together in passionate, carnal ways. God, how was it possible to desire a man so keenly? A man so utterly *wrong* for her in every way.

Not wrong in bed.

They'd never even seen a bed. She yearned to see him thus. Sprawling and naked, every gloriously hewn muscle on display for her ogling pleasure. Heavens, her imagination was like a runaway horse.

Oh, stop!

By some miracle, Bronwyn kept her face even, no small feat considering the flames of lust threatening to immolate her from the inside out. "Isn't it obvious?" she said, tapping at her golden crown and waved a handheld peacock mask. "Juno, Goddess of Marriage. One cannot say my mother is without a peculiar sense of humor or urgency."

A low huff of laughter rumbled through him, making her desperate to hear it again.

"That dress is…" His voice emerged like gravel and cut off, as if the passionate spell that had come over her had taken him in its grasp, too. He shifted ever so slightly, and she felt the graze of his fingers on her upper part of her spine laid bare by the gown—those five points of pressure like burning embers against her skin—and froze in place. The duke was much closer than was proper, and she still wanted to press backward into him. Each nerve in her body yearned for more of his touch. "You're stunning, Bronwyn."

Pleasure spun through her. "Thank you."

"I heard an announcement might be in the wind tonight," he said softly.

Her fogged brain fought to catch up. "Announcement?"

"Engagement. Yours."

Bronwyn's eyes fluttered closed. Gracious, her mother was dreadful. The Duke of Ashvale still had to give his permission to any marriage discussions, but given recent developments, he would find no fault with the very safe, very lackluster, and very enthusiastic Lord Herbert. The young gentleman was exactly as expected when she'd met him earlier—a pretty, polite, and polished boy. The perfect match for a perfect debutante. Who *wasn't* her. She was ruined goods. Willingly and deliciously ruined by the duke at her back.

The one her body craved still.

She did not want a boy. She wanted a man. *This* man. Carnal options for one last tryst raced through her head—an empty music room, the arbor, a scullery, the library—but if this was to be the last time between them, Bronwyn desired only one place.

"Your Grace," she whispered. "I feel dizzy. Will you escort me home?"

Valentine frowned at the woman seated opposite him in his carriage. She did look rather flushed, her eyes glittery and bright, her cheekbones burning with color. That rosy stain distilled down her elegant throat to the deep vee of her embroidered décolletage. That bloody gown had nearly unmanned him when he'd seen her in it. Shimmering panels of scarlet satin and obsidian lace left little to the imagination, outlining curves and hollows and her exquisite limbs. She'd been a enchanting vision…a blood-stirring study in temptation.

Queen of the goddesses, indeed.

Even Ashvale had looked like he wanted to drag her to safety from everyone who couldn't tear their eyes away from her lush form, but that would have caused a scene. The poor man had had to compose himself on the balcony before returning to the ballroom and not throttling his stepmother who had outfitted her daughter for one purpose.

Husband entrapment.

For one Lord Sodding Herbert.

The boy was perfect for her. Everything Valentine was not. He was old; Herbert was young. He was nothing but seething, swirling darkness, and the boy was a maiden's golden dreams personified. Youthful, idealistic, and ready to settle down with a comely wife and spout out a handful of perfect, beautiful progeny. Herbert would give her everything a lady like her deserved. Valentine would only swallow Bronwyn up and twist her into something she wasn't.

She craved danger, but she wasn't like him.

He would only ruin her for the future she deserved.

Then why was he in a bloody carriage with her alone, driving her home like some knight in broken armor, when all he wanted to be was the villain in the story who stole the heroine to satisfy his own jaded desires? The knight didn't have visions of dropping to his knees and plundering the treasures that lay under those teasing yards of crimson fabric with his tongue. Or commanding her to turn and hold the squabs while he fucked them both into oblivion.

Valentine dropped his palm to his lap, viciously willing his erection to subside. He hadn't even taken proper leave, only giving word to a hovering footman to let the Duke of Ashvale know that his sister hadn't felt well and was being escorted back to her residence. No doubt the marchioness would be livid that her fatted goose had slipped away from beneath her nose, but by all accounts, Lord Herbert was already besotted by his future bride. An offer would be imminent.

The coach turned down her street, and he steeled himself. He would see her home like the gentleman he was somewhere deep down inside. "We're nearly there."

"I meant *your* residence, Your Grace," she said softly.

He blinked. "I beg your pardon?"

"I wish for you to take me to your home."

Hell, if arousal didn't explode inside of him like

gasoline poured onto a banked fire. He shifted in his seat, his cock nearly punching through his trousers. "Bronwyn."

More color bled into her cheeks. "I am not ill. I simply wanted to leave with you." She eased out a breath. "If I am to be forced to marry some brainless young fop, then I will take the choices open to me while I can, and this is one of them. I want you. Now."

"We cannot." By God, why was he protesting?

"We can," she insisted. "Don't you want me?"

Devil take it, what kind of question was that? He craved her with every bone in his body, with every spark of desire in his depraved soul. He wanted to ruin her, over and over again, until no part of her body would ever forget him and she was wrecked for any other. Until he was etched all over her just as she was inscribed all over him. No other woman would ever compare to the tempest that was Bronwyn Chase. His perfect storm.

"You know I do," he ground out.

"Then I'm yours. Give me this tonight. That's all I ask, please."

She was begging *him*.

Valentine stilled, indecision and obligation riding him hard—the knight and the villain warring for dominance—and then he flew into action, tapping the roof of the conveyance twice so that the coach rolled to a smart stop. "Are you certain this is what you want?" he asked her in a low growl, the lust in his blood garbling his words.

"Yes."

He gave curt instructions to the driver and then they were off again, rolling past her residence...and the point of no return. The minutes passed and the tension grew until it was a solid thing vibrating between them with a life of its own. Valentine was so hard that he could feel each heartbeat echoing along his painfully aroused length. Her breaths formed in pants, hands clasped tightly and demurely in her lap, though they trembled. Those blue eyes bored into his, so much yearning in them that he wanted to bask in it.

She hid nothing—not her desire, not the need turning those irises to blue flame.

Bronwyn did not move from her position, each of them remaining in place as if they knew once either of them moved, there would be no stopping the wanton candescence that would occur. His skin felt hot and itchy, the slightest rasp of his clothing adding fuel to the fire.

Could a man have a spontaneous orgasm from a single protracted look? He felt the silken press of that blistering blue stare everywhere. In his lips, in his chest, in his cock. He pressed down on his groin with the heel of his hand, the spike of pleasure so intense that he nearly groaned with the relentless agony of it.

"How far is your residence?" she whispered in a rasp that prickled over his dangerously raw senses.

"Not far. A few minutes."

She bit her lip and then licked it. "Touch yourself."

"What?" he asked, blinking.

"Stroke your cock," she commanded, and holy hell, he

wanted to die at the commanding growl in her voice. His eyebrows rose, but he'd humor her, just this once.

Valentine splayed his legs wide and removed his hand from his lap, revealing the obscene bulge of his erection behind the placket of his trousers. He was so swollen that the length of him pushed down the side of his thigh, outlined under the fabric in vulgar detail. Her gaze went wide, a soft gasp escaping parted lips as she sat forward on the bench. She licked her lips again, those eyes of hers so bright with lust that they shone in the gloom of the carriage.

The angle wasn't ideal, but holding that feral gaze of hers, he ran his fist down his rock-hard length and hissed at the pleasure that filled his veins. Valentine stroked back up, wishing he could free his staff from the fabric and grasp it properly, but he was much too close and erupting like a geyser in her face would not leave the best impression.

"Take it out," she said.

His brows crashed together, fingers tightening to stop the impending explosion. "I'll spend, Bronwyn."

"I know. I want to see you come."

His hands fumbled at the fastenings of his fly, and then he was free, the air of the carriage kissing his hot, over-heated flesh. Wetness covered the broad tip, the rest of him purple and pulsing in his palm.

"Good heavens," she murmured on a shivery exhale, eyes fixed to his crotch. "It's...beautiful. And b-big."

Valentine let out a gasp as he stroked over his hard flesh again. The first was hardly the word he'd used to describe a man's cock, but he was glad she thought so, considering all of this was for her. The savage, hungry look in her eyes, coupled with the tight glove of his fist, made his body tighten.

"I'm close," he grunted.

"Show me."

And the sound of her husky voice was all it took before lightning crashed into the base of his spine and he was spilling in long ropes of seed onto his trousers. He worked himself through the release, milking every spurt and every pulse until the waves of pleasure ebbed, and all the while those blue eyes held fast in complete fascination.

"My word," she breathed, a glowing stare rising to his.

"You're next, never fear," Valentine growled and squeezed his still-hard cock, ignoring the wetness that seeped into his pants. "Last chance to change your mind because I am going to ruin you, Bronwyn, for any lover you'll ever know."

Her throat worked at the dark promise, but she didn't tell him no.

Twenty-one

OH DEAR GOD, SHE WAS A SODDEN, SOPPING MESS UNDER her skirts! Just from watching him take himself in hand. It had been beyond erotic, beyond anything Bronwyn had imagined. His staff had been thick and turgid, almost angry in its appearance as he'd throttled the full, impressive length. Her own core had clenched on air with every wicked stroke...the memory of his thrusts deeply visceral, coded into her body like a special cipher made for her.

And when he'd found his release, the expression on his face—that moment of utter bliss softening those hard, rugged features—had been mesmerizing. Plush lips had parted on a moan, and she'd wanted to crash into them. Swallow those sounds for herself. Even now, his passion-glazed amber eyes sought hers, promising nothing but sweet, sinful retribution.

An overheated Bronwyn watched as he put himself to rights, fastening his soiled trousers—thank goodness they were dark—and scowling as his hands brushed the wet fabric.

She let out a wry laugh. "Seems fair that I'm not the only wet one in this carriage."

Those golden eyes flared, lust gathering anew. "You are a tease, Lady Bronwyn."

"If I'm not direct with you, Your Grace, you tend to miss much subtler cues," she said with a coquettish flutter of her lashes. "And besides you like when I'm unspeakably blunt, don't you?"

"I do." The soft growl made her thighs quiver with anticipation.

The coach rolled to a stop and Bronwyn peered out the window, squinting into the darkness. They were not on a well-lit front street. Instead, they seemed to be in the mews behind the residence. That didn't mean that eyes weren't watching. In the last year, she'd learned that someone was *always* looking. She pulled her cloak over her head so that her face was hidden by the cowl. Thornbury descended and offered her his hand along the uneven cobblestones before ushering her inside the manse to a dark hallway.

She frowned. "Where are your servants?"

"Out or abed," he said, discarding his hat, greatcoat, and gloves on a table before moving to take hers. "When there is a ball and I am in residence, I give them the rest of the night off, once they've finished their duties."

"That's generous of you," she said.

"It would be an excruciatingly dreadful measure of a man if he could not open the door to his own home himself."

"Isn't that what they are paid for? I don't mean that in a haughty way," she said quickly. "Butlers are supposed to stand at the door and greet their master or guests."

He winked. "Not my butler. At least not when I need him in another capacity."

Bronwyn's pink mouth fell open as his intent became clear. "Your servants are informants?"

"I know you are pretending to be shocked right now, Lady Kestrel. There is an extraordinary network of information and secrets out there. I would be a fool if I didn't take advantage of it with loyal servants under my employ. In our world, information is gold bullion."

Valentine didn't blink at the fact that he'd said *our* world, but she heard it and a strange warmth filled her breast. The sooner he stopped treating her like a child who had wandered into her father's cigar room, the better it would be for everyone. He peered down at her. "Would you like a tour or shall we get straight to the main event, considering the whole of Scotland Yard might come looking for you once you're not discovered sick at home?"

It would be so like her mother to send the entire Metropolitan Police force after her. Bronwyn stifled a giggle and glanced around, eyes wide with interest at the muted but beautiful details of the foyer. "A tour, of course! I've always wondered where you lived, and now getting to see it is…like a glimpse into who you are." The look on the duke's face was priceless! She'd never seen someone look so dejected and try to shore it up with false energy. She snorted. "Good Lord, your face! The main event, you silly man. I don't care about any of the rooms in your house unless it contains a very sturdy bed."

With a laughing oath, Valentine scooped her up into his arms and tossed her over his shoulder, filling his palm with a handful of skirts, petticoats, and feminine charms.

God, he was strong. "Put me down this instant, you over-bearing ogre!"

He was already up the staircase and onto the landing by the time he replied. "Ogre? Ouch! That deserves retaliation." Her sinful tormentor yanked up her skirts, baring her silk-covered posterior, turned her body slightly and took a bite.

"You brute!" she nearly screeched.

He smacked his lips. "Tastes like apples."

"It's my soap as you very well know," she muttered inanely, her buttock on fire where he'd put his mouth and the rest of her aching to be licked, sucked, and bitten. Her sex was practically throbbing against his shoulder, until he kicked open a door to a very large bedchamber and deposited her next to an enormous bed. A fire danced in the grate, illuminating him in shades of flickering golden light.

For a moment, they just stared at each other. It was odd since they had coupled twice before, but this felt monumental. This felt more intimate than either of the other two incidents. Toeing off her slippers, Bronwyn spread her hand over the dark silk of the counterpane. The bed was massive, to accommodate his large frame, but the rest of the room was sparsely decorated. A mantel on one end and an armoire on the other, a pair of stuffed armchairs near the fireplace, and a potted plant. How many women did he bring back here? She forced that thought away. None of them were here now. *She* was. "I like your bed."

"Bronwyn," he began, and she held up a finger.

"I don't want to talk, Valentine," she whispered. "It ruins everything with us. We both know what we're doing here and the consequences of our decisions. If you are in agreement, then let us pretend whatever we need to for the sake of it. I don't wish to argue or defend my choices because I'm a lady and you're a lord, and neither of us is married."

He cleared his throat. "I was going to ask if you wanted a drink."

"Oh," she said, and then frowned when he ducked his head to hide a guilty smile and moved toward one of the armchairs to remove his boots and shuck off his coat. She studied him as he silently rolled each of his cuffs, and burst into laughter. "You cheeky liar. You were going to ply me with all the reasons this is wrong and we shouldn't be doing this, weren't you?"

A now barefooted duke stood to his full height and prowled toward the bed. She took a step back and bumped up against the mattress. "Am I so transparent when it comes to you?"

Bronwyn could barely breathe from the raw desire choking her when he bent over the edge of the bed, thick, bare forearms holding up his big frame and bracketing her in place. Clad in a midnight-blue waistcoat, a diamond stickpin winking from the folds of his cravat, tawny hair falling into his brow and cheeks, and eyes glinting with lust, he looked like a dissolute hedonist. Even his cheekbones were in firelit shadow, giving him an otherworldly look. A fairy-tale prince come to snatch her away from the world of mortals. Heavens, when had she become so fanciful?

"No, but you're careful with me, and you want to make sure I am here in full possession of all my wits and not coerced in any way."

Because he was a gentleman. A duke who had offered to wed her but for all the wrong reasons. Bronwyn didn't want him to resent her for it one day, and he would.

"And?" he asked.

"To be clear, you're what I want." Her hot stare clashed with his, as she eased out a breath from her tightening throat. "I want you to pleasure me so well that I all can see and feel is you. Make me yours, Valentine."

The growl that broke from his chest was so primal that all the hairs on her body stood on end. All of her nerve endings, every pulse point in her body, throbbed to violent life. Oh, she had no doubt this man *would* ruin her for any other man. Already her body craved his and only his. With a pained grunt, he tore off his waistcoat, buttons flying in his haste, and yanked off his cravat until he stood there in plain shirtsleeves.

The Duke of Thornbury was the most beautiful man she had ever beheld.

The most sinful. His shroud of ice had melted, leaving behind only fire and passion.

Bronwyn wanted to combust.

Holding his gaze, she reached up to the pins in her hair and removed them, letting her hair tumble loose, and climbed further back onto the bed. With one lazy hand, she walked her fingers down her bodice, slowing over the mounds of her breasts in a languid caress that had his jaw clenching before drawing up her skirts to bare her black knit silk hose.

He stared, mesmerized, nostrils flaring.

"Like what you see?" she whispered, suddenly unsure. Each of their past couplings had been hard and fast...with no slow seduction and heady perusals. The feel of those hungry eyes on her was as powerful as the stroke of his fingertips over her heated skin. One look and he could send her aching body to the precipice of release.

"I love what I see."

She parted trembling thighs. "Then undress me, Your Grace."

Her breath hitched when his knees hit the side of the mattress, and he stared down at her like a backlit god about to wreak havoc on the world. On *her* world. Her teeth sank into her lower lip with a moan, and his eyes dilated. "My word, you're exquisite."

With reverent fingers, he unrolled each of her stockings, warm lips caressing her skin all the way down. She wanted him all the way *up*...right to where it ached the most, but he took his time at her ankles, at the sensitive skin behind her knees, the delicate muscles along her thighs, and by the time he removed her drawers, she was a writhing, disconsolate mess.

He stared, eyes memorizing every curve. Reality intruded, and Bronwyn felt a flicker of uncertainly. No man had ever stared at her naked body or her exposed sex with such blazing intensity. "What's wrong?"

"Nothing, you're fucking perfection."

Need contorted his face, making those golden eyes half-wild as he bent and Bronwyn braced. *Lick me*, she wanted to scream. As he'd done on the ship. But all she felt was the barest kiss of his breath on her overheated flesh and his moan of pleasure as he inhaled.

"Turn over," he commanded in a hoarse voice.

The horrid, heartless beast.

"I want to see you without a stitch on this perfect body, my lovely Kestrel," he said. Bronwyn almost squirmed in pleasure. When had her handle become such a wickedly sinful moniker instead of a curse on his lips? "I want to touch every inch of you so that you never forget."

Bronwyn obeyed, the friction of her wet thighs moving together almost impossible to bear, and then his hands were working the laces of her dress and corset. Every press of the fabric against her flesh made her skin prickle. She was so aroused that each second felt like she was about to shatter. The mattress shifted with his weight as Valentine eased the garments off her body. Air kissed her bare skin and then…nothing. With her face buried in the bedclothes as she was, she couldn't see him, but she could feel him staring at her. It made her chest squeeze that she could bring him thus, to such a speechless state.

Bronwyn turned and propped herself on her elbow, glancing at him where he knelt on the bed, jaw slack and eyes so burningly bright they almost outshone the fire behind him. "You're the most beautiful woman I've ever seen, Bronwyn. I admit I did you a gross injustice by not worshipping this body in the manner it deserved. Twice." A fingertip chased down her spine, causing her to arch wantonly. It traced over the place on her arse where he'd bitten before dipping into the crease between her legs and making her gasp.

"Then do it now," she urged. "Hold nothing back. Not here, not with me. It will be our gift to each other." *A gift before parting.* Bronwyn closed her eyes, refusing to think of the end before they'd even started. "Your turn. I wish to see you as well."

He pulled the shirt over his head as she pushed up to her knees to unfasten his trousers. He kicked them loose. When they knelt facing each other in the altogether, bare of everything but skin and burning passion, in the middle of his bed, Bronwyn felt an odd sense of accord. That this was right where she was supposed to be in this moment. Here with him, her body making a forever pledge that only his could hear.

I am yours.

She reached up to touch his tight jaw. "Make love to me, Valentine."

The choice of words did not escape him. Strangely, they did not scare him either. This would not be like either of their previous encounters—he knew that for sure. Valentine had never brought a woman back to this chamber. Even when he'd been "married" to Lisbeth, any consensual relations took place in her room or when they were on assignment.

Kneeling toward each other as he and Bronwyn were now with no clothing or barriers between them, he felt a deep sense of vulnerability, as if every part of him, including his pounding heart, were laid bare before her. And for once in his life, Valentine didn't want to hide. He wanted to give her everything...all his flaws, his scars, his darkness.

Her fingertips traced over his smooth jaw, then traced over the parted contours of his mouth. First the upper lip and then the lower. Valentine resisted the urge to lick the pad of her finger. His eyes met her brilliant blue ones, almost glowing in the muted firelight. He could get lost in those eyes. It was as though she wanted him to see into her, too.

When her hand moved to cup the back of his neck and draw him close to her, Valentine didn't resist. Her lips brushed softly over his once, then twice, the achingly gentle strokes making his heart flutter quite unnecessarily. Hinging nearer so that her pert breasts grazed his chest, she kissed his nose, his cheeks, then his brow, the soft pulses bursting across his skin like the most treasured of touches. The tenderness of them sank deep into his marrow.

He let her, because he wanted it, too.

Valentine knew it was dangerous, this game they were playing with each other as if they had a future beyond this moment and this room...as if they were a duke and his duchess retiring for the evening in languorous familiarity. For one night, he could pretend that she was his. That they were each other's.

He slid his arm around her waist and drew her flush to him, making a gasp fly from her lips when her breasts flattened against him and his cock found a home in the juncture between her thighs. He chased it with his tongue, capturing her next heated breath. He couldn't get enough of her mouth, her scent, her taste. Valentine wanted to memorize it all. He almost wanted to force himself to slow down, but the passion was already beyond him, sweeping him up into the storm that was her.

"Bronwyn," he groaned when her fingers tangled into his hair and tugged, angling his neck to one side so that she could slant their mouths together more deeply, as if she, too, could not be sated with a few shallow nips and licks. Valentine wanted to bury himself in her heat, climb inside her skin and live there for all eternity. His thoughts were nonsensical, of course, but his brain was functioning at half capacity, if that. He'd never thought himself capable of such foolish, impulsive thoughts. Climb into someone? It was absurd.

But still, a part of him yearned... What would life be like with her, if circumstances were different? If he'd courted her properly. If she wasn't Ashvale's sister. If they hadn't collided the way they had. Before the ocean liner, Bronwyn Chase had always been a girl, the forbidden younger sister of his best friend, an option he could never entertain. But now, he couldn't imagine how on earth he'd ever managed to stay away.

A small voice tried to argue that it was nothing but lust, but Valentine knew it was far beyond that.

Bronwyn Chase was...life changing.

"Valentine," she moaned over his lips, dragging her taut nipples across his mat of chest hair and making them both gasp at the friction. He was so on edge, his skin felt like it was going to split apart at the seams, and yet, he couldn't stop touching her, mapping every velvet inch of her curves. He never wanted to forget what she felt like.

How responsive she was. How fucking beautiful.

His hands roved her back, from her slender nape along the deep sultry channel of her spine to the sweet rise of her buttocks, drawing her closer until there wasn't a sliver of space between them. Then he took her lips again in a drugging kiss before lying back on the bed and pulling her to straddle him. He groaned as the new position notched him right in the wet, warm haven between her thighs. "Take your pleasure, Bronwyn," he said huskily.

Those blue eyes went wide as she rocked against him, the slow, slick glide making them both shudder at the sensation. God, he couldn't wait to be inside her, but this was all for her. Valentine wanted every second of this interlude to be directed at her whims.

"I've read about this position," she whispered as he settled his palms over her hips.

"You'll like it," he said and winked. "Gives the lady all the control."

Her lashes fluttered down. "Does it now? It is rather scintillating to have such a strong, powerful man at my mercy."

He stared up at his goddess in all her glory with her wild brown curls and perfect creamy breasts tipped with the most luscious dusky-pink nipples. They were mouthwatering handfuls and suited her frame perfectly. Valentine's mouth watered, and he sat up for a taste, lapping his tongue over one of the taut buds and then drawing it into his mouth. When she moaned her approval, head arching back, he switched to the other breast, paying it the same devoted attention he'd given the first. The tight position had his cock lodged against her, and it twitched between them, the need for more friction searing.

"Put me inside you," he said hoarsely.

Bronwyn notched him at her entrance and then began the slow, deliciously excruciating descent. She was so wet and ready that gravity did most of the work, sheathing him to the hilt in one satisfying stroke. "Oh," she breathed. "It feels so extraordinarily full. It wasn't like this before."

No, because the previous times had been heated and rushed. This coupling was at the opposite end…every kiss savored, every touch cherished, every look revered. Even the clasp of her body was different. Joining with her had felt like coming home. Like he *was* home.

"You're made for me," he said through clenched teeth. "So perfect."

She peered down at him. "Then why do you look like you're in pain?"

Valentine forced his face to relax, but it was a strain keeping himself from spending before making sure that she reached her peak first. He was holding on by a damned thread. "Not pain, love, pleasure. Intense pleasure."

She rolled her hips with a sigh and he nearly swallowed his own tongue. "Oh, that feels good."

It was both bliss and torture watching her learn this newfound power of her own body. The slow, languid movements made his eyes roll back in his head, the furtive grind of her hips not nearly enough friction to give him the release he craved.

"Ride me, Bronwyn," he begged. "Hard, please."

A wicked smile graced her features as she tightened her thighs, but kept up the tiny pulsing motions that were driving him to madness. "I like this pliant version of you."

"You are a ruthless mistress."

"I had an excellent tutor," she shot back before bending forward to kiss him, nipping at his lower lip hard enough to make him gasp. She soothed the sting with her tongue. "Don't pretend you don't like it. You love me running roughshod over you."

Her channel gripped him like a glove as she straightened. His muscles strained as he struggled to keep himself from thrusting his pelvis, seeking the release that was nearly upon him from the soft pulsations. What was it about her that turned him into a fumbling novice? But then he couldn't think because she took pity on him and started to move, lifting her hips off of him and hurtling back down in a motion that made them both groan in pleasure when she was seated again. Eyes rounding, she quickened her movements, mouth parting as she chased the bliss that hovered just out of her reach.

"Valentine," she wheezed. "Please."

He couldn't even open his mouth to tease that the tables had so quickly turned, that she was the one begging him. It wasn't a competition. The only thing that mattered was her. "I've got you, love."

He lifted a hand to palm her breasts and squeeze her nipple. The answering whimper was reward enough, but it was when he slid his thumb down to the damp, needy apex between her thighs that her motions became more frantic. A sob broke from her as she rode a hell-for-leather pace, his own release looming on the heels of hers. Valentine circled with his thumb and he could feel her walls clamp down on him. He watched in indescribable wonder as her entire frame seized, her beautiful body caught up in the first throes of pleasure.

"Oh God."

Bloody hell, he'd never seen anything more stunning in his life!

"Time to rise and spread those wings, my beauty," he whispered, giving the swollen bead of flesh under his fingertips a decadent pinch. She screamed, eyes flying open, and pure euphoria crested over her features, mouth going slack as her body quivered over his. The undulations made his ballocks tighten, lightning driving through him as he bucked up into her before yanking himself free and spending onto his belly.

Bronwyn rode out the last few pulses, eyes unfocused with bliss. "That was different for us," she whispered after a beat, staring down at the mess he'd made on his belly with an odd look over her face that she sought to hide when she saw him looking. It was almost…regretful. He blinked—she was so adamantly opposed to marriage and a future with him, and yet, she seemed almost sad. "I'm glad one of us was thinking."

Valentine dragged a corner of the bedclothes and wiped his seed off his stomach. He gathered her into his arms and tucked her in to his chest. His heart was beating much too fast, but there was only one thought in his head.

"Marry me, Bronwyn," he said.

He could feel her stiffen before her muffled answer came, "I can't."

"Why?"

Her shoulders lifted with her short breaths as if she was struggling to find the right words to soften the blow he knew was coming. "This is sex, Valentine. You know that. We both know it. I can't let my heart get involved because I'll only set myself up for heartbreak." Her voice went soft. "You don't believe in love, and I…do. Someday, I want that for myself. Maybe that will be with Herbert, maybe not."

Valentine blinked, glad that she could not see his face… see the utter chaos that the soft words had caused and the sudden sensation in his chest as though something inside was cracking into pieces. She wasn't wrong about him. He was a pragmatist, a man ruled by wit and will, and not by his passions, and yet he'd never felt more like a stranger to himself than he did in this moment.

He'd never resented himself more.

Twenty-two

BRONWYN HAD LIED TO VALENTINE. HER HEART WAS well and truly involved, and heartbreak was *definitely* in her future. Hell, it was already here. Though she had no one to blame but herself that she had fallen stupidly and irreversibly in love with the duke.

Why couldn't she have fancied a sweet, uncomplicated man like Lord Herbert? If Thornbury was a roiling, stormy ocean, the charming young lord would be a placid, glassy lake. No, perhaps a pond with no depth whatsoever. Even the Marquis de Tremblay, dancing so gaily with her aunt, would have made a better option of a husband. Not that he *would*, considering how infatuated he was with her aunt and she with him, though they both tiptoed around it as if that would make it disappear.

Love didn't care about age.

Her mother had seen through Tremblay in half of a second, staring him down as if he were an insect that needed to be squashed when he'd offered to escort her to the ball. Be her foil, as they'd planned. But even he, with his perpetually pleasant mien, had withered like a flower facing the cruelest frost at the force of the marchioness's glare. Later on, Bronwyn heard him whisper to Aunt

Esther, "I am sorry, *chérie*, but I always thought you were exaggerating about your sister."

"No, which is why we have to save Bronwyn."

Bronwyn eased out a breath. There was no saving her now. Her future was a foregone conclusion, even with her heart pledged firmly elsewhere. She had known exactly what she was getting into by offering her body to Valentine Medford. This was her own fault. He hadn't wooed her and then lied, like other men in the aristocracy, or pretended to be someone he wasn't to impress her. In fact, he'd loathed her on cue, and she could have easily kept him at arm's length. And even after they'd run for their lives and given in to their mutual lust, she could have made different choices.

Could she have? Could she have resisted him? Resisted her own need?

Would it have made any difference?

No, not likely. Bronwyn did not regret her choices. She'd lain with him and she'd caught an inconvenient fistful of feelings, not that they hadn't been there before, simmering under the surface. She had been foolish, however, to believe she could keep her heart separate from her body. Truth was, she'd been half in love with the Duke of Thornbury ever since she'd met him at Courtland's home. It'd had started out as distant hero worship, and then evolved into something more. In her head, he was the perfect choice.

In real life, he'd been the *only* choice.

Even if his participation had been driven by lust or

the barest measure of fondness, Bronwyn had let herself believe it could be enough. Regrettably, she'd only succeeded in letting herself fall deeper and deeper into his quicksand.

"More like prick-sand," she muttered drily to herself and then giggled into her glass of champagne.

She lifted it, toasting his manhood silently. He did have a magnificent prick, and he certainly knew how to use it. Bronwyn chuckled again. Gracious, she was silly!

"What are you toasting?" an amused voice asked, and she turned to see her sister-in-law. Bronwyn choked on her sip. She could hardly admit the subject of her scandalous toast to her brother's duchess, of all people. One, Ravenna would laugh to the rooftops and draw too much attention, and two, the subject of the duke's rather excellent man parts was something Bronwyn wanted to keep to herself.

"Nothing, something about Thornbury." She wrinkled her nose. "Aren't you supposed to be in your confinement?"

"I'm with child, not infirm."

"Some people make it out to be the same thing," Bronwyn replied.

"Why are you avoiding everyone, loitering on this balcony like a lonely pariah?"

Bronwyn let out a bark of laughter. "Goodness, you're full of compliments tonight, aren't you? If you must know, I'm keeping an eye out. Lord knows why my mother decided to host a ball." She sniffed and gulped the rest of her too-warm champagne. "I mean, I know why she did—she wants to marry me off to that man over there." She surreptitiously pointed to Lord Herbert, who was wandering around the ballroom with a very put-out look on his face and clearly looking for someone. Her, obviously…which was also why she was here and *not* down there.

Bronwyn knew she'd disappeared for a handful of dances, two of which had been promised to him, but the thought of dancing with another man made her feel ill.

It's just a waltz.

Until it wasn't. There was a reason she'd safeguarded all her waltzes, and deep down, there was only one partner who would do. A man who wanted her, but did not love her.

"Does Thornbury know how you feel?" Ravenna asked softly.

Bronwyn blinked, the name sending the slightest of shudders through her. "Don't you mean Lord Herbert? That's who I pointed to. Him, the pretty blond in the light-blue waistcoat with the cherubic cheeks and Byronic smile."

He was too pretty, too soft, too agreeable.

Too *not* Valentine.

Good gracious, why couldn't she stop thinking about him? Herbert would be an excellent match. They would marry and make gorgeous cherubic children.…and she would be miserable in matrimony just like her mother. Heavens, she was twenty times a fool. She'd told the duke she would only marry for love, but what she had meant was that she would only marry *him* for love. Any other would do just fine.

He's not for you, Bronwyn. He's a solitary creature. A lone wolf.

"I don't mean Lord Herbert." Ravenna took hold of her hand. "Sister, what happened between the two of you? I know something did. My intuition has never failed me, and Courtland has been an absolute bear since you all returned from France. I've only seen him like that when something's amiss with you or Florence. Rawley is tight-lipped, too, and his eyes shutter every time I mention your name."

"Nothing happened," Bronwyn said.

Everything happened. She swallowed, her throat dry, and wished that she had more champagne, but that would mean going back downstairs and mingling. It would mean flirting with a man she did not esteem and giving *him* her precious dances.

"I don't believe that for one second," Ravenna said quietly.

Of course, she didn't. Her sister-in-law had always had an uncanny ability to see right to the thick of things. Bronwyn felt the warning sting behind her eyelids, the pressure in her chest expanding until it was impossible to contain. "What do you want me to say, Ravenna? That I love him? That he does not love me? That he's only here for duty's sake?"

She burst into tears, the emotion—and the admission—too much to take.

Beyond her sharp, spiky feelings, she knew very well why Valentine was here. He'd never leave her unprotected in public.

"Oh, my darling," Ravenna said, gathering her close, as much as her round abdomen would allow, and patting her back. Mortified at her loss of control, Bronwyn sniffed and reached for the handkerchief in her reticule. She hadn't cried since she was a girl, and here she was turning into a veritable waterspout...over a *man*, no less. "You love him, then?" Ravenna asked.

"As much as anyone could love a mangy, feral dog who licks your hand only to snap at it the minute you let your defenses down."

Ravenna laughed at her tone. "You're definitely in love. What are you going to do about it?"

Besides throw her naked body at him? Bronwyn bit her lips. "Nothing. He's not the marrying sort."

"Isn't he? Ashvale said he offered for you and you refused him."

Bronwyn gave her a helpless look, ugly feelings churning in her belly again. Perhaps she should have said yes, allowed Valentine to be the hero he needed to be. He could marry to protect a supposed damsel in distress...but one mention of love and the man was gone. It was his out, Bronwyn realized. In a few years, he could say, *You're protected and safe, so now I can leave.* By then, her heart would be inextricably wound up with his...and impossible to extract.

"He wanted to marry me as a safeguard."

Ravenna stared at her, brows rising, compassion in her eyes. "I see. Not the right kind of offer, then. One of very logical convenience." Clasping her hands over her belly, she inhaled a deep breath and perused the milling crowd. "You know many marriages start in strange places but get to where they need to be."

"Not everyone has true love binding them together since childhood like you and Courtland."

The duchess burst into laughter. "Not the case at all. I wanted to murder your brother on a daily basis. Still do. My point is our beginnings don't always veer to where we think they're going to go. Everyone's path is different. Courtland and I might have been forced to the altar, but I wouldn't have married him if deep down I didn't know he'd be an excellent husband." She patted her belly. "And father."

A twinge of envy ran through her before Bronwyn squashed it. No use hoping for things that could never be. "That's not the same here. In truth, we've both known from the start that getting involved would be a mistake. There's no room for love in whatever this is." She let out a breath, worried that she'd revealed too much. The last thing she needed was her overbearing brother forcing them to the chapel. "Besides, my mother has Lord Herbert at the end of her line. He's suitable and checks all the boxes."

"Except love."

Bronwyn eyed her sister-in-law. "You just said beginnings can be fickle. Perhaps my story with Lord Herbert will have a wondrous ending like yours."

"If that is what you want," Ravenna said.

It wasn't the least bit what she *wanted*. "Maybe that's what I need."

Stability. Constancy. Companionship.

Bronwyn's eyes swept the guests, searching for the one face she knew would be there somewhere…and the opposite of all those things. Valentine was passion and heartbreak, lust and impermanence.

Her gaze veered left as a face—one she did not expect to see and that made her stomach drop—disappeared behind a column. Bronwyn balked. The ugly brute from Philadelphia?

No, it couldn't be him!

But as she searched the crowd, her skin crawled as though a hundred spiders had been let loose upon her. Every instinct screamed for her to defend against a threat. If he was here in her mother's ballroom, and even if she'd conjured him out of misplaced fear, she could not take the chance that she'd imagined it and let any harm come to her pregnant sister-in-law. "Ravenna," she said in an urgent voice. "I need you to find Courtland or Rawley and get to somewhere safe. If you happen to see Thornbury, tell him I'm looking for him."

"Why? What's the matter?"

Bronwyn wasn't sure how much the duchess knew, and she also did not want to cause her undue worry. "Find my brother, and tell him the Kestrel is in flight. Please, Ravenna."

Her eyes widened, but she nodded and disappeared in a flash of blue skirts.

Keeping alert, Bronwyn made her way down the stairs. How her mother had managed to fit so many people into the ballroom was a mystery to her. A huge hand wound around her arm at the base of the staircase, and she nearly screamed when an equally large body crowded her into an alcove. "You scared the spit out of me!" she accused Valentine.

"I've been looking for you." He frowned at her, eyes canvassing her face to view the panic she could not hide. "Why so jumpy?"

"Why were you looking for me?"

His frown deepened when she didn't explain, but he answered. "The boy in France regained consciousness and is awake."

"What did he say?" she demanded. "Anything about accomplices?"

That gold stare narrowed on her. "As a matter of fact, he did. The man from the tavern in Philadelphia is cousin to one of the men on my report, the men responsible for the assassination."

She felt the blood drain from her face, the warning signals in the pit of her stomach making it roil. The American president had not survived the brutal attack at Ford's Theatre. If they could kill such a man, what would they do to her? Her body swayed.

"What is going on, Bronwyn?"

"I think he's here," she whispered and then shook her head. "I was on the balcony, and I thought I saw him."

The duke swore. "Here? Are you certain?"

"I don't usually forget a face," she said. "But it was so

fast, I can't be sure. I told Ravenna to find Courtland and get to safety."

"Good move." He eyed her. "Do you have a weapon on you?"

She patted both sides of her thighs, and those golden eyes flared with a combination of approval and heady desire. "Ravenna told me the Duchess of Embry used to cut holes in the pockets of her gown to access her knives, kukri she called them. I've done the same but with pocket pistols."

"Good girl." It should have been patronizing coming from him, but all it did was make her weak in the knees. Something was officially wrong with her head. She peered at him with narrowed eyes, expecting him to order her to stay hidden like the helpless damsel she was, but he gave a firm nod. "I'm going to walk through the ballroom. Keep an eye on the exits, if you can. If you see anything, break the biggest vase you can find."

Her brows pleated. "You're going to trust me on my own?"

"Yes, two sets of eyes are better than one," he said on an exhale and then rubbed the bridge of his nose with a sigh. "I must be out of my mind, but well, there it is." Bronwyn stared at him in utter shock. Had the most decorated spy in Britain deemed her an asset instead of a hindrance? She could not hide her grin.

"I suppose I'm official now. Do we get embossed calling cards? Is there a secret spy handshake? A special wink, perhaps?"

"God, that mouth. It's incorrigible." The duke started to move away, but then turned around and closed the distance between them with three brisk steps. With a blazing look, he hauled her to him and planted a hard kiss on her lips before releasing her. "Be careful. Don't get shot."

"You don't get shot," she tossed back. "Partner."

She was still smiling when he walked away with lengthy strides, already observing the guests as he walked the perimeter. Perhaps she should head back up to her small balcony. It provided an exceptional view of the entire ballroom. Bronwyn turned and promptly crashed into someone. "Forget something?"

The words died on her lips as she stared up into the ugly face of the man from the tavern. Even dressed in a bespoke suit of clothing, nothing could hide the craggy harshness of his face. The barrel of a gun pressed into her stomach. "You've caused a lot of trouble, little bird. Are you going to come quietly? Or shall I make an example of someone? How about the pregnant woman with you earlier?"

All the bravery bled out of her. "I'll come quietly."

It wasn't her fault that on the way out, she stumbled clumsily and crashed into a giant vase of flowers in the foyer. As she watched it smash into a million pieces, she hoped the noise would be enough to alert the Duke of Thornbury, wherever he was.

If not, she was on her own.

Valentine's head ached. The further he walked away from Bronwyn, the more troubled he felt. And it wasn't as though he didn't think she wasn't capable of defending herself. He did. She astounded him, to be honest. How a sheltered heiress had gone from being a debutante to running messages for the Home Office and crossing international borders to do so was beyond him. He used to think that it was foolish whimsy, but he was coming to realize that Bronwyn was far from a fool. She had a cunning mind and bravery that most men lacked.

And he was letting her go like water through his fingers.

She doesn't want to marry you.

His chest squeezed as if a huge hand had taken his heart in a tight fist. His feelings on everything were so muddled—tied up in the life he'd lived and expectations for the future. If Bronwyn knew some of the things he'd done in the name of Crown and country, would she look at him differently? She would. That was his penance. He was meant to be alone with that burden. Not foist it on someone else. The only person who'd ever understood had been Lisbeth because they were the same.

Bronwyn was light, and as much as his darkness craved her, he could not drag her down with him. She deserved someone like Herbert, whom everyone loved. Who was safe and steady. And who knew, maybe he would be the grand love she deserved. Valentine couldn't stand the thought of that wishy-washy boy kissing Bronwyn, *touching* her. Being the recipient of those wily smiles and weighted looks from those brilliant blue eyes.

He'd noticed her the minute she'd entered his sphere, his every sense attuned to her. In a stunning rose-colored gown that floated around her slender form, she was the loveliest lady in the room. From the tips of the ostrich feathers in her hair that had been dyed to match to her jeweled slippers, she was a vision. He hadn't been the only one in the ballroom left slack-jawed after her entrance.

A man came abreast of him. "Rawley," he said. "Good. Bronwyn said she saw someone in the ballroom."

Rawley gritted his teeth. "I told Ashvale to tell his step-mother that a ball was a bad idea with someone after Bee. She probably thought it was a hoax or some attempt to thwart her plans to barter off her daughter like a side of beef. And now that man is here. *Inside.*"

Valentine exhaled forcefully. "He would have found a way to get her to him, no matter what. Where is Ashvale?"

"Seeing the duchess home, and also fetching the Metropolitan Police."

"This is too much of a crush. If he is here, he could be anywhere. We need to draw him out somehow." But even as he said the words, he felt his skin pull tight. Typically, one drew a target out with bait, but not if the bait was on the other side of the ballroom.

He was running before he could even finish his thought. He'd left Bronwyn on her own when he really should have kept her with him. A part of him had wanted to let her know that the way he saw her had changed, but even her bright burst of delight was not enough to stop him from kicking himself. The man from Philadelphia was here for *her*!

The loud crash of something large splintering on the floor had him lengthening his stride, his heart thumping in his chest. He was almost running by the time he neared the entrance to the residence. Efficient footmen and maids were already sweeping up the mess.

Rawley caught up to him, his chest heaving.

"She's gone," Valentine said.

The other man blinked. "Taken by force?"

"Yes, I suspect so. From right under our goddamned noses." He clenched his fists. His entire body felt heavy and uncoordinated as if he were wading in mud. Even his brain felt unnaturally slow. "They can't have gone far, unless they're still inside."

"I'll search the house," Rawley said. "You go outside."

Valentine wavered on his feet. It was unlike him to be so undecisive, but he felt frozen with fear. At an urgent look from Rawley, he lifted a palm to his throat, inhaling great gulping breaths of air as he ran down the steps, his eyes checking all the carriages lined up for any sign of rose-colored skirts. She'd looked so beautiful tonight, too. Beautiful and *lethal*. He recalled the impudent look when she had tapped at her thighs, indicating her hidden weapons.

At least she was armed. That was one comfort.

Bronwyn was smart. If she was being taken somewhere, she would have left crumbs, knowing he wouldn't be too far behind. With several harsh breaths to cleanse his foggy head, he surveyed the top part of Upper Brook Street, watching each coach and each person, and then turned to the bottom. *There!* What looked like part of one of the pink fronds from her coiffure lay on the ground in a patch of mud.

Clever girl.

Valentine raced past it until he saw another on the corner of the road, turning onto Park Street. Bronwyn wasn't that far ahead of him, a few minutes at the most, but feathers could fly if there was a bit of wind, and then he would be in dire straits. Cursing, he ran faster, catching sight of yet another ripped frond. She wouldn't have much left at this rate. He ran down the street past the mews toward South Street and blinked at the crossroads. *Hell.* There were no more sodding feathers in sight, or if there had been, they'd blown away.

Which way, damn it!

Retracing his steps, he stared at the ground, searching for something, anything. *Come on, Bee, you know I'm right on your heels.* She'd be tickled pink to know that he was calling her by Rawley's nickname. Hell, he'd call her whatever she wanted when she was safe. That strange feeling rose from deep in his chest into his throat again, as if he was choking. He *had* to find her. Every second that went by—every sodding heartbeat—meant the odds of that were dwindling. Valentine had never felt so helpless in his life as he glanced one way and then the other.

Right or left?

Either decision could be wrong. The choice could mean life or death.

Toward Hyde Park or back to Mayfair. If the man was

going to kill her, Hyde Park would be the logical choice. Ice bled into Valentine's veins. Scrubbing a hand through his hair, he nearly roared his frustration. *Make a decision.* He turned right to go to the park and then saw the glint of something that caught the light from the gas lamp on the ground to his left.

A lady's hairpin. It could be anyone's hairpin.

His breath rushed out at the sight of the gilded lily. A second hairpin lay a few feet away—this one with a jeweled butterfly at the curve. Yes, these were Bronwyn's. He recognized them from the folly.

Valentine praised her dauntless, clever, brilliant self. He picked up his pace, running as fast as he'd ever run in all his life.

Twenty-three

BRONWYN TUGGED ANOTHER HAIRPIN LOOSE WHILE the man dragged her along like a rag doll. He was huge and strong, and she struggled to keep up, not because she was actively trying to slow them down—well, she *was*—but she couldn't with the brutal hold he had on her arm. With her luck, he'd wrench it off. His strong grip was more than likely going to leave bruises. The street had been too clogged with carriages for him to get them into a hansom, so they walked. Correction, *he'd* walked. She had been forced to run to keep pace.

Oh, she hoped Valentine had found her bread crumbs.

Her coiffure was practically mangled, while she was attempting to surreptitiously pluck the feathers and then when she'd realized how foolish that was because feathers were apt to *float*, she had resorted to her favorite hairpins. Not much better considering it was late evening and the things were barely visible in good light, but Valentine was shrewd and missed little. He wasn't known as the greatest spymaster in England for nothing.

"Move," the man at her side growled.

"Where are you taking me?" *To my death?*

Something worse?

But he only grunted and nearly yanked her arm out of

the socket. Bronwyn reached up for the last of the hairpins, the linchpin that was holding her mass of curls in place, when they made an abrupt left onto the Balfour Mews. She dropped it, and her hair, along with the rest of the ridiculous headpiece her mother had insisted she wear, fell down her back.

"What the hell happened?" the man growled, stopping to snatch up the jeweled decoration. He didn't care that it would be a clue for anyone following…. The piece had real gems clustered to its base and would be worth a few bob.

She stared innocently up at him. "What do you expect when you've been jostling me like a rag doll for the last quarter of an hour? This hairstyle is meant for light dancing, not vigorous activity."

"I wish he'd let me get rid of you."

Bronwyn perked up. So she wasn't going to die…yet. And who was *he*? Obviously, this man was not in charge and there was someone here in London, or from France or the United States, who was calling the shots. Who was the knave working for?

"Why haven't you?" she asked. "Seemed like that was the intent in Paris and Philadelphia."

He hissed as if she'd pressed on a raw wound, his mouth flattening into a hard white line as his fingers closed around her arm and made her wince. Cursing, he sent her a vexed look and then yanked her into the empty stables. The soft nicker of horses reached her ears, but no one of the human variety was around.

Bronwyn let out a breath and revised her statement when a shadowy form carrying a lantern loomed into view. Her heart kicked in her chest, hoping that it was the duke, but then a different feeling, one of relief filled her when the new arrival was made clear. He held a gun in his hand and looked quite fierce. Bronwyn wanted to whoop and stomp on her captor's instep, but she stayed still, waiting for his signal.

"Lady Bronwyn, my most unexpected success and the biggest fucking pain in my arse. Where's my goddamned list?"

She blinked at Wentworth. "Sir?"

But he only stared, waiting for her molasses-slow brain to catch up. *Oh dear God.* The employer of the man whose grip was currently crushing her arm was *him.*

Everything seemed to unravel in slow motion—the fact that her mentor in the Home Office was sneering at her, that the gun was pointed at her instead of her abductor, and the utterly numbing realization that the man she had trusted most in the world was not on her side.

Stay calm. Control your emotions. Valentine's words from the Bois de Boulogne arose as she faced down the deadly weapon.

"When did you decide to throw me to the wolves?" she asked, keeping her voice measured.

"You were always disposable, Lady Bronwyn." He strolled closer, waving the gun carelessly in the air. She clenched her teeth. If the brute released her, she might have a chance of getting to one or both of her weapons or even disarming him as she'd practiced. Wentworth was a trained operative, however, not a careless, hired cad. "You know, when you first approached Sesily and then me so boldly, wanting to do your part for God and country, I almost laughed, but you wanted to prove yourself so badly." He shook his head and tapped his chin with the gun. "Imagine my surprise when you turned out to be better than Sesily."

"Where is she?" Bronwyn asked, keeping her stare on him and her shock at bay. "What have you done with her?"

The bastard laughed. "Nothing. I married the bellicose chit."

"*What?*"

He shrugged. "Though lamentably, I had to send her back to San Francisco. She threatened to expose me and I couldn't have that. At least, not until I dealt with a few loose ends that could see me lose my position." Wentworth laughed. "She's the one who tried to extort you, you know. After I cut her off, she was hoping for money to hide from me and remain in England."

Poor Sesily. Valentine had been right—that note had been sent out of despair. To be that trapped and desperate, Bronwyn couldn't imagine. But that was the thing with a patriarchal society—a wife became her husband's property.

At least she was safe with her mother if Wentworth was telling the truth, but that would explain why she would not have received or responded to Bronwyn's correspondence from France. Which meant *Wentworth* had sent the note about meeting him at the masquerade.

"If you despised her so much, why marry her?" Bronwyn froze as the answer came much too readily. She exhaled. "You wanted her fortune."

"My very own American dollar princess. You see? This is why I love her," Wentworth said to the silent man still holding her in an iron grip, a proud look in his eyes that made Bronwyn want to spit on him. The lily-livered liar! He'd played both her and Sesily like a fiddle and they had fallen for it. "She's fast on her feet and intelligent to boot."

"She walked like her legs were made of lead," the man muttered. "Stumbling every two seconds. Crashed into a vase in her own home, lost her headpiece."

Bronwyn stiffened right as Wentworth stilled, his sharp eyes settling on her messy hair. Unlike the one with his paws on her, her former handler wasn't a fool. She saw the moment he realized that her hair would not have gotten into such a state without help or by her own design.

"Damn it!" he thundered. "Did you see anyone following you?"

"No."

Wentworth let out a coarse oath, his face going red with rage. "Go keep a lookout. Shoot if you see anyone."

When the man did as he was bid, Bronwyn forced herself not to move too quickly as blood rushed into her numb arm, prickles burning hot beneath the skin. Any big movements would be noticed, and she needed to be slow...excruciatingly slow to avoid notice. With an eye on Wentworth, she eased her hands to her sides where the false pockets had been sewn. *Slowly*, she urged herself, despite the need to rush. *There.* She was in. As if he could sense the uplift in her state, Wentworth frowned, eyes darting to her once more.

"Wait, Larry, did you check her for weapons?"

Halfway to the entrance to the mews, the man glanced over his shoulder. "Why would I? She was at a ball and she's wearing a ball gown."

"You're a bloody—"

But he didn't even finish his sentence as Bronwyn slid her pistols from their holsters in a well-practiced movement, cocking both barrels with the thumbs of each hand, and pointed one at each of them. "Never underestimate a lady in a dress."

Wentworth's mouth went tight, a vein pulsing in his forehead. "Give me what I want and no one will get hurt."

Bronwyn lifted a brow, despite her racing pulse, and fought to keep her arms steady. No need to offer him a shaky countenance as more ammunition against her. Her heartbeat thundered in her ears, but she refused to show this man any weakness whatsoever. "I have two guns, one trained on each of you, and believe me I'm more than capable of shooting straight with both. Hands where I can see them, Larry."

"Just get me the bloody list," Wentworth ground out. "And I'll never bother you again."

She frowned, torn between shooting each of them so she could get away and finding out what had driven Wentworth to this point. "Why do you want it so badly? *You* gave it to me."

"Because *he*"—Wentworth glowered at his surly counterpart with his hands in the air—"was supposed to retrieve it in Philadelphia and sell it to the Union general. Two birds, one stone."

That made sense. Information cost money. Wentworth would have gotten himself a pretty payout by selling it. "I thought you were married and rich now."

He scowled. "The dowry is gone."

"Why did you try to have me killed in Paris?"

"That was before I learned that Larry here lost the list."

Bronwyn's frown deepened. Something wasn't adding up. Wentworth was turning his back on everything he'd ever worked for, everything he'd *stood* for. He also wasn't lacking in fortune, even with Sesily's depleted dowry. In fact, in the year she had known him, he'd always been impeccably dressed. He could be up to his ears in debt, she supposed, but her instincts were firing. No, there was something else…something more than money.

"Why do you want the list so badly? Tell me the truth and we'll talk about a deal." She was playing with fire now, but confidence was the biggest part of this game. That and a whole lot of bluster.

Wentworth wasn't a man used to being questioned. She'd seen it when he'd interacted with Sesily, and also with her on occasion, but she had always put it down to the usual male arrogance and power posturing when a female's intelligence was involved. But now, she looked at him with fresh eyes. He loved power. He loved his position. What was threatening either of those?

"The shooter in France is on that list. He is linked to me."

She swallowed, her arms beginning to ache from holding up two small but heavy guns. "Linked how? Was he like me? An operative."

"Not exactly. A...relative."

Bronwyn blinked. He'd sent an assassin who was family to kill her? That wasn't it though. Her senses were still buzzing. "How is that related to an arbitrary list of names of American spies? You're wasting time here, Wentworth."

His face went dark. "You stupid, vain, puffed-up—"

"I'll stop you right there. Save you getting a bullet in your mouth for your efforts," a mocking voice drawled as the Duke of Thornbury sauntered into the mews with his own gun cocked and ready. "She's a marvelous shot. Seen her in action myself. Anyway, the lady can't give you your precious list because she doesn't have it. I do."

―――――

Valentine had the most untimely half erection ever. If there was anything more magnificent than the sight of Bronwyn Chase with a mass of glossy, wild ringlets tumbling down her back and over her shoulders, in that gold-threaded, rose-colored ball gown and holding two guns wide at twelve and six, then he didn't know what it was.

Because by God and everything holy, this woman took every breath of air in his lungs. She stood like a commander on a field of battle, stance wide, cheeks red, and eyes sparking with fire. She put on a good front, but Valentine could see the strain in her shoulders in the barest tremble of her hands. And if he could see it, he knew Wentworth could as well.

Valentine had overheard quite a lot of the conversation, and he, too, had been hoping that Wentworth would expose his reasons. The big brute, Larry, shifted and redistributed his weight to the balls of his feet as though about to launch himself in an attack, and Valentine tutted, moving the barrel of the gun into the man's side. "Don't even think about it. You and I have unfinished business. I'd hate not to get any fun in before I turn you in."

"Go fuck yourself," the man snarled.

Valentine made a shocked sound. "Such language, good sir, and in front of a lady no less. Wentworth, what kind of riffraff are you surrounding yourself with these days? Didn't your mama ever tell you that if you lie with curs, you'll get fleas." He sniffed. "I suppose not."

"Fuck you, Thornbury. You always thought you were too good for everyone else."

Valentine perused the man, pretending to falter in memory even though he knew exactly who the bastard was. "I remember you. The courier who fetched the newssheets and took the reports to the filing chambers for the senior staff."

"I worked my way up. There's nothing wrong with that."

"Yes, but there are ways—honest ways—of climbing the ladder and yours were rather questionable, weren't they, Mr. Wentworth? Then when you decided to steal confidential files and sell them to the highest bidder, that kept you flush for a good long while." Valentine nodded, even as he could see Bronwyn goggling at him from the corner of her eye. "Your son is awake by the way."

Bronwyn gasped. "Son?"

"The relative he mentioned," Valentine explained helpfully. "And the one who knows all of his big brother's aliases, including one on my very list."

"You have no proof of such a thing," Wentworth bit out, though his face had gone a little ashen, his control of his own weapon starting to waver.

Damn and blast! Valentine wanted to rattle him, but not enough to make him get a nervous shot off. Bronwyn could get hurt, and after the last half hour of sheer dread, that was something Valentine did not wish to experience again. He did not think his poor traumatized heart could take another scare.

"The French Sûreté offered him leniency in exchange for what he knew. Turns out, he knew a lot, especially about you. What do you think about that, Mr. Wentworth? Or should I call you Mr. Malcolm Sommers? Half brother to Brent Sommers. How long have you been working against the Crown? Going against the oaths you swore to God and country? You were helping your brother, weren't you, while lining both your pockets?"

Some of this was conjecture on Valentine's part, based on a decade of extracting information and putting clues together. When the list of names had been read to the boy in Paris by Rawley, on Valentine's direction, his reaction had been telling. It had only taken a bit more pressure for him to envision the rest of his life in the worst prison in Paris, Fleury-Mérogis, and blurt out that his father was a powerful agent in England. Rawley had tried, but no names had been given. Accusing Wentworth was an educated guess based on all the evidence. He could be wrong, but his gut told him he wasn't.

Valentine had arrested Brett Sommers and had him summarily deported, but he'd never been able to figure out how Sommers had been a step ahead of them. Well, now he knew. A traitor in the Home Office would have been valuable.

"You have no idea what you're talking about!" Wentworth growled, but the sweat beading on his forehead and the nervous shift in his eyes belied his words. He'd done an excellent job of covering his tracks but now his son could confirm that his father did, in fact, have an alias…and one tied to a notorious group of criminals.

His career was over, and he knew it.

"You would use your own son?" Bronwyn whispered. "He's barely out of school."

Wentworth's gaze swung to her. "Don't you dare judge me! That boy was a mistake. Always listening, poking his head in, rifling through my private correspondence. He took it upon himself to go to France and *help*." His gaze hardened. "Shooting at the sister of a duke in the middle of Paris? He deserves a stint in prison for his stupidity."

"At least he had the ballocks to do it himself," she shot

back. "And not hire ruffians to do so to keep his own nose clean."

Wentworth scowled. "It would have been so easy to dispose of you in Philadelphia. But who knew you'd have the most famed operative in Britain at your side?"

Bronwyn's shoulders shook. "I trusted you! I trusted you with my life."

"Look at the bright side, my lady. You thwarted an abduction."

"The president was still killed!"

Wentworth waved his free hand. "Our friends needed incentive, and an abduction was never going to be decisive enough to turn the tide."

Bronwyn broke into guttural laughter. "That's not going to turn the tide, you stupid man. Whether you're trying to preserve your lands or your privilege, people deserve equal rights. People like my mixed-race brother, like my friend Rawley who is a free Black man still fighting for others in America deserve to be heard. You might have shot a man who had these principles, but his values and opinions won't stop with him."

"Your *brother*," Wentworth spat out, "isn't worth the seat he occupies in the Lords."

"Is that what you think?"

Valentine could see the thoughts racing through her head, the signs of self-doubt and recrimination, the fact that she hadn't seen the scoundrel for what he was, but he could not comfort her. Not now, not even if every instinct in his body was roaring for him to protect and defend.

To *shield* the one he loved most in the world. But he also knew that taking his attention away from Wentworth would be a mistake.

The man snorted. "It's a fact."

"So you were just going to kill me?" She wasn't quite as adept at hiding the waver in her voice…addressing the man she'd trusted for an entire year.

He shrugged. "Accidents happen, and what on earth was the daughter of a peer doing gallivanting to America anyway? Meeting a clandestine lover? Caught in a lover's quarrel in a tavern?" Valentine cringed, remembering that he had wondered the same at first. Wentworth lowered his gun in a show of good faith, but neither Valentine nor Bronwyn lowered theirs. "Give me the list or destroy it, and we can all move on from this. You'll never hear from me again."

"You know I cannot do that." Valentine's jaw was hard. "I took the same oaths you did, only I still honor mine."

Wentworth narrowed his eyes, beginning to sense he was losing the battle. "What's it to you? You have no leg to stand on here. You have no proof besides hearsay from a boy with no claim to me. My word as an upstanding officer of Britain will stand."

"Will it?" Valentine asked softly. "He also gave up letters you wrote him with confidential information. Coded ones, with a cipher that belongs to a certain protégé of yours." He glanced at Bronwyn, taking in the suddenly sharp stare and mulish set of her mouth. "Which I'm sure she will be more than happy to share with the Home Office."

"I shall," she said immediately.

A high-pitched ugly mewling noise was all the warning Wentworth gave before diving toward Bronwyn. In the same moment, the silent Larry swung, his meaty body blocking any shot Valentine could have gotten off and knocking the pistol from his grip. The blast of a discharged weapon and the smell of spent gunpowder filled the air, and out of his peripheral vision, Valentine could see two bodies crashing into the wall. He had no idea whose shot it was, or whether anyone had been hit. He had his hands full with Goliath who was attempting to crush his windpipe with his bare hands.

Fighting loose by dropping like a deadweight and dislodging from the man's grasp, Valentine kicked out at his legs. The minute the brute was down, Valentine was on top of him, his fists flying at top speed. How *dare* he lay his filthy fingers on Bronwyn? He'd seen the purple marks of his manhandling on her arm.

"Valentine, stop." The sweet voice came to him as if from a distance, and then her beautiful face was in front of his, eyes wide and concerned. The bloodlust faded and he looked down at the mess of Larry's face. He was still breathing, if the thick wheezing, wet sounds were any signal, but Valentine didn't care.

"Where's Wentworth?"

Her mouth firmed as she hooked a thumb over her shoulder. "I threw my gun at him and it knocked him right out." She grinned. "You did advise me to throw anything handy."

Valentine couldn't help it; he let out a dark chuckle. "Well done."

Bronwyn stared at him, all heated, needy eyes and chest heaving with exertion and energy. Lips parting on a ragged pant he felt in his own lungs, her fingers curled into her skirts. Valentine could barely form a coherent thought but the one pounding a tempo to his heartbeat. She had done it. She had saved them both.

"What now?" she asked.

His voice was a hoarse, deep rasp. "What now what?" He was aware he sounded like an echoing imbecile.

"Valentine." The name on her lips was a whisper, a plea.

He stepped toward her in a trance and then reality intruded as the two men on the floor interrupted his vision. Reaching into his coat pocket, he removed the set of hand-cuffs he always carried and secured the much bigger Larry to a pipe along the floor. Then he found a leather lead from a nearby bridle hanging on a hook and used that to tie the unconscious Wentworth to a post.

There. Neither of them was going anywhere anytime soon.

Slowly, he turned to face Bronwyn, who had not moved a single inch, her eyes glued to him. "Did you have those handcuffs on your person all along?" He nodded, and her throat worked over an indelicate swallow, pupils dilating. "Do you have another set at home?" Valentine nodded again. "Can you restrain me sometime?"

Every single drop of blood in his body descended south.

If his erection didn't kill him, she certainly would. "Come with me."

Twenty-four

THE TINY TACK ROOM HE'D LED HER TO COULD BARELY qualify as a room, but it would do. Apparently the duke thought so as well because within seconds of the door closing behind them, Bronwyn was nearly bent over in half, face mashed up against a worn sidesaddle hanging over a bench.

The position was lewd and everything she needed as her throbbing pulse points rubbed on the rounded edges of the saddle. The warm scent of leather filled her nose, but she could barely appreciate it, her attention caught by the man lifting handfuls of her skirts. He kicked her knees wide, yanked down her drawers, and she moaned when air kissed her bare behind.

Within seconds, he thrusted into her, hot and thick, a groan pulled from the depths of him when he seated himself to the hilt. "I love being inside you."

"Yes." It was the only word she was capable of. No, wait...there was another. She pushed back against him with impatience. "More."

A breathless chuckle left him as he moved, filling her with hard, glorious strokes she felt so deeply that she wasn't sure where he began and she ended. Pleasure coiled along her nerves, spiking and gathering, as each powerful thrust rubbed her sensitive nipples against the saddle. Bronwyn's eyes nearly rolled back into her head when he tilted her hips even more, one hand flat at the base of her spine and the other reaching up to wind in the mass of her hair. She groaned.

"Is this what you want?" he demanded, never once slowing his desperate pace.

"Yes." It was practically a sob.

"You want me to fill you?"

She whimpered. "God, yes."

"Are you thinking of Tremblay? Or Herbert?" The strange question pierced through her lust-fogged senses, cold washing over her even as the sudden loss of him made her gasp. He lifted her from the saddle in those strong arms as though she weighed nothing and turned her to face him, eyes scouring hers. "Are you?"

What kind of a question is that, she wanted to retort, but somewhere deep, she recognized the shine of despair in those golden eyes as if it had torn him apart to ask. To expose himself thus…to be so vulnerable. This proud, hard man who had never bent before anyone.

"No," she answered honestly. "I only think of you."

His reply was to ease between her spread legs and push back into her, but the stark gratitude in his eyes was worth the bit of honesty. They both groaned at the fit from the new angle, and her eyes fluttered shut when he hit a particular spot inside of her that made her vision go white. "Open your eyes, Bronwyn. Look at me."

She did. His eyes blazed gold as they held hers. He

was so handsome, it made her heart hurt. She loved his face. All harsh lines and slanted hollows, heavy slashes of brows, bold nose, prominent cheekbones, and that lush mouth that was so spare with sweetness unless she was tasting it. She loved all of him, and he could never know how weak she was when it came to him. If he asked her to marry him now, she wouldn't prevaricate. Bronwyn felt him where they were joined, and she felt him moving in her heart and under her skin.

His stare drilled into hers, taking something from her soul that she wasn't sure she was willing to share. Not yet.

Something inside of her gathered and built, even as his control started to become ragged. He kissed her, his mouth claiming hers as if there wasn't a part of her he meant to leave unconquered. They might still be fully clothed, but every single important part of them was bare. "Stay with me, Bronwyn. Choose me. Please."

The whisper lanced through her, making tears prick her eyes. "I can't... You know—"

"I love you."

Bronwyn's world exploded in a shower of fireworks so bright that her body felt like it would bow in half from the force of it. She squeezed her eyes shut, muffling her cries with her own hand. Valentine rode her through it, strokes changing to something slow and delicious as the pleasure rolled and ebbed through her. Dear God, had she imagined what he'd said? Had he said it in a mindless haze?

His pace slowed and he withdrew from her, while supporting her boneless body against his. Confused, she glanced down at his obviously unsatisfied state and blushed. "You didn't... You haven't..."

"No." Valentine ran a hand through the damp tendrils of hair curling onto her cheeks, the touch so tender, so *unlike* him that she blinked. "I don't want you to think my confession was in haste or in the throes of passion," he said softly. "I meant it. I *love* you, Bronwyn. When I realized you'd been taken and that I might lose you tonight, I've never felt a fear so deep. And worse, I never told you how I really felt."

"Oh."

Everything inside of her started to tremble. Her lover, the very handsome, very virile Duke of Thornbury, had just declared his love in the most incongruous place in London. While in the middle of sexual congress. In the tack room of a public mews. With two vigilantes tied up in the next chamber.

Bronwyn could not help it. She burst into soft laughter and ran her nose down his jaw, inhaling him. "Hardly the place for a romantic declaration, Your Grace," she whispered with a smile.

"It's the perfect place and time for a declaration. Whenever I am inside you is the perfect time and place."

She bit his jaw. "You're not inside me anymore."

His arms tightened around her back as he gathered her close. "Not until I've said it all. I've never truly had anything to lose, until you came along, crashing into my well-ordered life with your charm and your cleverness, and I was spellbound. The truth is, Bronwyn, I don't know when you stole my heart, ragged, undeserving thing that it is, from right beneath my nose, but you have. It's yours, even if you decide you don't want it."

She wanted it. She wanted *him* more than anything. But perhaps it was time for a little retribution. "I shall require convincing, sir. In fact, I shall require you to beg for my favor."

Valentine met her eyes, and Bronwyn lifted a brow. "Dukes don't beg."

"Since when do you ever do anything society expects of you?"

"That is true." He snorted. "I am admittedly an abysmal duke. I expect most of my tenants will scatter at the sight of me when I eventually go to Scotland."

"Why would they?" she asked.

"I'm a harsh man, Bronwyn. I'm not likeable or young or perfect high society fodder. I've done and seen things that have changed me. I don't know how to be a duke. How to be...the perfect gentleman." Bronwyn's breath hissed out. He wasn't talking about Scotland at all.

"Be yourself. That is enough."

"Is it?" When she nodded, he kissed her nose, eyes glinting with so much warmth—and *love*—that her breath fizzled in her throat.

Bronwyn slid her arms up around his neck, needing to feel him close. It felt as if she was imagining the whole interlude. His openness. His sweetness. His tenderness. This vulnerable side of him that only she got to see. "You've always been enough, Valentine, whether you were an earl, a spy, or a duke. You just weren't ready to accept that."

————————

Valentine bent to bury his nose in the crook of her neck, the skin there already cooling from the fine layer of perspiration on her velvety skin. She smelled of spiced apples, and he wanted to devour her whole. Her pulse rose and crashed at the base of her nape, but she remained excruciatingly silent on the subject of her true feelings. Of her *love*. He supposed he deserved that…just because he had been ready didn't mean she was. The thick wall of ice surrounding him had done its job well. *Too* well. Perhaps she did not believe him.

His hopes plummeted, like a falling star. "I didn't mean to spring this on you. I'm sorry."

"Don't be sorry," she rasped, the soft waft of her breath blowing into his hair. "I just need a minute."

"I understand," he whispered.

"What about everything you said before? That love wasn't for you?"

He huffed, gliding his lips along her soft skin and feeling his cock twitch. His desire for her hadn't abated in the least with his declaration. Instead, it had increased. "I guess I'm the fool then, aren't I?" He kissed her eyelids. "To be bewitched by a pair of bright-blue eyes and a luscious mouth." His lips moved to hers, for the sweetest graze from corner to corner before pressing into their plush depths. "A wicked tongue that could reduce the most hardened of men to mush." His tongue licked hers in a move that made her gasp and writhe against him. "A brain that could bring any foe to mercy."

"Valentine?"

"Yes, love?" he asked.

"Are you ever going to stop talking and finish what you started?" His little virago tightened her arms around his neck, hitched her fallen skirts, and hooked her legs over his hips. "Inquiring minds need to know."

"As my lady wishes."

When he slid into her anew, it felt like home. Where he belonged. And when he began to move, Valentine's whole world shifted. So this was what it felt like to offer himself up fully, without holding back. He made love to her tenderly, despite their location, though when had that ever mattered to them? She hadn't said she loved him back, but he would wait.

Bronwyn was worth the wait.

He felt her body tighten deliciously around him before she gasped out, fingers digging into his shoulders. "Faster."

Valentine quickened his strokes, wanting to find his release with her, wanting this moment to be perfect. She was beautiful, caught in the throes of passion, lips parted, pupils dilated, her creamy skin marked with a beautiful flush. She would always be the most exquisite woman he'd ever seen. When she cried out, her muscles clenching around him as she tumbled over the precipice into bliss, again he gladly followed.

He'd follow her anywhere. Into pleasure. Into purgatory. Into the unknown.

His release went on and on, as if that part of him, too, refused to let her go.

"Valentine, kiss me," she said breathlessly and he did. He kissed her with everything he held in his heart…all the warmth and the budding trepidation, the joys and the heightening worry that he might have been a hair too late in his avowals. That she might have set her sights on someone else. That she might never love him back. Why did people ever give in to love? It wrecked and it took, and left devastation in its wake.

Her fingers cupped his jaw as those heavy-lidded blue eyes bored into his. He let her see it all. He had nothing left to hide, not from her.

"I love you," she whispered.

He blinked, sure that he'd imagined the soft declaration. "What did you say?"

"I've always loved you." She blushed and ducked her face as if to hide, but he wasn't having any of that. Valentine wanted to see every emotion, relish everything that crossed her expressive face. He tipped her chin up, the sight of those blues a benediction he would never tire of, not in his lifetime. "I wouldn't have given myself to you so easily if I hadn't."

Sighing softly, he pressed his mouth to hers. "I'm sorry I'm such a buffoon and it took me so long to realize it. I didn't know what I had until I nearly lost you." He kissed her again, unable to help himself, and gently withdrew from her body, before tending to her and then to himself with his handkerchief. Smoothing the skirts of her gown into place and fastening his trousers, he suddenly felt unsure of where they went from here. All his cards were on the table. Would she refuse him now? He supposed he could take the coward's way out and wait.

Or he could…

"Be my duchess," he blurted out. "Please, Bronwyn."

She laughed, the light sound filling him like nothing ever would. "A proposal in a tack room?"

"Suits our story, don't you think? We've never done anything the proper way. Our courtship has been arse-backwards from the start."

Still chuckling, she leaned forward to brush his lips with her own before her eyes met his. They were full of mirth, love, and wonder. "Yes, Your Grace, I'd say it suits us rather well. And yes, nothing would make me happier than to be your duchess."

A thumping noise from the next room had them leaping apart, giving Valentine no chance to celebrate her answer before the door crashed open and a wild-eyed Wentworth advanced on them, a gun in each hand—the ones Bronwyn had dropped when he'd barreled into her. A bruise had formed on his temple, and a thin trickle of blood meandered down his cheek and jaw.

Valentine let out a bitter curse—he should have found some rope. Leather was good in a pinch to restrain someone, but it loosened too quickly, and he hadn't actually planned to take Bronwyn into this room and have his way with her. He grunted, putting his body in front of her and blocking her from view.

"She has nothing to do with this," he said. "Let her go and we can sort through this like men."

"She has everything to do with this! If it wasn't for her running off in Philadelphia, none of this would be necessary," Wentworth seethed, his eyes crazed. "This report. That stupid boy. No, no. I won't go down like this and I won't go to prison." He shook his head as if to clear it, as if he couldn't think.

Valentine felt a beat of real fear. The man was unhinged. People tended to get like that when they felt cornered. He held out his hands in a placating gesture. "What do you want? The list? I can get you the list. I can get rid of it. But you have to let her go."

"I can just kill both of you."

Valentine nodded, keeping his voice modulated. He could feel Bronwyn pushing against him, but at least she was smart enough to stay behind him for the moment. He had a pistol tucked into his boot, but with the way that Wentworth was flailing around with the guns, he didn't want to take any chances. The best way, for now, until he could figure something out, was to keep the man talking. "You could, but then there would be two bodies and an investigation. You know how it is. Someone might have seen you or your man outside."

"You always were smart, weren't you? I told my brother to stay away, but he wouldn't listen. His own arrogance cost him. But you, you, Thornbury, always a step ahead." He scowled. "Even with her."

Wentworth twitched again, and Valentine wondered if Bronwyn's hit hadn't knocked something loose in his head. He seemed deranged, tapping his head with the handle of one of the guns, and mixing insensible words with coherent ones. He glanced around, eyes widening on them, his head lolling from side to side.

"You were swiving in here, weren't you? I can see the lust written all over you." He leered. "Was she good? I always wondered if she was loose in morals. Perhaps I should kill you and avail myself of her sweet body. Then I'll shoot her. It will be like a scandalous lovers' quarrel."

Valentine felt Bronwyn stiffen behind him and turned his palm at his side slowly to where she could see it. He had no idea if she was looking down or not, but he pointed toward his right boot. There was very little chance that someone wouldn't get shot, but with two guns in play, he wanted to even the odds that it would only be him in danger. A few short taps with her fingers on the middle of his back let him know that she understood. It would take some coordination and finesse, but first they needed an opening.

"No one would believe you," Valentine said evenly. "I proposed to Lady Bronwyn just this evening before your man abducted her. Ashvale would never believe it. There would still be an investigation."

Wentworth shrugged. "I could say that the lady and I were seeing each other in secret for months, and you were a jealous lover."

"People, like her mother, would ask questions."

Wentworth stared at him and let out a frustrated roar that went to the rafters, making the horses in the nearby stalls whinny and stamp. "I need to think. I can't bloody think!"

"Let Lady Bronwyn go, and then you and I can talk."

Wentworth shook his head, pacing back and forth. "You're trying to trick me. Let her go so she can call for help? I'm not a fool, sir."

The seconds ticked by with their options dwindling. Perhaps he could make a dive for the guns and hope to take Wentworth down before he got a shot off. He seemed distracted, which could bode well or ill. Either way, there was no guarantee Valentine wouldn't get killed by being rash. Or Bronwyn.

"Your Grace," he heard her say from behind him. "I don't feel well. It's too hot in here. Oh, dear me, I'm going to swoon."

Wentworth's eyes fastened on them, but he didn't do anything but watch as Bronwyn let herself slump in a slow graceless slide down to the floor. Valentine didn't dare look down. He kept his gaze firmly on the man with the guns.

"One down," Wentworth said. "Guess she doesn't really have the stomach for this business after all. Or did you tup the strength right out of her?" Valentine knew the vile rotter was trying to get a rise out of him. He might have a few screws loose, but he was still the same man who was drunk on his own power. "There, you wanted me to let her go, and she has handled the matter nicely for both of us. Where's the list?"

"At my residence," Valentine said.

"Then that is where we shall go," Wentworth said, his tone becoming firmer as he nodded to himself. He pointed a gun at Bronwyn's prone form. "Pick her up, and don't trying anything clever. I have no problems shooting you both and letting the chips fall where they may. Jealous lovers, cutpurses, any story will do. Now, move."

Valentine nodded, turned, and crouched down slowly. Bronwyn was pale and listless, her chest rising with barely any motion. He frowned. Was she pretending or had the faint been real? But as he gathered her limp form into his arms, he realized with some relief that it was the former when he felt her fingertips ease into his boot and then quickly tuck against her stomach. Carefully, he half rose with her in his arms bridal style when she pretended to awaken, eyelids fluttering, her lower half sliding down the front of his. The pistol was concealed between them.

"Are you well?" he asked.

His beautiful, clever future duchess smiled, her blue eyes clear and bright. "Never better, my love."

Then she stepped to the side and fired.

Epilogue

THE DUCHESS OF THORNBURY STARED AT HER HUSband, who was in the process of fixing a broken window in their bedroom that had fallen off its hinges after his herculean attempt to pry it open. Did she mention that he was shirtless? He was, mouthwateringly so. She let her eyes drift over his wonderful musculature and felt her breath quicken. Even though she was well and truly sated. Moving any muscle of her own required intense concentration. Except for her eye muscles... Those could move quite well apparently.

Heavens, he had such clever hands. Fixing a broken hinge...stroking her body to indecent heights. Her lower half warmed.

"Enjoying the show?" her husband asked, watching her over his shoulder as he reattached the hinge.

"I like watching you do menial things," she said from her indolent position on their marriage bed, her bottom half covered only by a loose silk sheet. Her duke tired her out thoroughly, and they'd steamed up the bedchamber so deliciously that they had to open a window to let in some cool evening air. Until it practically fell off one hinge, that was. She peered at him from a hooded gaze, knowing the picture she presented.

"Besides, I cannot move, remember?" She jangled both arms still loosely attached to the headboard. "Do you plan on letting me out of these anytime soon, Your Grace?"

"You were the one who asked for the handcuffs," he shot back, turning to give her a breath-snatching view of the front of him. She loved looking at him, almost as much as she loved putting that honed body to use.

"You did promise I'd be in them at the end of all this."

The corner of one lip curled into a sultry smirk. "That is true."

They had only been married a few weeks and were still in Scotland. Their wedding in the Highlands had been intimate and tasteful with mostly family in attendance, but even the Willingtons had made the journey. Courtland and Ravenna, along with their latest addition, Isla, had come as well, though to no one's surprise, the Marchioness of Borne had been conveniently ill. Aunt Esther had more than made up for her absence, however.

Since their vows, Bronwyn and Valentine had been insatiable. Occasionally, they ended up in bed, but her husband had a penchant for finding her in the most incongruous of places—from the gardens to the attic, and practically every usable nook or cranny in the residence. He'd even pulled her into a bedding closet once, and they'd scandalized the daylights out of the housekeeper. But they were enjoying their honeymoon so they were supposed to make mischief...and love. Constantly, it seemed.

Thank goodness, there were no more clandestine adventures.

The Duke of Thornbury was a respected peer, and she was now a duchess with a role to play. Bronwyn hadn't given up all her plans, though she was accomplishing them in a less subversive way via charitable endeavors that raised funds for families displaced by the American Civil War, especially those of people of color forging new lives in England, the West Indies, and America. And when she saw opportunities to better conditions for immigrant workers in Britain, particularly those who weren't white, she was sure to raise discuss the issue with her brother in the Lords. Courtland had meant every word he'd said about valuing her voice.

The scandal had taken the newssheets by storm: *Corruption Tarnishes the Home Office.*

When all was said and done, Wentworth, who had survived Bronwyn's shot to the abdomen, and his accomplice, Larry, had been arrested and charged with numerous counts of criminal activity, including coercion, fraud, and attempted murder of a peer. Thanks to Bronwyn's rather thoughtful and excellent husband, Sesily was no longer tied to their lying, manipulative former handler. Their marriage was annulled and she had decided to remain in San Francisco to help in her mother's tireless efforts toward civil rights and equality. She and Bronwyn wrote to each other often.

The Duke of Thornbury and the Countess of Waterstone had received the queen's own commendation for their part in bringing the villains to justice. When a malicious Wentworth had tried to pin the identity of the infamous operative, the Kestrel, on Lady Bronwyn, he'd been derided by the gossip rags.

As if the daughter of a marquess, the sister to a duke, and a future duchess could ever be a spy! Bronwyn and Valentine had laughed, mocking the terribly small minds of the aristocracy, but he had appreciated not having to apprehend or testify against his own wife. Lisbeth had confirmed that the Kestrel, who was purportedly working under secret orders from her, had been killed in action in Philadelphia while attempting to thwart the treasonous acts against the American president.

Not long after the arrests, Rawley and Cora had tied the knot in Antigua, where they'd decided to live, and the celebration of their union had been one of joy and love. It had been one of the most beautiful ceremonies Bronwyn had ever seen.

When Bronwyn and Valentine announced their own engagement to her mother after they returned from Antigua, however, as well as their intention to have an engagement of only a few months, the Marchioness of Borne had been horrified.

"I won't allow it," she'd said in a half shriek as if on the cusp of a fit of the vapors. Aunt Esther had rolled her eyes and reached for the smelling salts, making her sister give her a withering glare. "I've promised you to Lord Herbert, Bronwyn."

Aunt Esther had scoffed. "She's not a goat to be traded, Evelyn."

"Stay out of this, Esther, or so help me…"

"Yes. You clearly need help." Her aunt had let out a snort worthy of a thespian. "Or a good round of blanket hornpipe to work out all that tension."

The marchioness had reared back, face going puce. "Good Lord, must you be so vulgar? Don't think I don't know what you and that sordid Frenchman are up to in this very house!"

"Must *you* be so straitlaced?"

They'd stared at each other in strained silence, mirrors of each other in appearance and yet so firmly opposite in nature. Bronwyn had shaken her head. Her mother could stand to let loose, and Aunt Esther, well, she could do with some boundaries, but they were both rather set in their ways.

"He's a duke, Mama, and he outranks Lord Herbert," Bronwyn had interjected before the twins started shedding blood. "Shouldn't you be happy? I shall be a duchess."

"A *Scottish* duke," her mother had muttered as if the very thing was blasphemy.

Bronwyn had almost laughed at her aghast expression. "Don't worry, you still have Stinson and Florence. Perhaps they will find the blue blood you so desire, and you can balance out us scoundrels in the family."

In truth, it didn't much matter what her mother thought. As much as Lady Borne had given birth to her, some of her opinions as well as her behavior were truly execrable, and the way she treated Courtland was unforgivable. It was difficult and disappointing when such intolerance was in a family member, but sometimes space needed to be taken. Bigotry was an ingrained thing—brought on by a lifetime of privilege—but that didn't mean people could not change, and Bronwyn meant to lead by example.

One day, her mother would learn. It wasn't Courtland's job to educate her on his heritage; that was *Bronwyn's* work, if she chose…and she did. Because it meant something. Broadening a single person's point of view could make all the difference.

"What are you thinking about, Duchess?" her duke asked, coming to stand beside the bed and staring down at her with an appreciative look. "You were frowning quite fiercely."

"Privilege…and my mother…and the fact that she might never learn."

He lifted his brows. "Heavy thoughts."

"Sometimes necessary ones."

Her duke tugged at the edge of the sheet, bringing it dangerously low on her hips. "But not in bed, however."

"One of these days, Your Grace, we will have to leave this bed and get back to the real world."

"But I love it here."

Bronwyn shook her head at him as he pouted that full bottom lip and looked positively edible. This was the problem with them. One sultry look and her brain dissolved into mush.

"Will you release me?" she asked, jangling the cuffs.

"You look like the *Venus de Milo* in repose with the sheets draped just so," he said, his golden eyes darkening as they took in her exposed breasts and belly with undisguised relish.

"That statue has no arms."

He smiled. "Yours are restrained. Seeing you thus does things to me."

It did things to her, too. A forgotten memory of her adolescent fantasies flitted across her thoughts. She let out a low laugh. "Did you know I used to fantasize that I was Andromeda chained to a rock waiting for the sea monster to come?" She licked her lips, cheeks heating. "Only the monster was you."

His eyes flared with desire at the image. "Was I fearsome and...*large*?"

"Now you're just fishing for compliments," she replied laughing. "Yes, very well, the largest I have ever seen. Actually, the only one I've ever seen. I've no basis for comparison with other sea monsters, you see."

"Yes, I see, and we shall keep it that way," he growled with possession in his voice. He kicked off his trousers as though he meant to stake his claim—*again*—then and there, and Bronwyn's eyes went wide, her throat dry. Monster, indeed.

"Good God, Your Grace, surely you have tired yourself out by now? Your duchess is famished and needs to be fed."

"I need to be fed." He climbed onto the edge of the bed with a playful growl and tugged the sheet off, his mouth going slack. Gracious, she loved the way he looked at her. Bronwyn had wondered as the months had gone by if he would ever tire of her or lose interest, but his eyes always glowed with that scorching combination of lust and love. "Not even the *Venus de Milo* can compare to your perfection."

She rolled her eyes, though she blushed at the praise. "I think the Duke of Thornbury is addled with hunger as well."

"Hunger for you," he said, climbing up her naked body and kissing each of her breasts and then her lips. With a deft twist of his fingers, he released the locking mechanism on the handcuffs and placed them on the bedside table. He brought her arms down and she moaned softly as he massaged her wrists. "Sore?"

"No, but that feels good."

She wrapped her arms around his back and traced the muscles she'd ogled before from the rounded tops of his shoulders to the firm globes of his arse. He was so hard. Everything about him was hard, including the part between her thighs.

He peered down at her. "I thought you were hungry?"

Her blush deepened. "Well, when it comes to you, I am voracious, it seems."

"The feeling is entirely mutual, my love."

With a laugh, he took her into his arms, burying his nose in her hair and inhaling deeply. He could never get enough of her scent, he'd told her. Valentine had loved it so much that she'd had to have another batch of the special soap made and delivered from the apothecary.

His stomach chose that moment to give an obnoxious growl, and she laughed, poking him in the chest.

"What do you say we feed each other," she suggested.

"And then we can spend the rest of the day playing try-to-catch-the-naughty-spy. That way you won't collapse when the dastardly and devious Kestrel puts you through your paces."

A slow grin limned his lips. "I knew I married you for that superior intellect of yours."

"Don't you forget it, Duke."

Her husband took her mouth in the sweetest of kisses, gentle but with enough bite to make her swoon. "Never, my brilliant, beautiful, wicked love."

Author's Note

Research is one of my favorite things to do, especially when delving into historical timelines and trying to figure out how to tie a fictional story into actual events. The idea for the Kestrel—my international female operative—going to Philadelphia with information to thwart Lincoln's abduction on March 17, 1865, came from the fact that no one really knew what made President Lincoln change locations at the last minute, which foiled John Wilkes Booth's abduction plans (even though the president was assassinated by the same man a month later). I thought it would be an interesting tie-in for the story.

Before I delve into that, however, I want to point out that the American Civil War was a very fraught and painful period in history. While this series aimed to be inclusive and incorporate people of color as researched during the Victorian era, the concept of race is not anachronistic, though more modern terms for racial identity might be. In the interests of being as transparent about race as possible so as not to erase the harms of oppression, for race identifiers, I opted to use skin tones for white, mixed-race, and Black characters instead of harmful descriptors of the period as well as the modern capitalized version to center the appearance of Black characters in the story.

It is my hope to encourage discussion about positive allyship and what this means in the context of current race relations without being performative, othering, or supremacist. On the advice of a sensitivity reader, these references were incredibly helpful to me: bell hooks's essay, "Eating the Other," from her 1992 book, *Race and Representation*; Toni Morrison's *Playing in the Dark: Whiteness and the Literary Imagination*; and Ta-Nehisi Coates's article, "What This Cruel War Was Over," in *The Atlantic*.

I based my heroine, the Kestrel, on real-life female spies during the era. Elizabeth "Crazy Bet" Van Lew was a white Civil War spy from Richmond, Virginia, who freed all her slaves when her father died and used every penny of her wealth toward the Union cause. To stay under the radar and fool everyone around her, she pretended to be vapid and witless, which was effective at making her invisible. Van Lew got the nickname "Crazy Bet" because she mumbled nonsensically to herself and pretended to be flighty and distracted in order to escape notice. In 1863, Union General Benjamin Butler recruited her to head up the espionage network in Richmond. She visited imprisoned Union soldiers and brought them clothes, food, and medicine, while ferrying coded messages hidden in vegetables and eggs and written in invisible ink that could only be seen when milk was poured on the messages.

Another real-life spy who makes a cameo in my story was Mary Richards, also known as Mary Bowser, Mary

Jane Henley, and Mary Jones. She was a free Black woman
who was an essential part of the Union intelligence ring.
She had a photographic memory and was a brilliant
actress. Working behind enemy lines, Mary Richards was
a maid in the house of Confederate President Jefferson
Davis and reported back on plans and documents that she
saw while cooking and cleaning. There are many different
stories about her identity as well as her role as a spy, but
there's no doubt that she was an intelligent and extraordinary woman. Known later on for facilitating education
for her freed fellow men and giving speeches across the
United States about her experiences during the war, she
was reported to be funny, smart, and sarcastic. The last
recorded sighting of her was in 1867.

Sesily Pleasant's mother was inspired by yet another
intrepid Black woman of the era, Miss Mary Ellen Pleasant,
a self-made female millionaire (nearly a billionaire by
today's equivalent) as well as a fierce abolitionist. In 1852,
she settled as a widow in San Francisco, where she worked
as a maid and a cook for a few rich investors. Though she
wasn't formally educated, she listened to tips, invested in
real estate as well as gold and silver, and bought a chain of
local businesses, including laundries and boardinghouses,
in the 1860s. To thwart discrimination, Pleasant put many
of her investments in the name of a white male business
partner and friend. Their combined fortune was worth
about $30 million then, which is worth just shy of $900
million in today's currency. She used her wealth to aid
slaves in escaping to the Northern states and Canada via

the Underground Railroad, gave them jobs, homes, and financial help. She became known as the "mother of civil rights" in California when she sued two streetcar companies for racial bias.

The Bell in Hand Tavern, where my heroine meets her spy contact, was an actual tavern opened in 1860 in Philadelphia by Irish immigrants Catherine and William McGillin. They raised thirteen children in the rooms above the tavern. I read that President Lincoln might have visited this historic location when he went to Philadelphia, but I couldn't find actual evidence that he did.

Although Viscount Palmerston, then prime minister of England, kept Britain's position neutral toward the American Civil War (1861–1865), British shipyards were still allowed to supply ships and munitions to the Southern states. He was a shrewd politician and one of the most important figures in Victorian England. He was also a womanizer whose nickname was Lord Cupid, even into his seventies. There was speculation that the cause of his death was a heart attack while in the middle of congress with a parlor maid.

On the subject of the self-defense scene in the Bois de Boulogne, I belong to a women's weapons and self-defense group, and we meet monthly to learn about protection for women facing assault, home invasion, and general personal safety. While some of the strategies I wrote about are practical, they are also dangerous and I'm by no means a professional, certified training instructor. I would encourage anyone looking for classes about self-defense to research local groups in their communities.

I also had a bit of fun researching the history of hand-cuffs. Hand restraints have been around and documented since 600 BC, but it was only in the early nineteenth century that they were constructed with hinges, keyed openings, and ratcheting mechanisms. Weighing over a pound, they were heavy and difficult to carry, however, and the screw key lock made things difficult, since locking and unlocking were both time-consuming processes. However, American W. V. Adams invented a pair of hand-cuffs with an adjustable ratcheting system in 1862, which improved on English handcuffs. He made his version smaller, lighter, and easier to conceal as well as fitted with a smarter lock system. A key was only required to release, not to lock. This is why my hero refers to his handcuffs as of ingenious American design and also why he could carry a pair around.

A quick mention on the architecture of France related to the scene in Paris where my heroine gets in trouble: From 1853 to 1870, Napoléon III tasked Baron Georges-Eugène Haussmann with modernizing the very over-crowded city of Paris, which was dirty and riddled with disease. Haussmann's solutions were new sewer and water systems, train stations, and wide, open boulevards. Some historians say the latter was to accommodate Napoleon III's large army. These architecturally unique boulevards are recognizable even today in Paris with their cream-colored, uniform apartment buildings. They all had the same rooflines, the same number of stories, and the same wrought-iron balconies on the top floor. Many French people of the era criticized Haussmann for changing "old Paris," especially Victor Hugo who apparently disliked him and accused him of destroying the city's charm. However, his work will be forever immortalized in the famous Boulevard Haussmann in Paris, which I have walked many times.

One last note: While I did my best to be thoughtful, mindful, and respectful in my representation, my experience as a woman of mixed-race West Indian descent and an immigrant to the United States will not be the same as someone who was born or raised in the United States, England, India, the wider Caribbean, or elsewhere. This means that as a writer, I might not be the perfect representation for members of another diasporic community. I can only write from my own lived experience and through the knowledge of my own sphere of existence.

I truly hope you enjoyed Valentine and Bronwyn's journey to their happy-ever-after!

xo,
Amalie

P.S. For those interested in Marlborough pie, here's the recipe and a brief history. Marlborough pudding pie is an apple custard dessert that dates to the 1600s and features sherry, cream, nutmeg, and a combination of shredded apples. It appeared in a 1660 British cookbook, *The Accomplisht Cook*, written by a Paris-trained chef named Robert May, before it traveled to the New World. Versions of the Marlborough pie appear in eighteenth-century English cookbooks as well as in *American Cookery* (1796) by Amelia Simmons.

MARLBOROUGH PUDDING PIE

4 apples, peeled and cored (2 Granny Smith and 2 Pink Lady) OR 2 cups applesauce
1 cup cream
⅓ cup brown sugar
⅓ cup granulated sugar
3 tablespoons lemon juice
3 tablespoons sweet sherry
2 teaspoons all-purpose flour
4 tablespoons butter, melted
3 large eggs
Dash of cinnamon and nutmeg, to taste
1 9-inch pastry shell
Whipped cream for topping

Preheat oven to 350°F. Grate the apples and cook them in a saucepan with a small amount of water on medium heat until tender, then drain excess water and puree (or use applesauce). Add cream, sugars, lemon juice, and sherry to the apples. Add butter. Beat the eggs and add to the mixture. Fold in flour. Add cinnamon and nutmeg. Mix and fold the mixture into the piecrust and then bake about 1 hour. After pie is cooled, add fresh whipped cream on top.

Acknowledgments

As always, so much gratitude goes to my fantastic editor, Deb Werksman, who keeps me on my toes and makes sure my stories are the best they can be. Thank you for all your notes and insight, Deb!

A huge thanks to the entire production, design, sales, and publicity teams at Sourcebooks Casablanca for your tireless efforts behind the scenes—I'm so grateful for everything you do. To Pamela Jaffee and Katie Stutz, thank you for your brilliance in publicity and marketing, and for giving my books the best chance to succeed.

To my stellar agent, Thao Le, words cannot ever express how much you mean to me. I realize this sounds like a love ballad, and it kind of is, because I'm all up in my feelings right now. They're up there with lyrics from Journey, Whitney Houston, and Taylor Swift. But in all seriousness, thank you for being such an incredible advocate.

An enormous thank you goes to the amazing women in my life who keep me company on this wild publishing adventure, call me regularly, read my manuscript drafts, gawk over cover concepts, blurb my books no matter how many times I ask, put up with my grumbling, send me funny TikToks, and generally make me feel appreciated, seen, and valued, I have so much love for you. Thank you. Your friendship means the world to me.

To all the readers, reviewers, booksellers, librarians, educators, extended family, and friends who support me and spread the word about my books, a heartfelt thanks to you.

Last but definitely not least, to my incredible family, Cameron, Connor, Noah, and Olivia, I love you so much. Thanks for putting up with me and reminding me to shower, eat, and not become a hobbit.

About the Author

AMALIE HOWARD is a *USA Today* and *Publishers Weekly* bestselling novelist of "smart, sexy, deliciously feminist romance." *The Beast of Beswick* was one of Oprah Daily's Top 24 Best Historicals to Read, and *Rules for Heiresses* was an Apple Best Books selection. She is also the author of several critically acclaimed, award-winning young adult novels. An AAPI, Caribbean-born writer, her interviews and articles on multicultural fiction have appeared in *Entertainment Weekly, Ravishly* magazine, and *Diversity in YA*. When she's not writing, she can usually be found reading, being the president of her one-woman Harley-Davidson motorcycle club, #WriteOrDie, or power-napping. She lives in Colorado with her husband and three children.

UP ALL NIGHT WITH A GOOD DUKE

A new sparkling and sexy Regency romance series
from award-winning author Amy Rose Bennett

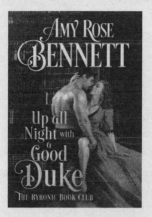

Artemis Jones—"respectable" finishing-school teacher by day and
Gothic romance writer by night—has never lost sight of her real dream:
to open her own academic ladies' college. When Artemis is unexpect-
edly called upon by a dear friend to navigate her first London Season,
she comes at once. Perhaps she can court the interest of a wealthy
patron for her school. As long as she can avoid her aunt's schemes to
marry her off. Little does she realize she's about to come face-to-face
with a Byron-esque widowed duke determined to find a bride...

"Infused with heat, energy, and glamour."
—Amanda Quick, *New York Times* bestselling author,
for *How to Catch a Wicked Viscount*

A GENTLEMAN SAYS "I DO"

Dazzling enemies-to-lovers Regency romance from *New York Times* and *USA Today* bestselling author Amelia Grey

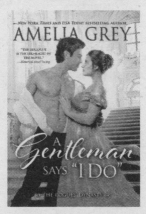

On the cusp of another missed deadline, burgeoning author Catalina Crisp takes matters into her own hands and completes her father's latest satire of the notorious Brentwood twins. Thinking she's saved the family for another day, she's shocked to find Iverson Brentwood on her doorstep seeking revenge.

Looking for the scoundrel Sir Phillip Crisp and finding his lovely daughter instead, Iverson might have finally met his match. Headstrong Catalina heats his blood like no other. But no matter how attracted he is to the intriguing Catalina, he can't give in to his desire...for she is the daughter of the man he's sworn to destroy.

"Amelia Grey never fails to entertain."
—Kat Martin, *New York Times* bestselling author